CONTEMPORARY AMERICAN FICTION

MARTHA CALHOUN

Richard Babcock, a graduate of
Dartmouth College and the Uni-
versity of Michigan Law School, is
an editor at *New York* magazine. He
grew up in Illinois, and now lives in
New York City with his wife and
son. This is his first novel.

MARTHA
CALHOUN
A NOVEL

By Richard Babcock

PENGUIN BOOKS

PENGUIN BOOKS
Published by the Penguin Group
Viking Penguin Inc., 40 West 23rd Street,
New York, New York 10010, U.S.A.
Penguin Books Ltd, 27 Wrights Lane,
London W8 5TZ, England
Penguin Books Australia Ltd, Ringwood,
Victoria, Australia
Penguin Books Canada Ltd, 2801 John Street,
Markham, Ontario, Canada L3R 1B4
Penguin Books (N.Z.) Ltd, 182–190 Wairau Road,
Auckland 10, New Zealand

Penguin Books Ltd, Registered Offices:
Harmondsworth, Middlesex, England

First published in the United States of America by
Random House, Inc., 1988
Reprinted by arrangement with Random House, Inc.
Published in Penguin Books 1989

1 2 3 4 5 6 7 8 9 10

LIBRARY OF CONGRESS CATALOGING IN PUBLICATION DATA
Babcock, Richard.
Martha Calhoun: a novel/by Richard Babcock.
p.   cm.—(Contemporary American fiction)
ISBN 0 14 01.1872 1
I. Title.   II. Series.
[PS3552.A174M37   1989]
813'.54—dc19   88–31674

Printed in the United States of America
Set in Goudy Old Style

For Gioia

MARTHA
CALHOUN

One thing about Bunny, she's got beautiful blond hair. It's the first thing about her you'd notice. Actually, she's got lots of great features—soft, clear skin, blue eyes, long, muscled legs. She's the most beautiful woman in Katydid, Illinois. But she was always proudest of her hair. She used to talk to me about it, showing it off. (Bunny is my mother. I call her Bunny because that's all I ever heard anyone call her. My father, Jeremiah P. Calhoun, ran away before I was born.)

When I was about six, Bunny went through a phase where she was upset because her hair was turning darker. It was still very blond, and she helped it along with a little peroxide—Sweden in a bottle, as she used to say—but it was no longer pure blond corn silk, the way it was when she was young. I guess the change had started after my brother, Tom, was born, when Bunny was eighteen. She understood that life goes on and that she had to grow older, but still she was sorry, and she always wished that Grandmother had thought to snip off a lock of her hair years ago, just so there'd be some souvenir of how things had once been. Then Bunny got it in her head that I should never suffer like that. My hair is plain brown. At best, just after it's been washed, it has a kind of reddish sheen. But Bunny was concerned that, like her, I'd lose something and then be sorry, so she clipped off a bit of my hair and put it in an envelope. That way, she said, I'd have something to save and show my own daughters, if I ever had any. But later she started worrying that we'd lose the envelope or forget where she'd put it. So she clipped some more hair, and then again and again and again. Over the course of a year or so, she kept taking samples and hiding them away. After a while, there were locks of my hair everywhere. I'd be looking over a bookshelf or rummaging through a drawer and suddenly come across an envelope with my name on it and a soft chunk of my hair inside. It always gave me an eerie feeling, as if I'd grown very old or gone far away.

That was around 1946, about ten years ago, just after the war. I've been thinking a lot about those times recently. Bunny's little house on Sycamore Street, where we'd lived since I was two, is closed up now. All our things are locked inside. I keep imagining that some time, years from now, someone will go in and discover everything—our clothes, the furniture, Tom's baseball-card collection, my locks of hair—and try to piece together our lives from the evidence. They'll never get it right, of course, but it's fun to think of the romance, the mystery they'll attach to us—"Another lock of hair! What can it mean?"—particularly given the way things really were, and the way they turned out.

This is my explanation of all that. My testimony, my confession, whatever you want to call it—the story I probably should have told before and didn't. My name is Martha Calhoun, and I'm sixteen. I turned sixteen three months ago. Looking back, I think that may have been part of the trouble. I turned sixteen—Sweet Sixteen—and I expected something to happen. To celebrate, Bunny took me to dinner at Walker's Chinese, outside of town. We got dressed up—me in a sweater and skirt, Bunny in a black sheath and heels. While we were sitting there, two men we didn't know—businessmen passing through town, probably—noticed us and sent over drinks. It seemed so romantic, Bunny and me being courted. Of course, I was too young to have a drink. Bunny finished both of them and then shooed the men away. But still, it seemed as if I'd passed a point, that things were starting to happen.

The next day, though, I woke up, and everything was the same. Bunny's house was still tiny and messy. My best friend was still Mary Sue Zimmerman, though she really only qualified through endurance—we'd known each other since we were both five. Katydid was the same little town, full of farmers and ex-farmers, living from one county fair to the next. And, of course, I still had the same brown hair, the same angular face, the same towering body.

Over the next few days, while Bunny was at work, I spent hours in the bathroom, studying myself in the mirror. I remembered that Bunny had once said that she could look at other kids and tell exactly how they were going to turn out. With me, she wasn't sure. "You defy me," she had said. "I see too much. You've got too many possibilities." Staring at myself in the mirror, hour after hour, I used to wonder what she saw. All I am is tall. I've always been one of the tallest in any group. Even as a child, I was an expert on the tops of boys' heads, a connoisseur of the incredible swirls of hair, sometimes double-barreled, that form just behind the crown, of the sweeping waves that push forward from the back. By ten, I was taller than Bunny, and even with Tom, who was a year older. At fourteen, I passed him and towered half a head above most of the boys my age. I finally realized what was happening and *willed* myself to stop growing, but by then I was almost five eleven, and it was already too late. To compensate, I developed a permanent slouch, almost a hunchback. That helped a little, and, over time, some of the boys started to catch up; a few even passed me. (Today, Tom and I are exactly even again.) But nothing ever erased my feeling that I was from a different race, one that was fundamentally a mistake. Leafing once through a social studies book, I came to a photograph and stopped. There I was: A totem pole carved by a tribe of Pacific Coast Indians, a thin, knobby log topped by an enormous, beaky bird's head.

It didn't help any being Tom's sister. Everybody knew about him, or if they didn't, he made sure they found out. He was always in trouble. Even when we were little and the best of friends, his face would light up at the prospect of doing something naughty. We'd be playing happily enough, and suddenly he'd get an idea—let's hide the neighbor boy's bicycle, let's put a scoop of Jell-O in Bunny's coat pocket—and he wouldn't be satisfied until he'd done it. I used to argue with him, but he always had some reason why it was really all right—he was just playing a joke, or only getting even. Then, as he got older, you couldn't argue with him at all.

Given my feelings of awkwardness and Tom's reputation, the solution was to stay quiet and out of sight, and by the time I started high school, I'd become almost a recluse. I'd venture out to school and to the usual school events, but I drifted farther and farther from the world of my classmates. Mostly, I just stayed home and waited, looking forward to the time when Bunny would get back from work or from her date, wherever she was.

I don't know why I thought that being sixteen would change anything. Perhaps I was carried away by boredom. Once school had let out for the summer, I didn't have much to do. Occasionally, I'd sub for Bunny or one of the other waitresses out at the Katydid Country Club. That probably sounds like a more glamorous place than it is. They call it a country club, but there aren't any tennis courts or swimming pools. In fact, the golf course only has twelve holes—to make a complete game, you have to play the first six over again. But there's a restaurant at the club where Bunny had worked as long as I could remember. Actually, the food wasn't bad. The cook was an Indian man called Gunga Din—that wasn't his real name, of course, just something people gave him from the movie. He claimed he was once personal chef to a rajah, and he was full of stories about riding elephants and tracking Bengal tigers. How he ended up in Katydid has never been clear to me. He lived in back of the country club, above the equipment barn in a room he shared with Shorty, the greenskeeper. They made a very odd pair. Shorty's deaf and he can hardly talk, and Gunga was always going on about his glory days in India. Bunny once told me never to go back to their place.

Anyway, the real trouble for me actually started a couple of years ago out at the country club, though I didn't realize it at the time. Business was slow that night, and Bunny had brought me along to keep her company. One of her tables was occupied by the Benedicts, a family I'd seen around for years. Mr. Benedict was an airline pilot and often out of town, but Mrs. Benedict was a country-club regular, a young, very dark, very stylish woman, a slacks lady, as Bunny put it. The three Benedict children had come along, and the family was having a pleasant dinner, perhaps happy to have the father around. After a while, I noticed that Bunny was getting depressed. This was right at a time when Tom was at his worst, and it weighed on her, seeing another family so carefree. Finally, she couldn't restrain herself. "Don't you have any trouble with these children?" she asked Mrs. Benedict. "I mean, don't they give you any problems?" Bunny was preoccupied and looking for reassurance or she never would have said anything, but Mrs. Benedict isn't the type to coddle people. "Children can only return the love they get," she said. Of course, that made Bunny feel worse. I tried to comfort her, but I couldn't. Just two days before, Tom had shot out all the windows on the back porch with his BB gun.

For some reason, though, ever after that evening, Mrs. Benedict took a special interest in me. I noticed it off and on, but especially when I started subbing at the club at the beginning of the summer. At first, she was just very friendly—she'd ask how I was doing, or comment about what I was wearing. Pretty soon, she began giving me suggestions on makeup and styling, and she'd bring me little samples of perfume or lipstick that her husband had picked up in his travels. Once after lunch, she took me down to the ladies' locker room and showed me how to put on a new lotion she liked.

"You stroke upward from the throat," she said, as we stretched our necks, craning toward the mirror. "Over the chin and across the face."

The lotion was chilly and tingly against my skin. I felt very adult.

"I like this stuff," Mrs. Benedict went on, vigorously rubbing it into her face. "It's new. They say it replaces the hormones you lose when you get old or when you're tense. Who knows? It's probably just advertising, right?"

"Right."

"But you do need something. Your skin wears out. What does your mother use?"

"Bunny?" It was strange talking this way, looking in the mirror. We were talking to each other but looking at ourselves. "I'm not sure. Mostly just lipstick, I guess."

"No creams? She better watch out or she's going to lose those looks of hers."

"Yeah, I guess."

"She needs more sleep."

"Yeah."

"More nights at home."

"Yeah."

Mrs. Benedict straightened up. Our eyes met in the mirror. "You don't mind if I talk this way, do you? Speaking frankly, that is."

"Oh, no."

"That's just my way."

"Oh, I understand."

"Here, take this," she said, giving me the jar of cream. "You use it. See if your mother wants to try it."

"Thanks."

Later, Bunny caught me in the bathroom at home, giving myself a facial.

"What's this?" she said, scrunching her nose and holding the little glass jar between two fingers.

"Mrs. Benedict gave it to me. It's a hormone cream. It helps your skin."

"Junk," said Bunny. "A waste of money. And what's all this stuff?" She waved her hand at the small collection of makeup jars I'd spread around the sink.

"Stuff."

"Junk. All the makeup in the world won't help if you don't have character in your face. Character's the thing."

"That's easy for you to say. You're beautiful."

"You would be too if you let your character come out."

The truth is, though, the makeup did make me look better. And Mrs. Benedict started complimenting me and pointing out things about me to her friends. I'd come to her table to take an order, and she'd make me spin like a model so everyone could inspect me from all sides and angles. After a while, she began referring to me as her "summer project."

When I told Bunny that, she blew up. "What's the matter with that old fat bottom?" Bunny demanded. "Doesn't she think I can raise my own daughter?"

But I figured Bunny was still sensitive about the comment Mrs. Benedict had made at dinner that time. And, to me, the comment didn't mean much, it was just the way Mrs. Benedict talked.

Then one day Mrs. Benedict tugged on my sleeve and whispered that she had a proposition for me. I was serving lunch at the time, and she promised to explain later, down in the ladies' locker room, where she was going to play bridge. Once lunch was over, I went down there. Mrs. Benedict hopped up from her bridge game and led me by the hand around a corner, out of sight of everyone else.

"I've had a wonderful idea," she said, breathlessly. "Why don't you come work for me? Our regular babysitter, Mrs. Johnson, is leaving to spend the rest of the summer with her sister in Minnesota, and I can't think of anyone I'd rather have replace her than you."

"Gee," I said. "That's nice of you." Actually, I was a little disappointed. I don't know what I was expecting, but I'd been a babysitter before and I thought waitressing—even as a substitute—was a better job.

"Well, what do you think?" asked Mrs. Benedict excitedly.

"I'll have to talk to Bunny."

"Oh, of course. Of course talk to Bunny." She backed up a step, cooling by several degrees. "But this is an excellent opportunity. And you're old enough to start making these decisions on your own."

Just as I thought, Bunny didn't like the idea. "Why didn't she ask me first?" Bunny grumbled, as we drove home. "Nobody thinks about mothers any more."

"Bunny, Mrs. Benedict is a mother. Besides, I'm old enough to be offered a job by myself." By then, I'd thought about it and decided the job might be all right after all—the work would be steady, the pay was reasonable, and I'd have something to keep me busy.

"But you won't make as much money. You'll earn more as a waitress."

"I'm not sure. She said she'd use me four or five times a week. That will mean at least fifteen hours."

"Fifteen hours! No mother leaves her children with a babysitter for fifteen hours a week."

"Bunny, you used to leave Tom and me alone half the night."

"That was different," Bunny said. "I always knew where you were."

"Huh?"

"You were in bed."

"Anyway, fifteen times 75 cents an hour means $11.25 a week. I've only made that much once out at the country club."

"But you'll start working more. Just be patient." Bunny drove once around the square and managed to find a parking space just down the block from Meyers' Grocery. We went inside to buy eggs and milk, and when we came out, Dwayne Spinelli, the simple man, was leaning against the hood of Bunny's car. His bicycle was resting against a pole. "That's retarded," said Dwayne when he saw us. It's what he always says. "Retarded" is the only long word he's ever learned.

"Hello, Dwayne," said Bunny. "Tell Martha she should work at the country club."

Dwayne's uncertain eyes searched Bunny's face for some sort of clue, and he plucked nervously at his black hair. His short-sleeved print shirt was buttoned high up under his chin, but the tail had worked its way out of his shorts and was flapping around his hips.

"Tuck in your shirt, Dwayne," said Bunny. Relieved, he grinned and jumped up and pushed the shirttail out of sight.

When we were back in the car, I said, "They don't need me out at the country club. Half the time, nobody sits at my tables. Three waitresses are enough, even if one of them's not working."

"Be patient. Maybe someone will go on vacation."

"Who's going to go on vacation? Beatrice and Millie only work there in the summer."

"But maybe next year you'll be full time. Mr. Higgins has taken a shine to you."

"It's you he's taken a shine to, Bunny."

Mr. Higgins was the bartender and also the manager of the club. He and Bunny went back a long ways.

"It's all the same," said Bunny.

That night, when Bunny came home, I asked her again about the babysitting job. "Haven't you forgotten about that yet?" she groaned. The little Franklin boy had thrown a scoop of chocolate ice cream onto Bunny's pink waitress uniform, and she was standing at the kitchen sink in her slip, trying to wash out the stain. There was a bare bulb over her head, hanging by a cord. She'd broken the glass shade years ago. Last winter, Eddie Boggs put in a new shade, but Bunny made him take it down. She said she was used to the bright light and shadows—they seemed the way a kitchen should be.

"I've got enough things to worry about," Bunny went on, "without having to worry that you're gonna give up a good summer job."

"Well, I did some arithmetic and I figured I can make an extra fifty dollars this summer babysitting."

"I was never good at arithmetic, and I never relied on it," Bunny said. "You've got to use intuition in these things, and my intuition says you should stay at the country club."

I was getting exasperated. "The only reason you don't want me to babysit is you don't like Mrs. Benedict," I said.

Bunny sighed. "Oh, take the damn job, then," she said finally. "I don't care."

The Benedicts lived in a brown-shingled house, big and angular, on Parkview Avenue, overlooking Katydid City Park—the opposite side of town from Bunny's place, but an easy trip by bicycle. My job started on Friday. That morning, I put on a blouse and pants, kissed Bunny goodbye and set out on my bike. I pedalled down Prosperity Street, past the Katydid Tool and Die—the KTD—the subject of constant worry, since half the people in town worked there and rumors were always going around that it was about to shut down. I crossed the railroad tracks and chugged up Center Street, skirting the square,

10

which would be crowded with traffic on a Friday morning. It was exactly eleven when I got to Parkview Terrace.

"Martha!" said Mrs. Benedict at the door. "I think this is perfect!"

"Me too!"

"I *adore* it!" she said.

"Me too."

She took my hand and pulled me in. I'd never been inside the Benedict house before. The rooms were high and spacious and the furniture all looked oversized. My first thought was that at last I was in a house that looked as if it had been designed for me. Mrs. Benedict led me into the living room where her children were draped around a huge, boaty sofa. I didn't really know them well. The oldest, the twins, were eleven. Brenda was a chunky, big-cheeked girl with a fast circle of friends who were always huddled together in some sort of conspiracy. Arnold—in addition to having to live down that unfortunate name—had the bad luck to be skinny and clumsy. More often than not, I'd seen him tagging along with Brenda's group. Butcher, the youngest, was nine. He was short and compact, with his mother's dark looks and heavy, sulky eyes. All three studied me grudgingly.

"Do you play poker?" asked Brenda. "That's our favorite game."

"No, but I'm sure I can learn," I said.

Brenda and Arnold exchanged sour glances.

Mrs. Benedict said she was in a hurry, but she took me around the first floor of the house, showing off the furniture and appliances. In the library, an enormous TV sat wrapped in wood, bursting with knobs and dials.

"It's new," said Brenda, who'd been trailing along behind.

Mrs. Benedict bustled to get her things together, then lined the children up at the front door. "Goodbye, now," she said. "The Kool-Aid and sandwiches are in the refrigerator. Be nice to Martha." She bent down and kissed each of them.

After she'd left, the children lurked around the door. It was clear that Brenda and Arnold were a team and that Butcher was left to fend for himself.

"Well, what do you want to do?" asked Brenda.

"What would *you* like to do?" I responded, trying to be agreeable. In fact, I'd have loved to get my hands on that television. Bunny's old TV had been broken for the last couple of weeks and she hadn't had the money to get it fixed.

Brenda said she wanted to play "purr kids."

"Yeah," said Arnold.

Butcher just stood there.

"What's that?" I asked.

"You know, *purrr* kids—little children whose parents don't have any money so they have to starve and try to find food in the forest."

"In the park," said Arnold.

"You mean *poor kids*," I corrected.

"Yeah. Purr kids," said Brenda. "Let's go." She ran into the kitchen and out the back door with Arnold just behind. I hurried after, bringing Butcher along with me.

Playing purr kids, I soon discovered, consisted mostly of wandering around the woods in Katydid City Park, while Brenda explained how we'd got into this horrible predicament: We were a family. Our mother had been run over by a train and our father was a drunk. I was the oldest sister, but I was retarded, so Brenda, the next oldest, had to make all the decisions. Arnold was the protector, so he carried a stick. Butcher just followed along behind, looking bored. Brenda and Arnold spent a lot of time telling him to pretend right.

"Now, it's nightfall," said Brenda after a while. "We'll have to make camp." She picked a spot on the path underneath a big tree, where not much grass was growing.

"I'm not lying down in the dirt," said Butcher.

"You do what you're told," said Brenda sharply.

"Yeah," said Arnold, waving the stick around.

"Now, now, let's be nice," I said.

Brenda and Arnold sat cross-legged in the dirt. I found a little clump of grass and sat on that.

"I'm not getting my blue jeans dirty," said Butcher.

"What a baby," said Arnold.

"You're a brat," said Brenda.

"Now, now," I said. "Let's get on with pretending."

"How can we pretend when he won't sit down?" asked Brenda.

"Let's pretend he's got a bad leg and can't sit," I suggested.

"That's stupid," said Brenda.

"Really stupid," agreed Arnold.

Brenda went on with her explaining: We were going to starve unless we could grow a garden. We'd grow carrots and peas and lettuce and take turns staying up all night to make sure animals or drifters didn't steal anything. Arnold started rooting around in the dirt with his stick, making holes to plant the seeds in. Butcher came over and stood by me.

After a while, the noon whistle blew down at the KTD. Arnold leaped up. "Noon," he yelped. "Time for *Noontime Adventures*."

"Arnold, I'm not finished," said Brenda.

Arnold was torn, but he sat down again.

"And so, if we have a big harvest, we'll have a day of thanksgiving," Brenda went on. "And we'll invite the Indians and the drifters. And so we'll have corn-on-the-cob and turkeys and peas, and we'll have a big feast, with dancing . . . and so . . . aww, let's go," she said, jumping up. She and Arnold ran back down the path toward the house. I walked back with Butcher.

"Do you like to watch *Noontime Adventures*?" I asked.

"Naaa," he said.

I served sandwiches and Kool-Aid on TV trays in front of the television. The show was mostly cartoons. Afterward, we tried some soap operas, *The Brighter Day* and then *The Secret Storm*. I was settled on a sofa, enjoying every minute. Bunny's TV is about the size of a toaster, and even when it works, the screen has black, squiggly lines running across it. But pretty soon Brenda and Arnold started grousing and chasing each other around the room. Then Brenda's friend Laura Brinkman came to the front door.

"Can we go back to Laura's house?" asked Brenda.

"I don't think your mother would like that," I said.

"Awww. Well, can we go out and play in the yard?"

"Of course." I started to get up.

"I don't want to do that," said Butcher. He'd been the only one besides me interested in the soap operas.

"We don't want you to play out there anyway," said Brenda.

So Butcher and I kept watching soap operas and Brenda, Arnold, and Laura went out to the yard. I wasn't worried because I could keep an eye on them through the back window.

Butcher, I started to realize, was a very strange little boy. He almost never smiled, and when he knew people were watching him, his face was contorted into a sort of squinty frown.

"Butcher, is something bothering you?" I asked, when *The Secret Storm* was over.

"No."

"You seem unhappy."

13

"Do you want to come look at my room?" he asked in a solemn voice.

"Sure." I checked outside, and the kids were doing fine. Butcher led me up two flights of stairs, his black sneakers leaving diamond imprints on the carpeted steps. On the third floor, the ceiling was low and slanted.

"Here," he said, opening a door with "Butcher" stenciled on it. I paused in the doorway to look. Inside, the room was filled with cowboys. There were cowboys on the wallpaper, cowboys on the rug. A giant horsehead was sewn into the bedspread, and ten gallon hats decorated the curtains. There was a lamp made out of a cowboy boot and a carving of a horse rearing up. A bowl shaped like a rolled-up lariat was plopped in the middle of the bureau, and an animal skin was tacked up above Butcher's bed.

"That's a gazelle skin," Butcher said. "My father got it during the war. It sweats in hot weather."

I climbed onto the bed to get a better look. Sure enough, drops of liquid were zigzagging down the wall under the skin. "Weird," I said.

"I don't let anyone come in here," he said. "Not even my mother. I clean the room and make the bed myself."

"Why?"

"I like to be alone."

"But don't you have friends?"

"I like to be alone."

I turned around and sat on the bed. Butcher had taken some wrinkled pieces of drawing paper out of a drawer and was clutching them in his hand. He stared at me for a moment and then came and sat beside me, thrusting the papers into my lap.

"What's this?" I asked. The papers were covered with crude, childish drawings of people strangely entangled. It took me a few seconds to realize that the people were naked, embracing. Balloons floated out of their mouths, circling words like "Oh, Oh," and "Mmmm."

"Butcher, these are ridiculous," I said.

"I drew them myself." He slipped off the bed and stood a few feet away, watching me leaf through his artwork. He was very intense, and I sensed his dark little eyes moving back and forth across my face.

"People don't even look like this." I pulled out a drawing of a woman whose breasts were entirely covered by her nipples.

"Oh yeah?" said Butcher. He was stuck in a kind of pose, one leg in front of the other, hands in pockets. Still, those eyes covered me. I felt uncomfortable and slid down the bed a few inches, but his eyes followed.

"Here, put these away," I said, handing him the drawings. "You should throw them out." I was hoping to break the spell, but he kept staring as he stepped forward to take the drawings from my hand. He slipped them back in the drawer and then stepped over beside me. He was standing too close, almost touching my leg, but he was acting so oddly that I didn't think to move away. Outside, the voices of the other children drifted up. Butcher's room was incredibly hot. The windows were all closed. I felt a little dizzy. It was almost like another world in that room.

"I like you," Butcher said.

I fought to restrain a high-pitched laugh. Here was this grumpy little boy, trying to act like a man. He was so wound up he was tight, a dark little ball of muscle, a fist.

"Let me take off your shirt," he said.

I should have said no, but instead I said, "Why?" I can't explain it. Everything was silly, and it just seemed to happen. I don't think I even thought about it. He reached out with one dark little hand and fumbled with the top button on my blouse. I put my hand up to protest, but then dropped it. He needed two hands to undo the button. Then, using two hands, he undid the next, and the next, and the next. His eyes were drawn down and I was watching his face. I wish I could explain it, but I can't. I've worried about it so much since. It was a kind of madness in me, really. I was hypnotized—not by him, but by his fascination with me.

My blouse fell open, and he stepped back to examine what he'd done. He was absolutely motionless. For a few seconds, I was actually enjoying it—feeling the way a snake-charmer feels, probably, exercising a power that he can't really understand. Then I looked beyond Butcher across the room. His bureau had a mirror on it. I saw myself reflected back in the glass, framed by the cowboy-boot lamp and the wooden bucking bronco. I was trying to understand what I was seeing when Mrs. Benedict walked into the room.

TWO

The Katydid Police Station is tucked into a corner of the Katydid County Courthouse, a solid, red-brick building that towers over one side of the town square. I'd been inside the police station often enough—sometimes to pick up my bicycle registration, sometimes with Bunny to pick up Tom. I always felt a secret thrill in there. A bulletin board hanging in the front room is covered with wanted posters, and I usually managed to slip over and examine the pictures of fugitives for a few minutes. My game was to try to guess the crimes they'd committed. I was never very good at it. Most often, the hardest faces would turn out to be accused of something like mail fraud, while the sweet-looking ones were wanted for armed robbery or murder. I always wished they'd include pictures of the criminals as children, just to see if you could spot something early on. Occasionally, I'd find a wanted woman tacked up on the bulletin board. Most of the women were accused of minor things, like writing bad checks, though once I saw a poster for a woman accused of shooting a man. The police apparently didn't have a mug shot of her, so instead they used an old snapshot. She was wearing a two-piece bathing suit and posing with a beach ball—the picture of silly innocence, lined up beside men with numbers across their chests. A few of the wanted women hadn't committed a crime but were being sought because they were believed to be "traveling with" so-and-so, some dangerous wanted man. I always tried to imagine what their travels were like—long silent stretches in big cars, nights at tiny, shingled motels, where bugs buzzed around yellow door lights, meals huddled together at truck stops or drugstore lunch counters. It was always summer in my imagination, and the fugitives were young, and there was something achingly wonderful in the way they passed over the country in constant flight.

Underneath the wanted posters, a long, wood bench was pushed up against the wall. I'd never paid any attention to the bench before, but Chief Springer told me to sit there while he phoned around to locate Bunny. He'd driven up to the Benedicts himself to pick me up. He's old, and his back is bent from arthritis, and waiting alone in Butcher's room, where Mrs. Benedict had left me, I had heard his slow, hobbling steps on the stairs. He opened the door without knocking and then stood with his hand on the doorknob, staring at me and breathing heavily. The walk up two flights had winded him.

"I didn't expect this of you," he said after a while.

"It's not what it seems," I whispered.

"What?" he said, still wheezing. "What?" He's also a bit hard of hearing.

I couldn't bring myself to say anything more. Deep inside, I felt a terror fighting to get out, and I struggled to hold it in. It wasn't even so much that I was afraid of what would happen—I didn't let myself think that far ahead. What really frightened me was a feeling I had that this had been bound to happen, that one day I'd make a mistake and from that moment everything would unravel. The feeling was terrifying, but calming in a way, too. It had always been just a matter of time.

I knew I had to keep my wits about me until Bunny got there. Above all, I must not cry. Bunny hated crying and she often warned me against it. She thought that when you cry, you lose all your strength, that tears flowing down your cheeks wash away your dignity. Through all her troubles in this town, refusing to cry had been her act of defiance. I wasn't even supposed to cry at the movies.

Chief Springer watched me from Butcher's doorway. He seemed unsure of what to do, and he took his glasses off and chewed on the frame. Finally, he said, "Well, come on, then, I'll drive you to the station."

17

I followed him downstairs. The hallway at the bottom was empty, and we got outside without seeing any of the Benedicts. In the car, he was quiet at first. After we'd gone a few blocks, he asked, "What do you hear from Tom?"

"Nothing," I said, in a tight, cracking voice. I almost started to cry. Chief Springer looked sharply my way. I'd frightened him.

Once we were at the station, he went in back to do the phoning and left me on the bench in the front room with Mrs. Donaldson, the police clerk. She was sitting behind a counter that's protected by a tall, wire screen. After I'd been sitting there a few minutes, she unlocked the gate in the screen and walked around the counter to me. Her slacks and blouse were made of the same blue material as the police uniforms.

"What are you doing here?" She asked.

"I don't know," I said. It seemed the easiest thing.

"There must be some reason," she insisted.

"No."

She shook her head and went back behind the counter.

Later, a policeman named George brought me a Coke. "Eugene V. Debs once sat on that bench," he said. "Do you know who he was?"

"No."

"He was a famous Communist. He started riots all over Chicago, so they put him in jail out here, where there wasn't hardly enough people to riot with." George stared, waiting for me to say something. "Didn't they teach you that in school?" he asked.

"Not yet."

"That's history," he explained.

Chief Springer came out and told me he couldn't reach Bunny at home, and no one was answering the phone at the bar at the country club. I suggested he try calling out to the room in back where Shorty the greenskeeper lives.

"Shorty?" asked Chief Springer, cocking his head back.

"Sometimes she goes there to rest between shifts."

"Ohhhh."

Chief Springer located Bunny at Shorty's, but before she could get down to the station, Tony Wesnofske, the youth officer, arrived. Because of Tom, Bunny and I had known him for years. He's much younger than Chief Springer, and everyone just calls him Sergeant Tony. He came quietly out of the back, and when I looked up, he was standing with his hands on his hips, examining me as if he expected to spot some evidence. He was wearing Bermuda shorts and a golf shirt, and his flattop looked freshly cut.

"Well, Martha," he said. "This is something, isn't it?"

I nodded.

"Maybe you better come with me." He led me down the hall to his office. A sign by the door said YOUTH BUREAU. He sat at a small, gray desk and gestured for me to sit in a gray chair beside it. The room was tiny and crowded with metal furniture—a metal bookcase, a metal file cabinet, a narrow, gray metal table piled with papers and folders. One small window faced out on the square.

Putting his feet up on the desk, he wiggled his chair forward a few inches. The grooves in the bottoms of his sneakers were packed with dried mud, and when he moved, little flakes of it rained down on his desk.

"You look scared," he said.

"I am."

"No need to be. I'm used to handling stuff like this. Much worse, in fact. This is nothing." He made a steeple with his fingers and stared thoughtfully into the air. "You wouldn't believe what I hear. This town, other towns, too. So different from a few years ago. It's a city infection. Our boys went to war, Europe, Korea, and fought beside city boys. Brought back some of their attitudes. Passed them on." He sighed. "You know what I mean?"

I nodded.

"Look at Billy Pick. I know his family, used to shop at their grocery store. He was a punk here, a nothin', he didn't even play football. Then he comes back from Korea, and he's a big deal, lots of girl-friends, just 'cause he won't take no for an answer. Now look at him. Hollywood. That's where he belongs."

I nodded again. Nobody knows what Billy Pick does in Hollywood. He's not an actor, but he's handsome and he dates starlets. Sometimes he shows up in gossip columns in the Chicago papers. People make jokes about him, but they say he's Katydid's most famous person.

"Hell, I don't blame the soldiers," Sergeant Tony continued. "You can't turn your mind off to that stuff. I fought in Europe, too. I know what it was like. Look at this." He leaned forward and pointed to the back of his calf. A small, hairless bubble of skin bulged out of the

19

muscle and moved in and out with his pulse. "A piece of shrapnel gave me that. Push on it."

I frowned, not understanding.

"Go on, push on it."

Tentatively, I reached out and pushed against the strange little dome of skin. The bubble deflated, then filled up again when I took my finger away.

"See?" he said.

I nodded, still not understanding.

He put his feet down and sat up. "Now, tell me what happened at the Benedicts'. Give me the whole story. Get it off your chest."

I stared at the floor, pale gray linoleum.

He waited, then went on. "I know it's a shock. I understand. That Mrs. Benedict—she can get very hysterical. Some of these women, they marry well, then lose all sight of things. I knew her before, you know. She was a few years behind me in school. She lived on Hacker Street. *Hacker!* You know what I mean?"

Hacker's a very short street that runs along the train siding behind the KTD. Mary Sue Zimmerman lives over there. "Yes," I said softly.

"You can't really know whether to believe a person like that, can you?"

I shook my head.

"I'd like to hear what *you* had to say, your side of the story."

Without taking my eyes off the floor, I said, "It's not really what you think."

"Oh? What do I think?"

I looked up at him. "That, you know, something was going on up there."

He shrugged. "Is that what I think? Hmmm. Maybe, maybe not." He put his hands behind his head. "I just know what Mrs. Benedict says. And then there's your mother."

"What's she—"

"Come on. Grow up."

My eyes dropped to the floor. I fought to hold back the tears. How could I tell him anything? He'd always been like this, always been cruel about our family. It was crazy to try to explain to him. It would only make things worse.

He saw that I was about to cry, so he waited a few seconds. When he spoke again, his tone was very casual. "Where's your brother these days? Sherwood?"

"Yes."

"What's he got? Four years?"

"Until he's twenty-one."

"Segregation, right?"

I nodded. They keep the boys convicted of serious crimes away from the younger boys.

"Whew." Sergeant Tony whistled softly. "That's rough. They're rough on boys down there." He paused. "You know, I didn't have anything to do with his case. That was adult."

"I know."

"I think he respected me. We had our differences, but, overall, I respected him and he respected me. You know?"

I didn't say anything. Tom has a lot of problems and a lot of anger toward people, but, for all that, there's a kind of harmlessness about him. He's soft-hearted. In sixteen years, the only person I ever heard him wish ill of was Sergeant Tony.

"That ought to tell you something," Sergeant Tony continued. "I'm someone you can talk to."

When I didn't say anything, he got up and stepped over to the window, looking out at the traffic going around the square. He's short, far smaller than I. Standing next to him over the years, I used to feel guilty—afraid he'd hold my size against Tom.

"Your mother goes out on a lot of dates, doesn't she?" he asked pleasantly. I didn't respond. "It must be lonely for you, sitting home alone, with her havin' all the fun. I mean, she's just about the hottest thing in town, and you're kind of on the discard pile, right?" He kept staring out the window. I could hear the cars honking and grunting as they edged around each other. Friday is a big shopping day on the square.

"She works," I said.

"Hmmm?"

"She works evenings at the country club. She's not out having fun."

"Oh, I mean after she's through work." He turned and sat against the window sill, crossing his legs. "They stop serving dinner out there around nine, don't they? And she doesn't come home right afterward, does she?"

"Usually."

"Usually? Hmmm. That's not what I hear." As an afterthought, he added, "That's not what Tom told me." I didn't believe him.

He studied the back of his hand. "Who's your mother dating these days? Anyone special?" He was used to my silences now. He just let them sit there and pound on my head for a few seconds before he went on. "Eddie Boggs, right? Yeah, Eddie." He waited. "Eddie," he repeated, sounding wistful. "Sad case. Tough. He ever talk about his wife?"

I shook my head.

"Tough." He stood up and walked over behind my chair. I felt him leaning on the back of it. I wanted to curl up, to shrink, to wrap myself in some thick blanket to protect myself from him. Too late, I realized my left arm was exposed, resting on the edge of the desk. His hand clamped down over my hand, squeezing too hard.

"You're different from them, Martha." His voice came softly, from just above my ear. "Don't get trapped in their kind of life." I stared at his hand, hardly bigger than mine. The veins made thick, blue lines among the pointy black hairs. "Let's get to know each other. Open up. It's the only way you're gonna get out of this. What was going through your mind?"

The door rattled suddenly, and Chief Springer walked in. "What's going on?" he demanded. Behind him, a blur of pink pushed into the room. Bunny was still wearing her waitress uniform. Jumping up, I wrapped my arms around her, burying my face in her neck. The sweet fragrance of stale perfume mingled with the cigarette smoke clinging to her hair. The combination was so familiar—I wanted to pull myself up and climb into her arms.

"We'll give you a few minutes together," said Chief Springer. "Come on, Tony." The chief gave a jerky, chicken wave with his arthritic arm, and the two of them left the room.

Bunny put her hands on my shoulders and held me at arm's length. "I didn't cry," I said.

She dropped her arms, and, without saying anything, she started pacing the office. She'd get about three steps in between the bookshelf and the filing cabinet and then have to turn and repeat herself. It was dizzying watching her. "First Tom, now you," she said finally.

"This isn't at all like Tom," I said. "It's nothing like Tom."

"It's trouble, isn't it?"

"But this is different. I can explain." While Bunny paced, I told her about the Benedicts' house and the children and playing purr kids in the woods, about Butcher's room and his pictures and his baby manliness. Bunny hardly seemed to be paying attention, but when I said I'd let Butcher unbutton my blouse, she stopped suddenly. "You let him *touch* you?" she barked. Her look was incredibly fierce, and I found myself gasping for breath. So what I'd done really was that bad, after all.

Bunny plopped down in Sergeant Tony's chair. She listened as I burbled on, hoping she'd start to understand, but I could see that her attention was drifting again. I felt so hopeless I was weak. My body weighed a ton. I had to go lean against the filing cabinet to support myself. No one would understand. Even I didn't understand.

I stopped talking and watched as Bunny listlessly studied the gray linoleum. After several seconds, she said, "Why'd this have to happen *now*, just when I'm starting to get things together? This town's been bad luck for me ever since we got here."

Something occurred to me. "Maybe we should leave," I said. I hadn't thought of it before, but suddenly I realized—why not? Bunny's just a waitress, and she could be a waitress anywhere. I've only got two more years of high school and there are thousands of other schools. My best friend, Mary Sue Zimmerman, I haven't even seen in a month.

Bunny was acting as if she hadn't heard me, so I said it again. "Why don't we move?"

"We can't leave here. This is where our house is."

"So what? We just rent. We could move someplace and start all over." I was getting excited. My strength was coming back. "People don't like us here anyway. Think of all the trouble that Tom got into."

"Trouble would probably follow us around."

"We could get a new house. You could get a job at a real restaurant. I could get a job after school. We'd have money."

Bunny jumped up and started pacing again. "We can't leave here," she snapped. "We *live* here. Besides, I'm starting to get it together with Eddie, and he could never leave his job at the KTD."

Eddie Boggs. Just like his brother Cecil. And just like Wayne Wadlinger and Johnny Tremone and Vic Mattox and Lester Vincent and who knows who else I can't remember. One thing about Bunny, she's got the worst taste in men of anyone I ever saw.

"Now, don't you say anything bad about Eddie," she said. "He's a lot different from his brother."

"But, Bunny, there are better men in Chicago. Or New York. We could go to New York and you could get a job in one of the restaurants where people eat before going to the theater, and then all the stars come in afterward. You could wait on Marlon Brando."

"Really?" Bunny paused and thought for a moment. "Gee. You know, he grew up around here. In Libertyville. His sister came into the News Depot once to buy a magazine."

"I know. That's why I mentioned him. See, *he* got away from here."

"Gee. And we could move into an apartment. I've always wanted to live in an apartment. I mean, an *apartment*. It sounds so sophisticated." Bunny came over and put her arm around me. "Gee," she said, thinking about New York and rubbing my back.

I pulled away. We were coming to something important. "How about it? Let's not even think about it. Let's just move. No more Katydid Country Club, no more Katydid High School, no more Mrs. Benedict."

Bunny frowned. "She was out in front, raving at Chief Springer when I came in just now."

"Did she say anything?"

"She called me a slut and you a slut." Bunny looked away in disgust.

"Both of us?"

"Yeah."

"What'd you say?"

"Nothing. I spat on the floor."

"You spat?"

"I know," she said, looking bewildered and shaking her head. "I don't know where it came from."

"Eddie spits."

"I had to do *something*," Bunny said.

"But spitting?"

"I know, I even surprised myself." She stared out through the water-spotted window, out across West Street to the square. Workmen there were cutting down an elm tree that had died. Elm trees are dying all over Katydid on account of Dutch elm disease. "What a way to grow old," Bunny said.

"For who?"

"For me." She turned around. "And you. For both of us."

Chief Springer returned with a knock. Sergeant Tony was crowding behind him, and there was a woman with them—a large, formidable woman with hair the color of carrots and a broad, pink face. The three of them pressed into the tiny youth bureau, driving Bunny and me behind the desk. There wasn't room; we were all struggling not to touch each other.

"This is Mrs. O'Brien," said Chief Springer.

"Peggy O'Brien," she interrupted.

"She's a social worker from over in Gordonton," the chief went on, talking to Bunny. "We're lucky she was here today and we could locate her."

"Why?" said Bunny, her eyes wide. "Why lucky?"

" 'Cause we want her to talk to your daughter," said Chief Springer. "We've got a problem here, and maybe Mrs. O'Brien can help."

Bunny grabbed my wrist. "She's not talking to Martha. Martha's not talking to anyone."

"Don't make this hard on yourself," Chief Springer said. "We just want to do some talking. This lady here is trained to give help."

"We don't want any help," snapped Bunny. "We're perfectly fine." She was still squeezing my wrist.

"You're not fine," insisted Chief Springer. "This is a serious thing, and this is a small town."

"Leave us alone," said Bunny, her voice rising.

Chief Springer motioned Bunny to calm down. "Don't force my hand," he said.

Sergeant Tony suddenly pointed a finger. "We've carried your family before," he huffed.

"Now, now," said the social worker. "There's no need to get excited. I'm just here to talk to Martha."

Bunny stared at all of them. Her eyes were wild. She started to say something and stopped, her mouth frozen in a perfect "O." Over in the square, a motorized saw buzzed a long, aching plea through the hot afternoon air.

"Come on, Martha," Bunny said. "We're leaving." Dragging me by the arm, she pushed roughly past Chief Springer and the wide, solid social worker. Neither tried to stop her, and Bunny pulled me out into the hall.

"Don't do this, Bunny," yelled Chief Springer, but by then we were down the corridor, banging out the lobby past Mrs. Donaldson. Bunny's car was parked in front, and we drove straight home.

When we got there, Bunny slammed the door and stomped around the living room, muttering in rage. After a few minutes, though, she started to wind down. By the time Chief Springer and the social worker arrived, about an hour later, Bunny was collapsed on the couch. I touched her on the way to let them in, and she rattled like a bag of sticks.

Chief Springer explained that a juvenile delinquency petition had been filed against me and that I was being taken to a temporary foster home. "I'm sorry, Bunny," he said. "I didn't want to have to do this."

Bunny sat without saying anything or looking at anyone.

"This is a lovely foster family," said Mrs. O'Brien. "We could have put Martha in the Children's Home, but I'm sure you'll agree this is better. The Vernons—do you know them? They lost their daughter tragically a few years ago. Of course, Mrs. Calhoun, you'll be able to visit. We'll get this all straightened out." She turned to me. "Now, come, Martha. Let's pack some clothes."

I hesitated.

"This is a serious thing," said Chief Springer.

The social worker wiggled two thick fingers at me, and I went numbly. I took the old, brown suitcase down from the shelf in the front closet. It's faded and dusty and coming apart at the seams, but it's the only suitcase Bunny owns. My father left it. Bunny once said that when he disappeared, he took everything worth putting in a suitcase and left the suitcase.

While Mrs. O'Brien watched, I opened it on my bed, then stood staring into my clothes closet.

"Oh, come on, just throw in any old thing," she said. "We can always come back for more."

I reached into the rack of clothes, grabbed a bundle, and dumped them in the suitcase. Mrs. O'Brien suddenly spotted something in the closet.

"A bathing suit!" she called out. "Bring it along. We'll go swimming."

A few minutes later, I arrived at the Vernons' house with a suitcase full of wrinkled clothes and my striped bathing suit.

THREE

I knew the Vernons well enough—or, at least, I knew Mrs. Vernon. Her only child, Sissy, had been in school with me from kindergarten on, and I had been at the class picnic last year, over at Durham's Pond, when Sissy drowned. She was a strange, frail, sickly girl, absent from school a good part of the time. She usually carried a wadded-up Kleenex in one hand because her nose was constantly running. When we were little and had to square dance or line up with partners— something where you had to hold hands—people fought to avoid Sissy because they didn't want to touch the hand that held the wad of Kleenex. But that was about as close as anyone came to paying attention to her. As far as plainness goes, I'm hardly one to speak, but at least I was unmistakably around and alive. Even before she died, Sissy was a kind of ghost, always just out of the picture, always just out of your mind.

She drowned on a cool overcast day—the kind of day that seems impossibly misplaced in summer. A few people were swimming despite the weather, but most of us were sitting along the grainy beach at the end of the pond near the parking lot. Bobby Peterson and Wayne Turner were out in a canoe and started hollering. They'd found her behind the big, wooden float. She was lying face down in the water with her arms and legs spread out as if she were making a snow angel. The boys tipped the canoe over trying to bring her in, and finally Mr. Malm, the gym teacher, had to swim her to shore using the cross-chest carry. He gave her artificial respiration, but you could tell it was too late. She'd always been pale, but stretched out on the beach under an overcast sky, her skin was the same steely color as the water in the pond. Her lips were a dark, purplish blue. She was the first dead person I'd ever seen, except at a funeral. It was the same for a lot of the kids.

Standing in the circle that gathered around while Mr. Malm worked on her, I had a painful feeling, totally selfish. I kept thinking that I'd lost a chance to do something good. I wished I'd said something to her—anything, a compliment on her bathing suit, a warning not to go in the water for an hour after she ate. I wished I'd noticed her, just that day. Later, walking home, I remember thinking that all of us who'd been there were tainted—that we'd allowed it to happen, and now our lives were forever changed. But the next day was sunny and warm. School let out, the lines grew at the Dairy Queen, the city pool opened, summer carried on. The only remembrance was a story in the paper in which Dr. Baker said Sissy hadn't been eating anything and hadn't got a cramp. He said he didn't know why she'd drowned, that it was an anomaly. I didn't know what the word meant until I looked it up in Bunny's dictionary. Then I understood perfectly.

Anyway, Sissy was seriously religious—even at school, she'd talk about "putting herself in the hands of God." (After she drowned, Tom went around saying that God must have held her under too long.) She and her mother belonged to a strict Protestant church—something Baptist, with no dancing, no makeup, no card-playing—that met in a small, converted barn just outside of town. The church—the barn—was terribly plain. Someone whitewashed it periodically, and a large, wood cross had been fastened to the door, but there were no stained glass windows, no soaring arches. The yard had even been cleared of trees. Every now and then, Bunny and I would happen to be driving by on a Sunday when people were streaming in or out. I would watch them and feel so sorry. Compared to my life with Bunny, their lives seemed so empty, so flat—as barren as the stark, white building in which they worshiped.

When I moved into the Vernons' house, they put me in Sissy's bedroom, on the second floor, at the end of the hall. The room, at first, was startling. Sissy had filled it with an enormous collection of religious figurines. All the shelves and tops of things were covered by little statues, most of them of Jesus. The statues were everywhere, lined up like toy soldiers. Mrs. Vernon said they were imported from Mexico, where artisans made them from plaster and gave them their bright coats of paint. Sissy ordered her collection from catalogues, starting when she was five. By the time she died, she'd put together a collection that ranged all over the life of Jesus. He was there as a baby—in a crib, being stared at by farm animals, or sitting in Mary's lap under a halo. As a teenager, He was portrayed pacifying beasts and doing carpentry and just talking to a few old men. And then there was the adult Jesus section, lots of statues of Jesus carrying the cross, or blessing someone, or simply standing in His robe, His arms stretched at His sides, and His palms open. With His long, solemn, bearded face, Jesus looked about the same in all the figurines except one—a little statue of Him walking along a rocky road. Sissy placed that one facing the wall on the end of a shelf above the bed. One day, as I lay there it occurred to me that something was strange: Why would she have Him walking into a wall? So I stood on the bed to get a better look. It was Jesus, all right, the robes were flowing behind Him, and His palms were open. But in this figurine, He didn't have a beard and His hair was short. He looked young and ordinary and a little like George Gobel. Sissy must have been embarrassed for Him.

Two other girls had stayed in Sissy's room since she died, but Mrs. Vernon told me she hadn't changed a thing. The room seemed that way—neat and perfectly arranged, like a room in a photograph. There was a wooden bureau, crowned with a doily, a small wooden desk with drawers underneath that still held Sissy's school papers and report cards. (One day, when I was bored, I thumbed through them— she got mostly B's and C's and incompletes.) Her teddy bear still sat in a chair in the corner. The bed was covered by a yellow crinoline spread. And circling all around the room was some terrible, light pink wallpaper, decorated with bunches of daffodils tied by a ribbon. Two pictures cheered things up a bit: a painting of Man o' War, standing in the winner's circle with a wreath dangling over his neck, and Sissy's fifth-grade class photograph. I was there in the second row, a sky-scraper against the horizon.

The room had one window, just above the bed, and for my first few days, I spent most of my time staring out. The window faced the back yard, looking into a creaky oak tree with a branch like an old gray dog's leg that passed just beside the house. On the other side of the lawn, over a fence, was a house belonging to the Porter family. Their only son, Ernie, was Tom's age and had joined the navy. Mr. Porter's mother now lived in Ernie's room. She was very old and sometimes, looking out, I'd see her staring back across the yard at me.

That first weekend, Mrs. Vernon came up every few hours to see how I was doing and to urge me to come down. She was a thin, pale woman, always wearing an apron and constantly wiping her hands on it. I kept telling her I needed time to think. As the hours passed, she became more persistent. Finally, she knocked and stepped tentatively into the room. "How are you feeling?" she asked.

"Okay, thank you." I still couldn't say more than a word or two at a time. The effort was too exhausting after all the thinking I'd been doing. I felt cut off, though. I wanted her to go away, but to like me.

"I'm sure everything will work out," she said.

I nodded.

"I'm sure," she repeated. She relaxed slightly and looked around the room. It was early afternoon. The air was so still I could see dust particles in the light shafts, and the only sound was the angry buzz of flies against the window screen. "I get such pleasure out of this room," she said. "It has so many memories. Sometimes, it seems that Sissy and I spent days up here together without ever coming out. I suppose you think that's silly."

"No, not at all."

"She was always so delicate. . . ." Her voice trailed off, then came back. "She thrived in this room, like a hothouse flower. I wish you two had been better friends." Mrs. Vernon took a few steps toward the end of the bed and placed her hand on the wall, touching it gently, as if it were a living thing. "Sissy picked out the wallpaper," she said. "Do you like it?"

"Ahh. . . ." I should have lied and said yes, but my mind was so tired I couldn't think quickly enough.

"I know," she said, smiling, catching me before I'd had time to recover. "There is a lot of pink." With her finger, she traced one of the bright yellow bouquets. "But Sissy loved daffodils. They were her favorite flower."

"They're beautiful."

"We were rather lucky to find this print," she said, stepping back to inspect the wall. "We got it from Fanzone's Hardware, but Mr. Fanzone was keeping it in the stock room in back. One Friday night we went down to the store and looked over everything. Nothing was quite right. Mr. Fanzone wanted to close up, but the Eberhardt girl was working there then. You know, the one with the port-wine stain on her cheek."

"Rosie."

"Yes, Rosie. What a shame. Such a pretty girl otherwise. Anyway, she'd remembered seeing this in back and finally brought it out. As soon as they'd blown off the dust and unrolled it, Sissy yelled, 'That's it!' She was so happy."

I could see it all: Sissy, the dust, the Kleenex squeezed in her hand. There was something deathly about the scene. "Gee," I said.

"Yes." Mrs. Vernon folded her hands at her waist and for a moment drifted with her thoughts. Suddenly, she stiffened and walked over to straighten the Man o' War picture. Then she fluffed the teddy bear and propped him up again in the chair. "Well, I'm glad someone can use the room," she said. "It's a room that's meant to be lived in."

"Yes."

She moved to the bureau and ironed the wrinkles out of the doily with her hand. "Now, I'm off to do some weeding," she said. "Would you like to join me? The fresh air and sunshine would probably do you good."

Her back was turned, and I quickly grabbed a book from a shelf under Sissy's nighttable. "I thought I'd do some reading," I said. She pivoted and I waved the book at her.

"Oh, how smart of you. What is it?"

I had to look. It was En Français, Sissy's French text. I held it out for Mrs. Vernon to see.

"Why, that's Sissy's book." Her face lit up, then darkened suddenly. "I suppose I should have taken it back to the high school."

"I'm sure they don't mind."

"You're probably right." Once again, her face swelled with happiness. Her body was so thin and fragile that the least emotional change was immediately visible. "And this way, you can bone up on your French," she said. "What a good way to spend your time. Mrs. O'Brien will be pleased."

"I hope."

"Were you in Sissy's French class?"

"No."

"No?"

"I took Spanish." No one who spoke French ever came to Katydid, but there were lots of Mexican pickers and factory workers. I'd thought I might be able to speak Spanish to one of them, but I never had the nerve to try.

"Oh, well, French is a beautiful language," Mrs. Vernon said. She backed toward the door. "I'll leave you now. Goodbye—how do the French say it?"

"Toodle-oo?" It was all I could think of. She didn't notice, just waved and closed the door.

On Saturday evening, she brought me dinner on a tray. Later, she sent up her husband, Walter, a big, growly man, who was a foreman at the KTD. He knocked and then filled the whole doorway, his chest hairs spilling out of a tattered, sleeveless T-shirt. He'd obviously come on this mission reluctantly, and he stumbled around trying to make conversation, asking me things like whether I was good at geometry and did I think President Eisenhower was going to dump Nixon. I couldn't talk to him, and finally he blurted out, "Well, do you want to come listen to the Cubs' game on the radio?"

I shook my head, and he went away.

Mrs. O'Brien called once, to see how I was getting on, and Bunny came on Saturday and again on Sunday afternoon, between shifts at the country club. By Sunday, she was smoking cigarettes, something she does when she's nervous. She stomped around Sissy's room, flicking ashes on the floor and stubbing out her butts in a manger that was part of a religious scene. She didn't mean any harm by it. She was distracted, and the thing looked like an ashtray. She kept talking about how the people of Katydid were against her and how we should have moved out after they sent Tom to jail. After a while, she started going on about how Eddie Boggs had said they couldn't do this to her, and how Eddie had said she should sue Mrs. Benedict and Chief Springer, and Eddie this and Eddie that until I started feeling worse than ever. Finally, I told her that Eddie had enough problems of his own without advising her on mine. Besides, I asked, what does Eddie Boggs know about anything? Her head snapped up, and she paused and looked around the room. "Ugh," she said. "What hideous wallpaper."

At night, I lay on Sissy's bed, stretched out on my back. I'd think for a while—and then, when it got bad, I'd try not to think. Before all this, the idea of suicide had never occurred to me. The thought was simply beyond my realm. People, animals, plants—every living thing fights to continue life, not to end it. But lying in the darkness on Sissy's bed, I became convinced that I had ruined everything for me and, worse, for Bunny. I felt so weak and hopeless that it seemed my life *would* end, whether I did anything about it or not. The string would simply run out, and that would be all. Later, after I'd lived with the situation for a few days, I started to daydream back, imagining that time had returned to Friday morning and that I was again biking up to the Benedicts' house. I'd have another chance, and everything would be different. But over that first weekend, the truth of what had happened was too close for there to be any comfort in imagining.

At about 8:30 Sunday night, after Mrs. Vernon had removed the tray of pork chops—still untouched—that she'd brought up earlier in the evening, the lights went out all over Katydid. I was already in the dark in Sissy's room, but outside, in the dusk, it was as if night had fallen very suddenly. I could hear the Vernons scrambling around on the first floor beneath me. Out of the stillness, a siren sounded, then another. The phone rang and, seconds later, Mrs. Vernon appeared at the door, holding a candle. Her face was a skeleton behind the flickering yellow light.

"Are you all right, dear?" she asked.

"Yes."

"Something awful's happened." She moved closer, and I could see that it wasn't simply the candlelight—her face had tightened with fear. "Someone's hit a light pole out on Willow Road. A terrible accident, they're sure to be dead."

Around us, the light from the unsteady flame made the statues move.

"Are you all right?" she asked again.

"Yes," I said. In fact, I was surprised at how calm I was. For two days, I'd been preparing for death. Now, it had turned out to be someone else's.

"Do you want me to leave you a candle?" she asked.

"No, thanks, the dark is fine."

"Sissy hated the dark. She always slept with a nightlight," Mrs. Vernon said. She added quickly, "I wish you'd take a candle."

"No, thanks, I'm just going to lie here."

"Well, all right. Call me if you need anything. . . . Call me." She looked at me longingly. For a moment, I thought she really loved me.

"I will," I said.

After she'd gone, I let myself cry at last. The tears poured down my face, soaking Sissy's pillow. I cried so hard and long I amazed myself—where does all this liquid come from?

The sirens carried on for an hour or so. Then everything was quiet again, except for an occasional motorcycle gunning down Oak Street. After a while, I started to notice a humming sound, a low, mechanical noise that almost made the air vibrate. The noise seemed familiar, like something I'd heard long ago, but I didn't recognize it until I sat up in bed and put my ear to the windowscreen. It was the sound of the machines down the street at the KTD, working right through the weekend and the blackout. Walking past the factory, I'd heard that sound a thousand times before, but only close up. The other noises of the town drowned it out as soon as I was a block or so away. But now, with the rest of the town silenced, the sound took over the neighborhood, covering things like a light snowfall. Later, at midnight, the factory whistle blew a moist, promising toot, and I imagined a whole shift of men stepping away from their machines and sitting down with their black lunch pails and pulling out the sandwiches that their wives had made up and wrapped in wax paper earlier that evening. And thinking about how things just kept going down at the KTD finally helped me fall asleep.

FOUR

On Monday, Mrs. O'Brien arrived to drive me to court. "Achhh," she said, as we walked to her car, a maroon station wagon with wood paneling painted on the sides. "I never should have eaten that second corn muffin this morning." She patted her stomach. "It's just sitting there like a brick."

She motioned for me to get in front and then slid behind the steering wheel, hiking her plain white dress up above her knees. The back seat of the station wagon was piled with files and notebooks, many of them spilling papers and documents. The materials were stamped here and there with seals and covered with bold, black type. They seemed to come from some place new and threatening, and I was cheered to see on the floor a child's baseball mitt, its worn, brown fingers splayed open.

"Did you hear about the accident?" she asked.

"Yes."

"Was your electricity out?"

"Yes, most of the night."

She shook her head slowly. "A boy, probably hot-rodding. He hit a utility pole so hard he knocked it down. He was killed, of course. Michael Cooper. Did you know him?"

"A little." For a moment, I thought that knowing Michael Cooper might be held against me. He was a thin, sandy-haired boy with pockmarks on his cheeks. He was two or three years older than I, but his sister was in my class.

"Well, it's a shame, of course, but I don't see why every teenager today has to run around in a car."

She guided the station wagon toward the square, traveling slowly and making looping turns around corners. "Do you have your license?" she asked after a short silence.

"No."

"You're sixteen, aren't you?"

"Yes, but I don't know how to drive."

"Nobody's taught you?" She sounded pitying.

"Eddie took me out a couple of times," I said, eager to show that I hadn't been neglected at home. "He tried to teach me, but I wasn't very good. He said I was too uncoordinated."

"Eddie?"

I realized that mentioning him had been a mistake. I have to think harder, I told myself. Guard things. "He's a man, a friend of Bunny's."

"Oh. He's not your friend?"

"No. I mean, yes, sort of."

She braked sharply and slowed to cross the railroad tracks. "He doesn't sound like much of a friend to me," she said.

We parked just off the square, in a lot reserved for court employees. Walking the steep trail of steps to the courthouse entrance, we ran into Mrs. Covington, who works at the library.

"Martha, what are you doing here?" she asked pleasantly.

I stopped and tried to think what to say.

"Martha's got business," said Mrs. O'Brien, lightly pushing me forward.

We entered the courthouse, crossed the black-and-white checkered stone floor of the big, echoing lobby, and walked down a corridor decorated with yellowing pictures of judges. At the far end, people were gathered around two closed doors. A sign standing on an iron stick said JUVENILE COURT IN SESSION—QUIET. Mrs. O'Brien walked over to a bench where two hoods were slouched, their legs stretched into the corridor. "Excuse me," she said, "could you two gentlemen possibly make room for two ladies to sit down?" The hoods stared at her in disbelief. Finally, one of them stood up and lit a cigarette. Mrs.

O'Brien sat on the spot he'd vacated. She patted the bench beside her. "Here, Martha," she said. I squeezed in and the other hood hopped up. The two of them glared at us. Mrs. O'Brien ignored them.

"I hope your mother gets here soon," she said. "I told her ten." A clock on the wall indicated that Bunny had five minutes.

I didn't recognize any of the people standing around. Besides the two hoods, there was a girl about my age, with red eyes and stringy hair, and a younger boy in a pair of overalls with dried mud around the cuffs. Older people, probably parents, stood morosely by. After a few minutes, one of the courtroom doors opened, and a lady with short, gray hair came out. She saw Mrs. O'Brien and walked over. "You're next, Peggy," she said.

"Hi, Josephine," said the social worker. Then she shook her head. "Awful about the accident."

"Awful," said Josephine. "And the family lost an older brother in Korea. Two sons gone."

"Awful."

"I lost a pork roast, you know. The electricity was out for eight hours, and in this heat the thing just spoiled on me. I was going to make it for dinner tonight."

"These times," said Mrs. O'Brien. She happened to glance at me. "Why, Martha, your jaw looks frozen solid."

"I'm a little nervous," I said softly.

"Nervous of what? The court? There's no need to be frightened." She put her hand on my knee. "I go to these hearings all the time. This is just preliminary. Judge Horner will ask the police a few questions, and he'll want to know if you're being well cared for. You *are* getting along with the Vernons, aren't you?"

I nodded.

"Yes, I thought so. Judge Horner might ask you. And he'll set a date for a full hearing. That's it. The whole thing won't take more than about ten minutes."

"Can I go home with Bunny then?"

"Oh, I don't know about that. These things have to go in stages." She paused, studying me, and then adjusted the bow on the front of my blouse. "Now, don't you look nice," she said. "Is the blouse new?"

I shook my head.

"Well, it's a smart outfit. You're lucky—you're tall, and you can wear smart things. Doesn't she look nice, Josephine?"

37

"Yes," said Josephine. "Dressed for court."

By 10:15, Bunny still hadn't arrived. She always had trouble getting out of bed on mornings after she's worked. Mrs. O'Brien began to look past me, searching down the corridor toward the lobby. "We can't keep the judge waiting," she murmured ominously.

Five minutes later, a young boy and his father pounded out of Judge Horner's courtroom. The boy's name was Louie. I'd seen him around town. He couldn't be more than eleven or twelve, but he was notorious in a way—he had an unusual, piercing voice, like a dentist's drill. Rather than keeping quiet, so as not to draw attention to the problem, he spent most of his time talking loudly, using his voice as if it were some kind of weapon with which to assault people.

Now, however, Louie was quiet. His head hung over his chest while his father—a big man, in work clothes and boots—guided him roughly down the corridor. I wondered what the boy had done.

"Hey! Lou-eee!" called out one of the hoods. But Louie's eyes never left the floor.

Soon Josephine came to the courtroom door and waved us in. "What about Bunny?" I asked Mrs. O'Brien.

"I warned her," she said. "We'll manage."

The courtroom looked far too big. At home, I'd heard Bunny and Tom talk of the "juvenile court," and the words had always suggested something small and homey—something, in fact, on a scale with juveniles. But behind the heavy wood door, Judge Horner's court spread out in vastness. Thin, dirt-speckled windows stretched far up the high walls. Two propeller-like ceiling fans turned slowly above our heads. Rows of empty seating, like pews, lined the floor, and at the front, the judge's bench sat on a raised platform, backed by an American flag and a flag of Illinois. The Great Seal of Katydid County—a cow sniffing a corn tassle—hung from the wall. It frightened me to feel so dwarfed by the place, to have all that space devoted to me.

Down front, Sergeant Tony was sitting at a table. He looked up blankly as Mrs. O'Brien and I took seats at a table across from his. A few seconds later, a man in a suit and tie came in and sat beside Sergeant Tony. The man nodded a greeting to Mrs. O'Brien.

"Hello, Mr. Moon," she said. Francis X. Moon is the prosecutor.

We sat for a few minutes, and then Josephine came out of a door in front and asked if we were ready. Mrs. O'Brien said Bunny wasn't there yet. Josephine frowned and disappeared behind the door again. Sergeant Tony and Francis X. Moon whispered quietly together. Mrs. O'Brien just sat there, her hands folded on the table. I didn't move at all. If only they had let me stay with Bunny, I thought, I could have got her here on time.

Finally, Josephine came out again. She stood on the platform in front and arched her back. "All rise," she yelled, and we stood up. In marched the judge, a middle-aged man wearing a checkered sports jacket. He sat down and nodded at Mrs. O'Brien, without seeming to notice me. Then he turned to the two men.

"Heard anything yet?" he asked.

"They're running tests," said Mr. Moon. He spoke in a quick, eager voice. I'd been expecting something deeper. "They found some glass in the back seat, maybe from a bottle. But then, there was glass all over."

"Did we have him?" the judge asked. "I think I remember the name."

Mr. Moon looked at Sergeant Tony. "No, your honor," the officer said. "I don't believe I ever picked him up. You may be thinking of his cousin, Kurt Cooper."

"Yes, Kurt Cooper," said the judge. "Setting fires?"

"Stealing batteries."

"Little guy? Father was chewing a toothpick."

"Yes, your honor."

"Oh, yeah," Judge Horner said. "Cooper."

"We can't quite figure out how it happened," said Mr. Moon.

"Drag racing?" asked the judge.

"Not likely. They drag race out on that flat stretch on Thompson Road, near the old McIntyre farm. This happened along that big curve, just before the Stewart place."

"Oh, I know where you mean. There's a line of trees there on the right."

"That's what's strange. The utility pole is off the road. Cooper managed to fly through the trees without hitting one. You and I couldn't push a wheelbarrow through there without bumping a tree, and yet this kid tears right through, missing every tree, and then hits the pole head on."

"Incredible," said the judge, shaking his head.

The men went on talking about the accident. Separately, each had driven past Kuhn's Garage to inspect the wreck, and Sergeant Tony had gone out to Willow Road to measure skid marks. Listening to their conversation, I thought of the campfire scenes from the old war movies that Tom loved to watch. The three of them seemed to take the accident personally, as if these were perilous times we lived in, and they were all slightly heroic for having survived as long as they did.

In the midst of their conversation, the courtroom door banged open, and I heard a familiar click-clicking coming down the aisle. It was Bunny, in high heels. She slid into a chair beside me. "Why don't they put something down on these floors?" she asked in a loud whisper. "I nearly broke my neck sliding around." Still ignoring Mrs. O'Brien, Bunny straightened up and stared at the judge. She looked wonderful, bright and sleek in her candy-stripe red dress.

"Hello, Mrs. Calhoun," said Judge Horner.

"Hello, Judge."

"Here we are again." He smiled weakly.

Bunny stayed stonily silent.

"How's your boy?" he asked.

"You know."

"He graduated from this court some time ago."

"He didn't get a fair chance."

"I'm sorry to hear you feel that way," said the judge. He turned away, but his eyes seemed to trail behind, as if reluctant to leave Bunny. "Well, let's get on with it, Frank," he said to the prosecutor. "What have we got?"

Mr. Moon stood and handed a sheaf of papers to the judge. Then he stepped over and gave one sheet to Bunny. At the top, it said, In re: M.C. Before I could read it, Bunny folded the paper into a small square and put it in her pocketbook.

Mr. Moon started to explain what the case was about, but Judge Horner waved him silent. The judge put on a pair of glasses and examined the papers. Bunny leaned over and put her mouth close to my ear. "Don't worry," she said. "It's gonna be all right."

"How do you know?" I whispered.

"I can feel."

Judge Horner finished, then took off his glasses and rubbed his eyes wearily. "I don't quite understand, Frank. She's found there in the bedroom with the boy, right? That's not a crime. I mean, we don't encourage boys and girls to get undressed in front of each other, but that doesn't mean we need to take up the time of the juvenile court with it."

Mr. Moon bounced up. "Your honor, the boy was nine years old. She was his babysitter."

"Nine? Does it say that in here?" The judge looked over the documents again.

"I believe so, your honor, on the first page—"

"Yeah. 'Butcher Benedict, nine years old.' Hmmm. I missed that." The judge moved his arm to scratch his head and the sleeve of his jacket scattered the papers on his desk. "Still, there's got to be some underlying crime," he said. "Unless you're saying she's a truant, or in need of supervision, which I don't see here, you need a crime for a delinquency petition. You can't just run her in for playing doctor."

Bunny couldn't restrain herself. "That's what I've been saying all along. There's no crime. It's all made up."

"Please, Mrs. Calhoun," said Judge Horner. Mrs. O'Brien reached over me to pat Bunny on the leg, but Bunny pushed her hand away.

"Lewd and lascivious conduct," said Sergeant Tony. "That's the underlying crime."

"Does that statute still exist?" asked the judge.

"It's got to be public conduct for lewd and lascivious," said Mr. Moon.

Sergeant Tony glared at the prosecutor. "It *was* public," Sergeant Tony said. "It was in front of someone."

"A bedroom's not public," said the judge.

"Your honor," said Mr. Moon, "I've already got a call from Father Wennington on this case. He's upset."

"So?" said the judge. The two men stared at each other.

"Well, contributing to the delinquency of a minor," said Mr. Moon. "That's the crime."

Judge Horner sat back. "But *she's* a minor, too, isn't she? At least for some purposes."

"Doesn't make any difference. Under the statute—"

"Do you have the statute?"

"Not in front of me."

Judge Horner turned to Josephine. "Get the code book," he said. She hurried out of the courtroom. "This is very interesting, gentlemen," said the judge, smiling. "We may have a case of first impression here."

While we waited for Josephine to come back, Sergeant Tony started whispering to Mr. Moon again. The prosecutor's brown suit hung lifelessly on his small shoulders, and strands of his thinning, black hair were combed over a bald spot on the top of his head. Sergeant Tony, making a point, jabbed a finger at him. Mr. Moon nodded. "Can we approach the bench?" he asked the judge.

Judge Horner said yes and the two men walked up, draping their arms over the front of the desk. The three of them talked quietly. Only an occasional hiss from Mr. Moon, who has a slight lisp, rose above the low murmuring.

"Why does everyone have to whisper?" Bunny asked in a loud voice.

I put my finger to my lips, and she groaned.

Josephine returned with the book. The three men looked at it, then sent her out again. Soon she returned with another. They studied that one. After a while, they called Mrs. O'Brien up to the bench. For a time, the four of them talked in whispers. Josephine stood silently to the side, listening. Occasionally, she'd look over at Bunny and me. Once, our eyes met, and she turned casually back to the group.

I remembered one time, years ago, when Tom came back from a court date, and I asked him what had happened. "I don't know," he said, shrugging. "How could you not know?" I demanded. "You're not *supposed* to know," he said. Later, that became a kind of joke for him. I'd ask what's for dinner. "You're not supposed to know," he'd say.

Finally, an agreement was reached. They all came back to their seats. Mrs. O'Brien sat down without looking at me, but, beneath the table, I felt her hand tapping my knee—a sign, I took, that things were all right.

Judge Horner continued to study the code book for a few seconds. Above his head, a ceiling fan spun listlessly, moving the air just enough to ripple the pages. He seemed to be looking over the book the way you sometimes read an encyclopedia—dipping in after a particular entry, but then hopping around, testing other subjects that happen to catch your eye. He apparently didn't care that all of us were waiting, and he certainly didn't seem about to pronounce anything serious.

Finally, he closed the book and put it aside. "Well, here we are," he said, glancing down at the documents on his desk. "This is J56—

129, In re: M.C. I'm satisfied, after careful consideration, that there are grounds for the county to get involved here. I can't imagine that this incident with the Benedict boy would have happened if the girl had been properly brought up at home. I'm not saying that I'm convinced yet that she's not getting adequate supervision—or, should I say, the right kind of supervision. But I'm satisfied that Mr. Moon has made the preliminary case. We'll have a full hearing in two weeks and just see what's here. In the meantime, I think everyone will benefit—particularly you, Mrs. Calhoun—if Martha continues her residence with the foster family, the Vernon family. It will be useful just to get everyone apart to study this thing carefully, and a foster family is certainly less severe than the Home. Of course, Mrs. Calhoun, you'll have unlimited visiting rights, provided you don't make a nuisance of yourself. Mrs. O'Brien, you'll work up a psychological evaluation of the respondent. And do a social history of the family, if you would." He picked up a small pack of papers and flapped them in the air. "I've got one here, but it's four years old. The girl only gets one sentence." He dropped the papers. "I suppose the father is still out of the picture?"

Mrs. O'Brien looked at Bunny. Bunny's head was sunk in her shoulders, and her eyes were glassy; she wasn't looking at anything.

"He's long gone," said Sergeant Tony.

"Well, all right," said the judge. "Anyway, you'll work that stuff up, Mrs. O'Brien, and Frank, you'll amend the petition in accordance with our discussions." He paused. "Now, I understand there was a problem interviewing the girl, that Mrs. Calhoun wouldn't cooperate."

"I think that's all cleared up now," said Mrs. O'Brien.

"Good."

The room was silent. The judge's voice was echoing around inside my head. I understood what he'd said, but the words he was using—words like "social history," "evaluation," "respondent"—didn't seem as if they could possibly apply to me. They were from another world, and I was still only a child, I was Bunny's little girl. Sitting there in that stiff, wood, courtroom chair, I felt tiny and innocent, the way I used to feel when I'd have a sore throat, or a stomachache, and Bunny would take me to Dr. Baker's office and put me up on the cold, leathery sofa in the waiting room, my legs sticking out high above the floor. There were medical magazines on a low, corner table, and

Bunny and I would look through them together, studying the illustrations of the diseases. Some of the pictures were hideous, but they were never frightening. They were from another world, and snuggled up under Bunny's arm, I felt perfect and safe in the world I knew.

"Have you ever been to juvenile court before?" Judge Horner asked me.

"No."

"Never came down with your brother?"

"No."

"He ever tell you about it?"

I shook my head.

"And your mother—"

I interrupted him by shaking my head again.

He frowned and looked down, overacting to convey his seriousness. "Let me say a few words, then." He started giving a little speech about the history and purpose of the juvenile court. "We offer you a second chance," he kept repeating. He sounded bored, spinning off the neat, practiced sentences with no enthusiasm and little energy. As he spoke, he arranged the papers in front of him into a careful pile. He was talking to me, so I kept my eyes on him, but, beside me, I sensed Bunny starting to fidget. Finally, the judge noticed. "What is it, Mrs. Calhoun?" he asked.

"Can I say something?" she said.

"Of course. What is it?"

"I can explain all this." She waved her hand, as if to indicate Mrs. O'Brien, Mr. Moon, the whole courtroom.

I leaned close. "No, Bunny," I whispered.

"Yes, yes," said the judge. "Go on."

"It's that woman, Mrs. Benedict—she doesn't like me, your honor. She's jealous, and jealousy is a powerful emotion and makes people do terrible things."

Judge Horner looked quizzically from Bunny to the prosecutor, then back to Bunny. "Jealous of what?" he said.

"No," I whispered again.

"Jealous because. . . ." Bunny started slowly, but suddenly the words tumbled out. "Jealous because I've got a beautiful, smart daughter, and she's got a dumpy, dumb one."

I bowed my head, burrowing my chin in my chest. Why'd she have to say *that*? Better to be marched off to prison, locked up like Tom, than to talk like that in the open. And the worst thing was, she probably believed it. She'd argue with the judge if he gave her half a chance: The town was conspiring against her; Tom got blamed for everything; now, Mrs. Benedict was acting out of jealousy. I could have recited the arguments by heart. I'd heard them all before—listening silently, holding them in as if they were our own dark secret.

Sergeant Tony let out a long, low, dirty-sounding whistle.

"What do you expect me to think, Mrs. Calhoun?" asked Judge Horner. He sounded gentle, almost helpless. "We've got a nice town here, a simple town. There are families here with six kids, ten kids, and not one of their children ends up in my court. You've got two, and now they've both been here. What am I to think?"

Bunny glanced quickly around, looking for an ally. "But she's been jealous of me for years. She tried to take Martha away—"

"Mrs. Calhoun," broke in the judge, "jealousy didn't put your daughter in that room with that little boy. She got there on her own. This isn't a trivial matter. I could have sent her right into the Home. Be grateful that I had some restraint." The judge arched his back, lifting his chin. "There's no reason on earth why the county should sit by and let you ruin another life. We've got a system in place here and expertise—the court, the social workers."

He stood, catching Josephine by surprise. "All rise," she yelled, scrambling to her feet and glaring at us. The judge held out his arm toward Bunny. A thin, pale, accusing finger jutted out of his sleeve. "My advice to you, Mrs. Calhoun, is to get your own life in order. Use these two weeks to settle your own affairs. I think you know what I mean. I'm not about to send your daughter back into the same environment that's produced all the trouble." He turned to Josephine. "Let's go," he snapped, and she hurried in front, holding the door for him as he whisked out of the courtroom.

FIVE

I sometimes think that this story is as much Sissy's as mine, that for everything I've learned about myself in the last few weeks, I've learned equal amounts about her. I see now how wrong I was about her, how much I depended on an idea that was fixed long ago and that I never bothered to reconsider. What I did was cruel, in a way—never giving her the possibility to change, until I came to know her, bit by bit, living in her room, in her house, with her parents.

The morning after the first court hearing, I awoke early. I felt tired in every part of my body, but I couldn't fall back asleep. I was too worried and unhappy. Lying on my side on Sissy's bed, as the early light turned the room a dull gray, my scratchy eyes were focused on the wall. After a while, I noticed that a spot on the wallpaper just in front of my nose had been disfigured. One of the daffodils was faded and slightly fuzzy, as if the wallpaper had got wet or been rubbed down. Leaning up on my elbow, I inspected more closely. The spot *had* been rubbed down; it had been erased. Some- one had drawn a heart in the cup of the daffodil and inside had written, "Sissy Loves Elro." Afterward, there'd been an attempt to erase the evidence, but the pencil point had made a permanent mark.

"Sissy Loves Elro." There was only one Elro in Katydid—how could there be anyone else with a name like that?

Elro Judy had been in my class for years. He had one of those farmer's faces that had been sunburned and peeled away so many times that it had become a permanent pink—though, in Elro's case, he'd looked that way ever since I knew him. He was strong and wiry and tall. From first grade on, he was one of the few boys taller than I. He and Tom used to get together occasionally for some minor mischief. Elro is younger than Tom, but Elro grew up early—physically, that is. He was the first boy in the class to start becoming a man, and it happened very quickly. In fifth grade, one day, the teacher told him to shave before he came to school again. He'd been growing a feathery little black beard. His voice got so deep you could hear him all over the playground. In gym class, when he sweated, his sweat smelled strong, like a man's. Over the years, he developed a personality to go with that body—awkward, rough, a little bullying. Though we'd been in the same classrooms, I probably hadn't said a word to him in five years.

Elro had always been a bit apart from everyone else, but to strike up a romance with Sissy? The idea seemed impossible. Aside from her constant cold, her dreadful, itchy sweaters buttoned up around her chin, her old-fashioned skirts, she was a captive of religion. There wasn't a place in her head for romantic notions, at least as far as I had ever been able to see. And even if she'd fooled us all, even if behind everything she'd really been secretly dreaming, she couldn't possibly have been dreaming about Elro. The two of them were just too different. They hardly belonged in the same world together, let alone together in a crudely penciled heart.

I didn't fall back asleep, but, before I knew it, the room was full of light. The sun was up. I'd passed a half hour, maybe an hour, contemplating Sissy and Elro, and not once had I thought of my own problems. There's a lesson there, I thought. Diversion. That's how to survive this. Sissy may rescue me yet.

Mrs. O'Brien came that morning for the first of what were to be our regular sessions. We sat in the parlor, a small, book-lined room off the main hall, with a sofa and several soft chairs. During the day, the oak tree outside keeps the room dark and gloomy. At night, Mr. and Mrs. Vernon sit in there and listen to the radio.

"Why don't you tell me something about yourself," said Mrs. O'Brien, after she'd settled herself on the sofa.

"Mmmm. Like what?" I watched her take a small notebook out of her bag.

47

"Oh, let's see. What about your interests. Do you have any hobbies?"

I thought for a moment. "Not really," I confessed.

"Do you sew?"

"A little, but our sewing machine's been broken for a year now."

"Cook?"

"I'm not very good at it."

"Do you go shopping?"

I shrugged. "Sometimes."

"Any school activities?"

"Sometimes I help in the library putting books away."

Mrs. O'Brien frowned. "What do you do with your time?"

"Oh, I'm busy," I said eagerly. "I read a lot, do my homework, clean up around the house, talk to Bunny. Sometimes I don't have enough time."

"What about religion? Your mother tells me you belong to the Congregational Church."

"Yes." I couldn't imagine why Bunny would tell her that. We'd been to church maybe three times that I could remember. The last time was two years ago, on Christmas Eve. Bunny made Tom and me get dressed up and she took us down for the evening service. Tom got bored during the sermon and started grumbling out loud to himself and making comments about the people around us. Everyone thought he was crazy. Finally, he stomped out. Bunny and I had to sit there, trying to pretend that nothing had happened.

"I thought I'd stop over and have a word with the minister," Mrs. O'Brien said. "Maybe he can come by and pay you a visit."

"Gee." The minister was a tall, thin, blond man, quite young, and he'd looked very unhappy while Tom was making all the noise. I wondered if he'd remember us. "Gee," I said, "do you think that's necessary?"

Again Mrs. O'Brien frowned. "It's now or never, Martha," she said sharply. "You won't get another chance. When we go back before Judge Horner next week, he'll want to know about the progress you've made. Do you understand?"

"Yes." Her anger startled me. It was so easy to go wrong.

"Then let's not have any more of this 'gee' stuff."

"Okay."

"Nix on 'gee.' "

"Yes, ma'am."

"Now, where were we?" She looked at her notebook. She hadn't written anything down yet. "Well, why don't you tell me a bit about your family. Go back as far as you remember."

I knew I had to open up, so I started talking about Bunny and Tom and our life together. I told Mrs. O'Brien about Bunny's house and the neighborhood, the trips to Grandmother's when we were little, the Sundays we used to spend at the city park or on picnics out at Mason's Farm. I tried to explain Tom as best I could, and I mentioned a couple of Bunny's boyfriends. But I didn't go into details on the touchier things. They would have been too hard to explain. Occasionally, Mrs. O'Brien asked a question or two, and every now and then she jotted something down. Mostly, she just let me talk. She didn't seem disturbed by anything I said; she didn't seem particularly interested, either. She just listened. Her manner was perfectly pleasant, actually. I sort of enjoyed myself. Even depressed as I was, I had the feeling that I could win her over, that she'd come around to helping me. The problem, I was afraid, would be Bunny. Mrs. O'Brien didn't like her. It wasn't just my imagination—when Bunny was around, Mrs. O'Brien was cooler, more formal, more of an authority. Even now, when Bunny came up in our conversation, Mrs. O'Brien's eyes darkened, her voice got lower. The signals were clear. But that left me with a dilemma: How was I going to befriend Mrs. O'Brien, earn her sympathy, without being disloyal to Bunny? I'd just have to be careful, I decided.

After we'd been talking for an hour or so, she folded her notebook, sat back on the sofa, sighed and closed her eyes. Her orange hair, the only bit of brightness in the room, stood out like a new summer hat. I wondered if she had to do anything to it to keep it that color.

"It must have been hard on you," she said after a while. "Your father running off like that and then all the trouble with Tom. It must have been hard."

"Not really."

"What?"

"It wasn't really hard on me."

She nodded. "Sometimes the person who's suffering most doesn't even realize the trouble she's got. It's like being born blind—you don't know what you're missing until you can see."

"But I can see. I can see perfectly—or, at least, I thought I could

49

until this trouble came up." I couldn't bring myself to mention Butcher's name. "I mean, I never knew my father, so I didn't have any reason to miss him. And Tom's getting in trouble was hard, but I knew I always had Bunny, we always had each other. We were close, no matter what. So I never felt deprived. It never even occurred to me."

Mrs. O'Brien smiled weakly. "Shall we turn on a light?" she said. "It's awfully dark in here, isn't it?"

I got up and turned on a floor lamp. The shade was made from a copy of the Declaration of Independence, and it threw off a yellowish light that seemed particularly false, given the bright sunlight outside.

When I sat down again, Mrs. O'Brien said, "I keep hearing about this Eddie Boggs fellow."

"You do?"

"Here and there. You mentioned him. And then the judge."

"The judge?"

"Sergeant Tony, too. When we were having the bench conference in court. He sounds like trouble—Eddie Boggs, that is."

"I really don't know him that well."

"How serious do you think it is between your mother and him?" Mrs. O'Brien's face was open and smooth. I couldn't tell what she expected of me.

"I really don't know."

"They've been going out for a while now, haven't they?"

"I guess."

The social worker let her gaze wander around the room. "It worries me," she said.

"Worries you?" I caught my breath.

She turned back. "Oh, it's just me," she said cheerily. She'd noticed my distress. "Don't you worry about it. I'm supposed to worry. That's my job." She threw her head back and laughed.

I managed to squeeze out a smile.

"I'm paid to worry. That's what a social worker does."

"Do you think things will work out for me?" I said. "I mean, do you think things will get settled."

She shrugged. "Look, at least you're not pregnant."

"Oh, no!" I held my stomach.

"That's irrevocable." She shook her head. "There's nothing I can do about that." She started telling me a long story about another case she was handling. It involved a girl over in Fogarty. She was sixteen, like me, and from a nice family, but she had a habit of hanging around with a bad crowd. She was fascinated by hoods for some reason. After a while, she started going steady with one. He was a rough character. His main preoccupation was fixing up his car, and he liked to steal things to put in it—hubcaps, fancy mirrors, things like that. He looked so ominous, however—long sideburns, slicked-back hair— that salespeople at the auto-supplies stores were always suspicious. So he taught the girl to steal the stuff, and she got quite good at it. When they finally caught her, they found a whole junkyard of auto parts hidden behind her family's garage. Anyway, she was in trouble, and he was on his way to reform school when they made their next big mistake. They took his car and ran away together. They got as far as Chicago and checked into a crummy hotel. He thought he was going to get a job at a gas station, but he didn't have a Social Security card. They ended up just hanging out in the hotel room until they ran out of money and the hotel clerk called the police. By that time, they were guilty of both stealing and running away, but worse, the girl had got pregnant.

"Think of it," Mrs. O'Brien said, her voice rising. "Sixteen years old, on the way to reform school, and about to become a mother. What's she going to do?"

I shook my head in exasperation and, satisfied, Mrs. O'Brien got up to go to her next appointment.

Afterward, I stayed down in the kitchen while Mrs. Vernon chopped vegetables for a church dinner. I offered to help, but she said no, that it was pleasant enough just having me for company. She poured me a cup of chamomile tea, so mild it was barely more than plain hot water, and I sat at the kitchen table. She'd been at her garden, and neat rows of carrots, beans, cucumbers, and tomatoes were lined up on the counter. She picked up a long knife with a wood handle and a blade that was wavery and bright from many sharpenings. As she pushed the vegetables forward, the knife kept up an even, metronome pace in her right hand. Watching her was a comfort, her work was so steady. All the while, she chattered on about Sissy.

I waited for my chance and finally, at a pause, I said, "Do you remember Elro Judy from our class?"

"Of course I know Elro," she said softly. Her eyes were downcast; she was hurt. Why had I assumed that she'd want to talk about this, that her daughter was a mystery to her, too? "The spring before Sissy died, Elro used to call on her," Mrs. Vernon went on. "They went out on dates a few times." She fumbled with the vegetables. Every knife stroke now was slow and carefully positioned. She'd lost the unconsciousness of it.

"Sissy went out on dates?"

"They only went to the movies. Sissy wanted to, and I couldn't see any reason to say no." Mrs. Vernon paused. "I think she had a crush on him." The word "crush" was hard for her, she struggled saying it. "I don't know why he stopped calling," she continued. "But it's been tough on him in the last year or so, what with his mother dying that slow death, and his father selling the farm. They live out at the Gardner place now, in the tenant house."

"Oh." I still couldn't imagine Sissy and Elro together. What happened when she talked about Jesus?

"Sissy was disappointed when he stopped coming around. She didn't let on, but a mother can tell." Mrs. Vernon put the knife down and looked up. "Walter never liked that boy, though. He never said anything specific, but he used to grumble a lot—that's Walter's way. He just didn't like the boy and was glad when it ended."

"Did you ever ask him why? I mean, Mr. Vernon—did you ever ask him why he didn't like Elro?"

"No, I figured he had his reasons." She took a white glass bowl off a shelf and pushed the piles of chopped vegetables into it. "Some boys are men's boys, and some boys are women's boys," Mrs. Vernon said. "And I figured that Elro must just have something that women notice."

That some women notice, I thought. Very strange women.

SIX

At about three that afternoon, I heard Bunny pull up outside. She owned a blue 1948 Pontiac that made a rattling noise when it moved, as if a stone were loose inside a hubcap. Eddie Boggs once checked, though, and didn't find any loose stones. "That car's just got a death rattle," he said. Anyway, I could hear it when Bunny was within half a block.

She parked at the curb and came up to the Vernons' front stoop. She was wearing her waitress uniform, and her hair was carelessly pinned up. Mrs. Vernon opened the door, but Bunny wouldn't come inside. Speaking through the screen door, she said she had to take me away for an hour or so to run errands. Mrs. Vernon was unsure— Bunny could certainly visit any time she wanted, but it wasn't clear whether she could leave with me. Bunny was indignant. "Do I need permission to drive my own daughter down to the square?" she demanded. Reluctantly, Mrs. Vernon let me go.

"I can't stand to set a foot in that house," grumbled Bunny as we got into the car. "It always smells like toast."

"Mrs. Vernon makes a lot of toast," I said. "She even makes her sandwiches with toast at lunch." I'd been rather impressed.

"Ugh," said Bunny. "Disgusting."

She drove down to the center of town and edged her way into the traffic crawling around the square. She honked and slapped the steering wheel in frustration. "Jesus," she said, "the businesses all move out, and you still can't find a place to park." She went around twice, stopping and starting and honking. An old man sitting on a bench yelled at her to lay off her horn. "It's these hot-rodders that crowd things up," she muttered. "They've got to show off their cars by driving around."

"The square's always been crowded," I said.

"Yeah, but with people who have some reason to be here."

She found a parking space, finally, in front of the courthouse. Just as we were getting out of the car, I saw a girl from my class, walking with two other girls I knew. I hopped back into the front seat and slouched down. "What's the matter with you?" Bunny said.

"I don't want to run into anyone."

"Don't be ridiculous," she snapped. "Hold your head high. You haven't done anything wrong."

"I just don't want to have to explain."

The girls walked by in front of the car, too involved with themselves to notice Bunny and me.

"See?" said Bunny. "Nobody knows."

She led me quickly across the green park that makes up the center of the square. People were out taking advantage of the tree shade, sitting on the benches or lounging in the grass. The bandshell was littered with hoods, who make it their special hang-out in the summer. A group of grade-school-age children was playing at the drinking fountain. As we passed the broad, black trunk of an elm, Bunny paused and pointed up at the sickly yellow leaves growing in sparse tufts in the upper branches. "Another dead tree," she said.

Leaving the park and crossing the street, we went into the tallest building in town, the Katydid Hotel. People say it used to be grand, but now it's mostly filled with offices. Since Chicago is only about two hours away by car, hardly anyone who's passing through needs to stay overnight in Katydid anymore. A wide, worn staircase cuts into the lobby of the hotel, and we took that up to the second floor. Bunny led me down a narrow hallway to an office with a sign on the door, SIMON BEACH, ATTORNEY AT LAW. Inside was a waiting room with several people in it and a secretary at a desk.

"Well, hello, Bunny," said the secretary. She was about Bunny's age, with brown hair teased up above her head. "Was Mr. Beach expecting you?" She smiled in a smug way.

"No," said Bunny tartly. She didn't like that smile. "Just tell him I'm here to see him."

"He's with someone," said the secretary. "I'll have to wait until he's between appointments."

Bunny surveyed the waiting room and marched over to a red vinyl couch. The couch sank when she sat on it, and she had to wrestle her uniform to get it over her knees. I plopped down beside her.

The other people in the waiting room watched us obliquely, pretending not to stare. There was an old, white-haired man in worn, casual clothes, and a young couple with a girl about four. The room was plain and windowless, except for the smoky glass in the front door and in the door that led to the lawyer's inner office.

Bunny closed her eyes and folded her arms across her chest. The old man and the family went back to the magazines they'd been reading, but after a few minutes, the little girl climbed down off her chair and walked over toward where we were sitting. She was wearing a fluffy pink dress and shiny, black Mary Janes. She stopped a few feet in front of us. She didn't say anything, but she stared intensely at Bunny, examining everything about her. I saw the little girl's lower lip tremble. She was entranced. She must have thought Bunny looked like someone from a storybook or a dream—someone too perfect and beautiful to be real. I smiled at her, but she didn't notice me. Her face was set, half in wonder, half in fear. Finally, her mother looked up. "Susie!" she called out. The girl backed off, her eyes still on Bunny, then she turned and scooted away, throwing a long look back over her shoulder. Susie's mother grabbed her and hissed something into her ear. The girl buried her face in her mother's shoulder, but, every few minutes, she couldn't resist peeking out at the wondrous figure across the room.

After half an hour, the door to the inner office opened, and Simon Beach came out, guiding a matronly woman by the arm. He stopped abruptly when he saw Bunny. "Hello, Mrs. Calhoun," he said.

"It's Bunny," said Bunny grimly.

The lawyer glared at his secretary and then went back into his office and closed the door. The woman who'd been with him frowned and marched out. A few seconds later, something buzzed on the secretary's desk, and she went into the inner office. When she came out, she told the family they could go in. She closed the door behind them and came over to Bunny and me.

"Mr. Beach won't have time to see you today, Mrs. Calhoun," she said.

Bunny didn't move. The secretary displayed her smile again and went back to her desk. I leafed through some terribly boring lawyer magazines. Bunny smoked.

After about an hour, the family left, and we went through the same act. The secretary took the old man into the inner office, then told Bunny it was no use. Bunny just sat there, exhaling smoke. I didn't know what she had in mind, but I'd seen her in one of these moods before, and I knew there was no use arguing with her or even asking what was going on.

Eventually, the old man left, too. The five o'clock whistle blew down at the KTD, and the secretary straightened her desk. She called goodbye to Mr. Beach, turned out the overhead light, and paused in front of us on the way out. "The door locks automatically, so you can just let yourselves out when you're ready to go," she said. She slapped us with that smile again as she left.

The waiting room was warm and filled with a dull, gray light. Clouds of Bunny's cigarette smoke drifted gently above our heads. For a while, the place was so still I thought Mr. Beach might have left through the back. Finally, I saw a shadowy form moving behind the door to the inner office, and I could just make out a face pressed against the glass. Suddenly, the lawyer flung open the door and strode into the room. "Now, Bunny—"

"Liar! You filthy liar!" Bunny jumped to her feet. "You liar!" Her voice exploded with cracks and pops, she'd been holding it in so long.

Mr. Beach was across the room, but his arms shot up instinctively in defense. "Bunny, my God," he said weakly. He glanced at me. "What's this, your daughter? Let's not involve her."

Bunny stood with her head forward like an angry bull. "You promised," she hissed. "You said any time."

He looked miserably to me for help, then dropped his hands, shrugged, and ushered us into the inner office.

Bunny and I sat in chairs in front of his desk. A window looked down on Parker Street, where the army recruiter's office is located in an odd little building made of corrugated pipe. In the heat, the recruiters had set up a card table outside, along the sidewalk. The table was covered with piles of brochures, each weighted down with a small stone. Two officers were sitting there alone, and the sidewalk was empty.

"This is Martha," said Bunny. "She needs a lawyer."

Mr. Beach smiled at me. "What happened? An accident."

"This." Bunny reached in her purse and brought out the paper she'd been given in court. She'd folded it into small squares, and the creases were already getting worn.

"This is a delinquency petition," he said, after unfolding the paper and looking it over. "It says here she's been behaving promiscuusly." His eyes shot over toward me.

"I can explain all that," Bunny said. "But I want a lawyer to do it for me."

"But this is juvenile court. They don't use lawyers there."

"Frankie Moon's there."

"He's just the assistant county attorney. I mean the defendants, the children, don't have lawyers."

Bunny turned to me. "Well, that's not fair, is it, Martha?"

I shook my head.

"See?" said Bunny. "Martha wants a lawyer."

"The only way you'll get a lawyer in juvenile court is to hire your own," said Mr. Beach.

Bunny stared at him. No one said anything for a few seconds. Mr. Beach swiveled gently, back and forth, in his chair. "Who was Tom's lawyer, the last time, when he was in criminal court?" he asked.

"Lewis Atwood. I didn't like him."

"Was he assigned? Did the county pay for him?"

"I didn't like him," Bunny repeated.

The lawyer slapped his hand on his desk. "Bunny, I can't take your case. I got a busy practice and I'm already overbooked."

Bunny glowered.

"I'm expensive," he said to me, shrugging. "Your mother can't afford me."

Bunny flicked her head in my direction. "Martha, will you leave us, please."

I went out and sat down again on the couch in the waiting room. Mrs. Vernon was going to be worried, I knew. I'd already been gone two hours.

The sound of voices rose and fell in the inner office. I listened hard, but couldn't make out what was being said. After a while, the voices got lighter and I heard an occasional laugh. Finally, Mr. Beach opened the door. He was holding a cigar, and smoke spilled out of the room behind him. "Do us a favor, wouldja, honey," he said to me. "Run down to the Buffalo and get us a glass of ice."

The Buffalo Tavern is on the first floor of the hotel, set off from the lobby by a pair of swinging doors. I'd never been inside, but I'd paused, once or twice, to peek through the crack between the doors. There was a long, curving bar, rows of bottles lined up in front of a huge mirror and bright-colored beer signs breaking the darkness. Men you d never otherwise see around town were always going in and out.

I walked down to the lobby, then stood by the swinging doors for a few seconds before pushing on through. The room was bigger than I'd imagined. The bar swept off in a slow curve and disappeared in darkness, far at the other end. A few tables were scattered to the left, and, at one of them, someone was hunched over. There was a mop of tangled gray hair, beer bottles all around—whoever it was seemed to be in disarray, and I didn't dare stare. To the right, on the wall above the mirror, someone had hung a buffalo's head and decorated it with a giant pair of earmuffs. The buffalo's blank, glass eyes looked down on the bar. Two men in suits were sitting on stools, talking to the bartender.

"It's all numbers," the first man was saying. He had a bald head and a crisp, efficient look. "They do it by numbers, and if the numbers don't add up, that's it."

"Yeah," said the second man. "There's nothing we can do about it. We just listen to the numbers guys."

"It'll be real hard," said the bartender. He had on a green knit shirt with a little palm tree over the pocket. "This town lives off that factory."

"Hey, I know," said the bald man. "I grew up in a factory town."

In the back, suddenly, there was a clumping sound, followed by the crash of breaking glass. A bottle had been knocked to the floor.

"Christ," said the bartender.

The two men in suits turned and gawked. The drinker slumped at the table straightened up groggily. I recognized Edith, an old woman I see around the square. In the summer, she likes to sit on a bench with her skirt pulled up and her stockings rolled down, getting a little sun on her knees.

"Jack, I shpilled it," she mumbled.

"I heard," said the bartender. "I'll get it."

"What's *she* doing in here?" asked the bald man. He made a face.

Edith's head rolled around her shoulders and she plucked absently at her gray curls.

"Look at her," said the bald man. "She's a mess."

"She's all right," the bartender said. "She's been sobering up for the last hour, just napping. She'll go home and go to bed now."

"No, I mean it," the man insisted. "Why do you let her in? She's disgusting."

"Hey, cool off," said his companion.

"Yeah," said the bartender quietly. Lifting the flap to get out from behind the bar, he noticed me. "How long have you been there?" he asked irritably.

"Just now. I came for some ice. A glass of ice for Mr. Beach."

"Ohhh," he said, putting down the flap. He scooped ice out of a big, open tray and handed me the glass. "Ice for the little lady," he said.

"The big lady!" said the bald man, leaning over to grin at me.

I thanked the bartender and hurried out.

Bunny and Mr. Beach stayed in the office for another hour or so. I could hear them laughing and the ice tinkling in their glasses. I considered using the secretary's phone to call Mrs. Vernon, but I was afraid Bunny would hear me and get mad. While the room got darker, I just sat on the couch and waited, hoping Bunny knew what she was doing.

At last the door opened and they came out. Mr. Beach's cigar was just an ugly stump, and he was holding it between his lips, though it wasn't lit. Bunny was rummaging carelessly through her purse. She was blinky, the way she gets when she's been drinking.

"Hello, Martha!" she said, too cheerfully.

I walked ahead of her into the hall. She stopped, still searching through her purse. Suddenly she tipped it, spilling her compact, some lipstick, a pencil, and—finally—the car keys onto the floor. "Aha!" she said, bending to sweep up everything. Mr. Beach patted her quickly on the bottom, while he winked at me.

"Come on, Bunny," I urged, but my anxious tone only confused her and slowed her down.

"What a fussbudget," she said, knowing I hated to be called that. "A fussbudget daughter." She carefully packed up her purse and strutted out, dangling the keys around her finger.

"What did he say?" I asked, as we walked down the stairway.

"Oh, it'll be all right," she said. "He's gonna work it out. It'll be all right."

"But what about the money? I thought he was expensive."

"He owes me," said Bunny.

Bright rays of the sun, surprising after the gloom of the waiting room, slanted across the square. The benches and lawns were almost deserted for dinnertime, though a handful of hoods was still lounging around the bandshell. I didn't pay attention to them, but when we were getting into the car, Dwayne, the simple man, came up behind us, running in his awkward way, with his arms and legs flopping in different directions.

"Where's your bicycle, Dwayne?" Bunny asked.

He stood in the street for a moment, huffing. Then he raised a bony arm and pointed at me. "Ho," he said. "Ho, ho." I knew what he meant even before a cackling sound drifted over from the bandshell.

"What?" said Bunny, sensing trouble. "What did you say?"

"Ho," he said uncertainly. His arm dropped. "Ho."

"He means, 'whore,' " I said.

Bunny stared at me, unbelieving, and then picked up the distant cackle. She slammed the half-open car door and stomped over to Dwayne. His face went limp with terror. He backed off, but he couldn't move quickly enough to escape Bunny. She put her finger at his throat, just above where his misbuttoned shirt opened onto a patch of pale skin.

"If you ever repeat that, I'll never speak to you again," Bunny snarled. "Never! Do you understand me?"

Dwayne nodded frantically. With the color washed out of his face, the dark stubble of his beard stood out. He's so childlike that I'd never really noticed it before, and I wondered suddenly whether he could shave himself or whether someone had to do it for him.

"Never," said Bunny.

"Nevva," repeated Dwayne, in a high, tight voice. He turned and ran back toward the park. Not watching, he cut in front of a car. It honked and swerved sharply to avoid him. Frightened, Dwayne skittered off in a different direction, down the street and around the corner. The cackling echoed behind him.

"Go home!" screamed Bunny in the direction of the bandshell. Then she climbed in the car and slammed the door again.

"It's bad," I said quietly.

"Silliness," she said. Her eyes were shining. The effects of the drinking had burned off. "The lawyer will handle everything. Put it out of your mind."

I told her I'd try my best to do that.

SEVEN

Bunny dropped me off in front of the Vernons' house. Hurrying up the stone walk, I saw Mrs. Vernon's head bob past the living room window. She'd been sitting, watching for my return. The door flew open when I reached the front steps.

"Lord, I was worried," she said, hugging me hard. "I almost called the police."

"We were at a lawyer's," I said. She kept hugging me. I didn't know where to put my hands, so I just let them hang at my sides.

"A lawyer's? Oh, Lord, I thought your mother had taken you and run away. I was afraid you were gone forever."

Mr. Vernon had already eaten, but there was a place set for me at the dining room table. Mrs. Vernon set down a huge plate of stew, brimming with chunks of lamb and vegetables. I still wasn't hungry, and with Mrs. Vernon watching every spoonful, I found it particularly hard to eat. That only made her fret more. "A young girl should have a big appetite," she said. "It's only old people like me who stop eating."

After dinner, I escaped to Sissy's room, but pretty soon Mrs. Vernon was at the door, asking if I wanted to join them in the parlor. I would have preferred to be alone, but, remembering Mrs. O'Brien's warning about making progress, I followed Mrs. Vernon downstairs.

Her husband was sitting in his chair, reading the Katydid *Exponent* and listening to the Cubs game on the radio. He looked at me for a second and something flickered over his face—a slight tightening of the muscles around his eyes that passed, apparently, for a greeting. Then he went back to the paper. I sat in a ladder-back chair beside the window. Mrs. Vernon took a pile of old *Life* magazines off a shelf and dropped them in my lap.

"Sissy used to love to look through *Life*," she said. Then she sat down on the sofa and picked up her knitting.

We didn't talk at all. The only sound in the room came from the radio as the announcer called the game. Mr. Vernon eventually finished the paper and picked up a copy of *Popular Mechanics* that was lying on the table next to his chair. Mrs. Vernon rocked gently up and back while she knitted. I leafed through the magazines. At one point, when Mr. Vernon got out of his chair to turn up the volume on the radio, I asked, just to be friendly, who the Cubs were playing.

"Pirates," he grunted.

In fact, I found I didn't mind sitting there. The wood bookshelves gave the parlor a warm, busy look, and the yellow light from the Declaration of Independence lampshade had a cozy effect at night. I started to think that staying with the Vernons for a few days might not be a bad thing after all. I love Bunny more than anything, but having a little vacation from her would probably be good for me, I thought. In some ways, we may be too close to each other. Even she used to say I should get out more, get to know more people. Leafing through *Life*, I came upon a story about a girl who was supposed to be a typical teenager, and she wasn't anything like me. According to the article, she spent all her spare time talking to her friends on the telephone. That's what made her typical. The magazine was filled with pictures of her with a phone pressed up to her ear. In one long sequence, her side of the conversation had been copied down. She was wearing shorty pajamas and lolling around the easy chair in her family's living room. The pictures were almost sexy—shorty pajamas don't hide much. Meanwhile, she was winding the phone cord around her legs and threading it through her toes, twisting herself into all sorts of contortions and all the time keeping the phone clamped to her ear. Her conversation, which was printed in italics, was hard to understand. She talked in half sentences and skipped from thought to thought. She kept saying, "Oh, ish," and calling

63

people she didn't like "ishy," words I'd never heard before. The article said the conversation had lasted for over an hour.

I felt a little funny reading about her. Not that I would have wanted to act like that, but her life seemed so different from mine. Half the time, our phone was disconnected because Bunny had forgotten to pay the bill. And, anyway, I didn't have any friends to talk to that way. I mean, I had friends, but they didn't have enough interesting things to say to go on for an hour while I lounged around in a chair and fiddled with the phone cord. Bunny was the only one I could talk to like that. Sometimes, when she came home from work and I was still awake, we'd start talking and stay up until two or three in the morning, even on school nights. We'd just chatter away. The time would disappear. We'd talk about everything. Nothing, really, but everything. Just talk.

I was thinking about that, not paying any attention to what was going on around me, when I started to sense that something was happening in the parlor. I looked around. It all seemed the same: Mr. Vernon was still in his chair and Mrs. Vernon was concentrating on her knitting. But something *was* happening. Mr. Vernon had set down his magazine and was gripping the arms of his chair. Mrs. Vernon was rocking faster, and every now and then, she'd glance anxiously at her husband. I couldn't figure it out: Not a word had been said between them, and yet she looked as if she were about to cry and he looked ready to explode. And then he did explode.

"Damn it!" he yelled, pounding the arms of the chair. Thunderclouds of dust rose in the air.

"Ohhhh," moaned Mrs. Vernon.

He jumped up, ran to the radio, and flicked it off angrily. That was it: the game. Something had happened in the game.

He glared at the curvy, gray Philco for a few seconds and then stomped to the window. Staring into the night, he ran his fingers through his hair, trying hard to settle himself down. After a bit, he came back, looking cooler, and turned on the radio again. A huge, scratchy crowd roar burst out of the speaker. The announcer broke in: "Well, that loads the bases, and Roberto Clemente is stepping to the plate." The announcer sounded depressed.

"Shaaaaa," hissed Mr. Vernon. He turned off the radio again. Mrs. Vernon didn't take her eyes off him. She let her knitting drop to her lap.

I couldn't understand why this was happening. They were only listening to a baseball game. I wondered if someone had been hurt or if one side had cheated. Was there something wrong with the man at bat? With all the tension in the room, I almost started to feel that I was somehow at fault. "Is Clemente a good player?" I asked Mrs. Vernon, trying to break the mood.

She stopped rocking for a moment. "He's a Pirate, dear," she explained, and she gave me a look that said I should never ask another question at a time like this.

Mr. Vernon paced in front of the silenced radio. Finally, he reached out and turned it on again. "Here's the pitch!" called the announcer. A smack like a cherry bomb going off came over the radio. The crowd started hollering, drowning out the commentary. When the announcer came back, he was screaming: "He's rounding third . . . here's the throw . . . he's saaaafe!"

For a few seconds, the parlor was very calm. All the energy was confined to the radio, which just sat there, like a small, gray animal, spitting out its scratchy roar. Suddenly, Mr. Vernon leaned back and lifted his chin. "Arggggg!" he screamed. The noise came from deep within him and overwhelmed the sound of the crowd. But when he ran out of breath, the crowd was still there. So he took a short, fierce swing and smacked the radio with his open hand, knocking it to the floor with a crash. That shut it up instantly, but the blow jarred loose the back cover, and inside I could see the little orange lights of the tubes fading only gradually, as if the old Philco were fighting against giving it up. Meanwhile, Mr. Vernon looked frantically around the room for something else to get mad with. I was afraid he might do something to me. Instead, he grabbed his copy of *Popular Mechanics* and heaved it against the wall. The magazine hit flat open and fluttered to the ground like a wounded bird.

"I think I'll go to bed now," I told Mrs. Vernon.

"Sweet dreams, dear," she said, trying to give me a smile but not having much luck at it.

I couldn't fall asleep again that night. The scene in the parlor had upset me and, besides, I had too many other things to think about. Too much had happened, just today, on top of everything else. The news from the lawyer sounded good, but I was a little wary. Bunny had a tendency to be over-optimistic. She wanted something to happen—and therefore it would. Still, having a lawyer had to help, I thought. Maybe he could make it all go away. I knew I was lucky that it had happened during the summer, when school was out. If I'd been in school, with everybody knowing, everybody asking questions—well, it would have been impossible. I just couldn't have managed. Some people obviously knew already—there'd been that incident with Dwayne and the hoods. The hoods probably learned about it from the cops. The hoods are always talking to the cops. But the hoods don't really matter, I told myself. I didn't care what they thought, and, anyway, I hardly knew them. They didn't really belong in Katydid, I realized. A lot of them moved into town with their parents for a few years and then just disappeared. They dropped out of school and went into the army or something. They just stuck around long enough to cause trouble. A couple of them had even teased me in the past, making remarks about how tall I was. Bunny's right, I told myself, don't think about it. Still, it was hard. It's an awful thing when people talk about you. Sometimes I heard people say things about Bunny. They didn't know I was there or didn't know who I was—or sometimes they just didn't seem to realize that what they were saying was hurtful. They almost expected me to agree with them. Were they cruel, or stupid? I thought of Edith, the old woman in the Buffalo Tavern. The bald man hadn't even been quiet about it, he'd talked as if she weren't there or couldn't possibly hear. Maybe she couldn't—she never flinched when he called her disgusting. I shuddered at remembering it. That must be about the worst thing a woman can be called. Disgusting. The word almost had an odor to it. She did seem to be in pretty bad shape, though. How did she get that way? I tried to imagine her as a young woman. Even now, she had a pleasant, round face, almost childish—she might actually have been pretty once. Didn't she have a family that cared about her? What had happened?

For a couple of hours, I flopped around on Sissy's bed, trying out my stomach, then my back, seeing how it felt under the sheet, then on top. Some hot rods chased each other up and down Oak Street for a time. Somebody walked by singing "Que Sera, Sera" to himself. At midnight, the whistle blew over at the KTD.

A little later, I heard a sharp pinging sound at the window. I sat up. The sound came again. Something had hit the screen. I climbed down the bed to look out.

The moon had set, and the street lamps on Oak stretched a few long, faint slivers of light over the lawn. The Potter house across the way was dark, and there didn't seem to be any light coming from the Vernons' house. Mr. and Mrs. Vernon must have gone to bed. Looking down through the leaves of the big oak, I stared at a silent black carpet of lawn. Suddenly, a tall figure stepped away from the tree. In my surprise, I thought it was Tom, come back from Sherwood to reassure me.

"Hey," said the figure, in a loud whisper. It wasn't Tom, but the voice was familiar.

"Who's there?" I asked softly.

"Elro." A pause. "Elro Judy."

"Elro?" I didn't understand.

"Yeah."

"This is Sissy's old room," I said, as if to explain to myself why he was here.

"I know."

"What do you want?" I had a sudden, frantic thought that he didn't know Sissy was dead, and I'd have to give him the tragic news.

He stepped farther out from the shadow of the tree. He had on dark pants and a dark work shirt. "Why don't you come down?" he hissed. "I've got some beer." He waved his hand, and I saw the glint of a bottle.

"No."

"Awww, come on. I'll show you some fun—show you how it is with a man."

I pulled sharply back from the window, afraid for an instant that his filthy hands could reach up to the second story and touch me. So he knew, too. Probably everyone knew.

He came forward, up to the side of the house, directly under the window. "Pssst," he hissed. "Hey! Martha." He was getting clumsy at keeping his voice down. The Vernons' bedroom was at the other end of the house, but someone was sure to hear him. From my angle on the bed, I could see the top of his head moving. He seemed to be working at something. Scratching noises came from below. Was he trying to climb up the wall?

As quietly as possible, I unlocked the screen and leaned out. The night air felt cool. Elro was standing right below me.

"Please go away," I whispered.

He shook his head. "I heard you were lookin' for action, and I figured, hey, I got plenty of action right here." He made a vague gesture with his hand and then snorted, holding in a laugh. He swigged the beer again.

"Please," I begged.

Cocking his head, he studied me for a few seconds. "You know, I always did think you were kinda cute—ever since sixth grade. I like big girls."

"Please."

With his empty hand, he reached in his pocket. "Look, I got money," he said, thrusting a fist of crumpled bills toward me. "I'm workin' the night shift at the KTD this summer." Standing with his arm upstretched, he swayed slightly, obviously drunk. He was hardly even trying to keep his voice down now. "Look!" he insisted, angrily. All there was to see was the tightly squeezed money. "Look!" he repeated, angrier and louder. "Look!"

I felt dizzy and had to grab the top of the windowsill. Out of the daze, a memory floated back. On a summer's night like this, years ago, an angry man was in Bunny's yard, yelling at the house, howling at a window, threatening, cajoling, always calling for Bunny. Inside, we were huddled together on a sofa, and I was scared—scared of the man, but scared, too, that Bunny didn't hate it as much as I wanted her to.

A light flicked on over in the Porters' house. Elro saw it and with two quick steps slipped behind the tree. I pulled back inside, then pressed against the edge of the window to look out. The light came from Grandma Porter's room. I watched her old, shapeless body roll out of bed and pad slowly out the bedroom door. A minute or so later, she padded back and came to the window, staring at the yard. She had a ghostly shape and a ghostly color. Her gray-white hair, released from its daytime bun, was surprisingly long, and it fluffed down over her neck. She was wearing a pale nightgown that hung loosely from her shoulders, exposing her big, fleshy arms. The darkness all around made her seem even closer. She turned her head slightly as she scanned the yard. Was she the only one who had heard us? After several minutes, she climbed back into her bed and turned out the light.

The yard now seemed even blacker. I searched the form of the oak's trunk for a bulge that would be Elro, but saw nothing. Maybe he'd managed to slip away. I stayed at the window a while longer, not really thinking, not really knowing what to think. The cool air felt good on my face and carried a fresh, grassy night smell. I breathed deep. My gaze was lost somewhere in the branches of the oak. I concentrated on the sound of the KTD, letting the comforting hum fill my head.

"Hey!" said Elro again. He'd stepped back under the window.

"I'll tell the Vernons," I whispered. "They'll call the police."

"Come on," he said, ignoring my warning. He was swaying, and his words were more slurred. "I got my dad's pickup." He swung his arm wildly toward the street. "We'll go to Wisconsin. You can escape."

"Shut up! Go away!" I drew back and relatched the screen.

Elro stumbled to the tree, staring all the time at the window. When his back was against the trunk, he slid down, collapsing in an awkward clump at the base. He took another drink of beer and examined the bottle. Then he slapped his forehead with his open palm. He looked unhappy enough to cry.

I pulled the curtains closed and lay back on the bed. Much later, about three, I heard the sound of an engine starting up on Oak Street. A vehicle drove away.

EIGHT

The telephone jangled me awake early the next morning. I sat up and looked out the window. Elro was gone, and he'd taken his empty beer bottles. All traces of his visit had disappeared. The sky was overcast and drizzly, but the small backyard seemed so empty and safe in the daylight that it was hard to believe he had ever been there at all.

I assumed the call was from Mrs. O'Brien. Yesterday she'd announced we would go swimming this morning, but, given the weather, she was no doubt postponing the outing. Lying back in bed, I waited for Mrs. Vernon to come upstairs with the news. She didn't, though, and soon there was another call and then another. The phone was on a table in the hall downstairs. From Sissy's room, I couldn't make out what was being said, but I could hear the urgency in Mrs. Vernon's voice and then in her husband's as the two of them responded to the callers. There was an urgency, too, in the Vernons' footsteps as husband and wife moved about the house in their morning routine.

I stayed in bed until just before eight, when I heard Mr. Vernon bang the screen door shut on his way to work. Then I washed, got dressed, and went downstairs. Mrs. Vernon was sitting at the kitchen table, stirring a cup of tea with one of her tiny, silver spoons. She brightened when she saw me and hopped up to start breakfast, but it was easy to see that something was wrong. Worry was weighing down her shoulders, slowing her actions as she moved around the kitchen. A few minutes later, after she had set a plate of scrambled eggs and bacon in front of me, she explained. "There's talk they're going to shut down the KTD. The company that owns it lost some contracts. There were men here yesterday making arrangements. There's a story in today's *Exponent*."

"I might have seen those men," I said, thinking of the pair in the Buffalo. "That's terrible," I added quickly. "Terrible news."

"I don't know how this town will survive," she went on. "Four hundred people work in that factory. Think of all those people out of work."

The unhappy situation gave me an excuse not to eat breakfast, and I gently pushed my plate a few inches away. "What'll they do?" I asked.

Her lips tightened in a hard, flat smile. "I just don't know." She paused. "There's been rumors of this for a couple of years now. Bartlett Industries, the company that owns the factory, is over in Cleveland, and it's been on hard times for a while. I'd heard the rumors, but I never put any stock in them. The KTD seemed like too big a thing for them ever to close it."

"What'll *you* do? I mean, Mr. Vernon—"

"Oh, don't worry about us," she interrupted. "Walter is a foreman, and he'll find work at another factory around here. They're always trying to hire him away. No, it's the other people I worry about, the people on the bottom rungs who don't have something to fall back on. They're the ones we have to feel sorry for. Them and Katydid itself. What'll be left after the KTD goes?"

I thought of the two-story factory building, red brick on red brick, stretching the length of a football field, and I tried to imagine it closed up and quiet, lying there along Prosperity Street like something that had died. I'd heard stories about the Okies and I'd read *The Grapes of Wrath,* and I could see hundreds of Katydid families packing their belongings in cardboard boxes, tying everything down on the tops of their cars, and moving out in a long procession.

Suddenly, something occurred to me: With a crisis like this facing the town, how could anyone take the time to bother with me? Surely, they wouldn't care about me, now that the whole town was at risk. They had other things to do, an emergency to deal with. I was nothing; surely they'd see that now.

"They say we've got three months," Mrs. Vernon said. "Think of it, three months, after some people have given that factory their life's work. There ought to be a law. A company shouldn't be able to take people like that, use up their best years, and then throw away what's left, like it was nothing more than a cornhusk." Her small, white teeth bit at her lower lip. Quickly, I had another thought, again totally selfish: No one will notice me. I'd been agonizing over what people would think, but now they'd have something real to worry about, something that really mattered. Three months was too long to wait: I wanted the KTD to close down immediately. "Can anything be done?" I asked.

Mrs. Vernon stood up in several slow, aching movements. Her anger had passed as quickly as it had come. "I guess I'll just pray," she said. "That's all any of us can do. Pray and ask God to try to explain what He has in mind for us with this thing."

She picked up my plate of cold scrambled eggs and scraped them into the garbage can. "News like this kills an appetite," she said.

By the time Mrs. O'Brien arrived, a little before nine, the clouds were rolling in just over the treetops, and the wind had quickened into sharp little gusts. Outings to the pool were being canceled all over Katydid. "Are we ready?" she asked, standing on the front stoop.

"Just let me get my suit," I said.

If Mrs. O'Brien had heard the news of the KTD's closing, she didn't bother to mention it as we drove to the pool. She'd been to the high school the day before, collecting my records, and she'd run into Ellen Griffin, the assistant principal. At first Mrs. Griffin hadn't remembered me, and they'd had to find my picture in the yearbook to remind her. "She remembered your brother, though," said Mrs. O'Brien. "In fact, she said something that I thought was quite perceptive. She said that one reason you were so quiet might be because your brother had been so well known—in a negative kind of way." She took her eyes off the street and glanced at me across the front seat. "I thought that was interesting," she said.

I stared down at the bundled towel in my lap. "I don't know why she didn't remember me. I've talked to her a bunch of times."

"Oh, well, some people just aren't good at names." We drove in silence for a few blocks. "I also ran into Mr. Morgenson, your algebra teacher," she added. "He said you might have been quite a good math student if you'd paid better attention. Your mind always seemed to be wandering."

Once, Mr. Morgenson had caught me reading *Great Expectations* in his class. Afterward, even though I never did a thing but stare at him and his strange, Brillo-pad hair, he constantly accused me of not paying attention.

"I did my best," I mumbled.

"Oh, by the way," said Mrs. O'Brien. "I met that minister of yours, Reverend Vaughn."

"You did?"

"Yes. A nice man, and very young. He can't be more than twenty-five or so. And tall. He ought to play basketball. I don't think he's very athletic, though. He's shy, have you noticed that? It's strange for someone in his job, but maybe it's because he's young."

"Did he remember me?"

"Yes, as a matter of fact, I think he did. Yes, he did."

We drove across town, following, I realized with a moment's discomfort, the route I'd taken on my bike just a few days before. But instead of turning off on Parkview Terrace, we continued on Pinkerton Avenue around to the front of the city park, entering on the main drive, between the two stone posts.

The city pool is sunk into the top of a grassy hill, the highest point in the park. The pool was built two years ago, after the town held a special election to decide whether to spend the money on it. Mayor Krullke and the council had argued that a public pool would give kids a place to go—get them off the square and out of their cars. No one expected the pool to win, however, since elections to spend money almost always lose in Katydid. But about a week before the vote, Tom and a group of his friends set fire to an old abandoned barn on the Snyder Farm. They all got caught, but the incident was given a lot of attention in the paper. There was talk that the boys called themselves a gang, and people started remembering other suspicious fires. Suddenly, everyone got so worried about juvenile delinquency coming to town that the pool won in a landslide. Afterward, my brother was always bragging that they should name it the Thomas P. Calhoun Memorial Pool in recognition of his contribution to its construction.

We arrived just at nine and got keys to the basket lockers from Mr. French, the tanned, white-haired man who runs the place.

"Haven't seen you lately, Martha," he said.

"I've been working," I explained.

The changing room was cold and damp. My nose stung from the

disinfectant they use to wash the floor at night. I folded my clothes and tucked them into my basket. The tiles felt icy against my bare feet. I hate swimming.

"I'm looking forward to this," said Mrs. O'Brien. "I don't get many chances to swim anymore." She ran her hands lightly down her sides, stirring the fabric of her baggy beige housedress. "I know it's hard to imagine now, but I used to be a very good swimmer. I was the Minnesota girls' champion in the hundred-yard freestyle my senior year in high school."

"Really?" She was right; it was hard to imagine. "How'd you get so good?" I asked.

"Discipline, discipline, discipline."

My bathing suit felt stiff from long disuse. I hadn't gone swimming all summer. Sitting on a wooden bench, my back to Mrs. O'Brien, I stretched the suit out in my arms. Then I stood and pulled it on. It was extraordinarily tight, and the blue-and-white stripes—horizontal, to counter my height—bulged and narrowed around my torso as if they'd been sewn by someone who couldn't keep a straight line. I hadn't gained weight in a year, but was it possible I'd started growing again? I bent down a few times to touch my toes, letting the material adjust to my shape. No, the suit just needed stretching.

When I turned around, Mrs. O'Brien had already dressed for the pool. She was wearing a plain black suit that might have been left over from her high school team. It was far too small, pinching the middle of her body like an old-fashioned corset. Huge puffs of snow-white skin overflowed the top of the suit and squeezed out the bottom. The straps dug into her shoulders, straining to hold the material against her bursting chest. Her thighs were like bed pillows. And I'd never seen skin that white before—a pure white, not even pinkish. It looked as if her body had never been exposed to the sun.

She saw that I was staring. "I guess I've outgrown this suit," she said. She wrapped a towel around her shoulders. "It'll probably loosen up in the water." She clumped away toward the door in a pair of flat wooden sandals that slapped against her feet with every step.

We were alone at the pool except for a group of small children taking a lesson near the shallow end. Mrs. O'Brien marched down beyond the diving board and made a neat pile of her towel and sandals. Then she put on her bathing cap and walked over to the edge. Without testing the water, she bent her knees, rocked her arms, and flung herself in. She landed flat on her stomach with a terrific smack, sending two curling walls of waves crashing against the sides of the pool. The entire swimming class looked up. As soon as she hit the water, her arms were churning and her legs were kicking and she was chugging along like a big boat. When she got to the far end, she looked up to gauge the wall, did a quick, graceful, underwater flip, and came up heading back toward me at the same, fast pace. I stood near the edge, and she paused at my feet. "Come on," she insisted. Then she turned around for another lap.

The water looked cold and choppy. I dangled my foot over the side and confirmed my worst fears. At the far end, the swimming class was huddled under towels, while the instructor, a young woman I didn't recognize, stood and demonstrated a stroke, swimming through the air with her arms. Even the class won't go in on a day like today, I thought. Just me and my social worker. I pulled on my bathing cap, carefully tucking in a few stray hairs, and walked over to a ladder. I backed down a couple of rungs. The pool water lapped at my toes, then my ankles, in shocking strokes of painful cold. I'll never make it, I thought. By now, Mrs. O'Brien had made her turn and was again plowing back toward me. I felt the start of a gnawing worry deep in my stomach. What if I really couldn't go in? These weren't ordinary times for me, and that icy water represented a shock that my system might not be able to take. A swim right now might actually be dangerous. Why hadn't I pointed that out to Mrs. O'Brien? Why hadn't she realized? Relentlessly, she was moving toward me, her strong kick making steady thug-thug noises against the water. I climbed up the ladder and ran back to the edge of the deep end. Only one way to do it—one quick commitment, and it will all be over. Still, I wavered at the edge, staring into the gray water. The heavy odor of chlorine made me think of a laboratory. I could feel the agony of the cold slicing me all over. Why do I have to be so good at anticipating things? "Put it out of your mind," Bunny always said. But I can never put anything out of my mind. I know exactly how it's going to be in all its terrible facets. Just once, I didn't think ahead, just once in that dizzyingly hot cowboy room.

The water made a fierce cracking sound as I broke the surface. The worst pain turned out to be in my teeth, which felt swollen, on the verge of popping out. I fought back to the surface, but I couldn't breathe. I just pounded the water with my arms and legs while Mrs. O'Brien rumbled past on my right.

Halfway down the pool, I slowed and tilted my head to suck in air.

I started to realize that this wasn't actually so bad. Once the initial shock had worn off, the water was rather invigorating. For the first time that day, I was wide awake and clear-headed. Even the sandpapery feeling in my eyes had disappeared. I was going on only a few hours of sleep, but suddenly I was full of energy. Taking a breath every third stroke, I paddled down to the shallow end, then turned and headed back. Mrs. O'Brien, showing no signs of letting up, passed on my left. I rather liked this, I decided. It was as if I'd been storing up energy for five days now, and the exercise gave me a chance to release it slowly, in carefully controlled bursts. Up and back, up and back. I'd never done more than a couple of laps at once before, but I seemed to be tireless. It's amazing what you can accomplish if you simply set your mind to it, I thought. Mrs. O'Brien was right: Discipline, discipline, discipline. I concentrated on taking square, efficient strokes and kept up a steady scissoring of my legs. In my mind, I pictured myself knifing through the water with incredible precision and speed. Arms and legs at once, arms and legs at once. Bunny had recited that, over and over, as she taught me to swim, years ago, up at Grandmother's farm. I was only about three at the time, and Bunny was worried because there was so much water on the place. What if I wandered away some day and fell in? She started me off in the big, steel trough that the cows drank from, on the side of the barn. Walking along the outside with her hands under my stomach, she pushed me from one end to the other. The water was fresh and cold and sometimes, when she leaned over, the metal buckle on her belt would bump against the steel side of the trough, and the noise would ring through the water, louder and purer than anything I'd ever heard before. Later, when I'd mastered the trough, she took me out to the pond, wading on the muddy bottom while she held on to the back of my suit and I paddled in a circle around her. The water was low that year, and the pond was full of slippery green algae that clung to our bodies when we got out. Emerald people, Bunny had called us: human jewels.

I lost track of how many laps I'd swum—maybe five, maybe six, maybe more. Mrs. O'Brien was still going, and I was determined to stay with her. She couldn't last much longer, I thought. Just a lap or so. But I was starting to feel the toll. My chest was aching, and I was taking a breath on every stroke. I hit the end of the pool and turned to head back. The chlorine was burning my eyes. I should have kept them shut. Why hadn't I thought of that before? Now I could hardly see. I took a few more strokes. The heaviness came on quickly, with no warning—a sort of liquid weight, flowing from my neck, across my shoulders, down my arms. Now my arms were lead things, too heavy to lift, ready to break off and sink to the bottom. My legs, too, were used up. They hung beneath me, heavy and helpless. Was I paralyzed? I tried to switch to the breaststroke, an easier way to move, but the rhythm of my motions had been upset. I got confused and sucked in a mouthful of water. Coughing furiously, my throat burning, I sucked in more water. The spark of my earlier worry suddenly exploded, sending out terrible panicky electric waves. What was happening? I went under, came up, went under. Something was moving beside me. Mrs. O'Brien. Would she help? I summoned everything to lunge for her, but moved only inches, and she churned by, oblivious. I sank in the vast emptiness she left behind. Deeper, deeper, like Sissy. The panic started to dissolve. Aha. I see. Like Sissy.

My toe scraped something rough, concrete. The bottom. I stood, and my head and chest heaved out of the water. The surface was at my stomach. A little boy wrapped in a bright red towel had turned from the swimming teacher and was watching me, his face a mixture of confusion and concern. What had he just seen? How could he explain so anyone would understand? I'd almost drowned in the shallow end.

Ten minutes later, after I'd dried off and was sitting against the tall, wire fence, as far away from the pool as I could get, Mrs. O'Brien climbed out. Squinting, she spotted me in the corner, then picked up her towel and walked over. "Whew!" she said. A few strands of her hair, looking blood-red in the wetness, had squiggled out from under her cap. She toweled herself off methodically, patting down each arm and leg. "What a great workout," she said.

In the locker room, I showered and dressed quickly. Mrs. O'Brien took her time, lathering up twice and spending long minutes with her face up under the blasting shower nozzle. I was dressed and waiting when Tammy Mirkov paraded in, her starchy white bermudas glowing against the gold of her tan. She's a lifeguard, a cheerleader, a successful flirt, flashy but pretty in a ponytail kind of way. Any normal person would have been struck dumb at coming across Mrs. O'Brien and her Moby Dick body, but Tammy was interested in something else. She saw me and came over, taking a locker a few feet away.

"It's cold for swimming today," she said.

"Yeah."

With her blouse off, she hardly seemed naked. The white of her skin was like cloth against the dark of her tan. "What's been going on?" she asked.

"Not much." She and I had hardly spoken in years, not since our class had started developing its own empires and royalty, based on attractiveness to the opposite sex.

"I'd heard you got in some trouble," she said.

"It's not really anything." I stood up. I'd seen this coming. I knew it the moment she walked into the locker room. "Who told you?" I said.

Tammy put her head back and pretended to consider. "Oh, I don't know. Somebody—maybe somebody down at the News Depot." She went back to pulling on her suit, a lifeguard model, with a red bottom and white top. But my question had closed the short distance between what she wanted to say and what she thought she could. "Are they going to let you back in school?" she asked.

"Of course. I told you it was nothing."

She tightened her ponytail, playing at being distracted. "My friends and I were thinking—you'll either get a lot of dates or none at all."

"Huh?" I said. There was nothing else I could think to say. "Huh?" The words came out as clenched-up little squawks, hardly audible. She pretended she hadn't heard.

"See you," she said, casually throwing a towel over her shoulders on her way out. "I hope they let you back in school."

NINE

The main headline in the *Exponent* that day announced that Governor Stratton would make an appearance at the Katydid County Fair next week. He'd had to change his schedule, the story said, but now he'd decided to come on Saturday and present the award for the farm animal of the year.

I spread the paper out and searched the front page. There was a picture of the state treasurer, Percy Granville, looking worried and tired. A long story explained that he and two other men had been indicted for cashing phony checks from the treasurer's office. At least $300,000 was missing. Another story announced that one of the passengers on the *Stockholm*, the ship that had collided with the *Andrea Doria*, was the grandfather of a Katydid family, the Robert Olsons. The grandfather had been returning to Sweden for the first time in fifty years, but now he was back in Boston, trying to decide whether to risk an airplane flight. A short story in the left column reported that the number of new polio cases in Chicago was up to nineteen, and doctors couldn't explain the epidemic.

The headline I was looking for was set in small, thick type on the bottom left center of the page, a position that immediately made me think of an appendix scar: TALKS HELD ON FACTORY'S FUTURE. The story didn't add much to what I'd already heard. Several representatives of Bartlett Industries had been in town to discuss the future of the KTD. "Nothing is certain at this time," a man named Gerald Vance was quoted as saying. "It would be wrong to jump to conclusions. We're just looking at ways to make the KTD and Bartlett Industries more competitive." The story was only a few paragraphs long.

Bunny wasn't coming that day because they were setting up for the Champions Banquet out at the country club, so after lunch I went up to Sissy's room to try to nap. I managed to doze off lightly, waking once, covered with cool perspiration, because that same panicky feeling I'd had in the pool was starting to come back. I opened my eyes; the fear had left a metallic taste in my mouth. I couldn't remember what I'd been dreaming and, eventually, I drifted off to sleep again.

At three, the doorbell rang and soon Mrs. Vernon came to the bottom of the stairs and called me down. I wasn't expecting anyone, so I didn't bother to freshen up, only combing my hair with my fingers and pulling on my blouse to stretch away the muss. In the hallway downstairs, Mrs. Vernon was shifting from foot to foot. "Hurry, dear, hurry, you've got a visitor," she said, grabbing me by the shoulders and pushing me into the parlor.

A very tall man, dressed in a dark suit and tie, was standing at the window, staring out at the rain-soaked backyard. He turned quickly when he heard our footsteps. It was Reverend Vaughn from the Congregational Church.

"I hope you don't mind me butting in like this," he said. "I don't usually go where I'm not invited, but Mrs. O'Brien said there was a bit of a crisis."

"Oh." Why hadn't she warned me he'd be coming today?

"She thought you might like to talk." I didn't say anything, and he uttered a high, nervous laugh. "Of course, you don't have to," he added quickly. "It's up to you. It's such a personal thing—who you can talk to." He had thinning blond hair and pale skin. A pink blush appeared on his neck, just above his carefully knotted tie, and spread up under his chin. For once, someone was tall enough to give me a view under the chin.

"Would you like some tea? Or would you two rather be alone?" asked Mrs. Vernon, sounding as if she were trying to arrange a romance.

"Nothing for me, thanks," said Reverend Vaughn.

I shook my head. Silence tortured the three of us for a few seconds. Then the minister said, "The rain's let up for the moment. Would you like to take a walk?"

"Okay." I grabbed a jacket, and he ushered me out of the house. When he walked, his long body moved in sections, all elbows and knees and angles. I thought of Ichabod Crane.

We started left toward the square, then turned up Prosperity Street, crossing to the other side to put a little distance between us and the commotion of the KTD. "It's so sad," he said, gesturing toward the factory. "What'll Katydid do if it shuts down?"

"Mrs. Vernon was wondering the same thing."

He stopped for a moment and stared at the side of the building, a plain brick wall, lifeless except for an occasional grime-encrusted window. The machine noises, so comforting at night from a few blocks away, were a bit too insistent this close. "When I first moved here," he said, "I thought it was funny to find this factory, a huge factory, right in the middle of town. I couldn't understand why they didn't build it outside someplace, where it wouldn't be so close to so many homes. But then I asked someone about it and he showed me how stupid I was being. When they built the factory, it *was* outside of town. The houses came later, when people moved here to be close to the place they worked."

"That must have been a long time ago." It was hard to imagine the neighborhood as ever being new. It had nothing of the flat, cleared look of, say, Pine Tree Manor, the subdivision they put in west of town a few years ago.

"Oh, the place was built half a century ago, long before you were around," Reverend Vaughn said. "Your mother's parents might remember."

"My mother's not from around here. She's from Wisconsin. She only moved here when she was seventeen."

"Really?" He started walking again. "Why'd she come?"

"It had something to do with a man," I said—and wished immediately that I hadn't. Bunny deserved more privacy from me than that.

"I guess that's as good a reason as any."

We turned off Prosperity and walked down Sylvan Street. Though the sky had lifted somewhat, rain had been falling, off and on, for the last few hours, and we had to dodge puddles on the sidewalk. A few other people were starting to venture out—a woman dragging an empty, wire cart down to the Piggly Wiggly; Janie Wilson and a friend, probably on their way to Osgood's Store to buy candy; Jack the mailman, a deflated mail pouch over his shoulder. He nodded respectfully when he saw the minister.

Reverend Vaughn started asking questions—nothing serious, questions about school and friends, about books I enjoyed and movies I liked. He was gentle and shy, as Mrs. O'Brien had said. When our eyes happened to meet, his gaze would dart away. He seemed boyish to me, and he listened to me with a kind of boyish enthusiasm, getting excited when I mentioned something he cared about. At least he seemed to be excited—I guess you can't really know. At any rate, I liked him. Walking beside him on the sidewalk, I had a strange sense of my own presence. I couldn't stay out of the way. We kept bumping together. I'm so clumsy sometimes, so big. He's much taller than I, and yet I seemed to be occupying more space than ever. A breeze brushed by, lifting my hair, and for a moment, I was afraid the odor of chlorine, picked up in my morning swim, was floating off me, like bad perfume.

After a while, a sprinkle opened up again, and we ducked into the little park behind Sylvan Street Elementary School. The playground equipment was glistening with raindrops, but there was a small shelter there, just a roof supported by four thick wooden shafts. We sat at the picnic table underneath. Someone had carved "Elvis" in big, fresh letters in the tabletop.

"Do you like him?" Reverend Vaughn asked, pointing to the name.

"He's all right. I kind of like his voice. It's so deep."

"He's not too loud?"

"Maybe a little, but you get used to that."

"And the wiggling?"

"I've never seen him. I just hear him on the radio."

"He's supposed to be on Ed Sullivan this fall."

"I know. I'll try to watch."

The minister's legs didn't fit easily under the picnic table, so he stretched them out to the side. Drops of rain dripped off the end of the roof and splattered on his polished black shoes. "I don't know about Elvis," he said. "He has an effect on people. He does something."

"He's a fad," I said.

"Yes, but why? Why him?"

"He's different. He sounds different."

"It's more than that. I'll give you an example, but you mustn't repeat this because it involves local people."

I nodded.

"A few weeks ago, a father in the church came to me. He's not a man who comes to church often, but I knew him, and I knew his family. I thought he was a nice enough guy, a well-meaning person. But he wanted me to do something for him. He asked me to talk to his daughter. She's about your age, maybe a year or so older, and it seems they'd been fighting about her Elvis records. He said he'd put up with all the Johnny Rays and Bill Haleys and whoever else she brought home, but Elvis the Pelvis was it. She was too involved. Elvis had to go. Well, I told the man I'd be happy to talk to his daughter, but I couldn't tell her to get rid of her Elvis collection—that was something they had to work out between themselves. So he told me to forget it. He was actually sort of irritated with me. He wanted me to be the enforcer."

The minister reached down and swept some drops of rain off the tops of his shoes. "So that was it," he went on. "But then, last week, I happened to run into the man on the square, and I asked how things were going with the Elvis records. 'Well,' he said, 'I just went in there and broke them all. Smashed them over the bedpost.' "

"Wow," I said. I tried to imagine who the girl was, but no one I thought of fit.

"Yes," the minister said. "It's sad. And, you know, he's not an ogre. He's ordinarily a normal guy, with a good job. I asked him if he didn't think his solution was a bit extreme, but he was adamant. 'No Elvis the Pelvis under my roof.' "

"He's just a dumb singer."

"I know, but the truth is, it's not Elvis the man's frightened about, it's his daughter. He's scared to death of her."

"Really?"

"Well, not really—but, yes, really. He'd never admit it, of course, but I think he is. It's the same with a lot of people. They're scared to death of you kids, and I can't figure out why. I mean, these things come and go—the fads, the music, the clothes. But today people act as if the world is so delicately balanced that as soon as one little piece of it changes, the whole thing will collapse. You know what I mean?"

"Yes," I said, though I wasn't quite sure.

"They get very defensive, very irrational." He shook his head. "Smashing up a record collection. Now the girl will probably want to *marry* Elvis, not just listen to him."

"Maybe she should buy the records and hide them."

"Maybe she *should* marry him. Teach her old man something about psychology."

I laughed. "That doesn't sound like a minister's advice."

"Oh, I don't know. Look at the New Testament some time. There's a lot of vindictive stuff in it. Jesus was very sure He was right."

"Wasn't He?"

The minister spread his arms. "Depends on who's counting."

Across the asphalt playground, a custodian was washing the inside of the windows in the elementary school. I'd spent six years there—seven, including kindergarten. Now, the corkboard walls had been stripped clean for summer, all the colored paper and crayon drawings and looping streams of alphabets were gone. The classrooms were barren and cold.

"Do you and your mother ever argue like that—over things like record collections?" Reverend Vaughn asked.

"No. We argue sometimes, but not over things like that."

"I've never actually met your mother," he said. "I've seen her, of course. She's very beautiful."

"I know."

"She's quite young, isn't she?"

"Thirty-five."

"Thirty-five," he repeated in a soft murmur. "How does she feel about this, about the trouble you've got into? Has she talked to you much about it?"

I hesitated, trying to guess where this was going. "She's depressed," I said.

He smiled weakly. "I can understand why."

"Yes."

"Did she get mad at you?"

"Not really. She doesn't really blame me. That wouldn't be like her anyway. Bunny doesn't really separate between trouble that happens accidentally and trouble that happens because somebody did something wrong. Either way, she figures, the thing is just trouble and something more to worry about."

"That's very unusual."

"I guess so." Even as I said it, though, I realized I was talking about the past, about Tom's problems. This time, Bunny was full of blame— for Mrs. Benedict, Sergeant Tony, Judge Horner, for the whole town of Katydid. This time was different.

Reverend Vaughn watched my face. "You're very close to your mother, aren't you?" he said.

"Yes."

"A lot of people your age have difficulty with their parents, they go through a kind of rebellion."

"I know. I could never understand that. A lot of girls hate their mothers. With me, it's just the opposite. Bunny's my best friend, she's the one I think about all the time." Something about the minister invited me to open up, and I started gushing about Bunny, about how funny she was, how pretty, how good to me. I went on for several minutes, until I noticed that his expression had changed, and he was looking at me in dumb, blank wonder. I stopped talking abruptly, but my words hung in the air, gonging like some stupid bell. Now he knew what a child I was. I felt crushed.

After a few seconds, he reached out beyond the roof with his palm open to the sky. "The sprinkle's stopped," he said. "Maybe we better head back."

Walking beside him, I hurried to keep up with his long strides, but I didn't talk. My stupid mouth, I kept thinking. My stupid, stupid mouth.

In front of the Vernons' house, he said to me suddenly, "I hope I wasn't too nosy back there. Sometimes I get a little carried away."

"Oh, no, not at all."

"You got so quiet. I was afraid I'd scared you."

"No, no."

"Would you like me to come again?" He stood above me. I looked into his face.

"Of course."

"Well, then, tomorrow—about three," he said. "It's a date." He turned quickly and strode off, hurrying down Oak toward the square.

TEN

"How was the Champions Banquet?" I asked Bunny the next day. We were sitting on folding chairs in the Vernons' backyard.

"A lot of drunk men," said Bunny. "It gets worse every year."

"Did they have movies again downstairs?"

"No, thank God. Some of the wives nixed that." She stubbed out her cigarette in the teacup she was using for an ashtray. "But there was a fight. Shorty might get fired."

"Why?" I was shocked. Shorty had been there as long as I could remember.

"Well, you know John Dent? He and this other guy, Mel somebody or other who was John's guest, decided to have a divot fight."

"What's that?"

"See who can make the longest divot." Bunny lit another Lucky. She inhaled, made a face at the cigarette, and then stubbed it out in the teacup. "So, anyway, they went out to the practice green. They used irons. Each of them had three swings, and they went at it real hard. It's amazing the amount of ground you can dig up with one club. Great big pieces of sod. They were kind of creepy looking, like furry green toupees or something."

"Didn't anyone stop them?"

"Are you kidding? Everyone went out there to bet on the winner.

They made giant holes in the green. And then a couple of other guys decided to try it, too. The green was covered with scars."

"That's awful." A piece of loose tobacco was stuck on Bunny's lower lip. I reached over to brush it off and startled her. Already, I could tell, we were losing that ease with each other that comes from living together.

"Anyway," Bunny went on, "in the middle of this, Shorty comes out. He takes one look at what's happened to his practice green, all that beautiful, soft grass torn up, and he throws himself at this Mel guy, who'd lost the contest but was still taking divots. Shorty just flew at him and knocked him right over. Started hitting him, too, though he's about half Mel's size. Mel was so drunk I don't think he knew what was happening. Then everybody else jumped in and broke it up, but they were really mad at Shorty—you know, getting on him about doing that to a guest and everything. Now they're gonna take it up with the executive committee."

"Poor Shorty. What'd he do?"

Bunny shrugged. "You know Shorty. He just kind of growled and crawled back to his room. He was out there today trying to patch up the green. They had it all roped off."

"That's so sad. All he ever wants to do is make the grass grow better."

"And then it usually dries out on him anyway," said Bunny. "This is the greenest he's had it in July in a long time."

The folding chair was tippy and uncomfortable, so I plopped down in the grass. Stretching out, I caught sight of Dwayne, around the corner of the Vernons' house. He was riding his bike along the sidewalk, staring back at Bunny and me. I waved and Bunny turned. "Oh, yeah, Dwayne was hanging around in front when I got here," she said.

Bunny had changed clothes before coming over, and she was wearing a sleeveless yellow blouse with buttons down the front. Her arms were beautifully thin and white. She doesn't care about tanning, and this summer she'd had even less sun than usual. She closed her eyes and leaned back in her chair. "We're supposed to have a session with Mrs. O'Brien tomorrow," she said wearily. "All of us together."

"I know. She told me."

"What more can we talk about? I've already given her the family history three times. Plus she's collected all your records from school. And Tom's, too. She knows all about him. She knows more about us than we do."

I plucked at the grass. It had spurted up with the rain, and the lawn was looking a little shaggy. "Sometimes I think I bore Mrs. O'Brien," I said.

"Congratulations," said Bunny, without opening her eyes.

The social worker had visited that morning, but instead of staying to talk, she'd taken me out shopping. She was thinking about buying a new washing machine, so we looked at models around town. She was remarkably diligent about gathering information, asking question after question of the salesmen. At Fanzone's, for example, she kept one salesman so occupied that customers were lining up. The salesman was a bald, nervous little man, and he started sweating through his shirt. He was too polite to move her on, even after it was obvious that she wasn't about to buy something. Later, Mrs. O'Brien told me she thought the man was "shifty."

Bunny was quiet for a long time. Somewhere behind us, across the maze of yards and fences, children were laughing and yelling.

"I hear you've been talking to that minister from the Congo," Bunny said. The "Congo" is what she calls the Congregational Church.

"He came to see me. How did you know?" I hadn't mentioned him to Bunny, and, now that I thought about it, I wasn't quite sure why. Ordinarily, I'm eager to tell her about someone new I've met.

"I'm your mother," Bunny said. "I'm supposed to know those kinds of things."

"He's a nice man. He's real smart."

"I'm not sure I like all these people pushing religion on you. Like this one here." Bunny nodded toward the Vernons' house. "Who knows what goes on out at that awful church of hers. Probably a lot of chanting and hocus-pocus."

"Reverend Vaughn isn't like that at all."

"Well, he's got his own problems," said Bunny.

Dwayne rode past in front of the house again. This time, he stopped. With his thin legs straddling the bicycle, he squinted at us, making a face.

Bunny stretched and moaned. "Ohhh, I'm so goddamned tired," she said. "Goddamned tired all the time." She slid down in the chair, folding her hands over her stomach, dropping her chin to her chest, stretching out her legs. There was something manly about sitting like that. She looked as if she were inviting someone to pick a fight.

"Remember when I had scarlet fever?" I said. "Seeing you sitting there reminds me. It seemed like I couldn't move, and you were always there." I was six at the time. Bunny was scared to leave me alone through the night, so she had someone carry the easy chair up to my bedroom. She practically lived in that chair. I used to wake up and roll over at night to see if she was still there. She'd be asleep, but with her legs stretched out in that same masculine way, as if death would have to climb over her before it could get to me.

"You were real sick," said Bunny. "The sickest you've ever been. You had a fever of 104, and it wouldn't go away. I remember one night you woke me up because you were talking nonsense—the fever had gone to your head."

"What'd I say?"

"Oh, nothing—nothing that made any sense. Words and phrases. Alphabet soup. Stuff about Tom. You kept calling his name. That's what woke me up. I was groggy myself, since I hadn't got much sleep, and I gave you four aspirin, like I used to take when I had a bad headache. The next day, Dr. Baker said I was lucky I didn't poison you."

"Dr. Baker came a lot. I remember him being there all the time." During the day, he seemed forever to be standing in the corner of the room, huddling with Bunny. They were always whispering, but his deep voice carried anyway. "Weak heart," he kept saying. He was worried that the fever would damage my heart. "Weak heart," I heard over and over, at least in my imagination. Tom picked it up, too. He started calling me "weakheart," saying the words together quickly, like "sweetheart." Weakheart. He still calls me that sometimes.

"Dr. Baker's all right," said Bunny. "He's the best man in town."

"Better than Eddie?" I asked, half teasing.

"Don't get smart," said Bunny testily.

"I was just kidding."

"Well, don't kid. This is no time to kid, especially about Eddie. He's done a lot for me. He's been there when I needed him. Besides, who are you to talk? We wouldn't be in all this trouble if you weren't thinking about sex all the time."

I didn't respond. One thing about Bunny, when she's upset, she'll say anything. I just looked away. But that was the first time I realized how serious it was with Eddie. I suspected he might have moved in with her.

After Bunny left, I picked up the *Exponent* and brought it outside, spreading it on the lawn to read. There was nothing in the paper about the KTD and not much exciting about anything else. Percy Granville, the state treasurer, was insisting he hadn't done anything wrong. An accident over near Emerson had claimed the county's twenty-fourth traffic fatality of the year. A boy, just out of high school, had been driving alone when his car swerved into the path of a truck. Another story said the farmers were having a good year. The corn was much higher than last year at this time, and higher than the five-year average. In a picture, a farmer was standing in a field, his arms outstretched, and the corn up to his neck. "Sea of green," said the caption.

I flipped through the pages quickly. On the next-to-last page, something in the letters column caught my eye. WITCHES, read the headline over one letter:

> Though the vast majority of people in Katydid are good citizens who lead decent lives, there are a few who insist on living like wild things. They think they're too good to follow the normal accepted rules of society. Instead, they respond only to their own, selfish desires and laugh at the proper lives the rest of us try to lead. When I think of these people, I think of witches, stirring a bubbling caldron and cackling over what they're getting away with.
>
> People like this never last long. They usually only destroy themselves. I've seen them come and go, so, normally, I wouldn't be too worried. But when I hear that one person in particular is passing on her tricks to her children, then I get nervous. Mayor Krullke and Chief Springer are doing all they can, I'm sure, but the dangerous influences on our children are everywhere these days. You only have to turn on the television, listen to the radio, or read the newspapers. In this kind of environment, the "witches" and their children have a chance to spread and do far greater harm. It's up to the mothers and fathers in this town to make sure that doesn't happen. We must demand that all the irresponsible parents are isolated and, if necessary, punished. We have a right to insist on this because it is our town, and because the welfare of our children depends on it.

The letter was signed "A Concerned Mother."

I studied the message carefully. I tried to imagine who A Concerned Mother was. Mrs. Benedict, maybe. If the letter was about Bunny and me—and I was certain it was—then she had to be a suspect. But the language sounded too formal for Mrs. Benedict, and it didn't seem like her to write a public letter. Besides, whoever had written it had only *heard* of the trouble. That wasn't Mrs. Benedict. It must be some stranger, I decided, maybe someone new in town. "Isolated and, if necessary, punished." What did that mean? I felt a chill and quickly folded the paper.

Getting up, I saw Grandma Porter, sitting at her window in the neighbor's house. She'd been waiting for me to notice her, and she waved at me to come over. I couldn't very well ignore her, so I walked over to the chain fence just below her window. She leaned forward when I got close. Her face was puffy and wrinkled, but her eyes sparkled.

"I seen you in the room," she said, lifting her arm from the sill and pointing toward the Vernons' house. Her knuckles were huge, like walnuts. "They got you locked up."

"No, I can leave when I want," I said. "I mean, I can come outside, anyway."

"They locked me up, too," she said eagerly. "They put me in here. But I'm gonna get away." She craned to look around me, making sure I wasn't hiding someone behind my back or down at my feet. "Harry is gonna come and get me and take me away."

"Oh, really? Who's Harry?"

She ignored my question. "He can't take you, though. Two's too many."

"That's okay. I'm not going anywhere anyway."

She stared at me while her jaw worked silently. I backed away and then waved.

"I'll tell Harry about you," she called out. "But you can't come."

ELEVEN

As three o'clock approached, I began to worry about Reverend Vaughn. It was important that he like me—Mrs. O'Brien had made that clear. He could be crucial to my case. More than that, though, I *wanted* him to like me. I wanted to prove that I was more than just a silly, mindless schoolgirl, like the Elvis fan he'd told me about. I wanted to prove that I was different—as Bunny always said I was— different from the other kids in Katydid. Different from the adults, too. He seemed like the kind of person who could understand. But the more I worried about him, the more I lost my confidence. What if I couldn't think of anything to say? Yesterday, conversation had come easily, one thing following another, but that was because I'd been surprised by his visit. I hadn't had time to freeze up. Today, my mind was a blank. Nothing would be worse than to sit there, helpless, knowing he thought I was stupid. I hated myself for having led a boring life, for not having interesting thoughts and opinions and experiences. All those years with Bunny, when talk was as simple as breathing in and out, now seemed like such a waste. He wouldn't care about the things I knew.

To reassure myself, I took a piece of Sissy's note paper and made a list of possible topics of conversation. My favorite movie. (I'd just seen *Trapeze* and loved it.) The fair. Monroe and Miller. (Did he think it would last?) Ringling Brothers closing up. But, no, those were all too trivial—Reverend Vaughn is more serious than that. He'd think I was frivolous. I tried to come up with some others. Dutch elm disease. Percy Granville. (For some reason, I'd always noticed him. Maybe because of that name—Percy. Who'd ever give it to a baby?) President Eisenhower's heart.

Nothing was quite right, but I folded the piece of paper and tucked it in my pocket. Every now and then, as I waited anxiously for him to appear, my hand dropped down, and I fumblingly made sure the list was still there.

He arrived driving a strange little bumper car, something called a Metropolitan. The front seat was far too cramped, and his body unfolded like an easel when he climbed out. From the living-room window, I watched him coming up the walk. He was frowning slightly, distracted by something, his eyes were on the ground. Still, as he got closer, he seemed to tower over the Vernons' house, too straight and tall to fit through the front door without stooping. Getting up to let him in, I felt light-headed for a moment. My heart was pounding, and I had to pause briefly until the feeling went away.

We took the same walk we'd taken the day before, down Prosperity Street, out toward Sylvan Elementary. He was quieter this time, more withdrawn, and I worried that it was because of me. Had he heard something since he left yesterday?

"It's warm," I said, as we scuffed along an unshaded section of sidewalk.

"Yes, the sun."

"And so humid." I let my shoulders slump, pretending to go limp. "That's the worst."

We walked along silently. My face burned. It was as bad as I'd feared. Now I was too distracted to remember what was on my list, and I couldn't possibly pull it out. I'd look like a complete fool.

He stopped suddenly across from the KTD. "I wish people would do something," he said. "Everyone just seems to accept the fact that it's closing."

"What can they do?"

He started walking again, looking down at his feet. "Oh, I don't know." He sounded irritated. "Maybe nothing that could help. But you can always do something, and anything is better than just giving up."

93

He was talking about me, I was certain. He thought I was just giving up on conversation, that I was an idiot, a small-town lump. I looked around—at the trees, the concrete sidewalk, the grass, the Byrnes's blue Chevrolet parked at the curb. Wasn't there *anything* to talk about?

"What do you think about the president's heart?" I asked, suddenly remembering.

"It's his head I worry about," said Reverend Vaughn glumly.

At Sylvan Elementary, we sat in the playground shelter, shaded from the hot afternoon sun. The picnic benches felt extraordinarily hard. I hadn't noticed that before. I watched as an occasional breeze stirred the canvas swings, each hanging limply above its own little dust bowl.

"How's your case coming?" he asked after a while.

"I don't know. Okay, I hope."

"It's hard to relax when something like that is coming up. Nothing else is important."

"I know." My mood picked up instantly. I had an excuse for being a dull companion.

"For what it's worth, I think this whole thing will blow over," he said.

"Why?"

"I think the judge will realize that whatever happened, if anything really did happen, it will never happen again."

"You think?"

"I bet. Besides, you'll have your minister there speaking up on your behalf." He pounded his chest, Tarzan-style, and I laughed.

"How'd you end up as a minister, anyway?" I asked.

"You mean, how'd I get into this line of work? That's the kind of thing boys ask prostitutes."

"Oh, no!"

"Just kidding." He leaned back, stretching out. "Actually, it was sort of an accident. I don't come from a very religious family. We were what I call potluck dinner Congregationalists. We'd show up on Sunday and for the big events but never think about church the rest of the week. At least, I didn't. But when I went away to college, I started hanging out at the chapel. I don't really know why, except that I didn't fit in well at school. It was just a little college, in Iowa, and everyone seemed to be a football player or a wrestler. But all the students had to go to chapel on Sunday, and, after a while, I found

I was looking forward to those chapel services more than anything. It didn't have much to do with religion—in some ways just the opposite, I suppose. I secretly gloated that everyone at this dumb little school had to stop whatever they were doing and come to the service. There was something equalizing about it. That, and I loved the organ music."

"Really?" I'd never taken organ music very seriously. The sound is so loud and pompous and windy. Tom can burp at will, and once, on one of our rare mornings in church, he'd belched in tune as the organist played a hymn. I was the only one who could hear him, fortunately. It was amazing—disgusting, but amazing. "Faith of Our Fathers! Living Still," exactly in tune, right out of his stomach. Afterward, I asked him to repeat it, but he couldn't manage without the organ blasting away. That was before Reverend Vaughn joined the church.

"An organ's so melancholy," the minister said. "The music fills me up. I could listen to it forever." He put his foot up on the bench and hugged his craggy knee. His pantleg slipped up a few inches and flashed a bit of color—he was wearing argyle socks, with streaks of bright red.

"But it wasn't until after college that I decided to become a minister," he continued. "At first, I went back to my hometown, Wilcox, Iowa. It's small, a lot like Katydid, only a lot farther from a big city. My dad worked in the bank there, and he got me a job in the bank, too. I hated it, though—all those numbers, everybody talking about money. I was miserable, so I started hanging out at the church. It was a nice place to go to be alone. And people used to go in there and practice on the organ."

"It sounds lonely," I said.

"Well, not really. I'd have a book and read, or sometimes I'd just sit there and think. I rather enjoy being alone."

"I guess you're lucky."

He shrugged. "Perhaps. But I wasn't even alone that much, because pretty soon the minister noticed me. He was an old guy who'd been there for years. I don't think he quite understood, but he was rather touched that I came around. Nobody else who was young wanted to get near the place. Sometimes, he and I would talk about religion—I'd had a couple of courses in college and knew some ideas. He was quite enlightened about some things, actually."

Reverend Vaughn sighed and put his foot down. "Well, eventually, he started telling me I had 'a calling' for the ministry." Reverend Vaughn made quote marks with his fingers. "'A calling.' It was mostly just that he was thrilled that someone was paying attention to him, poor old guy. But I suppose I halfway believed him. So I quit the bank and went off to divinity school."

"What was that like?"

"Oh, it was like any other school. You had to learn things, take tests. There was nothing special about it just because we all had a calling, supposedly. But what was wonderful was that it was in Chicago. I couldn't believe Chicago." His face lit up. He had white, perfect teeth. "Do you ever go there?"

"Sometimes. Not often. Last year, Bunny took me down to the Museum of Science and Industry. They've got a display set up so you can see yourself on television."

"That wasn't far from where I went to school." He sounded pleased. "I'd never been to Chicago before. I'd hardly been out of Iowa, and here were these beautiful, giant buildings, these streets crammed with people and cars. I got there and it was like that scene in *The Wizard of Oz*, when the picture suddenly goes from black-and-white to color. A whole world opened up. Everything had seemed so obvious and certain in Iowa, and suddenly, in Chicago, there were possibilities."

"And then you had to end up in Katydid," I said.

He smiled. "Katydid's not so bad. It's pretty, it's got the square. I like the people here."

"But it sure isn't Chicago."

"One thing Chicago taught me, and that's that you make of a place what you want," he said. "The possibilities are always there. It's just a question of recognizing them." He placed his hands on the table in front of him, folded, one across the other, as if in the small space beneath them he was hiding something. His fingers were long and slender, like tapered candles. Little tufts of blondish hair saved them from being too delicate. I thought they were the most beautiful hands I'd ever seen.

By now, I'd forgotten all about my list and about my worries of not having something to say. We kept talking, and I started telling him about life with Bunny. Perhaps I was too talkative; thinking back later, I worried that I'd said too much. I wasn't careful, as I'd tried to be with Mrs. O'Brien. Bunny would have been furious. I even told him about the night Bunny burned her dress, though I'd never talked to anyone except Tom about it. He and I were very young at the time. It was very late, and we were both in bed when Tom smelled something funny and came to my room to wake me. Together we padded down to the kitchen. Bunny was in her bathrobe, kneeling on the floor. In front of her in a messy pile was a dress—a strapless gown with a yellow organdy skirt. It was an old dress that she never wore, but to me, it was the most beautiful piece of clothing she owned. She had put it on once just to show me. Her bare shoulders were white and with all that organdy spreading out around her legs, I thought she looked like a princess. When Tom and I found her, though, she was trying to set fire to the dress, using a lighter somebody had left at the house. The fabric smoldered and smoked but wouldn't catch. The organdy just turned into black spider webs and dissolved. Bunny didn't know we were watching. She was sobbing, and she kept flicking the lighter and holding it under the material until the lighter got too hot to hold. Then she'd drop it and suck on her fingers and pick it up again. Meanwhile, the kitchen was filling with gray smoke. Of course, when Bunny saw Tom and me, she stood right up and pretended that nothing had happened. She said something about there being a spot on the dress that she couldn't get out. She bundled the material up and stuffed it in the trash can. Tom and I just stood there watching.

"What was going on?" asked Reverend Vaughn.

"Well, it happened not long after Bunny had broken up with Wayne Wadlinger. She never said anything, but I knew there was some connection."

"How did it make you feel?"

I had to think for a moment. "It made me feel that I wished I could bring Bunny back down to Tom's and my level, so she would only feel the things we felt. This was so different. Most of the time, she seemed like us—that was why she was so much fun. But every now and then, something would happen, and I'd realize how different we were. Like the burning dress. Why would anybody burn a dress? It worried me. It still does, I suppose."

"But don't you think a mother is supposed to be different?" he asked. "She's older than you. She raised you. The generations are always different."

"Yes, but Bunny never hid things from us—or at least she never seemed to. It was as if we were all kids together. And that's what made her so unusual. I knew that all along. I mean, even before I went to school and saw what other mothers were like, I knew Bunny was special. It was wonderful, having a mother like that, but I always knew I had to be careful. It wasn't the kind of thing you could go around talking about."

Reverend Vaughn nodded and stood up. It was time to head back to the Vernons'. "You were right to be careful," he said, cracking a thin smile, so faint it hardly seemed meant to be noticed.

TWELVE

After Reverend Vaughn left, I mooned around the Vernons' house.
I couldn't get him out of my mind. I knew it was silly to get carried
away like that, but I decided it was good for me—thinking about him
relaxed me for the first time in days. I reviewed our conversation.
Trading confidences, we'd almost made a pact, I thought. Maybe I
had gone too far, but he'd gone far too; at least, it seemed so. He was
so open about examining himself. There was no boasting, no anger,
no point to prove. He was so . . . honest. And those hands. I couldn't
stop thinking about his hands.

That evening after dinner, Mrs. Vernon went off to a church
meeting, and Mr. Vernon went out bowling. I thought I'd try to read,
so I browsed through Sissy's bookshelf. It held a strange collection
that included mostly children's books—Bible stories, picture books
about talking animals, that kind of thing, as if Sissy had stopped
reading long before she died. There were a couple of volumes of
Reader's Digest condensed books and, by itself at the end, a lone copy
of Hard Times, by Charles Dickens. I'd liked Great Expectations, so I
pulled out Hard Times and started to read. I saw right away why Sissy
had collected the book: The main character was named Sissy. Still,
Hard Times at first looked promising, perhaps even useful. "In this
life, we want nothing but Facts, sir; nothing but Facts," said one man

early on. But the tone overall was so blustery and overblown that I couldn't quite tell if Dickens was being humorous or realistic. Plus the adult characters all had funny names. Thomas Gradgrind. Mr. M'Choakumchild. My thoughts soon drifted.

I put *Hard Times* down and wandered into the bathroom next door. Sissy had used this one; her parents had another at the far end of the hall. Two bathrooms in one house—three if you counted the half bathroom off the kitchen. Bunny and Tom and I had made do with one all those years. I wondered how much money Mr. Vernon made. A lot more than a waitress at the country club. Leaning over the bathroom sink, I stared at myself in the mirror. I felt kind of free, knowing I was alone in the house. I even felt a little wild. I made faces at myself, trying to find expressions that helped pull my features together. I tested my profile, straining to look out the corners of my eyes. With my chin held up, there was something almost dignified about my silhouette, something angular and flat, like modern art. Maybe Reverend Vaughn had noticed that. I wished I had some of my makeup—a bit of rouge to highlight my cheekbones, some lipstick to improve my mouth. Unadorned, my lips seemed so weak, so trembly. But makeup had been the farthest thing from my mind when I'd packed. I'd never thought to bring some. Now, everything was in the bathroom cabinet at home—that is, if Bunny hadn't thrown it all away.

I opened Sissy's cabinet, behind the mirror. Empty. Just a flimsy, metal container of throat lozenges, rusted at the hinge. The narrow glass cabinet shelves glinted under the bright overhead light. How could anyone have an empty bathroom cabinet? It was depressing. The thought of Sissy irritated me, and I slammed the cabinet shut.

Maybe Mrs. Vernon had some makeup. Every now and then I'd noticed a slight reddening on her cheeks and lips. I'd never use her lipstick, of course, but I might just investigate to see if she really had any. The door to the other bathroom was ajar. I pushed it open and turned on the light. The room sparkled with whiteness and tile. A can of Ajax sat on the back of the toilet. The shelf behind the sink was empty, except for a wrinkled tube of Colgate and a bouquet of old toothbrushes sitting in a cup. I looked in the cabinet: Band-Aids, Bayer aspirin, emery boards, Q-tips, Bactine, Noxema shaving creme, a razor, blades, Jergen's hand lotion. And one small, green plastic bottle of pills from Conrad's Drug Store. The prescription was from

Dr. Baker for Mrs. Vernon: Take two daily, one in the morning, one at night. I picked up the bottle to study the contents: big, dangerous-looking orange capsules. I tipped the bottle and nothing moved. They'd fused together, obviously untouched for years. I put the medicine back and closed the cabinet. Even in their private places, these people were uninteresting.

Leaving the bathroom, I paused in front of the door to the Vernons' bedroom. I'd never been in there; in fact, I'd never even looked inside. Mrs. Vernon had a way of sliding in and out, ghostlike, with the door three-quarters closed. I got the impression she thought that a bedroom was somehow too personal to open up. I pushed the door open.

The fading light of the sunset passed through the flimsy drawn curtains and gave the room a yellowy, historic aura, as if, once, something terribly important and tragic had happened there. A double bed jutted into the center of the room. Beside it, a small night table held a Bible and an empty glass. Two tall bureaus stood side by side. On one was a pincushion, a Chinese box, and a nativity statue; the other was topped by a school picture of Sissy and nothing else. A couple of mournful paintings of Jesus hung on the wall. The windows were closed, and a faint, syrupy smell, too sweet for perfume, clung to the air.

I stood in the center of the room. Going through the bureau drawers looking for makeup was out of the question, but I felt a small excitement at being there—the kind of thrill I used to get from seeing how long I could hold my breath, testing how well my nerve stood up against my better judgment.

Suddenly something banged downstairs. Someone was at the door. I felt awful, even before being caught. More noise downstairs, a thumping. I ran to the bedroom door and grabbed the knob. Hurrying out, I pulled too hard, and the door slammed. A crash echoed after me. I ran down the hall to Sissy's room and closed the door. It had to be Mr. Vernon, home early. I lay on the bed, trying to imagine what had crashed in the bedroom. In the hall, below me, footsteps creaked. That didn't sound like Mr. Vernon, or like Mrs. Vernon either. I went to the door and opened it a crack. Silence. I tiptoed down the hall to the top of the stairs. Someone was down there. My heart was pounding so fiercely that it was hard to listen, but I was sure someone was there. I came two steps down the stairs and tried to look along the front hall. Light from the parlor window cut across the darkness, but the far end of the hall disappeared in shadow.

"Hello?" I said softly.

"Whoosh!" Someone made a noise, like a cushion letting out air. Footsteps pounded down the hall, and the front door flew open. The screen door slammed. I ran downstairs and saw a thin, flailing figure dash across the lawn.

Outside, I stood on the front step. Nothing moved on Oak Street. The houses were all lit from within. Someone was playing a phonograph: The wavery voice of a male singer drifted through the air. Dwayne's bicycle was sprawled in the grass beside the sidewalk, and up the street Dwayne was peeking out from behind a tree.

I waved to him to come over. He ducked back. I waved again, and he came slowly, watching all the time, as if he thought at any second I could reach out over the lawn and grab him.

"What were you doing?" I demanded, when he was at the bottom of the steps.

"Na, na, nuthin'," he said. He stuttered sometimes when he was nervous.

"Yes, you were. You were doing something."

He searched my face, and I could see the fear in his eyes. People are always saying he's lucky to go through life being a child, but I could see then how hard it was for him, never trusting what he heard, always having to rely on signals he picked up from people's expressions, from the sounds of their voices, from the way they stood. Think of all the times he must have been betrayed.

"I saw you," I said, as gently as possible.

His eyes dropped. "Lookin'," he said.

"For what?"

"If-fa-fa-fa."

"Say it."

"You was there." He scrunched his eyes, and his mouth went through a contortion, with his lips pressed out, like the front of a bugle. It almost seemed he was trying to kiss me, from four feet away.

"Well, I'm still here, so you go home now, Dwayne. You understand?"

"Yeah," he said, backing and then turning to scamper away. He picked up his bike and climbed on it. "Bye-bye," he called out, pedaling furiously down the sidewalk.

I looked up and down Oak Street. No one was coming. There was still time to go back to the Vernons' bedroom and see what had crashed. Whatever it was, maybe I could do something—fix it, hide it, think of an excuse. I hurried up the stairs and opened the door softly. That smell again—now it seemed thicker. Had I broken a bottle of something? I walked toward the bed. The drinking glass still stood safely on the night table, the nativity statue was intact, the pictures were all hanging securely. Then I saw it: The framed photograph of Sissy had fallen flat down on the second bureau. I picked it up. The frame was heavy. The glass was thick and, in the bottom left corner, a spidery crack angled from one edge to the other. Had the fall caused that crack? Maybe no one would notice. I stood the photograph upright again. Sissy must have been in about fifth grade when it was taken. She was wearing silly bangs that were a curtain across her forehead. A self-conscious smile tilted her face. Poor Sissy, maybe she knew.

I went quietly to the door, then closed it slowly, keeping an eye on the photograph to make sure it didn't fall again. Sissy and I stared at each other across her parents' bedroom, then I pulled the door shut.

THIRTEEN

"Did you notice that it was particularly hot in the house last night?" Mrs. Vernon asked the next morning at breakfast. She was taking an intense interest in preparing for the session coming up with Mrs. O'Brien and had spread out the elements to make sandwiches.

"Not particularly," I said. "Not any hotter than normal."

"Well, that's odd. A piece of glass cracked in our bedroom, and the heat's the only thing I can think might have done it."

"How strange."

"Isn't it," she said, her voice lifting, leaving a wispy trace of suspicion in the air. Or perhaps it was only my imagination.

Bunny arrived first that morning. I met her at the door, and she stood glumly on the stoop for a few seconds, reminding me that she still didn't like the idea of stepping into the Vernons' house. She'd been dreading this meeting, and, if anything, her mood had turned even sourer than it had been over the previous few days.

"Well, here we are," she said.

"How come you're wearing your uniform?" I asked. I'd put on my court outfit—the white blouse with a bow and my pleated summer skirt—and I'd been hoping that Bunny would dress up a little, wear something to demonstrate her seriousness. "You'll have time to go home and change before going out to the country club," I added.

"I don't want that social worker to forget she's dealing with a working woman," Bunny said. "I'm not the kind who sits around all day."

"Mrs. O'Brien knows that," I whispered. We were on our way into the living room, and I didn't want Mrs. Vernon, in the kitchen, to hear.

"It's good to remind her every now and then," said Bunny loudly.

Mrs. O'Brien came a few minutes later. Sitting on a sofa opposite ours, she rummaged in her pocketbook, a large, battered, patent-leather bag with a shoulder strap, and pulled out a stubby pencil and her notebook. The book was well used since the time I'd seen it last. The first half had a rumpled, thick look, as if it had been thumbed and worn. With me, just a few days ago, she'd started on practically the first page.

She explained that she wanted to use this session to explore my relationship with Bunny—how we felt about each other, what our mutual interests were, how we got on at home. I could have talked for hours on the subject, but Bunny was immediately hostile. She answered questions in monosyllables or in short, sullen sentences, empty of information. I didn't want to anger her by cooperating too much, so I wasn't very forthcoming either. As a result, we didn't get anywhere. The conversation was stiff, and I felt stupid. But Mrs. O'Brien kept pushing forward, asking questions and jotting things down, even though nothing we said was worth remembering. Worse, she seemed to be concerned about all the wrong things. She was fascinated by the fact that I called my mother Bunny instead of Mom or Mother, and she returned to the point over and over, as if it were the key to solving some lurking family mystery.

"What about your teachers?" she asked. "Didn't they encourage you to call her Mom, like all the other children?"

"I don't remember kindergarten," I said, "but Mrs. Rogers, my first-grade teacher, told me not to say Bunny in front of the other kids. I could never remember, though. Bunny always came out, and, after a while, I guess everybody just got used to it."

"Weren't there children who teased you about it?"

"Why should they care?" interrupted Bunny.

"Children care a great deal about things that are different," said Mrs. O'Brien.

"They all called her Bunny, too," I said.

"It's contagious!" said Bunny, with a laugh.

"Yes, well, contagious might be just the right word for it," Mrs. O'Brien said.

At last Mrs. Vernon brought in several plates of sandwiches and a pot of tea. The pot was covered with a quilted warmer in the shape of a cow. "Isn't that darling," said Mrs. O'Brien. There was a set of flowered teacups I hadn't seen before. After pouring for each of us, Mrs. Vernon hovered awkwardly, unsure of her role.

"Why don't you sit down?" invited Mrs. O'Brien. "You've come to know Martha in this last week. I'm sure she and her mother would appreciate your contribution."

"Well, I . . ."

"Sit, sit," the social worker insisted.

Mrs. Vernon quickly perched on the front edge of the sofa across from us. No one said anything for several long seconds. Mrs. O'Brien studied and ate two sandwiches. Bunny was curled up in a corner of our sofa. She hadn't touched her tea.

"Any news on the KTD?" I asked, to break the awkwardness.

"Just that they're talking," said Mrs. Vernon. She turned to Bunny. "How's your work coming?" she asked.

"Hard," said Bunny.

"I've never eaten out at the country club," Mrs. Vernon went on. "Mr. Vernon has, though. I don't remember why. We're not members." She waited. Bunny made her nervous. "The cook's an Indian man, isn't he?" To Bunny's silence, she added, "I've seen him around the square."

"An Indian?" said Mrs. O'Brien. "Does he use a lot of curry?"

"Oh, I don't know. Walter never said."

"It's just regular old food," I volunteered. "No special spices or anything."

"That's a shame," said Mrs. O'Brien. "We should use more curry in this country. It aids digestion."

"Really?" said Mrs. Vernon.

I turned to Bunny. "What's happened to Shorty?"

She shrugged.

"Did they fire him?"

"Not yet."

"He's the greenskeeper," I explained. "He got in a dispute out there the other night."

"He's a deaf-mute," said Mrs. Vernon. "Or only deaf. I can't remember which."

"Has he recovered from the fight?" I asked Bunny.

"He's resentful," she said. "He's always been resentful. He's a resentful person."

"That's a shame," said Mrs. Vernon.

"Why?" said Bunny.

Mrs. Vernon looked blankly at Bunny for a moment and then glanced at Mrs. O'Brien, as if to establish that it was all right to continue with this line of talk. The social worker was concentrating on another sandwich. "It's a shame anybody would feel that way," Mrs. Vernon said cautiously. "When you think of all God has given us."

"But he's deaf," I said.

"Ha!" said Bunny.

Mrs. Vernon's eyelids fluttered. She was hurt that I'd sided with Bunny against her. Now I wished I hadn't said anything. "That he's deaf shouldn't make any difference," she said softly. "God gave us life and faith, and they're what count. He gave us His only begotten son."

"Well, whatever God gave Shorty," said Bunny, "He didn't give him enough. He can't hear a thing."

Mrs. Vernon again glanced at the social worker without getting any help. "It's a tragedy, then," said Mrs. Vernon, her voice trailing off.

Bunny sat up. "That's not tragic," she said. "Shorty never had a chance. What's tragic is when you have something and then lose the chance. You do something, and it turns out to be the wrong thing, and everything after that is a little different and a little worse. That's tragic, and there are tragedies happening every day, but they don't have anything to do with this God and Jesus stuff." Bunny paused and looked away. On the far wall was an oil painting of Sissy as a little girl. "And tragedies don't have anything to do with dying, either," Bunny added, "at least not always."

"Well, that seems inconsistent," Mrs. O'Brien put in. "Under your theory, dying should always be tragic because it always involves a lost chance—the chance for more life."

"Some people just don't get that much out of life," Bunny said.

Mrs. Vernon rocked gently, kneading the apron in her lap. Bunny had gone too far. She realized that and softened a bit. "That's what I think, anyway," she added.

Using a cocktail napkin, Mrs. O'Brien removed a crumb from the corner of her mouth. "Maybe we should get back down to business," she said.

"Should I leave?" asked Mrs. Vernon.

"No, sit," said the social worker. "I think you should stay." She moved back on the sofa, sliding away from the coffee table and the collection of uneaten sandwiches. She settled herself and faced Bunny and me. "Now, tell me, if you can, how the subject of sex was handled in your house."

Bunny and I looked at each other.

"What do you mean?" asked Bunny.

"I mean just what I said. How was it discussed, what did you talk about? What kind of an education did Martha get?"

"It was discussed," said Bunny. "I gave her the facts of life, just like any mother would."

"Did you give her any advice?"

"Of course. I told her she'd ruin her life if she got pregnant."

"I know this is a difficult subject," said Mrs. O'Brien, "but please try to be a little more open."

"About what?" Bunny spread her arms. "I don't know what you want me to say." Her speech about tragedy had keyed her up. She was jumpy and excited.

"Well, let's start here," said Mrs. O'Brien. "When did Martha first menstruate?"

"Early," said Bunny, smiling.

"I was the first girl in my class," I said.

"She was very excited," said Bunny, looking at me and giggling. "She told the whole neighborhood."

"What?" said Mrs. O'Brien.

Bunny clutched her stomach and doubled over to keep from laughing out loud.

"I got it in school, and I couldn't wait to tell Bunny," I explained, struggling to hold in my own urge to giggle. "But when I got home, she wasn't there. So I waited out on the front step." I stopped and took a breath. It was a little frightening, this powerful need to howl. Bunny's fight to keep it in was shaking the whole couch. "And when I saw her coming, I went running down the street, yelling"—I paused again and closed my eyes for control—"yelling, 'I got it! I got it!' "

Bunny roared. " 'I got it! I got it!' " she gasped, then she roared

108

again. "Everyone came out to look. The neighbors thought she was crazy."

A damp, shrill giggle burst out of me. Once the first of it had escaped, I had to let it run its course. My whole body heaved. "I'm sorry," I finally squeaked to Mrs. O'Brien. Bunny and I rocked back and forth together. We were having a kind of fit.

"Oh," gasped Bunny, at last, getting control. Her eyes were streaming with tears. She nuzzled my ear. "Oh, what a time," she said, sighing.

The two women on the opposite sofa had watched us silently. Now, Mrs. O'Brien wrote something in her book. "Well, I'm glad there was no trauma involved," she said.

Afterward, Bunny and I fell quiet again. The laughing fit had wrung something out of me. I was wearied by the tension of sitting there, wearied by Mrs. O'Brien's questions, wearied by Mrs. O'Brien herself. Except for our brief outburst, she had controlled the entire session. It wasn't this way when I was alone with her, but with Bunny there, things were different. Mrs. O'Brien never said anything specific, but her whole manner gave the impression that Bunny and I were doing something very wrong. It was almost as if by her sheer size and her stony silences, Mrs. O'Brien had a kind of rightness about her. The room tipped in her direction, and the furniture, the tables, and most of all Bunny and I slid down to her feet.

When she finally announced that she had to go visit another girl in trouble, it was almost noon. As it turned out, Bunny didn't have time to go home and change; she had to head straight out to the country club for lunch. I walked her to her car.

"I don't think that went too well," I said when we were outside.

"What's there to go well?" she asked. "Nothing could go well with that busybody."

"But I think she can help us. I mean, I really think she's sort of sympathetic—she's on our side."

Bunny stopped at the door to her Pontiac. "On your side, maybe."

"Well, that's something, anyway."

"Is it? Shouldn't you and I be the ones on the same side?" She looked down and picked imaginary pieces of lint off the front of her uniform.

"We *are* on the same side, Bunny." I reached for her hand and she looked at me again. "That's crazy."

She sighed. "Maybe." She shook me loose and climbed in the car. "Anyway, Beach is the only one who's really on our side."

"Have you heard from him?"

"He's around." She turned the ignition. The car groaned several times before starting up. "I gotta get Eddie to look at this again," she said. "Bye, now."

As she was pulling away, I thought of something and yelled. She stopped in the middle of the street. I ran up to her window. "I wanted to ask," I said. "What you said inside about tragedy and lost chances—was that me you were talking about?"

She frowned and thought for a moment, as if she couldn't recollect what I was referring to. Then her face lit up. "Oh, no, not at all. You're thinking too much. That was just philosophizing back there. It was all baloney. It was just to bother those two busybodies, to show them I'm smarter than they are. I could say the exact opposite tomorrow."

"I thought so," I said. "It didn't really sound like anything you'd ever said before."

The Scott's Milk truck came down Oak and stopped behind Bunny. The driver, a bald man named Pete, who's supposed to be the best bowler in town, had room to pull around. Instead, he sat there and honked.

Bunny looked in the rear-view mirror. "Jerkface," she said. She turned back to me. "Besides, if I was talking about anyone when I said that, it was me. You're too young."

The driver honked again, this time leaning on the horn. Bunny poked her head out the window. "Shuddup, loudmouth!" she yelled. "Can't you see I'm talking to my daughter?"

"Do you really feel that way?" I asked.

"Get out the way, goddammit," screamed Pete. The top of his head was flushed red.

"I told you it was all baloney," said Bunny. She looked in the rear-view mirror again. "Jesus Christ, this town is full of jerks. See you later." She pulled away, with the milk truck on her tail.

FOURTEEN

I wasn't entirely reassured by what Bunny had said. Her remark about lost chances wasn't just baloney—nothing she said was ever just baloney. Since I'd moved to the Vernons', she'd been acting differently, thinking differently, too. Part of it was just the fact that I wasn't with her for hours every day. But something more than that was going on. She'd never been one to look back with regrets, but now, I sensed, regrets were starting to eat at her. Practically the first thing she'd said, that afternoon at the police station, was that she never should have come to this town. Then there'd been other remarks—quick asides, mostly, thrown off as if they weren't meant to be listened to—about her childhood, her old boyfriends, even about my father. In her hours alone, she was recollecting, wondering what had happened, maybe even trying to pinpoint the moment things had started going wrong. Thinking like that can get you crazy.

I worried about Bunny, but, as had happened so often during the last couple of days, my thoughts kept drifting away. I really wanted to think only about Reverend Vaughn. It was wrong, I knew. I owed Bunny my full attention. I tried to discipline myself, to guide my thinking methodically back to the problems at hand, but it was no use.

Argyle socks. What made him decide to wear argyle socks? I'd seen them advertised in *Life* and *Look*, but I'd never seen a pair on a man in Katydid, at least not that I remembered. They were so . . . frumpy, and yet he made them work. On him, they looked sophisticated. Was that just luck and charm, or did he know what he was doing when he shopped? And his haircut. Yesterday, while we talked, he got excited, and the hair in front fell down over his forehead like delicate, yellow bangs. He needed to get clipped. But there was something sweet about his carelessness, something very lovable. I wondered how he ever decided to get a haircut. Did he just look in a mirror and form an opinion? Did he spend time thinking about it, weighing it, holding imaginary conversations with himself? I wished he would ask me. Thinking about him, I longed to be there when he fumbled in his sock drawer, figuring out what to wear. I was dying to be asked whether, yes, it's time to climb the stairs to the itchy room above the dry-goods store and sit in that chair that swivels and bucks and let Mike Havranek clip just a bit off the top and the sides. I wanted to get personal.

He arrived that afternoon in a bit of a rush, and the first thing he told me was that he had an errand to run. He had to visit a man on Jefferson Street—Ewell Johnston, a Katydid councilman, who'd worked for years at the KTD. Mr. Johnston was now retired, but Reverend Vaughn wanted to talk to him about what the town could do. Would I like to come along?

We walked out Oak and headed for the area everyone calls New Town. The name is left over from years ago, when the KTD built its own subdivision. The houses that the factory put up are smaller and a bit flimsier perhaps than others in Katydid, but in general you'd hardly notice that New Town was something different, except that the streets form an insistent, regular grid, First Street to Fifth Street, Washington to Monroe.

Reverend Vaughn walked briskly in his disjointed way. He had on a short-sleeved dress shirt, and his tie flapped as he moved. "I can't believe this is happening," he said after we'd gone a few blocks.

I thought he was talking about my case. "Oh," I said cautiously.

"Nobody seems to care." He sounded bitter.

"I know."

"Either they're all stupid, or they just can't face it."

I nodded.

"Hundreds of people are going to be out of work."

"Oh," I blurted out, "you're talking about the KTD."

"Well, yes." He looked at me quizzically. "What did you think?"

I considered trying to fake it but gave up the idea almost immediately. "Me," I said sheepishly.

"You? Well, of course, you." He laughed. "I suppose the same stuff all goes for you. Only I think we're going to solve your problems, and the KTD is still going to close."

"I hope not." I felt a twinge of guilt for wishing earlier that the factory would shut down immediately.

"By the way," he asked, "how are you and Mrs. Vernon getting along?"

"Oh, fine," I said. "She's different from what I'm used to, but she's been very nice."

He shook his head. "I happened to talk to her minister the other day. Reverend Wallenback. What a sour character he is."

"Really? I've never met him. She thinks he's wonderful. She even suggested that I talk to him."

"Are you going to?"

"I don't really want to."

"He's pasty," Reverend Vaughn said. "Do you know what I mean? He has a very pale, pasty complexion, and he talks with a heavy drawl, as if the words are stuck in his mouth and he has to pull each one out."

I laughed. "I had an image of someone different."

"Whatever you do, don't tell Mrs. Vernon I was complaining about him. She's suspicious of me already. Probably because I'm a Congregationalist. Too soft on Satan, that sort of thing."

"Oh, she's crazy about you," I said. "She thinks you're wonderful." In fact, though, I'd noticed that her enthusiasm for him had dropped a few degrees since his first visit. Once or twice, I'd caught her staring at him with a look that was almost hard.

"I'm not so sure," he said.

At the corner of Fifth and Monroe, we passed the New Town Variety Store. Three children were in front, standing on the scruffy lawn, picking sugar drops off a long, white sheet of paper. They looked up and stared hard at the tall, storky man who was passing down the sidewalk.

"Ichabod Crane," whispered a pudgy boy in baggy shorts. I glared at him, and he returned to the candy.

"Why were you talking to Mrs. Vernon's minister?" I asked.

"I had an idea, something I'd been working on," Reverend Vaughn said. "I tried to get in touch with all the clergy in town. I wanted to see if we could organize something on the KTD, some kind of protest or, at least, something that showed we were concerned."

"Oh."

"But it was like moving rocks. You could barely budge them."

"What kind of protest?"

"I don't know. I just wanted to talk it out. In fact, I shouldn't have used that word 'protest.' That was one of my mistakes. I mentioned it to Jack Forrester—you know, the Lutheran minister—and I suggested that the square would be a good place for a rally. And you know what he said? 'We don't want any of that ban-the-bomb stuff here. That won't go over in this town.' Can you believe it? You just mention the word 'protest,' and he immediately gets visions of people marching around with placards. He'd probably seen a picture in the papers once or something on TV."

"So nobody wanted to do it?"

"Everybody had an excuse. 'Let's wait a bit.' 'We don't know enough.' 'It'll just make the owners mad.' At least Wallenback was straightforward about it. 'A minister should concern himself with spiritual issues,' he said, 'not these day-to-day events.' "

At hearing him say "Wallenback," I felt a flash of warmth, like a sudden spot of sunlight on my cheek: Three days ago, he would have said "Reverend Wallenback" in front of me.

"But day-to-day events!" Reverend Vaughn went on. "How can you call the closing of the largest employer in town a day-to-day event? And the thing that's amazing is that Wallenback must have dozens of families in his church who work at the factory. I mean, that's not a wealthy congregation. Those are working-class people. Wallenback himself could be out of a job if enough people have to leave town."

"Did you talk to Mayor Krullke?" I asked.

"Huh? Krullke's a joke. If the owners of the KTD saw who was supposed to be running this town, they'd probably pack up tomorrow and be glad they got out when they did."

Sidney Krullke owns a tire store outside of town, near the new Montgomery Ward's. I know him slightly from the country club.

"No, Krullke's no good," Reverend Vaughn continued. "I tried Harry Childs, though. He's on the council, and he's in our church, but he wasn't any help. He sounded as if he hardly knew what was going on. He's a businessman, pretty successful. I don't think factory workers are really his constituency. So that's why I want to talk to this guy Johnston. At least he used to work there."

We came to Jefferson Street, in the heart of New Town, and turned left. The street was deserted. The flat, patchy lawns baked silently under the hazy afternoon sun. Reverend Vaughn consulted an address he'd jotted on a piece of paper and turned to follow the walk leading to a trim, two-story white house tucked under the branches of a healthy-looking elm. The Cunningham house. I held back for a moment, pausing on the sidewalk. The Cunninghams had long since moved away, but when I was about five, an upstairs bedroom had burned, killing the family's twin boys. They were younger than I, maybe two or three years old at the time, and I remember seeing their mother wheeling them, side by side, in a double stroller that looked incredibly big, as wide as a porch swing. After the fire, someone had taken me past the house. I don't remember who it was—I can't believe it was Bunny, it must have been one of her boyfriends. The fire had come in the winter, and, in my memory, the elm is prickly and gray, but the house looks just as it does today, except for a border of smudged black soot around one upstairs window. It looked as if you could take a damp cloth and a container of Bon Ami and wipe the smudge away. Then it would be as if nothing had ever happened.

"What's the matter?" asked Reverend Vaughn.

"I didn't know Mr. Johnston lived here." I said.

He consulted the piece of paper again. "Two-twenty-two. That's what he told me."

I hurried to catch up. No reason to mention the Cunningham twins. I didn't want him to think I was morbid.

Mr. Johnston came to the door wearing a raggedy brown bathrobe over a pair of brown pants. His thinning gray hair was disheveled, and he looked as if he'd just got up from a nap.

"Oh, yeah," he said, when Reverend Vaughn introduced himself. "Come in."

"And this is my friend, Martha Calhoun," the minister said. "She came along for the walk."

"Yeah," mumbled Mr. Johnston.

Inside, the house felt closed up and dusty. I wondered if the councilman's wife was sleeping somewhere. He led us down a narrow hallway. A large painting of a boat hung on one side. Suddenly, he stopped and turned. "Is that Bunny Calhoun's daughter?" he asked.

"Yes," said Reverend Vaughn, smiling.

Mr. Johnston studied me. "She's big," he said.

"Ah, where can we talk?" said the minister.

Mr. Johnston took us into the living room, darkened by a drawn curtain. "The girl can wait here," he said.

"Why can't she listen in? She won't be a bother."

"This is council business," said Mr. Johnston gruffly. His irritation gave him energy. His shoulders straightened, and the front of the robe fell open over his worn, sleeveless undershirt. "Can't have a girl here for that."

"Do you mind waiting?" Reverend Vaughn asked me.

"Not at all."

The two of them went out and down the hall. They must have gone to the kitchen, because in a few seconds I heard a chair screeching against linoleum.

Now that I was alone, the living room appeared to grow darker. As best I could estimate, I was probably directly under the room that had burned. The air had a faint, stinging odor to it. Smoke. Was it my imagination, or could you still smell the fire? How did the Johnston's stand it? From down the hall, the muffled voices of the two men drifted through the stillness. Sitting quietly on a sofa, I became aware of scampering noises over my head. I strained to listen. Again, I wasn't sure whether it was my imagination or something was really moving around upstairs. I stood up to get closer to the ceiling. Now the noises changed, becoming playful and watery, like the far-away sound of a waterfall. The faintness, however, was maddening. Was the noise inside my head or out? To get even closer, I kicked off my shoes and teetered on the spongy cushions of the sofa. My ear was just inches from the ceiling. The scampering returned, then the water. The sounds mixed and overlapped, then moved in circles over my head. I wasn't imagining things. Something was up there. Ghosts.

Reverend Vaughn and the councilman came back in ten minutes. We walked to the door, and the two men exchanged cool goodbyes.

"What an idiot," said Reverend Vaughn, when we were back on Jefferson Street, heading home.

"He couldn't help?"

"Oh, he could have helped all right. He just didn't want to. He was scared to get involved. He kept saying it wouldn't do any good, that

116

we shouldn't make the company mad." The minister threw up his arms in frustration. "He's too dumb to recognize his own self-interest."

"What are you going to do now?" I asked.

"I don't know. Maybe nothing. If no one cares, why should I?" He thought a bit, then added, "I think I'll give a sermon on it. Maybe I can stir something up in the church."

"Oh, I almost forgot. I think we're going to come this Sunday—Bunny and me." I'd suggested it to Bunny the day before. She hadn't been enthusiastic, but I knew she'd go along.

"Great, terrific," he said. "That'll double the size of the congregation."

We turned down Fourth Street. The day had been hazy and hot, but now some puffy gray clouds nosed into the sky. A breeze flipped the tree leaves to their silvery undersides, usually a sign of rain.

"Can I ask you something?" I said after a while.

"Of course, anything." He'd been staring at the ground, but now he looked at me kindly.

"Do you think it's possible to make one mistake—just one, simple mistake, when everything else is basically all right—and then have that mistake ruin your life?"

He tilted his head slightly, getting a different angle on me. "Did you make a mistake? We haven't talked much about it."

"I don't know. Maybe. I didn't necessarily mean that."

He thought for a few seconds and then shrugged. "Well, I suppose it is possible. I suppose it happens."

"Yes. I suppose so." I felt leaden all of a sudden. I guess I'd been expecting some reassurance.

He stopped on the sidewalk. With his face just inches from mine, he pushed some willowy strands of hair off his forehead. "But, look," he said, "a mistake has nothing to do with it. The world is full of people who haven't done a thing wrong, and their lives are ruined anyway. There's no cause and effect. It happens all the time."

"Oh."

"All the time."

A squat black dog, sulking on the stoop in front of the house where we'd stopped, picked up its head and sniffed at us. Suddenly it barked sharply, leaped up, and hurtled in our direction, its eyes and fangs flashing. The four powerful legs pounded on the lawn. Too late

Reverend Vaughn reached out to pull me back. We'd never get away. The dog was almost on us when it uttered a terrible, choking roar, and its legs flew up in the air. For a second, the animal hung upside-down a few feet off the ground, and then it dropped and landed with a thud on its back. The thin chain fastened to its collar and tied to the house had abruptly run out. Undaunted, the dog bounced back up and strained against the chain, making ugly, hoarse, rasping sounds trying to breathe and bark through the too-tight collar. You'd never see a dog like that on, say, Oak Street. New Town is just far enough away that things are a little wilder.

"Shut up!" said Reverend Vaughn, glaring at the animal.

A woman with her hair in curlers pushed open a screen door and stood on the stoop. "Carla! Hush. Hey, Carla!" she yelled. The dog ignored her and kept snarling at us. The woman cupped her hand to the side of her mouth. "It's all right, Reverend," she called. "She's friendly."

Taking me by the elbow, Reverend Vaughn guided me down the sidewalk. Carla followed us the length of the lawn, snarling and coughing the whole way. Over time, chasing pedestrians and pulling against the chain, the dog had trampled a quarter moon on the grass. The outer edge formed an arc so perfect it could have been drawn with a compass.

"Are you all right?" Reverend Vaughn asked, as we moved safely away.

"Yes, fine," I said bravely. Actually, I was in shock. Entranced, but in shock. In the commotion of pushing me away, his shirt sleeve had flipped up, exposing for an instant the top of his arm. He had a tattoo—a tiny, blue, rippling design that might have been a wave at sea or a billowing pennant. "A tattoo," I murmured, unable to hold it in.

"Oh, no." He grabbed his sleeve to pull it down, though the tattoo was already hidden again. "You weren't supposed to see that—no one's supposed to see that."

"I'm sorry." He was frowning, and I was afraid he was mad at me. But after a few steps, he shook his head and started smiling.

"Talk about a mistake," he said. "I'd give anything to have that night to live over." He patted his arm on top of the tattoo. "Now that, my friend, is a mistake."

FIFTEEN

On Saturday, I was reading in the backyard, when Mrs. Vernon called me to the phone.

"Martha?" said an excited voice. It was Mary Sue Zimmerman.

"Hello," I said wearily.

"How are you? I mean, how are you?"

"I'm okay. How are you?"

"Well, Jimmy and I decided to take a little vacation from each other, I mean, just a little vacation. We aren't going to see each other today or tomorrow." Mary Sue had been mad for Jimmy Phillips since seventh grade. Last spring he finally returned her interest and asked her to go steady. "I mean, we still love each other and all," she went on, "but absence makes the heart grow fonder, you know?"

"I'm sure it'll work out," I said.

"Oh, it is working out. I mean it *is* working out. Even married people need a vacation sometimes." She paused. "But, gee, I haven't seen you in a long time. It seems ages. So much has happened."

"Yeah."

"What's it like at Sissy's house? That must be weird."

"It's okay."

"What does Bunny say? She must be really upset."

"She's all right."

"Mmmm. I was thinking, I might come over to visit, you know, just pop over."

"I don't know." The thought of spending time with Mary Sue depressed me. Usually when we got together, we'd sit around and I'd listen as she filled me in on the latest news about people in our class. She was a sharp observer, full of opinions, and I didn't hesitate to pump her, since it was really only through Mary Sue and her endless gossip that I had any relationship to anyone else in school. Still, I didn't feel much like listening to gossip about the class now. "I'm not sure this is a great time for it," I said.

"Gee, they don't let you have any visitors?" Mary Sue was always eager to assume the most shocking details.

"Of course they do. Oh, all right, come on over."

Ten minutes later, Mary Sue and I were in the parlor, drinking Cokes. Mary Sue bounced from the sofa to the window to a chair. She leaned over and whispered, "It's so creepy here—I can't stop thinking of Sissy. How do you stand it?"

"You should see her room. Nothing's been changed."

"Yuck. She was creepy even when she was alive."

"Shhh." I pointed silently toward the kitchen.

"I remember," said Mary Sue, putting her mouth close to my ear. "The holy mother."

"Don't!" I stifled a laugh and pushed her away. She bounced up and went to the window, looking out across the backyard as if she half expected a party to materialize at any second. She was wearing yellow pedal pushers, and her hair was teased up, a style she'd adopted last spring, just before winning over Jimmy. There was something comforting about her, I realized.

She turned and sat against the windowsill, creating a wide, yellow lap. She had, as Bunny used to say, a "permanent fat bottom." She'd had it since she was little. "You've missed all the excitement this summer," Mary Sue said. "It's not your fault, I know, but so much has gone on." She twiddled with a thin silver chain around her neck. "Let's see. Ellie had a party last week, and her father came home and found Betty and Wayne down in the basement. Nothing was going on—it's filthy down there—but, still." She paused to let the word "still" echo suggestively. "And Mary Figaro moved away. Her father's store went bankrupt or something. And, let's see. Linda Matthews has got real fat. She's working at the fountain at the drugstore, and she must be sneaking ice cream, though she says she's not, because she's turned into a blimp, I mean, a real blimp." She took a breath. "And, oh, there's this great new song, only it's not that new really, it came out last winter but only made it to number twenty or something. Jimmy has it. 'Tutti-Frutti.' Did you ever hear it?"

"No."

"I gotta play it for you. You should hear the words. They're crazy. I mean, sexy but just crazy."

"Who's it by?"

"Little Richard."

"Who?"

"His name's Little Richard. He's really weird. He's a Negro but he looks just like a girl."

"Hmmm."

"Yeah. And what else?" Mary Sue looked off into space. "Oh, Andy and Sue broke up because he's not a Catholic, even though she never goes to church. And you heard about Tammy Mirkov, didn't you?"

"No, what? I ran into her once at the pool."

"At the pool?"

"I was there once."

"Did you see that cute lifeguard? He's from Fogarty or someplace. He's real cute."

"No. What about Tammy?" I sensed Mary Sue had something here that I'd like. I still carried an image of Tammy flouncing out of the locker room, her arrogant little ponytail poking at me.

Mary Sue got off the sill and sat beside me on the sofa. She lowered her eyelids, trying to look furtive. "She and Arthur were out parking last week at the Ledges. He did something with his finger, and she bled all over his car."

"Really?" I thought of the moment last Sunday when the siren screamed into the evening, as an ambulance headed uselessly to Michael Cooper's crash. Cars and blood.

"Really," said Mary Sue. "That's it for Tammy." She sat back and dipped her chin, opening her eyes wide as a sign of knowing. "Pop!" she said.

Mrs. Vernon bustled in with a plate of raisin-oatmeal cookies. The cookies had been coated with a sugar glaze so thick it looked as if someone had poured heavy cream all over the plate.

"I'll just have one," said Mary Sue.

"How's your mother?" asked Mrs. Vernon. "I used to see her all the time at Ward's. Every Friday morning. Our shopping schedules were the same."

"She goes out to the new Ward's now," said Mary Sue. "It's open later so she can go there any time. Sometimes she shops at night."

"That must be why I don't see her." Mrs. Vernon's hands churned in the apron at her waist. It seemed as if a little animal were burrowing in her stomach.

"I guess." Mary Sue took a second cookie.

"Well, give her my best." Mrs. Vernon backed toward the door.

"Thanks for the cookies," I said.

When Mrs. Vernon was out the door and down the hall, Mary Sue whispered, "She looks so old. I mean, she looks like an old woman."

"She's probably less than fifty. Way less. Forty-five maybe."

"All that gray hair, and those wrinkles. Her skin's like an old towel. I bet it was Sissy that did it to her."

"She always seemed old to me. I remember, even in first grade, when the parents came around, it was like everyone else had a mother, and Sissy had a grandmother."

Mary Sue put her hand on my forearm. She'd painted her nails shiny red. "What's it been like? I mean, I can't imagine. What's it really been like?"

"You mean here?"

"Here." She waved her hand, making streaks of red in the air. "The whole thing."

"Not so bad," I said. "Everyone's been pretty nice."

She grabbed my arm again. "But what happened? I mean, I can't figure it out. You were always so . . . nice."

I shook her hand off. "Nothing happened. That's the point. Everyone thinks something happened, but nothing happened."

Mary Sue sat back quickly. "Oh, I didn't mean that. I'd never think that. It's just—"

"Everybody's talking."

She fiddled with a tuft of hair on the top of her head. The tuft had been teased straight up and then over, into a semicurl, making a sort of half palm tree. "Not really," she said. "I mean, yes and no. Some people are, but it's not like Betty and Wayne in the basement. Everybody was talking about that. You could practically have written a book." She came close again and lowered her voice. "See, I have an idea. I think I figured it all out." Her eyes gave off spiky flashes. "That Butcher Benedict. I've noticed him before. He's a little sex maniac."

"You think so?"

"I've watched him. He really is. I've seen him down at the News Depot. He stands in front of the magazine rack and looks at the magazines that have pictures of girls. He's so little he thinks nobody notices. But once Mr. McClain caught him and chased him out."

"Gee." I'd hardly thought about Butcher since it happened, I'd been so preoccupied with myself.

"Am I right?" Mary Sue pushed her head forward. She really could be very perceptive sometimes. Underneath it all, she probably understood people better than I did. I guess that's why I was always drawn to her, even when we were very young. Still, I could see she was getting too excited about this. Standing up abruptly, I went to the window.

"The whole thing is too confusing," I said. "I just want it to end." I spun and faced her. "I hope you're not gossiping about me, Mary Sue. Too many people are talking as it is, and I'd hate to get that from you."

"Oh, no," she said. "I wouldn't ever do that." To avoid my stare, she picked up another cookie and studied its underside. "Hey! I've got an idea," she said, dropping the cookie. "Let's go down to Wally's. I'll play 'Tutti-Frutti' for you. He's got it on demonstration down there."

"I don't know." Wally's Record Emporium is on North Emerson, just off the square. "Too many people might be hanging around. Besides, I don't want to get close to the square. All those hoods."

"No one will see you. We'll go the back way. And once we're there, we'll stay in the sound booth."

I considered for a moment. The idea of getting out for a while was tempting. And I realized I wanted to spend more time with Mary Sue—it was a relief to talk to her. I checked with Mrs. Vernon, and she thought a visit to Wally's was a fine idea. She seemed pleased to get the two of us out of the house. So after I'd washed up and put on a fresh blouse and shorts, we headed downtown, walking along Prosperity, past the KTD. Mary Sue's father has worked at the factory for years, and I asked if he'd talked about what would happen if it closed. She said he hadn't mentioned it.

Crossing the railroad tracks, I bent down and laid my palm flat on the rail.

"Why'd you do that?" Mary Sue asked.

"To feel if there was a train coming."

"Yeah, but we used to do that years ago. You haven't done that in years."

"I just felt like it," I said.

A few steps later, Mary Sue asked, "Well, was one coming?"

"No."

She stared at me. "What do you do in there all day? I mean, it's summer. It seems so boring."

"It's not bad. Bunny comes almost every day." I stopped myself from mentioning Mrs. O'Brien. Too hard to explain a social worker. "And I've made friends with a minister. He's wonderful. He comes a lot."

"A minister?" Mary Sue scrunched her nose. This might be hard to explain, too.

"From the Congregational Church. Reverend Vaughn. He's not like, you know, a *minister*. He doesn't talk about God or anything. He's young."

"Is he cute? What do you do with him?"

"We take walks and talk. He's incredibly smart." I let my enthusiasm bubble over. "He's kinda cute, and he's so tall, Mary Sue. He towers over me."

She turned and looked up at the top of my head, then just above it, as if trying to imagine what it would take to tower over me. "Hmmm," she said.

"Oh, here's something weird," I said. "Guess who came one night and threw a stone at my window."

"Who?"

"Elro Judy."

"Elro?"

"And guess what else. He and Sissy used to date."

"Elro and Sissy?" She shook her head. "No, never."

"That's what her mother says, and I believe her. They went to movies together."

"I don't believe it. Anyway, what'd he want with you?"

"I'm not really sure. He was drunk and yelling about stuff. I guess he wanted me to come out with him."

"Did you?"

"Are you kidding?"

She frowned. "I never liked Elro. He's a creep."

"Yeah."

"Remember those magazines he brought to school in fifth grade? He's a sex maniac."

"Yeah." Practically every boy Mary Sue knows is a sex maniac. I wondered about her relationship with Jimmy.

We stayed on the east side of Center Street to avoid passing right in front of the News Depot. Even from across the street, I could see people sitting at the fountain, their dark silhouettes lined up in perfect order, like bowling pins. Behind them, the magazine rack filled an entire wall. It was funny to think of Butcher standing there, waist high to the older boys. When I was younger, I used to hang out at the magazine rack, too. Butcher and I had that in common. The movie magazines were what attracted me. I felt so guilty about it, Bunny was always saying that they only printed lies and trivia; she wouldn't let me bring them in the house. But I loved those magazines. Not so much for the stories—I only leafed through, glancing at the pictures—but for the way they looked and the way they felt, their shiny, gaudy covers, their thin, pulpy paper. The paper had a special smell, sweet and fresh and nutty. It smelled like excitement, and I always had the urge to rip out a page and chew on it, as if excitement were a kind of food you could actually eat.

We circled around the square, cutting over on Mabel Street, past the telephone company, and then hitting North Emerson and coming back down. Wally's Record Emporium was empty, except for Wally himself, who was sitting at a raised checkout counter watching a baseball game on an old television.

Mary Sue found the song she was looking for in the little section of records that were available for customers to listen to, and she led me back to the sound booth, a cubicle equipped with a phonograph. There was barely room for two of us in there. Mary Sue sat in the lone chair, and I stood beside her. The walls were made of white posterboard that had been scribbled on and dirtied and pealed away in spots. In a corner, I saw "T.C. 11–16–54," and I knew Tom had been there. Mary Sue closed the door, shutting in a sudden strong odor of stale cigarette smoke.

"You're gonna love this," she said. She slipped the 45 out of its cardboard sheath and put it on the phonograph. The sound booth suddenly exploded with noise. Little Richard came on with a kind of squawk, and he sounded panicky to get all the words out. Mary Sue swayed and bobbed her head back and forth, completely out of time to the music.

"What'd you think?" she asked when it was over and my ears were vibrating in the silence.

"It's awfully loud, isn't it?"

"That's the new sound. I think it's fantastic. And the words. What did you think about the words?"

"They seemed kind of simple to me."

"I mean the chorus." Mary Sue sang and snapped her fingers, reciting a string of nonsense syllables that were approximately what Little Richard had sung.

"How can you understand what he's saying there?"

"I listened to it. I probably listened to it five hundred times. We wore out Jimmy's record. Here." Mary Sue put the needle in the outer groove and started the phonograph again.

When Little Richard had finished, I said, "Once more." The song *was* pretty catchy. Mary Sue played it through four more times. I closed my eyes. I was tingling all over. I wondered if this was what Reverend Vaughn meant when he said that organ music filled him up. After a while, with my eyes closed, it started to seem as if the normal sound of the world was Little Richard screaming "Tutti-Frutti." Everything that went on—people talking, cars screeching around corners, birds singing and dogs barking—went on over and above that.

When Mary Sue finally put aside the arm of the phonograph, her face was red, and there were tears in her eyes.

"What is it?" I asked. She was always getting emotional.

"Jimmy," she said in a squeaky voice. "The song makes me think of Jimmy."

She'd turned so bright red and feverish that I couldn't help laughing. "Mary Sue, that's the most unromantic song I've ever heard," I said. "It's all loud noises."

Her eyes brimmed over, and the tears cascaded down her cheeks. "It's our song," she said.

"Oh, I'm sorry. Don't get upset." I knew it was useless, but I tried to explain myself. "I just meant the song didn't sound very romantic. Think of 'Autumn Leaves' or 'Sentimental Journey.' Those are nice, soft, romantic songs."

She stood up and slammed the record into its cardboard sheath.

"How would you know?" she said. "You don't know anything about romance." Brushing past me, she returned the record and hurried out of the store. I caught up to her on the sidewalk. "Why do you have to make fun of everything," she said bitterly. "Why can't you take me seriously?"

"I do take you seriously," I protested. "I loved 'Tutti-Frutti.' Maybe I'll buy it."

Dwayne came ambling up the sidewalk, pushing his bicycle. "That's retarded," he said and spit at Mary Sue's feet.

"Dwaa-yenn," she said, drawing out his name.

He uttered a choking laugh and moved on. When he was about fifteen feet away, he stopped and turned and watched us.

"He's always around now," I said.

Mary Sue wasn't interested in Dwayne. "You always have to spoil everything by picking it apart," she said. In her anger, she made her arms stick-like at her sides. "It's 'cause you think you're better than me. Even now."

"Mary Sue! I can't believe you said that." I reached over and took her hand. "You're my best friend."

Her lower lip pushed out from her face and trembled slightly. "No, I'm not. Bunny's your best friend."

"She's my mother."

"Even still."

We looked at each other for several seconds. Then she pulled her hand away and took a few steps down the sidewalk toward the square. "I've got to get home," she said.

"Well, come this way." I nodded up the street, the way we'd come.

"I'm in a hurry," she said, backing away. "I'm going this way."

"But that's past the square."

"I don't care. I told Jimmy I'd call, so I've got to get home." She gave me a stiff-armed wave. "Well, bye," she said. She took another step back, then turned and hurried off down the sidewalk. I watched her go. She was moving at about half again her normal pace, and the effort made her body sway from side to side. She reached the end of the block, crossed against the light, and continued down the next block, without looking back.

Finally, I turned and started for the Vernons' alone, going the long way around, away from the square. Dwayne followed the entire distance, always staying about half a block behind.

SIXTEEN

Bunny and I got permission to spend Sunday together, away from the Vernons' house. She had agreed to take me to church, and then we were going on a picnic at Mason's Farm. Bunny had arranged it all with Mrs. O'Brien. The idea was for us to spend time figuring out how we were going to pull ourselves together as a family.

On Sunday morning, Bunny was late, as usual. The church service starts at eleven, and it was already a few minutes after by the time I heard her Pontiac rattling down Oak Street. She had her excuse all ready. "I had to iron my skirt," she said, after I'd run down the walk and hopped into the car. She was wearing her tight, black skirt and a white blouse with ruffles around the neck. She also had on high heels.

"Everything else was dirty," she explained when she saw the disapproval in my eyes. "Besides, the Congo's hardly like church." She stepped on the accelerator, and the car zoomed past the KTD, heading toward the square. She didn't ask me how I was or comment on my outfit. She was frowning, and I could see a muscle twitching in her jaw, as if her head had its own tiny heartbeat. After we'd driven a few blocks in silence, she started going on about how I was always criticizing her, how I didn't treat her like my mother anymore. She'd obviously been thinking about it, and the words and ideas just tumbled out of her mouth, without any real order. Meanwhile, she had her foot planted on the accelerator, and she wasn't paying attention to the street. We hit the railroad tracks and bounced so hard that I bumped my head on the top of the car. "Watch your head," Bunny snapped.

The square was quiet, with everyone off at church. A couple of solitary hoods were hanging around the water fountain, smoking cigarettes. Bunny found a parking spot in front of the drugstore, and we hurried along the sidewalk to the Congregational Church on a side street a couple of blocks away. With its squat thick walls of red stone, the Congo suggests a fort more than a house of worship. Outside, the only religious sign is a small cross hanging above the main door. Inside, a big wooden cross stands behind the altar, and the high, white walls are broken by vaulted windows of stained glass. Over the years, the walls have become crisscrossed with dark, wandering cracks, like the veins in an old person's hand.

The congregation was singing the first hymn when we arrived. There were only thirty or forty people, families gathered in bunches, and they were all scattered in the first six or seven pews. Bunny and I walked down the center aisle, past row after empty row, and slipped into a pew just behind everyone else. Reverend Vaughn stood in front at a pulpit made of dull, brown wood. He saw us and smiled at me. I thought we'd entered quietly, but when the hymn ended and everyone sat again, several heads turned to see who'd arrived late.

In the rustling, I whispered to Bunny. "Isn't he handsome?" Standing on the raised platform, draped in a billowy black robe, Reverend Vaughn was larger than life, even a bit frightening. The robe gave imaginary bulk to his body and exaggerated his height. He seemed all out of balance with the inside of the church, like a man standing in a rowboat. Too big, too controlling, he could rock and spill us all into the water.

Bunny just shrugged. She smoothed her skirt and folded her hands in her lap. Viewed sitting down, with her skirt and heels safely out of sight, she looked perfectly proper, perhaps even a little old-fashioned in her ruffled blouse. As Reverend Vaughn shuffled the papers in front of him and paused for the congregation to settle, his gaze flickered across the pews and rested for a moment on Bunny. I thought I saw a spot of pleasure in his face. I imagined he was surprised at Bunny's radiance—she startles and stands out so when you're not expecting her. I even thought that, in his eyes, a touch of her radiance might have passed to me.

The mimeographed programs that we'd picked up on the way in announced that the sermon was titled "Abundance Lake: The Life and Death of a Small Town." Reverend Vaughn waited until the congregation had focused on him and then began, speaking in a tone that was confident and relaxed. "I need to start by making a couple of apologies," he said, smiling out across his audience. "I think I've mentioned before that some sermons are twenty-hour efforts—that is, they represent twenty hours of research and writing over the previous week or so—and some are more in the nature of ninety-minute jobs. I'm sure you've learned to distinguish one from the other." A smattering of laughter passed among the congregation. "Well, I'm afraid this sermon belongs in the ninety-minute category, as you'll soon discover." Again, a few people laughed. "In my defense, though, let me say that it's not because I was panicked and preoccupied trying to cook a noodle casserole for the potluck dinner Friday, or tied down by any of the other crises that normally divert me. The fact of the matter is that I had trouble with this one, and I knew that no amount of research or reading could pull me out of it. So, although what you get today represents ninety minutes of writing and rewriting, there's a good deal more undocumented thinking behind it. You'll just have to take my word on that." He leaned across the pulpit and wagged his head, luring laughs from the same few people who'd been amused all along.

"The second thing I want to apologize for," he went on, "is oversimplifying. The issue that I'm going to deal with is very complicated, and it's one that touches all of our lives. I realize that what I'm about to say lacks much of the nuance of the subject—and I'm well aware that many of you know far more about it than I do. Nonetheless, to make a point, you sometimes have to whittle down a large mass of facts. I guess it's up to each of you to decide whether I've whittled the facts in this instance beyond recognition."

He paused and looked down for a moment, then lifted his head solemnly. "Well, enough disclaimers. What I want to do today is tell a story. It's not a story you'll find in the Bible or in any other book. It's not even a true story. It's one I made up myself.

"Once, not long ago, in a certain country, there was a small town. The town was situated on a fertile plain that sat among a range of low, green mountains. A single stream of icy, clear water came down out of the mountains and ran through the town. Indeed, that stream was the lifeblood of the town. People came to the stream to get water to drink and to cook with, to give their animals, to use in the countless ways people use water in their daily lives. The stream was small, but it was steady: It didn't have to be big, since this was, as I said, a small town. There were a few farms, a few stores, a cluster of houses, nothing more.

"Then one day, a rich man arrived with a new idea. He wanted to buy a parcel of land, just outside of town. The stream flowed through the parcel, and the rich man's plan was to dam the stream and build a lake. With an entire lake of water to tap, the town would be able to grow. The farms could get bigger, the businesses more elaborate. More people would come to the town, and there'd be more money to make. Of course, the rich man would charge something for his water—after all, he was building the lake and it was on his property. But his rates would be fair. He even agreed to sign a contract assuring that.

"Now, to the people of the town, this seemed like a reasonable plan. More than that, it seemed like a good one. Everyone wanted to get bigger; everyone wanted to get richer. The idea of building a lake seemed progressive, the way things were supposed to be. So the rich man bought the land, dammed the stream, and created a lake; he called it Abundance Lake, for all the good it was going to bring. Soon the town started to grow. The farms expanded and spread up into the foothills of the mountains. New granaries opened to accommodate the farmers. Other businesses arrived as people moved in to work on the farms and in the stores. Soon, the town had filled the entire plain. After a while, the beautiful green mountains were dotted with homes. People were pleased with what was happening, particularly the original residents. Now there were many more opportunities. The rich man who'd built the lake had got much richer, of course, but other people had made more money, too. Indeed, things were going so well that one day the town fathers decided to rename the town. From then on, it too was known as Abundance Lake."

Reverend Vaughn paused and surveyed his audience. The congregation was listening in complete silence. No one coughed. No one squirmed. Even the children had been caught up by the sermon and were staring intently at the tall, robed figure rising above them. Beside me, Bunny sat stiffly erect, wound to a fine tautness by the minister's words. For some reason, I suddenly remembered his tattoo. It pleased me to think that of all these people, only I knew.

"Well, of course, time passed," he continued. "New people came to the town, and old people died. Eventually, the rich man died, and his property, including the lake, passed to his son. Now the son wasn't like the father. The son hadn't had to work for his money; he hadn't been part of building something up. He was spoiled, and he was used to getting what he wanted. And one thing he wanted was a house beside a clear mountain stream. There used to be such a stream on his property, but now it was part of the lake. So the son had a simple solution: He'd tear down the dam and empty the lake. Why not? He didn't need to sell water anymore. He already had more money than he could ever spend in his lifetime. What he wanted was to enjoy his money—and to do it in exactly the manner that pleased him.

"When the people of Abundance Lake heard what he planned to do, they of course were distraught. The town fathers went to him and tried to talk him out of it, but he remained adamant. Indeed, their entreaties may actually have stiffened his resolve; after all, he reasoned, it's a free country. Who were they to tell him how to use his property? The original contract with the rich man was pulled out and studied. It said clearly enough that the water rates would always be reasonable, but it said nothing about keeping the lake there forever. By now, the people who'd drawn up the contract were long dead. There was no one to explain the oversight. There wasn't even anyone to blame, really, except for the son, and he didn't care whether people blamed him or not.

"There was a lot of talk in the town of what the people could do. Some said they should petition the government, though the government never seemed to care much about people as unimportant as the farmers and shopkeepers of Abundance Lake. Others said they should sue the son, though lawyers warned that the law wasn't really on their side. The angriest citizens of Abundance Lake said they should storm the son's property and kick him out, but that talk never got much beyond the barrooms of the town. Most people just shook their heads and worried and figured that it was somehow in the nature of things that the lives they'd built for themselves could get ruined on a whim.

"So the rich man's son took down the dam, and Abundance Lake drained and shriveled to the original stream. Of course, without the water to support it, the town of Abundance Lake started to shrivel, too. The farms got smaller, people left the houses on the mountainsides. The businesses in town lost customers and had to close up. Within a few years, most people had moved away. The population returned to about what it had first been—only now the setting was far less lovely. The rich man's son had his mansion beside the stream, of course. But as for the rest of the town, Abundance Lake was nothing more than the shabby husk of something that had once been large and vibrant." The minister looked around, pausing for his audience to absorb the image. "For all practical purposes," he said, clipping his words to signal the end of the story, "the town was dead."

Around the church, there was an easing, a slight relaxation. Reverend Vaughn waited patiently for it to pass. After a few seconds, he took a breath, then started again. "Now, obviously, this story is designed to provoke a comparison between Abundance Lake and Katydid. Just as obviously, the comparison is a bit farfetched. As I said at the beginning, I've whittled a very complex subject down. For the most part, I'll let you people decide whether I've done that fairly."

He brushed a few strands of yellow hair off his forehead. "I don't think the story needs much elaboration," he continued, "but I do want to make two points. The first is that sometimes, in the hurly-burly of everyday life, we don't stop to look ahead by a week or a month or a year. Predicting the future is a most imperfect science, of course, but occasionally it has to be done. Just think of Dickens's *A Christmas Carol.* Would Scrooge really have changed his ways if the ghost of Christmas future hadn't demonstrated what lay ahead for the old man? In our case, I sense that no one is really thinking about what lies ahead for Katydid if the KTD closes. How can this town survive? Think of the people living on your block. How many of them would still be here in a year, or two years, if the town's largest employer suddenly packed up? Do we want to see Katydid wither away?

"The second point I want to make is that it doesn't necessarily have to be this way. Most of the people of Abundance Lake just shrugged their shoulders and figured there was nothing they could do. I'm here to say that's wrong. There's always something you can do. Perhaps, in the long run, it won't be effective, perhaps it won't work, but that shouldn't stop you from doing what you know is right. It is true, as the people of Abundance Lake believed, that the world is sometimes an inhospitable place that can crush your dreams in a moment. But the forces of the world aren't all impersonal and unresponsive. There isn't one giant wheel of life that rolls inevitably foreward, crushing everything in its path. People, institutions, nature—they all mix together to move life forward, and, sometimes, that mixture responds to a little poking, a little prodding. Not always, but sometimes.

"Friends, let me say it more baldly." He slapped the pulpit with his open hand and a cracking noise echoed through the vast, quiet church. "The largest employer in Katydid is threatening to leave town. Hundreds of people will be out of work. Misery is upon us. The very survival of Katydid is in question. And no one is doing anything. Not the town fathers, not the religious leaders, not you, not me. We have our heads in the sand, and it's not right. More precisely, it's not Christian. Friends, there is nothing inevitable about being crushed. If history teaches us anything, if Christ's life has any meaning whatsoever, it's that one person, one idea, one hope can make a difference. We have to work to fix what's wrong. That's the message of our faith, and that's what we must believe if we are to continue to lead honorable, Christian lives." He bowed his head. "Amen," he said gently.

In the great, soft commotion that followed, as people shifted and cleared their throats and allowed themselves to relax, I leaned toward Bunny. "Isn't he wonderful?" I whispered.

"I wish he didn't talk about such depressing things," she said.

Afterward, Reverend Vaughn greeted people at the door as the congregation slowly filed out. Bunny and I got in line behind the Pratt family. The four young Pratt boys were all wearing matching navy sports coats and clip-on bow ties. The two oldest kept turning around to stare at Bunny. They didn't have to say anything to each other. Bunny pretended not to notice.

The line stalled for a few minutes. Mr. Pratt, a compact man who walks with a kind of swagger in front of his troop of boys, was berating the minister. He was obviously angry, talking through a tight jaw and twisting his torso to lead with his shoulder. Reverend Vaughn listened and nodded impassively. I tried to edge forward to catch what was being said, but the angry man kept his voice down so others wouldn't hear. "Damned irresponsible," was all that floated out of his mutterings.

Finally, the Pratts moved on and Reverend Vaughn took my hand.

"I'm so glad you could come," he said. "What a friendly sight your face was."

I introduced Bunny, who held out her hand stiffly, like a man.

"Martha has said so many wonderful things about you," Reverend Vaughn said. Bunny seemed to be studying his starched, white collar. "I hope you liked the service," he added.

"I like organ music," Bunny said.

"Oh!" He caught his breath, momentarily taken aback. "So do I," he said, his face brightening. "Martha can tell you that. So do I."

Bunny and I walked down the steep stone steps. She held my arm for balance. Back on the sidewalk, I said, "I never heard you talk about liking organ music before."

"Well, I had to say something nice. He was just begging for a compliment."

"But what about the sermon? I thought the sermon was great."

She quickened her pace, and we left behind the groups of people chatting on the sidewalk in front of the church. "Maybe. I don't know. I told you it sounded depressing. Anyway, I didn't listen that carefully. I couldn't concentrate. His voice bothers me. It kind of drones."

"It does not," I said angrily.

"My, my." She raised her eyebrows and looked sideways at me.

"Anyway, you could have been nicer to him," I said. "He's been terrific to me, visiting almost every day."

"I *was* nice enough," said Bunny, crossing the intersection. "Besides, what do you two talk about, anyway?"

"Things."

"About me?"

"Bunny, we just talk—about anything. You know how it is."

She shot a glance at me, over her shoulder, and her temper flared. "Well, I don't like it. Everybody's got something to say to you these days but me. What I say doesn't matter. The mother doesn't count." She started walking faster, taking short, Chinese steps in her tight skirt. "It's all Judge Horner this, or Mrs. O'Brien that, or Reverend Vaughn something else. And that crazy Jesus lady they've got you living with, she's the worst of all. I've noticed the way she checks out whatever I'm wearing. You know what I think? I think she believes I'm the devil, and she's looking to see how I've hidden the tail under my dress."

"Bunny!"·I was almost trotting to stay up with her.

"I can just imagine her thinking, 'Let's see, does she wrap it around one thigh? Or maybe tuck it between her legs?' I bet that gives her a thrill. Hunh!" She brayed out a harsh laugh.

"Bunny, no," I said.

"I may not be perfect, but at least I'm your mother, and that should count for something. Why can't they just leave us alone?" She was a step or two ahead of me, talking to the world in front of her. I'd never seen her this excitable.

Half a block ahead, the Methodist Church was letting out, and the sidewalk was crowded. We'd have to wade through people to get to the car. Bunny didn't appear to notice. "Don't they understand?" she wailed. "It was bad enough with Tom, and now this. What do they expect? I've got to work. I've got to make money so we can eat. I can't stay home all day and chaperone." People on the sidewalk heard her coming, and a path, lined with familiar faces, opened up. I moved right up to Bunny's shoulder.

"It'll only be for a little while," I whispered. "Simon Beach will get us out of this." I hoped the lawyer's name would soothe her. I could see the Pontiac, just ahead, the rusted rear bumper jutting out from a line of cars.

"Martha!" an eager voice suddenly called out.

I pretended not to hear and kept moving.

"Hey! Martha! Yoo-hoo. It's me." It was Janie Owens, a classmate of mine. She goes to the Methodist Church.

I stopped, and she scampered up. She had on a blue dress, something new, with a lacy top. "Gee," she said. "I heard." She played with a fold on her dress and waited for me to say something. Bunny had stopped a few feet beyond and was watching us. "Are you out now?" Janie asked. "Did they let you go?"

"I'm with Bunny," I said. I wasn't about to explain anything. Bunny took a step back toward us.

"Oh." Janie came up and took my hand between hers. I felt the silky grease of hand lotion. She'd probably been rubbing it on secretly during the church service. "What's going to happen to you?" Her mouth hung open for an instant. Through her hands, I could almost feel her tingling joy at the horror and wonder of it all. "God, your reputation," she said.

Suddenly, Bunny was beside us. "Beat it, you little fat bottom," she hissed. Janie jumped back. Her hands stroked frantically at her dress, as if to protect it from what was happening. "If I catch you spreading any more rumors, I'll sue you for every cent you've got." Bunny stabbed at Janie with her finger, and then turned and walked elegantly toward her car.

"See you, Janie," I mumbled, before hurrying after Bunny and climbing into the safety of the Pontiac.

SEVENTEEN

Back in the car, Bunny was suddenly cheerful. Her explosion at Janie seemed to have calmed her, and she chattered away as if nothing had happened. How many times had I seen her blow up like that in the last week? She'd always had a temper, of course, and, occasionally, she'd lose it, but never so uncontrollably or so publicly. She used to seethe and then rage at home, mostly for my benefit, I thought. At home, she almost seemed to be showing off, and secretly I kind of enjoyed it. Her anger was harmless and she could be funny with it, saying ridiculous, outrageous things about whoever had offended her. But now she kept making these public displays—at the lawyer's office, twice on the square—as if she had to flaunt her anger in front of the town. It wasn't like her.

We drove back to the Vernons', and I ran in and changed into shorts and gym shoes for the picnic. Then we stopped at Bunny's house and picked up the red-checkered tablecloth and a grocery bag stuffed with sandwiches, potato chips, and apples. It felt strange to be back in the house again. I had the sense that the place had changed in tiny ways that I couldn't see. My room—all white and lacy and soft with pillows—looked childish to me, and even the kitchen, where Bunny and I had whiled away hours sitting around the old Formica table, seemed dreary and cramped.

We didn't stay long. Bunny said she wasn't going to change her clothes. "If these are good enough for the Congo," she said, "they're good enough for Mason's Farm."

I had an idea something was up, and once we were back in the car, instead of heading out of town, she swung down Beetle Street, toward Eddie Boggs's place. I turned and stared out the side window. We passed the V.F.W., Katydid Ford, Southside Elementary School. In front of the Poskas' house, the entire Poska family, with all its white-blond hair, was piling into the family car, probably going out to the Estonian Center to sing songs and eat sausages all afternoon. Why did Bunny have to do it? Why couldn't she give up on men for a while? Why couldn't she see that Eddie Boggs was wrong for her? Why, why, why—my head was starting to ache.

Bunny knew what I was thinking. "I want you and Eddie to be friends," she said.

I wanted to ask her: What about Mrs. O'Brien? What about Judge Horner? What about getting your life together? What about me? I wanted to ask those questions—I wanted to yell them, because I knew there were no answers. But my throat had tightened up as if some-body's fingers were clamped around it. I didn't say a word.

Eddie Boggs lives by himself in a room above Rose Dry Cleaners. Bunny says it's a sorry place, barren, except for a mattress, a few chairs, and a hot plate for cooking. But there's a big, gravel parking lot in front of the dry cleaners, and on Sundays Eddie and his friends can hang around and work on their cars.

When we pulled up, Eddie had his shirt off and was leaning over the engine of Tony Burger's red Chevy. Eddie's got one of those wiry male bodies on which all the muscles and veins stand out, as if the skin's too tight. He looked up and saw us and gave his wrench to Tony and then loped up the stairs on the side of the building. Tony came over and looked in Bunny's window. "Hey, lil' darlin'," he said.

"Shut up," said Bunny, and the two of them grinned at each other for a while.

Tony noticed me and stuck his head in the window, leaning over Bunny. "Well, hello, there," he said.

"Get out," snapped Bunny. She pushed him back and rolled up the window.

Eddie appeared again shortly and slid into the back seat. He'd toweled himself off and put on a soft cotton shirt with palm trees all over it. He was carrying a paper bag and immediately he pulled out a Hamms beer. "You see the light?" he asked Bunny, as he opened the can and a mist of beer squirted out. He was talking about church.

"It was very nice," said Bunny. "The sermon was about the KTD."

"That don't sound very religious to me," said Eddie. "I mean, I've heard of heaven and hell and the Garden of Eden, but I never heard anyplace in the Bible where it mentions the KTD." He smirked at me. That's typical Eddie Boggs. He won't come right out and say hello, like any normal person. He'll act as if you're not there until he wants you to laugh at a wisecrack.

Mason's Farm is a swampy piece of property about five miles south of Katydid, along the Little Carp River. Nobody knows anymore who Mason was. All that's left of his farm is a grassy pile of stones where the barn used to stand and a few old wagon paths. The rest of the place is overgrown with reeds. If you follow the most worn-down path, you cross a field and come to the Little Carp and to a grassy stretch shaded by a few big willow trees. The river—it's really not much more than a creek—makes a sweeping turn there, and the bank has been pushed up into an overhang. People from town have been picnicking at that spot for years, supposedly since Katydid was founded, over a century ago.

Bunny parked the car along the side of the road, near the start of the main wagon path. Just ahead, someone had left a pickup truck. "I hope nobody's beat us to the spot," said Bunny.

She gave me the bag of food, and Eddie carried his beer. The path was dry and scuffed down to the cracking, gray earth. Bunny still had on her high heels. She walked on the balls of her feet for a while, but pretty soon her ankles tired, and her heels started spiking into the ground, leaving long, thin holes, the way a planter would. Finally, she stopped. Resting one hand on my shoulder, she took off her shoes and her stockings. She stuffed her stockings into her purse, and dangled her shoes from the fingers of her left hand. Then she continued barefoot.

The path was just two parallel wheel ruts carved in the ground. No wheels had rolled over them in years, but wagons had once driven that route so regularly that even the thick marsh grasses couldn't quite erase the markings. There was no breeze, so the air along the path was thick and heavy with the strange, sweet fragrances of a swamp. Eddie walked on ahead, leaving Bunny and me to trail behind, walking side-by-side along the path. "We're each in our own rut," I said, and Bunny laughed. I was still angry about Eddie being there, but I could see how his presence reassured Bunny.

The yellow stand of willows rose like a golden oasis at the end of the path. Farther up the river, two men were spearing carp. Otherwise, we were alone. Bunny spread the tablecloth on the ground and dumped the sandwiches, potato chips, and apples in a pile in the middle. Eddie found a place in the Little Carp beneath the overhang to set the beer and a few bottles of Coke he'd brought along for me. Then we all stretched out. The ground was spongy and coolly damp.

Bunny undid a few buttons on her blouse and slid her skirt up to just below her hips, for comfort. She's got great legs with curved, muscled calves. She says they got that way because Grandmother's house in Indian Falls was on a hill, and every winter, when the pump froze, Grandmother would make Bunny haul water up from the stream at the bottom.

"Damn!" said Bunny, slapping at her neck. "I forgot the bug stuff."

"Too hot for bugs," said Eddie. He took off his shirt—Eddie takes off his shirt every chance he gets. He rolled the shirt in a ball and stuck it behind his head for a pillow. He's learned to drink a can of beer lying on his back without using his hands, just by holding the edge of the can in his teeth. Something went wrong this time, though, because a little stream of beer trickled down his cheek and dripped onto his chest. Bunny mopped it up with a napkin.

After a while, I passed out the sandwiches. "This is just like a regular family," said Bunny, smiling at Eddie and me.

Eddie took a couple of bites of his sandwich and then heaved it into the river. "Maybe the carp will eat it," he said. Bunny had made the sandwiches using some baloney that hadn't been covered right and one edge of it had turned dry and leathery. She must not have noticed. She's not too interested in cooking. Eddie ate some potato chips.

"You know, I read yesterday that the last Union Army veteran died, from the Civil War," said Bunny. "He had a funny name, Wolfson, or something."

"How old was he?" I asked.

"One hundred and nine," said Bunny. "He joined when he was seventeen. He was a drummer boy, and he signed up after his father was killed in a big battle."

"Gee," I said. "Imagine."

"He's the last Union man, but three Confederate vets are still alive," Bunny added.

"I guess that means the South won after all," said Eddie, pleased with himself.

"Very funny," said Bunny.

The shrill buzz of a swamp bug got fiercely loud and intense, then faded away to nothing. "Adlai is coming to the fair next week," said Bunny. "It's a campaign stop." She didn't seem to be speaking to either of us in particular.

"Big deal," said Eddie, after a couple of seconds.

"I like him," she said. "I feel sorry for him."

"He's an egghead," said Eddie.

"How about you, Martha?" asked Bunny. "Who would you vote for if you were old enough?"

"Oh, I don't know." I don't follow politics or sports much, but to help Bunny out with the conversation I added, "Mr. Vernon likes President Eisenhower. He has a sticker on his bumper."

"Walter Vernon?" said Eddie. I nodded. "That's quite a statement for him. That's practically an entire conversation. Whooo-eee. I worked next to him one night on the power press, and he didn't say a goddamn thing the whole shift. He just stood there scratching his ass all the time. He must have hemorrhoids."

"Eddie!" said Bunny. "Not in front of Martha."

"Well, it's true. He just stood there all night with one hand on the press and the other on his butt, like some kind of statue." Lying on the ground, Eddie rolled over and demonstrated what he meant.

Bunny shrieked and rolled on her back. "You ought to see his wife," she said, when she got control of herself. "All things considered, I think I'd rather feel up *his* butt than hers." She shrieked again and then pulled me close, rubbing her forehead into mine. "Oh, I'm sorry, Martha. I just couldn't help it."

Eddie grinned grudgingly. He doesn't like other people making jokes.

"Anyway," said Bunny, "Martha won't be with the Vernons long. Only till next Friday, when the judge hears our side of it."

"Yeah," said Eddie dully.

His tone worried me. "Do you know Judge Horner?" I asked. "I've heard he's very fair."

"Who told you that?"

"My social worker. And Reverend Vaughn."

"He's Martha's new friend," said Bunny. "The minister down at the Congo."

"That fairy," muttered Eddie.

"Hush!" snapped Bunny.

I pretended I didn't hear. Eddie's always calling everyone a fairy.

"We aren't going to talk about it anymore," said Bunny. "We aren't going to let this stupid town spoil this beautiful day and this beautiful picnic."

Eddie crawled over to the bank and pulled out another Hamms for himself and one for Bunny. "I guess you're right," he said, settling down on his back again. "There's not much better than cold beer from a stream on a hot day." He set the can in his teeth and lay back and started drinking.

"There's not much better than a beautiful daughter," said Bunny, petting my hair. She was feeling her beers by then, too, and her eyes got big and moist as she looked at me.

Presently, Eddie announced he was going down to see how the carp fishermen were doing. He took another beer out of the river and trudged away along the bank. Bunny watched him go. "I know you don't believe me," she said, "but he's different. I can just feel it, I really can."

"But that's what you always say."

"Oh, don't argue. Maybe I always say it, but this time I mean it."

"Doesn't it make you feel strange, though—going through so many men? I mean, even here." I swung my arm to indicate the picnic spot. "We've been out here with Wayne and Johnny and Lester."

"Oh, that's nothing," Bunny interrupted, grabbing my arm. "You'll never guess who I came out here with."

"Who?"

"Guess."

"I can't. Who?"

"*Guess.*"

"Mayor Krullke."

"No!" She put her mouth to my ear. "Your daddy," she whispered.

"Really?" I pulled away.

"Jeremiah P. Calhoun himself." Bunny rolled over onto her stomach. "And what's more, you'll never guess what happened."

"What?" I didn't really want to play this game. I didn't really want to know that much about my father, at least not at this point, with so many other things to worry about.

"Guess," said Bunny.

"He proposed."

"Better. We made you."

"What? Right here?" I squirmed. It seemed wrong to be lying on top of the spot.

"Right here. God, was that a surprise." Bunny stared up through the willow branches, off into the sky. "What a day."

"I'm not sure I want to hear about it."

"Sure you do," said Bunny, looking at me again. "It's about your daddy. Every girl wants to know about her daddy."

"You told me there wasn't anything to know."

"Well, there isn't, but you're old enough to decide for yourself." Bunny rolled over to face me and leaned up on her elbow. "It was when we were living in that little house on Trundle Street—62½ Trundle. We were the only half-a-house in Katydid. That was nice." I picked a few pieces of dried grass out of Bunny's hair. "Anyway, I was staying home, taking care of Tom—he would have been about six months old—and your father was bagging at the A&P."

"He was a bagger?"

"You knew that."

"I knew he worked at the A&P, but I thought he was an assistant manager or something."

"Well, he was young. He would have moved up. Your father had a lot of questionable qualities, but he did know how to work hard when he had to."

"A *bagger?*"

"Put it out of your mind. Anyway, he was working hard and I was always up all night with Tom, who was a colicky baby. It seemed like we'd gone for years without doing anything fun. So one Sunday morning—it was a beautiful day, like today, only later in the year—I suggested that we go on a picnic. Jerry wasn't too crazy about the idea. I think he just wanted to drink beer and lie around, which is what he did every Sunday, but I finally talked him into it. So we wrapped Tom up and put him in a little basket and came out here. We had a wonderful picnic. I was a much better cook in those days, and I'd made some fried chicken and potato salad, and we drank some beer.

And the next thing I knew, I'd fallen sound asleep. Conked right out on the tablecloth—in fact, it was probably this one right here." She lifted an edge of the red-checkered cloth. "And did I sleep! You know how it is when you're real tired on a hot day? The air, the ground, the whole world feels like a huge pillow? That's what it felt like to me. Well, when I woke up, there was Jerry, leaning right over me, with a big grin on his face. 'Guess what?' he says. 'We're gonna have another kid.'"

"Huh?"

"That's right," said Bunny. "We made you while I was asleep."

"Is that possible?" I couldn't believe how careless Bunny could be.

"It worked with you," said Bunny. "And don't look so disappointed. A lot of babies are surprises to both parents. You only surprised one."

"I'm not disappointed," I said, more snappishly than I'd intended. "I don't care." In fact, I wasn't sure whether I *should* care. I mean, I'd never stopped to consider whether I'd been planned. It wasn't a fact about myself that I'd been relying on. Still, given the choice, I suppose everyone would rather be a conscious decision. And it seemed strange that the person who'd intended me had disappeared, leaving Bunny with the consequences. Of course, Tom was unintended by both of them. He came six months after the wedding.

Bunny looked away. "Jerry didn't last long after that," she said. "He was gone by the time I started to show you."

I remember how Tom and I used to study the few bits of evidence my father had left behind. There was a heavy wool suit. ("He'd run out during a false spring," Bunny had explained.) It was mossy colored and hung limply in Bunny's closet, all traces of creases having long since drooped out. There was a thin little box of mechanical pens and pencils that all looked too dangerous, or at least too complicated, to use. There was the old suitcase, of course, and for some reason there was a bottle of Aqua Velva that sat for years in the medicine cabinet. Sometimes, when Bunny wasn't around, Tom and I would take the bottle down and sniff it. Today, I don't know much about my father, but I do know what he smelled like. And there was also one snapshot—I haven't seen it in years now. My father and Bunny are in overcoats, standing in a snowy street. They're looking at the camera and smiling. My father could have been anyone. He had the most unrecognizable face I'd ever seen.

"Why did he leave?" I asked. Bunny smiled to herself and stretched languidly. In the dozens of times Tom and I had asked that question, her response had always been the same, almost down to the last word: He was weak and a drifter and he couldn't face the responsibility of a family. This time, she repeated all that, but after thinking for a moment, she went on. "There was more, I suppose. He'd been hearing stories about me."

"Were they true?"

"It didn't really matter. After a certain number of stories, I think he'd just heard enough." She yawned. "It would never have worked anyway. There's no use looking back, 'cause it would never have worked." She put her arms around my waist and snuggled her head against my side. "But look what he gave me," she said.

By the time Eddie returned, wading up the river and carrying his shoes in his hand, Bunny was asleep. Eddie pushed through the water to the overhang, grabbed a Hamms and pushed on a few more yards to a stretch where the bank was lower. He hauled himself up and sat in the sun, his feet dangling in the water.

After a few minutes, I walked over to him. He didn't ask me to sit, so I stood awkwardly for a moment and finally plopped down beside him. He kept staring out across the Little Carp, toward the reeds on the other side. You could see bugs swarming over there in the hot afternoon sun. They'd come close enough together to form a dark cloud and then spread out again and disappear.

"I wonder why they move," said Eddie. "They aren't landing anywhere. They don't seem to be eating. You'd think one clump of reeds is as good as any other. Why go through all the effort?"

"Maybe it's instinct," I offered.

"But what for? Instinct's got to have some purpose. Like a fish swimming upstream, or a foal climbing up on its legs as soon as it's born. But what's the purpose if you're a swamp bug of just movin' over a few feet? You want a beer?"

I shook my head. "Bunny's asleep," I said.

"Figures," said Eddie, looking at me. His eyes are a color blue that's so pale they're bright, like tissue paper that someone's shining a light through. They don't give you much of a reading on what he's thinking, and that's probably okay with Eddie.

It's been years now since his wife left him, but people still mention it whenever his name comes up, as if it were the only important thing about him you had to know. He was in the army and got stationed overseas, and while he was away, his wife fell in love with a mailman. She was pregnant with Eddie's baby, and still she carried on with the mailman, even going out dancing and to restaurants in her maternity dresses. It was a huge scandal, but everybody liked the mailman, so they hardly blamed the girl. Even Eddie never speaks badly of her, Bunny says. Anyway, just before he was supposed to come home, his brother, Cecil, wrote him a letter and told him what was going on. Actually, Bunny helped write the letter, since she was dating Cecil at the time. They didn't know how to break it to Eddie, not wanting it to sound too bad. Finally, someone suggested, "You've been replaced in her affections." I guess that came from a book somewhere and sounded gentle enough. So that's how Eddie learned. They got divorced, but she never did marry the mailman. It turned out he wasn't such a nice guy after all. She and the baby just moved away, and Eddie turned wild.

Watching him now, as he stirred the river water with his feet, his blue jeans soaked to the thighs, it was hard to imagine how he must have felt once. "You've been replaced in her affections."

I asked him how the carp fishermen were doing.

"Awww, they're goin' about it all wrong," he said, sounding pained. "They're walking around in the water, stirrin' things up. That's no way to catch carp. What you got to do is find where they hang out. See, every carp has a favorite place that he always goes back to. Once you find it, you lie on your stomach on the bank above it and hold your spear in the water. Eventually, the carp will come back and park hisself right there beneath you. As soon as he's relaxed, WHAM! You got him."

"Then what do you do with him?"

"You hold him up and look at him and show him around."

"Do you eat him?"

"A carp? Hell, no. I guess niggers do, but I sure wouldn't. A carp's got flesh like mud. Carp fishin' is just sport. You throw him up on the bank and go after another."

An empty beer can, probably dropped by the fishermen, came bobbing down the river. Eddie pulled a clump of sod out of the bank and bombarded the can, trying to sink it. He missed, and flicked his cigarette at it as the little tin boat floated around the bend and out of sight. We sat there listening to the swamp noises. Every now and then, there was a shout and some splashing upriver. I'd come over here to have a talk with Eddie, but now that the time had come, I was having trouble finding my nerve. That's one thing that used to worry Bunny about not having a father around the house. Actually, two things. For me, she was worried that I'd grow up shy and wouldn't know how to talk to men. For Tom, she was worried he'd turn into a fairy. The fairy part really worried her more—so much so that she took us camping up in Wisconsin once because she thought that's what a father would do. Then it rained, and Tom decided he hated camping. He cut a hole in the tent with his new knife. We ended up coming back early. As for me, I never thought that talking to men was different from talking to anyone else, except that maybe they like to joke more.

"What do you think about the KTD closing?" I asked finally. Eddie's worked there ever since he got out of the army.

"Don't bother me none," he said.

"But what'll you do?"

"Somethin', I suppose. Or else nothin'." He kept stirring the river. Under water, his feet looked amazingly white, as if they were bloodless, or made of snow. "I used to have ambition but I got rid of it," he said. "It didn't do me any good. Just made me feel bad, and I'm better off without it."

I was still wearing my sneakers, so I kept my feet just above the water. Now, I kicked at the surface a few times, chasing a water bug that was lurking in a quiet spot under the bank. "Can I ask you a question?" I said.

"You already is."

He knew it galled me to hear him talk like that. Bunny uses excellent grammar. "It's a personal question," I said.

"Go on."

"Do you love Bunny?"

"What kind of books you been readin'?"

"No books. I was just wondering."

"Well, you're askin' the wrong person. I don't know nothin' about it. Not by a long shot."

"But you must feel something when you're around Bunny. You know, when you see her across a crowded room and all. *Something* must happen."

"Yeah. I take my hands off the chick I've picked up. Ha. Ha ha."

Eddie tried to laugh, but he could see I wasn't going along with it. "Ha, well, I don't know what happens. Whatever does, it just does, and I don't think about it."

I plucked a few strands of grass and dropped them in the river. "But you're sure that something does happen?"

"I told you, I don't know. See, you gotta understand. Things don't just happen for Eddie Boggs. Nothin' happens. I take every day straight." He started getting excited. "See, when I get up in the morning, there never was yesterday. You understand? And tomorrow is nothin'. Tomorrow is shit. Look." He held up his wrists. "I don't even own a watch. During the week, I live by the KTD whistle. For the rest, there's no time, there's nothin'. Bunny and I are together 'cause we ended up together, and that's it."

I waited a few seconds. "Well, what do you think will happen—I mean, with your job and with Bunny?" I asked finally.

"Nothin.'" He was staring at the water.

"Nothing?"

"Nu-thun. You heard me."

"Bunny's got to make plans," I said. "She's got to, you know, decide whether to stay in Katydid—"

Eddie whipped around and grabbed me by the wrist. "You don't know what you're talkin' about, girl." His words made hissing sounds through his teeth. "You're messin' in adult stuff, and you got no idea what's goin' on. That's how you messed all this up to begin with. You're still a child but you're pretendin' to be a woman."

I tried to shake loose, but his hand was locked around my wrist. His other hand fidgeted. I was afraid he might hit me, so I ducked and pulled back, but he yanked me toward him, still torturing my wrist. Suddenly, Bunny shouted behind us. "Hey!" she yelled. Eddie dropped my arm. "Hey!" Bunny yelled again. "There's a weird raccoon here." Eddie jumped up and ran toward her.

"Don't get near it," he screamed.

Bunny was on her hands and knees in the middle of the tablecloth, eye-to-eye with a raccoon, about three feet away. The animal looked sick. It was shivering and foam was coming out of its mouth. I ran up beside Eddie just as the coon seemed about to collapse. Its eyes rolled up in its head, and it teetered a few steps to the side, but then it pulled itself back and glared at Bunny again, baring its teeth and making a gurgling growl.

"Rabies," whispered Eddie.

"Get it out of here," moaned Bunny. She seemed mesmerized by the animal's stare. She crawled back a few inches, and the coon lurched forward, as if about to attack. "Aii-eee," she screamed.

"Don't move!" ordered Eddie. Then he shoved me away. "Go get the fishermen," he said.

I backed up a few steps. "But, Bunny—"

"Go!"

I turned and ran to the river, then dashed up the thin path along the bank. My feet sank in the wet soil, and mud soaked my sneakers. Low weeds sliced against my legs. I started yelling when I was still twenty yards away. The fishermen heard and hurried toward me, running in slow motion in the thigh-deep water. I recognized one of them from the News Depot, a short, stocky, dark-haired man with a flattop. His friend was younger and was wearing a White Sox cap. They both had on wading boots that came to their chests. They clambered out of the river, shook off the water and ran down the path, carrying their spears in front of them like a couple of native hunters.

Back at the picnic spot, Bunny was still on all fours, slowly backing away from the coon. Eddie was crouched beside her, one hand on her backside and the other holding an empty Coke bottle, gripped around the neck for use as a weapon. He guided her with his hand, making sure she moved gently. Still, the coon jerked closer, its eyes locked on Bunny's. No one spoke. The animal's madness seemed to poison the air. I didn't want to breathe. Finally, Bunny slipped her knees off the tablecloth and then her hands.

"Now, stand up slowly," said Eddie, in a low voice. She rose cautiously onto her bare feet. The raccoon gurgled and suddenly hopped forward. We all stumbled back. It snarled. "Now, back off," Eddie told us. The man with the White Sox cap held his spear in front, pointing at the animal. When the rest of us were about ten feet away, Eddie stooped slowly and picked up a corner of the tablecloth. The coon stared at Eddie, shaking its head, a long string of drool dropping out of its mouth.

With a growl, it sprang at him.

"Yowww," screamed Eddie, leaping back and flipping the table-cloth over the animal. The remnants of the picnic scattered in the air, but the coon got caught in the cloth. The more it struggled to get free, the more tangled it got.

"Should I spear it?" asked White Sox.

"Don't," said the other fisherman. "The blood's poison."

Eddie turned to Bunny and me. "Get back," he said. "Go to the river."

Bunny pulled me away. The raccoon was still thrashing around under the tablecloth, making growling noises, like the sounds of a car engine trying to turn over on a cold morning. Its claws kept ripping through the cloth and then getting tied up. The men circled around. Eddie still held the Coke bottle and the fishermen waved their spears. White Sox kept setting up and taking aim, but then dropping his weapon, as if he couldn't get off a clear shot.

"What'll we do?" said flattop finally.

Eddie stopped circling. "You got a gun in your truck?"

"No. Back in town."

"A rock," said Eddie. "Find a rock."

The men searched the ground. Bunny and I looked along the river edge. "There aren't any rocks in swamps," said flattop after a minute.

"How about a log?" yelled Bunny. She pointed to a branch about four inches thick that had drifted down the Little Carp and was lodged in the bank on the other side. Eddie ran over. Without pausing, he leaped off the bank into the middle of the river. He came down in a mud hole and sank up to his shoulders. "Jesus!" he cried.

"Don't drown," shouted Bunny, flapping her arms to show him how to swim.

Eddie hauled himself out of the mud and pushed through the water to the other bank. He pulled out the branch and then came back, flopping on his belly and dog paddling over the mud hole. Wheezing and coughing, he pulled himself out of the water and ran back to the spot where the fishermen were still circling the coon.

"You gonna club it?" asked White Sox.

Eddie stared down at the balled-up tablecloth. Little tufts of brown fur were visible through rips in the material and a thin, bony leg poked out underneath. The coon was almost still now, the only movement was an occasional twitch. "Looks like it's dyin' on its own," said Eddie. The three men cautiously leaned down. "Maybe it's already dead," he added.

"You better kill it," said flattop.

Eddie stared some more. The log dangled at his side. "I guess you're right," he said. He spread his elbows to make room. The other men stood aside. With both hands, Eddie raised the log up over his head, as if he were chopping wood. The animal wasn't moving at all now. The checkered cloth fluttered gently and was still. At the top of his swing, Eddie stopped. I can't say why, but I knew he was going to. In that instant, I felt that my arms, too, were locked above my head, my fingers were gripping a wet and heavy club that now seemed somehow mean. White Sox shot a hard glance at Eddie, and finally Eddie brought the log down with a soft thud. Bunny grabbed my arm and covered her eyes. Eddie struck three more times, going easier with each blow.

"Now it's dead," said White Sox.

Eddie looked down at what he'd done and then heaved the log, end over end, far out into the swamp.

"I'm glad I didn't bring Grandmother's good tablecloth," Bunny whispered to me.

For the ride home, Bunny made Eddie strip down to his underwear and sit in the backseat, so he wouldn't get the Pontiac full of mud. "There'll be hell to pay if the cops catch us like this," said Eddie, grinning.

Bunny was worried about getting stopped for speeding, so we crawled back toward town. Coming in on Fogarty Road, a line of cars got stuck behind us because the road curves, and they couldn't pass. Someone started to honk. Eddie laughed. "Go slower," he said. "I'm enjoyin' this."

Suddenly, a squad car was beside us. The cop gestured for Bunny to pull over to the side of the road. He parked behind us and walked slowly up to Bunny's window. He was a big, barrel-chested man. I recognized him, but I didn't know his name.

"Somethin' wrong with your car?" he asked.

"No, officer," said Bunny.

"You know, there's a minimum speed limit," he said. "Twenty-five miles an hour."

"I guess I forgot."

He looked past Bunny to the back seat, where Eddie was sitting with his legs crossed. The policeman straightened up. He stepped over to the back door and flung it open so hard the hinge screamed. "Out," he ordered.

Eddie climbed out, grinning. He looked ridiculous in his underwear beside the cop.

"His clothes got wet when I was attacked by a raccoon," said Bunny.

"Yeah, yeah," said the cop. He spun Eddie around. "Are you drunk, Boggs?" he said.

"Not enough," said Eddie.

"This is Sunday, you know," said the cop, without explanation.

Eddie smirked. "There's a dead raccoon with rabies out to Mason's Farm," he said. "You ought to go bury it."

"I don't do work like that," said the cop.

An old, brown car passed by, and a passenger, seeing Eddie, hooted and waved.

The cop leaned down and reached into the back seat of the Pontiac, pulling out a Hamms can. He jiggled it next to his ear, and you could hear the liquid slosh. "Open liquor," he said.

Eddie climbed back in and slammed the door. The cop took Bunny's license and walked to his car to write a ticket. Bunny looked at Eddie in the rear-view mirror. "Thanks," she said.

Eddie grunted.

When the cop came back, he gave Bunny her license and a copy of the ticket. He put his face in the window and looked at Eddie. "You got no pride," he said.

"Don't need none in front of you," said Eddie.

"Thank you, officer," said Bunny quickly. "We'll go now."

The cop straightened up. As Bunny pulled back onto the road, he slapped the trunk of the car with his hand, making a loud, ringing smack.

"Jesus!" said Bunny.

She kept at exactly twenty-five miles an hour the rest of the way back. When we got to Rose Dry Cleaners, the parking lot was empty. Bunny pulled up beside the stairway leading to Eddie's room. He climbed out and took his sopping clothes from the trunk. Then he stood in front of the car and did a little hula dance in his underwear, swinging his hips from side to side. "Get going," said Bunny angrily. She gunned the car and spit gravel all over the building as she pulled away.

We didn't say much on the way back to the Vernons'. I was thinking about Eddie, and I was starting to see how hard it was going to be for Bunny to let him go.

EIGHTEEN

"How was your day with your mother?" Mrs. O'Brien asked the next morning. We were driving through a misty drizzle out to Ward's, which was having a white sale.

"Oh, fine," I said. "It was fine."

"I think she's starting to catch on," Mrs. O'Brien said. "I had my doubts at first, but I think she's starting to catch on."

In the half rain, the wipers on the station wagon scraped methodically against the windshield. We passed the fairgrounds, which was starting to come to life for Thursday's opening. A few of the long, low 4-H tents were already up, and the silver skeleton of the Ferris wheel, not yet outfitted with seats, jutted into the gray air. Several men in dark, shiny slickers were marching over the soggy turf. They moved slowly, as if overwhelmed by all they had to do. The scene was gloomy and I turned away.

Ward's was gloomy, too, starting with the broad expanse of empty, wet parking lot, a field of lifeless gray. Mrs. O'Brien pulled up to the front, near a cluster of cars whose drivers had come early for the sale. "I'd have to go ten times around the square to find a space on a morning like this," she said with satisfaction.

Inside, she hurried away toward the linen department, while I wandered off on my own. I turned down a wide aisle that stretched back endlessly with new school supplies, all horribly yellow. How could school start without me? I wanted everything to stop until I was free again—until all my problems were only a memory. What had Reverend Vaughn said? There's no giant wheel of life that rolls inevitably forward. Maybe not, but looking around Ward's, with its aisle after aisle of racks and displays, its pots and pans, socks, refrigerators, pencils, toys, books, suits, chairs, paint, thumbtacks—it seemed there was just too much *stuff* around for the world to wait up for me.

I found my way over to the Sweet Sixteen Shoppe, which was set off by a lacy white canopy draped from the ceiling. I hadn't bought clothes from Ward's in years. The store apparently assumed that girls only grew tall by getting fat, so anything the right length for me was flappingly wide and boxy. Still, I strolled among the racks of skirts and dresses, rustling the clothes with my hand. A flowery fragrance hung above everything; I imagined a blue-jacketed Ward's lady blowing perfume into the air each morning, trying to give the clunky clothes the smell of something delicate.

The store was pushing a circle skirt of clingy cotton, red with a pink print of small flowers. The design was rather nice, actually, compared to the general drabness, and a whole rack of the skirts was set out, stretching thirty feet or so. I fumbled my way among them, looking halfheartedly for a size ten, then gave up. In a month, the skirts would be all over the high school, bright spots of red in the halls, each one signifying a kind of flaw. I went off in search of Mrs. O'Brien.

She was unhappy, too; the linen selection had been meager. "That's why they have these sales," she grumbled as we splashed back to the car. "To get rid of stock no one would notice otherwise."

Driving down Dunlop Street, back in town, Mrs. O'Brien braked suddenly in front of Kuhn's Garage. A fresh wreck, a crumpled green pile of metal, had appeared overnight. The front end of the car had been crushed and pushed back, creating a flat, wrinkled face with a gaping, grillwork mouth.

Several people were standing around under umbrellas, and Mrs. O'Brien pulled into the driveway. She rolled down her window. "Terrible!" she called out to the space around her. A tall man with a red, puffy face walked up. He reported that the car had hit one of the concrete abutments on the Route 59 overpass. A boy from Willowbrook had been driving, taking his girl for a joyride. Amazingly, the boy had hardly been scratched; the girl's legs had been crushed. Mrs. O'Brien took in her breath sharply and said she supposed the

155

girl was lucky to be alive at all. A woman named Florence, one of the checkers at Woolworth's, walked over, bumping umbrellas with the puffy-faced man. "It's so awful," said Florence. "You can see her little white pocketbook in front, just squooshed in the metal."

The man went over to look. "I hear she'll never walk again," said Florence.

Mrs. O'Brien shook her head. We stared at the green hunk of metal, shiny with rain. The puffy-faced man walked over to two other men, who were standing on the other side of the wreck. He said something to them, but they didn't seem to pay attention, so he walked back over to Mrs. O'Brien's car. "What I don't understand," he said, "is why these things happen alone. Those kids were out there on the road by themselves. It wasn't raining yet and visibility was good. They just crash into whatever's there. It's like something pushes them off the road. It don't make sense."

"These times," said Mrs. O'Brien.

The *Exponent* that afternoon said the girl's name was Ellen Pigott, and both legs had been amputated above the knee. The front page had a photograph of the car crushed against the abutment. I studied the dark, grainy picture and tried to imagine what had happened. Had the boy who'd been driving been distracted suddenly? Maybe he'd been showing off or he'd tried to steal a kiss. In the instant, it had happened. One mistake. His was probably quicker and simpler even than mine. It didn't seem right that things were so fragile, that in one unthinking moment you could destroy everything. What's the use?

I had the paper spread out on the kitchen table, and Mrs. Vernon looked over my shoulder. She made clicking noises with her tongue. "It's like a war," she said.

Percy Granville was on the front page, too. Over the weekend, he'd given an interview to the Chicago *Tribune*, admitting he'd pilfered the money from the treasurer's office and explaining how it all had happened. The *Exponent*'s account of the interview was long, and I read it from beginning to end. Granville claimed he was just a small-time banker, a simple, country boy who had got into politics almost by accident. But politics was the great corrupter, he said—the dinners, the drinks, the speeches, the attention. He'd been seduced by it all, and soon he was spending lavishly on parties and trips and women. All his life, he'd been a frumpy little banker, and suddenly he was the state treasurer, a man with power and fame. He loved the excitement, but it was like a drug—he always had to have more. And the excitement was expensive. That's why he'd started to steal. "I must have been temporarily insane," Granville told the reporter. That was his excuse—he was crazy, but just for a while. He was over it now.

I studied the sad, baggy face in the *Exponent's* photograph. He looked so frail. It seemed as if the tiny dots of ink on the page might spread, and he'd disappear like the cloud of bugs hovering over the swamp. I almost wanted to write him a letter, but what could I say—that I'd always liked him because of his funny name? That I thought mistakes—even big ones—should be forgiven? That he and I would always be together, in my mind, because we'd suffered our downfalls at the same time?

Nonsense. I flipped the page of the paper, looking for something to cheer me up. The Cubs had lost again, this time to the Cardinals. Take that, Mr. Vernon. Ava Gardner was starring in *Bhowanii Junction* at the Grinstead. An ad showed her dressed for safari, looking totally out of place and uncomfortable. In the letters column, I noticed a small headline, MORE ON WITCHES. My stomach burned. The letter was signed "A Loving Mother," but I knew immediately it was from Bunny.

> Somebody who calls herself "A Concerned Mother" (Letters, July 27), claims to be worried about "Witches" in Katydid. Well, I don't believe in witches, but I do know that bad mothers exist, and Katydid seems to have more than its share of them. I'm talking about mothers who spend more time at the beauty parlor than they do with their children; mothers who are more interested in their neighbors' families than in their own; mothers who worry about losing their husbands instead of taking care of them; mothers who talk to their friends more than they talk to their children; and mothers who think they should be able to tell everyone else how to run their lives. This used to be a nice, simple town, where people were left alone to do as they pleased. Now, everyone is snooping around so much we might as well be in Russia. I'd like to meet this "Concerned Mother." I'd like to look her in the eye. Maybe she's right about there being witches in Katydid after all. Indeed, I think she is right. After rereading her letter, I'm convinced. As a matter of fact, I bet she saw a witch this very day—when she got out of bed and looked in the mirror.

I read the letter over several times. It had all the signs of Bunny's thinking—the talk about motherhood, the accusations about snooping, the belief that Katydid had once been different, and better, than it is today. There was even a sort of rhetorical flourish to the language that sounded like Bunny when she got riled up. I could almost hear her reciting the letter line for line, punching the air with her fist at each semicolon.

Mrs. Vernon came up behind me again and looked over my shoulder. She'd seen the letter earlier, and now she reached down and put a thin finger on top of it. "I can't imagine why they printed this thing," she said. "Whoever wrote it is obviously disturbed."

NINETEEN

It was too rainy to take a walk that afternoon, so Reverend Vaughn suggested that we drive over to the Dairy Queen for a couple of chocolate-dip cones. I scrunched into his Metropolitan. With knees and elbows poking in all directions, the minister and I filled up the front seat. I tried to press against the door panel, but I was practically sitting in his lap. Reaching for the ignition, he brushed my leg. The windows steamed up and, in the close air, I imagined my breath smelled terrible.

When we got to the Dairy Queen, a line of customers stretched out in front of the service window—even in the worst weather, the Dairy Queen always has a line. We waited under the tin awning in front while the rain drilled gently overhead and dripped down in a soft, wet curtain around us. At the window, finally, Reverend Vaughn bought two medium chocolate-dip cones, and we sat on a protected bench along the side of the building.

"Mondays are such a letdown," he said, after nibbling the chocolate tip off his cone. "I hate Mondays."

"I thought it was the start of your weekend."

"That's the trouble," he said. "I get all worked up over a sermon, and then, on Sunday, it just disappears into thin air. What have I got to show for it?"

"People are thinking about it."

"Yeah? Maybe. Sometimes I wish I was, say, a cobbler or a furniture maker—someone who actually produced something, you know, an object. Think of working all week and then having a nice, solid chair. You could show it to your friends, take a picture of it. Hell, you could sit in it."

"But this way you're using your head."

"My head only gets in the way." His ice cream started to drip, spilling down the side of the cone onto his fingers. He slurped along the edge of the chocolate with his tongue and then borrowed my napkin to mop up. "Why can't they make this stuff colder, so you can at least have a normal conversation before it melts?" he grumbled.

A maroon Chevy packed with hoods cruised down Walker Street, slowing to check out the action at the Dairy Queen. A boy in the front seat spotted me and called out something I couldn't understand.

"Was that a friend of yours?" Reverend Vaughn asked.

"No, he's just a hood. His name's Larry. He used to be in my class, but he flunked."

"Oh. Charming guy."

The car swerved and turned left up Church Street.

The minister stood and walked over to the trash bin. "I suppose I shouldn't complain," he said, dumping a wad of sticky napkins into the metal container. "By Friday I'll be wrapped up in another sermon and won't have time to think about whether it's worth it. At least this keeps me occupied. Shall we go?"

Suddenly, the screech of skidding tires tore through the damp air. The sound rose, then fell, then rose again. Reverend Vaughn stopped and turned his head to listen. With a long, rubbery whine, the maroon Chevy shot out of Gora Street and made a skidding turn onto Walker. An approaching milk truck jolted noisily to a stop, and the Chevy slid sideways across the pavement, stopping just short of the sidewalk. The wheels dug in again, and the Chevy raced up toward the Dairy Queen.

"What the hell's this?" mumbled Reverend Vaughn.

The hood named Larry was leaning out the front window on the passenger side, and a hood I didn't recognize was halfway out a window in back. They were yelling and waving their arms. From the side, the car looked like some kind of big insect with a head full of jointed feelers. The Chevy roared up to the Dairy Queen and swept into the gravelly parking lot. The wheels on the right side missed part of the driveway and bounced off the curb.

"Jesus Christ!" yelled the minister. He grabbed for me, wrapping a long arm around my shoulder and turning his back on the car as a shield. The Chevy braked and swerved across the parking lot, just a few feet in front of us, churning up a cloud of gravel and dust. Larry and his buddies kept screaming. I took a moment to nestle my head into the soft place on Reverend Vaughn's chest, just beneath his shoulder. A clean, starchy smell, faintly dizzying, came off his clothes.

The Chevy finished its turn and without stopping roared out of the driveway and on down Walker, the hoods still leaning out the windows making nonsense noises. At best, the sounds were like a recitation of vowels, screamed at full volume: "A-E-I-O-U! A-E-I-O-U!" The noise trailed off as the car rocketed down Walker.

The girl working in the Dairy Queen rapped on the glass window, and Reverend Vaughn dropped his arm from around my shoulder. "Did you *know* those boys?" she asked in an excited voice.

"Hell, no," he said.

The girl looked startled. She'd probably never heard a clergyman swear before.

Reverend Vaughn dumped what was left of his cone in the trash can. He asked if I was all right, and I nodded. "Then let's get out of here before Attila and the Huns come back," he said.

"Oh, you *do* know them," the girl called out as we left.

TWENTY

In the evening, the sky cleared and the moon came out. As I lay in bed, a shaft of moonlight, so thick and silvery it seemed to have weight, poured through the slit between the curtains and pressed down on my legs. My pulse had started pounding back at the Dairy Queen, and it hadn't slowed, beating along like something apart from me, a tiny motor racing with the much larger engine in the hoods' car. Is it possible to have a heart attack at sixteen? To calm myself, I sat up and looked out the window. The backyard was all shades of gray and black, like a wood carving in a book, or an old, faded photograph. The Porter house was completely dark. Mr. and Mrs. Porter always went to bed dreadfully early, and, of course, Grandma Porter was usually ahead of them. Several times, from across the yard, I'd watched her tuck herself in, probably eager to start dreaming again of her escape. What was his name? Harry. Harry was coming to rescue her. It occurred to me that we all had our white knights. Grandma Porter had Harry. Bunny had Eddie. Mrs. Vernon had Jesus. And I had Reverend Vaughn.

I lay back down on the bed. There, I told myself. That ought to prove how realistic I was being. Harry, Eddie, Jesus—and Reverend Vaughn. What an idiot I was. It was ridiculous to think he cared a whit for me—or, at least, a whit more than he cared for any of the other people in the Congo. He was a minister doing his job, that was all. He was *supposed* to seem interested in people and their problems. Still . . . what about all the time he'd spent with me and the talks we'd had? Those weren't normal, preacherly conversations. He didn't open up like that with everyone. And at the Dairy Queen, he'd pulled me to him at the first sign of trouble. He didn't push me to safety, or step in the way. What he did was . . . well, he gave me a kind of embrace. I could still feel, on my cheek, the slippery softness of his fine white shirt. Had I closed my eyes? I shouldn't have, but I think I did. I actually fit there, right under his arm.

I remembered that when I was little, I used to cut out paper dolls and save them in a shoebox. After a while, I had dozens of paper dolls—mothers, fathers, sons, daughters—dolls of all shapes and sizes. Day after day, I'd take them out, shuffling them constantly into new families, testing how a blue cardboard son fit with a family made of drawing paper, or how a father clipped from an illustration in the *Saturday Evening Post* got along with a mother in a *Life* photograph. Thinking back, I realized that I'd obeyed only one rule with the families—a single, constant rule that was frightening for a tall girl, but still I never broke it: The father had to be taller than the mother. How do you fight an instinct like that?

I wished Bunny were more help in all this. She should have picked up some romantic insights over the years—though maybe that was wishful thinking, given the men she'd chosen. Anyway, I could tell she didn't like Reverend Vaughn; at least, she didn't like to talk about him. I'd bring him up and she'd complain or change the subject. It was funny, Grandmother had been the same way about Bunny when Bunny talked about her boyfriends. Of course, Bunny was almost obsessive about it. Something about being at Grandmother's house made Bunny babble on about the latest man in her life. It drove Grandmother crazy. Bunny would be going on, and Grandmother's knitting would get faster and faster, the needles clicking away like the sound of a typewriter.

She never actually criticized Bunny, though once, at the end of dinner, after Bunny had been rambling on about Lester Vincent and about some terrific job he was about to get, Grandmother got up to clear the dishes and said in a soft voice, "A woman's only supposed to have one man in her life." Thinking about it later, I realized that she said it when she did so there couldn't be any arguing. She just dropped the idea there for all of us and went into the kitchen. Of course, for her there was only one man. She was married for thirty-one years to Arthur Stoneham, a farmer. He died long before I was born—before Bunny was born, too, as a matter of fact. He and Grandmother weren't Bunny's real parents. Bunny's not even sure who her mother was, probably some farm girl from around Indian Falls who got in trouble. The girl needed someone to take her baby, and Grandmother was lonely without Arthur around. Grandmother had had four children of her own—three boys and a girl—but by the time Bunny arrived, they'd grown up and moved away. We never saw them much, and they were hardly ever mentioned, by Bunny or by Grandmother.

Bunny was devoted to Grandmother and we used to go up to the farm all the time when she was alive. Tom and I hated those trips. To us, the farm seemed terribly lonely and primitive. The animals were gone by then, except for a few old geese that dirtied up the yard and nipped at you if you got too close, and the rickety old house was usually chilly. Grandmother always wore layers of wool sweaters.

In those days, she was too old to keep things up by herself. Grandmother was in her eighties when we knew her. She had been small to begin with, and as she grew old, her back had developed a slight curve, so she was always hunched over. She was sweet to Tom and me, but she never talked much. By then, she was warm and content there inside her sweaters and didn't need anyone else to keep her company.

Bunny took it hard when Grandmother died. It happened in the winter, when I was eleven. The Indian Falls sheriff called on a Saturday afternoon. Grandmother had been found in her bed, she'd been dead for several days. The heat in the farmhouse had gone off, and she was frozen solid, though people said she'd probably died of natural causes and only froze later.

We drove up to her funeral on Tuesday. Tom and I had to miss school. She was laid out in a metal coffin on the table in the dining room of the farmhouse. The coffin was lined with puffy, silver satin, and Grandmother was so light that she floated on top of the material, barely denting it, the way a water bug rides on water. Grandmother's four other children were there, along with lots of people from the town.

Tom and Bunny and I were standing apart when one old man came over. Thick puffs of gray hair like cotton balls sprouted from his ears, and more gray hairs were sticking out of each nostril. He ignored Bunny and me and talked to Tom. "I asked her to marry me, but she turned me down for Arthur Stoneham, heh, heh." He had a faint, raspy laugh. Tom scowled at him, and the old man looked confused.

"I bet you were a pretty good catch yourself," said Bunny.

He brightened again. "Up until fourteen years ago, you could have asked my wife that, but she's dead now." He again turned to Tom for encouragement, but Tom was still scowling, so the old man shuffled away.

"That was Tim Butterick," said Bunny. "Grandmother said she turned him down 'cause he was sickly. Now, he's outlived them all. You just can't ever tell."

The coffin was closed, and we drove it down the road to a little cemetery that had been carved out of a pine woods. The frozen needles crunched under our feet as we marched to the burial site. The night before, a bonfire had been built so the ground would thaw and a grave could be dug. Grandmother's sons lowered the coffin into the hole with ropes, and the minister read a prayer. It was a sparkling bright day, but very cold, and his breath floated in beautiful, pure-white clouds, framed against the dark green of the pines. When he finished, everyone walked by and threw dirt on the coffin, using a small, black spade. Afterward, we left quickly, and Bunny hardly said a word to her stepbrothers and stepsister.

Later that winter, the farmhouse burned down. It had been empty since Grandmother died and vandals finally got to it. Bunny only learned of the fire several weeks after it had happened, but she insisted that we drive up for one last look. All that was left was the stone foundation, covered with soot and charred wood. I was shocked. I had known a huge, creaky, slightly frightening house. The flat, square foundation that remained looked terribly small, like a child's thing, hardly larger than a hopscotch game we'd draw on the sidewalk with chalk. Lying now in Sissy's bed, I remembered standing on the damp, cold lawn on a miserable March day and staring at the black scar in the top of the hill. "There goes home," Bunny had said.

The midnight whistle blew at the KTD. Several people walked down Oak Street, their heels clicking in the quiet air. After a while, a vehicle drove by, then stopped just down the street. The engine shut off, but the tinny sound of a car radio trailed on in the night. Someone was sitting there, listening, with the windows open. The sound kept up for about twenty minutes, the tinkling, distant lilt of the songs alternating with the staccato jabber of the disc jockey. The tunes, the words were unrecognizable, but familiar. When the radio was finally turned off, the night seemed empty.

Five minutes later, there was a very light bump on the side of the house below Sissy's window. I crawled down the bed and pulled back the curtain. Elro Judy was outside, standing on a ladder. His head was just below the windowsill.

"What are you doing?" I hissed through the screen.

"Visitin'." He was holding a bottle of beer.

"Go away!"

"Come on, just a little," he said. "It'll be fun." He took another step up the ladder, which ground against the side of the house.

"Are you crazy? They're going to hear you."

"So what?" In his drunkenness, he forgot to lower his voice. The loudness of his words amused him, and he laughed.

"Please, Elro, go away," I begged. "I'm already in too much trouble."

"You come out then," he said, talking in a whisper again. He thought for a moment. In his condition, it appeared to take some effort. "We'll go to the fair."

"It's not open yet."

"This is the best time—before it opens. They stay up all night partyin.' My brother's workin' there, and he says they got great stuff this year. They got a wrestlin' bear, and, oh, a two-headed baby in a glass jar. The heads come out of its shoulders like a V-8 engine." He waved his bottle, took a drink, wiped his mouth with the back of his hand and took another step up the ladder. Putting his lips close to the screen, he whispered, "You know you want to come. You know you do."

"Shhh!" Someone was at the bedroom door. I pulled the curtains shut and scrambled down the bed and under the sheet. The doorknob rattled and the door opened a crack.

"Martha?" Mrs. Vernon called out softly. "Martha, are you all right?" She stepped into the room, her slippers sliding over the wood floor.

"Who's there?" I tried to sound half asleep.

"It's me, dear. You must have had a nightmare. You've been

talking in your sleep. I could hear you all the way down the hall." She came to the bed and leaned over me. The scent of talcum powder was so strong that it was hard to breathe. She was wearing a light-colored robe that she clutched together at the front with one hand. I'd never seen her in bedclothes before.

"I'm sorry," I said.

"Oh, don't be sorry. Should I turn on the light?"

"No, thanks. It's all right."

She was silent for a few seconds. I imagined her studying me and the room. Finally, she said, "Well, why don't I just sit here until you fall asleep again. When Sissy was a little girl, she used to have nightmares, and I'd come and sit with her, right there in that chair."

"I don't think you need to stay. I'll be fine now."

"Are you sure? You sound a little jumpy."

"I'm sure."

"Well, okay, then." She padded toward the door. When she was a few feet from it, she stopped and turned. She stared toward the window. Even in the darkness, I could see her face changing shape, tightening, narrowing. Suddenly, she stepped back toward me, wringing the front of her bathrobe. Her eyes were diamonds in the room's faint light. "Oh, Martha," she wailed, "there's so much evil in the world, so much evil." She came quickly and knelt beside the bed. "That's what nightmares are—evil thoughts bubbling out." She grabbed the sheet and pulled it up to her mouth. "I lied to you before. I told you that Sissy had nightmares when she was little. She had them when she was older, too. She had them a lot. The week before she died, she had them almost every night. Ugly, evil nightmares, so she'd wake up screaming, and I'd have to come and lie with her. Sissy. Sissy."

She covered her face with her hands and started to sob. Suddenly, she reached out and grabbed the top of my nightgown, pulling me close to her face. "It's the serpent," she hissed. "That's where the evil comes from. The serpent. They tried to blame Eve, but it was the serpent. I know, I know, I know." She buried her head in my chest, rubbing her face back and forth. "Oh, Martha," she moaned. "I know, I know, I know." The words had a kind of rhythm to them, almost as if she were singing.

Reaching out slowly, I put my arm around her shoulder. It seemed strange and unnatural to be comforting her, but I stroked her back softly. After a few minutes, her sobbing slowed and then stopped. She lifted her head and used a corner of the sheet to wipe her eyes. She stood up, bracing herself on the bed. She sighed. "I hope you're over your nightmare," she said. Her voice was limp. "I'll leave you alone, if you think you'll be all right." She backed away, toward the door.

"I'll be fine."

"Then, good night, dear. Sweet dreams." She slipped into the hall and closed the door gently.

I couldn't hear her walk away, so I lay in bed for a long time. Finally, I climbed out and went to the door. The hall was dark and empty. The house was quiet. I turned and faced the window. The ghostly silhouette of a man was unmistakably shadowed on the curtain. I climbed back on the bed and put my face close to the screen. "Go away," I whispered.

"That lady's nuts," said Elro. "She's gumballs."

"Please, please, she'll be back. Go away."

Elro climbed a few rungs down the ladder. His chin was just at the level of the sill, and, through the curtain, his head seemed to sit there by itself, like a flowerpot.

"This is a bad place," he said. "It's dangerous."

"Please, Elro."

"I hate it. I'm gonna run away."

"Please."

His head disappeared below the sill. I pulled the curtain back and watched him climb down. At the bottom, he picked up the ladder and tucked it under his arm, then he ran silently across the lawn and around the corner of the house. A few seconds later, I heard his truck start up.

TWENTY-ONE

"What a glorious day!" trilled Mrs. Vernon the next morning when she appeared at the door, a little later than usual but with an otherwise unchanged routine. She flung back the curtains that had hidden Elro just a few hours before. Outside, past the leaves of the oak, I thought I saw a dark, gray cloud curling around the sky. "Sissy always loved these warm summer mornings," she said. She folded her hands in her apron and asked if I'd slept well. Nothing in her face gave away anything about nightmares or serpents. I told her I'd slept just fine.

She chattered on through breakfast, talking about her friend Mrs. Carmel, who kept getting terrible backaches until the doctors found a tumor the size of a lemon in the back of her neck. They took the tumor out and that helped for a while, but now the backaches were coming again, and Mrs. Carmel wouldn't tell the doctors because she was afraid they would think she was only imagining the pain.

The phone rang. Mrs. Vernon had her hands in the sink with the morning's dishes, so she asked me to answer.

"Martha? I didn't expect you to pick up," said Reverend Vaughn. Confined to the telephone, his voice sounded smaller and slightly unreal, though hearing it immediately put me in a playful mood.

"Only in emergencies," I said.

"An emergency?"

"No, no, I'm only kidding. Mrs. Vernon's hands were wet."

"Oh, I see. Well, how are you?"

"I'm okay. How are you?"

"Good, good. I'm great. No more visits from Attila, I hope. After the Dairy Queen, that is."

I sensed uneasily that he was pushing on to something. "No," I said.

"Good. I think that was just an isolated incident. It won't happen again."

"I hope not."

"Yes." He paused. "Ah, I wanted to let you know that I have to go out of town for the next couple of days. Nothing serious. A kind of business trip. But I won't be able to come by."

"Oh." I felt a sharp pain in my stomach—not really a pain, more a tiny explosion that seemed in danger of getting bigger.

"But I'll be back Friday. That's still the date of the hearing, isn't it?"

"Yes."

"I'm sorry. I know this is very ill-timed for you. But I'm afraid it can't be helped."

I worked to control my voice. "That's okay," I said.

"Anyway, Friday's the important day, and I promise I'll be here for that."

"Okay." Friday was now a straight, downhill fall away. All the possibilities had been wrung out of time until then.

"Will you be all right?" He had heard the disappointment in my voice.

"Oh, I'll be fine, thanks. Thanks for thinking about me."

"All right, then. I'll see you Friday. If I get back Thursday night, I'll give you a call. Okay? Chin up."

"Chin up," I repeated stupidly and put down the phone. In the kitchen, the water wasn't running in the sink anymore. I stood there in the stillness in the hall, and in a few seconds Mrs. Vernon stuck her head out the door. She was startled to find me looking right at her.

"Oh," she said. "Who was that?"

"Reverend Vaughn. He's going away for a few days."

"That's a shame. What bad timing." She stepped into the hall, drying her hands on her apron. "If you'd like, I can arrange for you to see Reverend Wallenback. He's a very nice man, very helpful."

"No, thanks." I wanted to say something cruel, something hurtful to her. How could she even think that that dismal man could take the place of Reverend Vaughn? But I fought the urge and ran upstairs. "I'll be all right," I called back.

Twenty minutes later, the phone rang again. Soon Mrs. Vernon was at the bedroom door to explain that Mrs. O'Brien wanted a session that afternoon with Bunny and me. There was a problem, though—Mrs. O'Brien couldn't reach Bunny at home or at work. I said I thought I could find her with the help of a phonebook. We trudged downstairs, and Mrs. Vernon handed me the Katydid directory. But then she stood there, apparently curious to see what I'd look up. I didn't want to let on, so I riffled the pages until I got an idea. Then I found the listing for the News Depot and asked the operator to ring that number. After the first ring, Frank Winwood, the counterman, answered.

"Is Bunny Calhoun there?" I asked.

"Who?" Frank was in Tom's class, and the two used to get into fights.

"Bunny Calhoun."

"Why the hell would she be here?" Frank demanded. "She never comes in here. Who is this?"

"Okay. Thanks." I hung up and shook my head.

"Oh, dear," Mrs. Vernon said. "Mrs. O'Brien really wants to find her."

"Why?"

"I don't know." She turned away. "Just concerned, I guess."

We went into the kitchen. Mrs. Vernon put the kettle on the burner and scooped some loose tea into the wire nest in the top of her orange pot. After a minute or so, I said I'd try Bunny again. I hurried into the hall, just out of Mrs. Vernon's sight, and thumbed through the phone book until I found Eddie Boggs's number. Then I whispered it to the operator. The phone rang eight times, and the operator broke in. "No one's home," she said.

"Keep trying," I whispered.

After four more rings, Bunny answered.

"Who is this?" she said.

"Me."

"You!"

"Did you get her?" Mrs. Vernon called out from the kitchen. "Tell her to come at two."

"What are you doing there?" I asked.

"Helping to clean up the place. It's a real pigpen. He's got engine parts all over the floor. There's grease on everything."

I tried to keep my voice low so Mrs. Vernon wouldn't hear. "Bunny, how could you?" I said.

"Don't talk to me like that," Bunny shouted into the phone. "You can't talk to your mother like that."

It wouldn't do any good to argue about Eddie now. "Mrs. O'Brien wants to meet with us," I said. "She wants you here at two."

"At two? How am I supposed to be there at two? I've got a job."

"Just be here," I pleaded.

There was silence on the line for a few seconds. "What's she want now?" Bunny asked finally.

"I don't know, but it sounds important."

"Why?"

"I don't know."

"You didn't tell them where I was, did you?"

"Of course not."

"We've got to be careful."

"I know."

A long, thin sigh hissed over the telephone line. It sounded as if the strength were draining out of her. "You'll be here at two, won't you?" I asked.

"Of course, sweetheart," she said softly.

She arrived fifteen minutes early. Sitting by the front window, I watched her park the Pontiac and come up the walk. She was wearing a white jacket over her purple sundress, and she had on her white leather sandals. Her hair made a yellow circle around her head. She took long, firm steps, her legs slicing through the air in clouds of purple cotton. Bunny had tried to teach me to "walk confident" like that. She'd marched around the living room, with me right behind, trying to imitate her strides and the purposeful swing of her arms. She could do it and look wondrous, a thoroughbred galloping over a field. But I was just clumsy, my gangly arms and legs always falling out of rhythm. There was too much of me. "That's it! That's it!" Bunny would yell as I circled the sofa and passed the TV—but I knew better. I never caught on, and the walking lessons fortunately stopped.

Mrs. Vernon hurried to greet Bunny at the front door and asked if we'd like to sit in the parlor.

"Sure, sure, sure," said Bunny, waving her hand.

Mrs. Vernon deposited us on the sofa and then left quickly.

"I make her nervous," Bunny said.

"She's really strange. She came into my room last night and started screaming about serpents."

"Serpents?"

"You know, snakes."

"Snakes?" Bunny wrinkled her face into a question mark.

"She was crying and saying how serpents were the root of all evil. It was as if she was in a trance." Bunny was still making a face. It occurred to me that this was probably not the smartest thing to talk about right now.

"Ugh," said Bunny after a moment. "Snakes give me the creeps."

"Me, too." I let the subject drop.

"What's this all about, anyway?" Bunny asked. "What's Mrs. O'Brien got to say that she hasn't said before?"

"I don't know. I didn't talk to her."

"There's something wrong with that woman. She asked me questions about Grandmother and about your daddy that just made me sick. I'd be ashamed to pry into people's lives like that."

"That's her job. That's what she's supposed to do."

Bunny leaned across the sofa. "But she's not supposed to enjoy it, that's what I'm saying. She *likes* poking around. She's not even humble about it." She sat back. "Anyway, it'll be a relief to get rid of her."

"Have you talked to Mr. Beach lately?"

"Don't worry. He owes me a lot of favors. He'll come through." She reached over and gave my cheek a soft chuck, the kind of pinch you'd give a baby. She took her hand away, and her face lit up. "Martha, God, with just a little color on those cheekbones you'd be the most beautiful girl in Katydid." She reached over with both hands and pinched both cheeks, and I twisted to get away. "Oh, come on," she said. "I'm serious. Those are classic cheekbones. I'd kill to have cheekbones like them."

Mrs. O'Brien arrived at the same time as the tea. Before sitting down, she studied the tray of tiny toast sandwiches that Mrs. Vernon had set on the coffee table. Finally, she picked out a triangle smeared with cream cheese and sat down in Mr. Vernon's chair. She carefully put the sandwich on a napkin on the arm of the chair, then sighed noisily and looked at Bunny and me. "We have a problem here," she said.

Bunny and I glanced at each other. "Yeah?" said Bunny warily.

"I think you know what I'm talking about."

"Yeah?" said Bunny again.

Mrs. O'Brien shifted in the chair. Her heavy, deliberate movements seemed to indicate that a great force was being brought into place. "Let's not be coy with each other, Mrs. Calhoun."

"I'm not being coy."

"Your daughter appears before Judge Horner in three days."

"I'm well aware."

"I don't think you are. I don't think you're even remotely aware."

Bunny turned to me and shrugged, raising her hands, palms up. "What's this?" she said.

"Sergeant Tony called me. He told me about the incident on Sunday. I didn't believe him—I didn't *want* to believe him, I should say—so I came down and read the police report myself."

"Jesus," said Bunny, staring at the floor.

"You disobeyed Judge Horner, you lied to me, you broke the law, and you ended up on a public road with a drunken, half-naked man in the backseat—the very man you're not supposed to be seeing. And your daughter was right there with you." Mrs. O'Brien uttered a false half laugh and turned to me, as if expecting to find some agreement. "It's almost funny, or a kind of mockery. You seem to think this whole thing is a joke."

Bunny stood up quickly. "I've had it," she said. "I want another social worker."

I reached for her hand to pull her down, but she brushed me away. "I mean it," she said. "Why shouldn't we have someone on our side?"

Mrs. O'Brien waited just long enough for Bunny to feel awkward, standing before us but not walking out. "You won't get another social worker," she said. "I'm your social worker. You can refuse to cooperate, but on Friday, I'll be there in court, giving my report whether you like it or not."

"Come on, Bunny, sit down," I said. I got hold of her wrist this time and pulled her back onto the sofa.

"You're beyond picking and choosing, Mrs. Calhoun," the social worker said. "You're way beyond that. The county is involved in your family now, and you can't shut them out. The county is part of your family now, too." Her tongue darted out and ran along her lips. Bunny was right—Mrs. O'Brien really did enjoy this. "When Judge Horner told you to clean up your affairs, he meant stop seeing Edward Boggs. And that's not just advice you can choose to ignore. He's a *judge*. He's going to decide what to do with your daughter." She moved forward in her chair, leaning toward us. "What's so special about this Boggs fellow, anyway? I don't know him, but he sounds bad to me, always drinking, drinking. He's dangerous, don't you see? I mean, half-naked in the backseat of your car!"

Bunny had curled up in a corner of the sofa. Her dress was pulled up, exposing a bruise the size of a quarter high up on the outside of her thigh. I reached over and pulled her dress down.

Mrs. O'Brien paused, and, on an impulse, I spoke up. "I can explain the thing with Eddie," I said.

She looked puzzled. "The thing with Eddie?"

"On Sunday, in the car. I can explain what happened. It's not as bad as it sounds."

Mrs. O'Brien's forehead folded into deep creases. She seemed on the verge of speaking but unable to find the right words. I got frightened and wished I'd never said anything. Finally, a pink flush crept into her broad, smooth cheeks. "You think you can *explain* it?" she gasped. A tiny drop of spittle broke from her lips and sailed in a gentle arc toward me. I felt it land on my arm, but I didn't take my eyes off her. "You could explain from now until Sunday, and it wouldn't get any better. This is what I've been trying to teach you, but you're as hopeless as your mother. You can't explain away trouble. Explanations don't do any good when the truth is so bad. Eddie Boggs was drunk and half-naked in the back of your mother's car. Explain it? What are you going to tell me—that you didn't know he was there?" Her face was bright red now under her carrot hair, and I could feel her breath when she talked. "It's the same with you, Martha. You were caught undressing in front of a nine-year-old boy. What can you possibly say? What? I'd like to know!"

I didn't say anything. Tears were welling up in my eyes and my throat was choked. Her anger had caught me totally unprepared.

She wiggled forward a few more inches. "You Calhouns think there's an excuse for everything. Nothing's ever your fault. Somebody always did it to you. But why are you always in trouble? Did you ever think of that? Why doesn't it happen to other people? Why is it always you? *Explanations!*" She tried to spit the word out, but her tongue got tied, and the effect was soft, like someone trying to flick a spot of tobacco off his lips.

The tears started streaming down my cheeks. I didn't dare look at Bunny. I knew my face was a horrid, splotchy, drippy mess. And yet I wanted to argue with Mrs. O'Brien. I wanted to fight her point by point. She was right in a way—but she'd missed it, too, and that's why I thought I could challenge her. She didn't understand how trouble can spiral, so that each little piece of it gets compounded by the weight of what's gone before. I wasn't trying to make excuses about what had happened, but simply to remove the latest piece of trouble so it could be judged on its own. That was my argument, and I wanted to force it coolly on Mrs. O'Brien, who was now sitting there silently, breathing heavily. I wanted to make her understand. But I was helpless, trapped by my sobbing. Tears were streaming from my eyes, my nose was running, and my throat was choked so tight I could hardly swallow, let alone speak.

Mrs. O'Brien let a minute or so pass in silence. She stared at both of us, then looked out the window. Finally, she turned back to contemplate the little cream-cheese sandwich, still untouched beside her. I knew she was thinking that she could finish it off in a single bite, that it would be in her mouth and gone in an instant, and she wouldn't have to suffer the embarrassment of holding a half-eaten sandwich in her hand while I wept and Bunny sulked in front of her. Her eyes lingered on the morsel, but she chose to pass it up. "I know it's hard," she finally said with a sigh. "You can't change overnight. It takes time and trauma."

She smiled. My sobbing started to let up. I soaked several cocktail napkins wiping my face. Bunny was still curled up on the sofa, gazing off distractedly.

"I've had worse cases than this one, God knows," Mrs. O'Brien went on. "You'd be shocked at the things that go on right here in Katydid County—things you wouldn't expect to find in the worst Southern trash novel." Suddenly, her manner softened. "Oh, I forgot. Remember that girl I told you about who stole the car parts and ran away with her boyfriend and then got pregnant? She miscarried! What a relief. I mean, it was difficult for her, but now, at least, she can begin to pick up the pieces. She can take a deep breath and start over."

On cue, I took a deep breath, letting the air out slowly through my nose.

"That's it," said Mrs. O'Brien. With her hand, she gave a kind of womanly salute, a little wave by the side of her face. In the same motion, she swept up the sandwich and popped it in her mouth. With a few nearly invisible movements of her jaw, it was gone.

"Now," she said, "where do we go from here?"

I smiled and shrugged. I felt weak.

"Well, there's no doubt it's got to start with Eddie Boggs. I'm sorry, Mrs. Calhoun, but I'll say it as plainly as I can: Get him out of your life."

For the first time in minutes, Bunny stirred. She looked at both of us, then stood up. "I've got to get to work," she said.

"So soon?" Mrs. O'Brien glanced at her watch. "I didn't think you had to be there so soon."

"I have to go," Bunny said, pulling on the bottom of her jacket to straighten it.

"Can't we talk a little?" I asked. "There's not much time."

"No, Martha," said Mrs. O'Brien. "It's up to your mother. She knows what the stakes are. It's up to her."

I looked at Bunny pleadingly, but she stared back coldly. "Walk me to the door, please," she said.

I followed her into the hall. She stopped just before the front door. "Why'd you let her make you cry?" she demanded.

"I couldn't help it. I didn't want to, but it just happened."

"She's trying to break us. We can't let her. We'll win." Bunny spoke as if each little sentence were a separate pronouncement, unconnected to anything else.

Mrs. Vernon stepped out of the kitchen, surprised to find us in the hall. "Oh, you're leaving?" she said to Bunny.

Bunny opened the door and then turned back. "You better watch out," she said to Mrs. Vernon. "I saw a snake on your lawn."

Mrs. Vernon's smile twisted and disappeared. Her hand darted up to her mouth. "No," she murmured.

"Snakes. A whole nest of them," Bunny called out, slamming the door behind her.

TWENTY-TWO

Mrs. Vernon's vegetable garden is a long, rectangular patch of uneven greens planted in the backyard, out of the shade of the oak. On Wednesday morning, at her suggestion, I put on an old T-shirt and jeans and went to the garden to weed. She said I was worrying too much, that I should keep busy to get my mind off my problems. For a while, I plucked diligently at the unwanted, leathery sprouts that circled and closed in on the vegetables. The garden was small enough that I got the idea you could make it completely weed-free —a perfectly controlled piece of land. That image of pure, black, cleared soil, the very neatness of it, kept me occupied. Kneeling in the dirt, I moved forward inch by inch. Every few feet, I'd turn up a shard of glass or a bent nail, or an ancient, rusted bottle cap. On soft nights, looking out Sissy's window, I'd seen the glint of moonlight off the junk in the garden, bits of glass and metal that had worked their way to the surface after a hard rain. The whole world is built on an old trash heap, I thought. You can't keep the stuff down.

My hand turned a gaudy green from the plant juice. Soon my back started to ache, and my thighs got sore. I had to stand up every few minutes to stretch my muscles. I'm so tall that I don't bend easily, and working close to the ground is terribly awkward for me. The more I worked, the clumsier I felt. Stretching once, I saw Dwayne standing on the sidewalk by the house, holding his bicycle and watching me. I ached too much to wave. The unweeded row seemed to go on forever. Mrs. Vernon worked on her garden every day of the summer, and still the weeds were unstoppable. It's amazing, really, all the weeds and junk in the world. It's a wonder anyone gets anything worthwhile done.

I'd been at it for about an hour, when Mrs. Vernon came out the back door. "Someone sent you a letter," she called out, waving an envelope. "The mailman just brought it."

The soiled and crinkled envelope looked as if it had spent time in someone's pocket. I recognized the handwriting immediately—stiff, blocky printing that broke occasionally into script. Tom had never had the patience to write properly. He talked that way, too—in bursts of words that sometimes came out so fast you didn't have any idea what he was saying.

"Who do you suppose it's from?" asked Mrs. Vernon, pushing the envelope toward me. The return address was only a long number and the name of a town, Sherwood. Everyone in Illinois, even Mrs. Vernon, knows what's in that town. It's as if the place has no other purpose, as if no ordinary person would possibly live there. I snatched the letter and took it over to a shady spot at the side of the house, sitting down with my back to the wall. I ripped open the envelope with my finger. The letter was written with a soft pencil on grayish paper that was thin and pulpy.

Dear Weakheart,

I heard the news! Some guy got here from Edmonton Monday morning (a car thief!!!) and he knew all about it. Now everyone wants to meet you! I guess us Calhouns are all college material after all. From what I hear, Horner will probably give you a full scholarship. You'll learn a lot of important stuff. Like I'm learning how to paint numbers on lisence plates and fold socks into pairs (you have to be able to count to two to do that). Plus, you'll meet a lot of interesting people, like Doug Thacker, who shot his gym teacher in the leg with a BB gun. I asked him why and he said because he was aiming at his ---- and missed! Well, that's about all I had to say. I just wanted to let you know I was thinking of you. How's Bunny? Sorry this writing is so hard to read,

179

but they won't let us have any sharp pencils so we won't stab each other.

As Always,
Tom

P.S. If you take my advise, you'll run away. You can't imagine how bad it is here. I know I'm going to die before I ever get home again.

I read the letter over twice quickly, then a third time more slowly. When I looked up, Mrs. Vernon was settled in on a folding chair near the back door, pealing and coring apples for a pie. She was pretending to be occupied by the work, but every now and then her head tilted, and her gaze sneaked over toward me. When I saw that, I wanted to do everything in my power to hurt her. So I folded the letter into a tight wad, and when I was certain she was watching, I reached down the front of my T-shirt and stuffed the wad into my bra.

I went back to the garden and took my place between a second planting of carrots and a row of young beans. The beans were sending out tendrils that curled along a suspended line of string. To try to get comfortable, I stretched my legs down the narrow path between the rows and rested on my side. My jeans were getting filthy.

I tried to imagine Tom, scrunched up at some worn and dirty reform-school desk, composing a letter to me. We'd been great friends once, when we were very little. Bunny's got snapshots from those days, grainy photographs in which I'm either looking up adoringly at him or clinging to the tail of his shirt. In a couple of the pictures, Tom and I are hunkered down, squatting on our haunches the way Indians do, inspecting something small on the ground. Sitting that way seems impossible now, it seems to defy balance. The memory of doing it has disappeared, just like the memory of when Tom and I were close. Once he got into school, he spent most of his time with his own friends—when he wasn't in the principal's office, answering for some sort of mischief. He was always up to something. On a dare, he ate a crayon. He dropped his arithmetic book down a storm sewer. He slipped out of class and hid all afternoon in the boiler room and only emerged to show off a mouse he'd caught with his baseball glove. The school was always calling Bunny, and it was probably during that time that I started to think of Bunny and me as somehow separate in the family from Tom. "What are we going to do with your brother?"

Bunny would ask. And though she loves Tom very much, there was a way in which she almost seemed to enjoy the situation—the two of us plotting a way to save him.

He grew angry with Bunny as he got older. He sulked around the house, hardly talking to either of us. He was defiant of all authority, but his problem with Bunny was something different, because she was never strict. She tried to talk to him and take an interest in his friends, even though some of them were dreadful boys, the worst Katydid has to offer. When he got in trouble, she would run down to the police station to try to work things out. After a while, I thought she was too forgiving. She certainly loved him hard. But Tom held a grudge against her anyway, almost as if he blamed her for all the rules and restrictions that other people were placing on him. It was a terrible thing when they sent him away, but Bunny's house was much calmer after he left.

A sharp corner of Tom's wadded-up letter pushed painfully into my left breast. My heart was pounding hard, and with each beat the paper stabbed. I didn't try to move it, though. Something about the pain was almost comforting.

What would happen to me at a place like Sherwood? How would I ever get by? We'd always heard stories—they'd beat you with straps, lock you in closets. You'd have to go weeks without talking to anybody. Vicious kids from the city were there with razor blades hidden in their shoes. You never knew how true the stories were. Even the thought of the Home terrified me. Once, Mrs. Rothermel, my fourth-grade teacher, found two runaways from the Home hiding in her barn. They told her they couldn't stand it there anymore, but all the same she turned them over to the police. It had pained her, she said, but what else could she do? Everyone in class was left wondering what had happened to those kids.

Tom had never said much about Sherwood before, at least not that Bunny had ever told me. She used to go down to visit once a week. I went with her a few times, though she never wanted me to come; she thought the place was too gruesome for me. The visiting room was a big, airless space with cinder-block walls and little tables and chairs, like a kindergarten. Guards were wandering all around, staring at the families as if to ask, Well, how'd you go wrong? How'd you let that boy turn out that bad? Most of the time when I was there, Tom just slouched in his chair and made jokes across the room with some of the other boys. Bunny used to bring him books, and he'd always refuse to keep them. Once, though, he kept a book on Eskimos. Something about it interested him.

He never said anything about dying there, but he wouldn't say it now if it weren't true, I thought. He's a kidder, but not about something like that. And if *he* can't take it, what about me? I'm not tough the way he is. I shrivel up when someone yells at me. I get depressed if I can't talk to Bunny. I know I have my limits, so I've always tried to avoid situations that could get me in trouble. There was just that one, stupid, stupid time. It's almost crazy, I thought. I'm usually so careful, so much more careful than other people. And then there comes a single moment when I'm not thinking about what will happen or whether what I'm doing is bad, and I get caught. It's unfair, it's so unfair it's even meaner than that—it's something off the scale of fairness, as if the whole situation had been designed to break me down.

The screen door on the back of the house slammed suddenly and snapped me back to attention. Mrs. Vernon had gone inside. I looked down at the section of garden that I'd been weeding, and it was all black. The earth was cleaned out. I'd pulled up everything, even the baby carrots. They were now lying in the weed pile, the carrot parts looking like tiny, helpless teeth among the leafy weeds. For several minutes, I tried to stuff the carrots back in the ground, but it was no use. The green stalks were already turning limp.

Back in the house, I telephoned Bunny, but there was no answer at her house or at Eddie Boggs's place. At the country club, Mr. Higgins said he hadn't seen her yet. I waited a few minutes, standing in the hall and staring at the phone. I had to do *something*. Finally, I called Simon Beach, the lawyer. It took several rings for his secretary to answer.

"Is Mr. Beach there?" I asked.

"Who is this?" She sounded suspicious. I remembered the smile that had made me uncomfortable.

"This is Martha Calhoun."

"Martha? Is that Bunny's daughter?"

"Yes. Can I speak to him?"

"Well, what on earth for?" Her voice had a laugh in it.

"About my case."

"Your case?" More of that hateful laugh. "Oh, your *case*. Is that why you and your mother were here the other day?"

"Yes."

"Well, I'm terribly sorry, but I'm afraid Mr. Beach isn't in today. He's down in southern Illinois on another matter, and he won't be back in the office until next week."

I couldn't say anything. After a few seconds, the secretary asked, "Would you like to leave a message?"

"I've got a trial on Friday. He's supposed to defend me."

"Friday? Oh, I'm sure not. Mr. Beach never misses a court date. I keep his calendar, and there's nothing coming up on Friday."

"He promised Bunny he'd do it."

"Are you sure? He never mentioned anything to me."

"I'm sure."

"What was the name of the case? Do you remember?"

"It was about me."

"Well, what kind of a case was it? Were you hurt in an accident?"

"It was juvenile delinquency."

"Ohhhh." She waited a moment. "Well, Mr. Beach never handles juvenile cases. At least, he's never handled one since I've been here." Another pause. "Well, let me look in the files. I always make up his files, but maybe this once he did it himself. You're Martha Calhoun, right? C-A-L-H-O-U-N?" She spelled it out.

"Yes."

"Hold on a second, and I'll look."

She was gone three or four minutes. After a minute or so, I realized I was holding the phone so hard against my ear that it was hurting me. I loosened up, and the receiver turned incredibly heavy, as if it were made of iron. Mrs. Vernon, who'd been upstairs, wandered down and looked puzzled to find me on the phone.

"Something wrong?" she asked.

I shook my head and turned to the wall. When the secretary came back at last, she opened with a sigh. "Well, I don't find it. I looked over the active and inactive files, and I went through the papers on his desk, and there's nothing there. I'm afraid there's been some kind of misunderstanding. Why don't you check with your mother again?"

"I don't need to check with my mother. He promised."

"He may call in later today. He's on the road, but he may call in, and, if he does, I'll give him your message. Why don't you leave your number?"

I gave her Bunny's number, the Vernons' number, and the number out at the country club. She read them back to me.

"Okay, got it," she said. "I'll give him your message. Good luck with your case. But you don't really need a lawyer in juvenile court anyway, do you?"

I put the receiver back gently and wandered down the hall. After a few steps, I stopped by a plant stand, a tall, spindly table made of wood. The hall didn't get much direct light, so Mrs. Vernon had set out a thin vase filled with pussy willow twigs. For no reason, I pinched one of the soft buds, and it broke into furry tufts, which clung to my fingers.

What a fool I've been, I told myself. I've been wrong from the start, wrong forever. No one can help me, not even Bunny. Nobody cares. Oh, maybe Bunny does, but she's got too many other problems. Everybody's got other problems. I'm all alone in this. Why didn't I see that before? What a fool.

I felt a charge of energy. Realizing how things really were gave me a new sense of power. It seemed for a moment that I could change myself right then, forever, just because I wanted to. No one's going to solve my problems but me, I told myself. Everything's up to me.

I turned and marched back to the phone. Fumbling clumsily with the directory, I found the number of the police station and gave it to the operator. When Mrs. Donaldson picked up, I asked to speak to Sergeant Tony. He came on the line and didn't sound surprised to hear from me. "Come on down, and let's talk," he said.

Mrs. Vernon offered to drive me, but I told her I'd rather walk. "Why don't you take Sissy's bike?" she suggested. She led me through the kitchen into the garage. Garden tools and fishing gear hung from the walls, and dark spots of grease patterned the cement floor. In a corner, she pulled away a large sheet of canvas, unveiling Sissy's lavender three-speed, still glistening with oil. "Walter looks after it every month," said Mrs. Vernon. "Don't know why, really, since no one ever rides it. You can imagine how a father gets about these things, though." She frowned suddenly. "I hope he's been checking the brakes, too."

"I'm sure they're okay."

"Are you sure you don't want me to drive?"

"This'll be fine."

She opened the garage door, flooding the room with midmorning sunlight. The seat was a little low—Sissy was much shorter than I am—but I didn't bother to adjust it. I just wanted to get there, to make something happen at last. Dwayne was still lurking outside. He jumped on his bike and pedaled after me, but his rickety, wide-wheeled one-speed couldn't stay with Sissy's smooth and almost unused machine. Besides, I had energy now, I had power. I knew what I wanted to do.

I sped past the humming KTD. An old, green station wagon filled with Mexicans passed me going the other way, and someone yelled something. I pedaled harder. The streets were almost deserted. The air sat in hot, puffy clouds between the trees, and the leaves hung listlessly. During the spring, if there had been storms in the area, this kind of stillness might be taken for tornado weather. At times like that, the air turns a kind of yellow, and everything that can move stops, as if the coming storm had sucked up all the wind to save for itself. But summer heat is different. There's no sense that something's coming and eventually will pass. It's just timeless, it's dead weather.

At the police station, I parked Sissy's bike in the rack in front. Mrs. Donaldson was sitting behind the screened-in counter. "Yes," she said without looking up. Then she did look up. "What do you want?" she demanded. I told her I was there to see Sergeant Tony. The bicycle trip had hardly winded me, and I bounced softly from one foot to the other. Mrs. Donaldson grunted and spoke into a microphone. "Tony, you got a visitor." Her words boomed out of loudspeakers around the lobby and down the hall in back.

"You can wait over there," she said, nodding toward the bench.

In a minute, Sergeant Tony came out from in back. He was wearing bermuda shorts again and whistling a tune I didn't recognize. "Hey! Martha!" he called out cheerfully. "Come on in." He unlocked the gate in the screen and held it open. To Mrs. Donaldson he said, "Hey, I seen your boy got a hit last night in Little League. He's gonna be a real slugger." Mrs. Donaldson looked at him grumpily and turned back to her desk. "Let's go, beautiful," he said to me, and he led the way down the hall to his office.

Inside, he held a chair for me and then sat down behind the desk, but a second later, he bounced back up. "Let's have some privacy," he said, walking over and flipping a lock on the door. "Just you and me, okay? Nothin' goes out of this room. Just you and me, okay, beautiful?" He sat down again. "Okay, beautiful, let's have it. What's on your mind?"

His energy was deflating me, stealing from mine. How could I keep up with him? I took a breath. "I came to talk about what happened," I said. "I mean, with Butcher." It hurt even to say his name out loud.

Sergeant Tony leaned back. "I'm here to help," he said.

I cleared my throat. This was harder than I'd expected. Talking about it made it real in a way I'd never allowed before. "What I want to say is that I know I did a stupid, stupid thing. Something that's totally unlike me—I'm not like that at all." His unflickering eyes were trained on me. His face gave away nothing. "And if there's any way we could get past this—you know, I mean, let it be forgotten—I'd never be in here again, I promise that. Never. Why, we'd move away if you wanted."

"Move away?"

"Yes."

"From Katydid?"

"Yes."

"Have you talked to your mother about that?"

"Not exactly. Well, sort of. But I know she'd agree."

"She'd agree to leave Eddie?" A smile teased his lips.

"Yes." I had to be strong about this. No doubts.

"Another tough call for ol' Eddie, huh?" He snorted, amused at the thought. I didn't say anything. He sat up and put his elbows on the desk. "That's a pretty strange idea of justice, Martha—that you can just promise to be good and leave town and the whole thing will go away. You don't think things really work like that, do you?"

"I thought, if we talked it out—"

"Have you been reading the paper? Did you see that letter in there about witches? That's you and your mother they're talking about, you know. And there's a petition going around, something they've given Judge Horner." He stood up. "I mean, people are worried about this town, about the way things are developing. They think examples need to be set." He walked around and sat on the edge of the desk, in front of me. "Let's face it, a lot of it's not your fault. It's your mother. Tom, too, but a lot of it's your mother. People don't like the way she acts."

"She's all right," I said softly, staring at the floor.

"A little man-crazy, wouldn't you say? I mean, if my daughter ran around like that, I'd strap her within an inch of her life." His daughter is a fat, pigtailed infant, barely out of diapers. He crossed his arms. When he spoke again, his manner had softened. "You know, I knew your father."

"You did?"

"Yeah, sure. Not well, but I knew him. I used to run into him at the Buffalo—though not the Buffalo so much, actually, that was a little top-drawer for him. More like the Doghouse, the Spa, places like that. He liked to drink." Sergeant Tony rubbed his chin, pulling on his face. "Yeah, sure, I remember him. He grew a mustache once. A funny little thing, real scraggly, hardly any hairs in it at all. You had to wonder what he was thinking of." He tickled his upper lip with his index finger. "And then he went away." He shook his head. "You didn't know him, did you?"

"No."

"Neither did Tom, at least not that he could remember." It pained me to hear Sergeant Tony talk like that, pretending that he was close to our family, that he knew us and knew about us. "A funny guy, your father. I wouldn't have figured him and Bunny, but you never know. I wouldn't have figured a lot of Bunny's men." He watched me for a reaction, and I tried to make my face go dead. I was breathing through my mouth, drying out my lips.

"Does your mother talk to you about her dates, about what goes on?" His voice was low, but prickly.

"No."

"What's she see in those guys? Eddie, Lester, Wayne. Doesn't she talk about 'em?"

"No."

"Don't get upset. I'm just asking. You came here to talk, right?"

"Yes."

He straightened up and walked over to the file cabinet and took something out of a drawer. Metal flashed and jangled in his hand. "Look at this," he said, dangling a pair of handcuffs toward me, holding them with his thumb and finger, the way someone might hold a dead mouse by the tail. "Did you ever see a pair of these before? Do you want to try them on?"

"No!" I pulled back.

He laughed. "They're not so scary. I've put them on some bad people in my time, though. Some real bad characters. Remember that guy who shot up the motel a couple of years ago?" I shook my head. "I collared him. A real bad guy. Look." Sergeant Tony took the key out of the lock on the handcuffs and then clipped the cuffs over his left wrist and his right. He dropped the key in the right-front pocket of his shorts. Holding his hands out, he strained against the metal. "See? The real thing." He thrust his hands at me. "Feel it. Go on, feel it."

I guessed he was talking about the chain between the handcuffs, so I touched it lightly.

"Tough, huh? Nobody's gonna break out of these. That metal's so strong you can't even saw through it. You see all these things in the movies where they take an ax and chop through handcuffs, but that stuff's a bunch of bull."

He came over and stood close to me. "Now, give me a hand here. Reach in this pocket and get out the key." He pushed his hip toward me, indicating the right-front pocket of his shorts. I didn't really think he meant it, so I smiled.

"Come on, come on," he said impatiently. "Help me get out of these. Reach in and get it." He pushed his hip closer, until he was almost leaning over me. My face was just at the level of his stomach; his gray, knit shirt gave off a strong, sharp odor. I turned my head away and put my hands behind the chair.

"Come on," he snapped. "What's the matter? Get me out of here. Nothin's gonna happen."

I buried my face in my shoulder. He wasn't touching me, but he was standing so close that I felt crushed by the weight of him. For a few seconds, he stayed there without saying anything, and then he walked back behind his desk.

"I don't know what you're scared of," he said. "It's just a toy." He held up his hands again and pushed a rivet on the left cuff. The clamp popped open, freeing his hand. "Trick, see," he said. Then he did the same thing with the other cuff. "Nothin' to be scared of."

I stood up quickly. All the energy had drained out of me, but I stepped to the door and started fiddling with the lock. I couldn't get it to work.

"I thought you wanted to talk," he said.

I kept working on the lock and pulling on the metal door, which banged in its frame. "Stop!" he barked. He walked over to me slowly. I turned, and my back was against the door. It was hot in the room and the door felt hot. He stopped right in front of me. Just below his flattop, his forehead bristled with fresh beads of sweat. "I feel sorry for you, Martha," he said evenly. "You don't know what you want."

He reached past me and flicked the lock, then pulled the door open an inch or two. "Go on," he said. For a moment, I hesitated. Was it possible I'd misunderstood? Then I hurried out the door and down the hall.

TWENTY-THREE

Bunny came in the middle of the afternoon, parking the Pontiac at the curb and honking until I ran out. She told me she refused to go in the Vernons' house again, so I climbed into the front seat beside her. Her uniform was rumpled and stained in spots, as if she'd got two or three days' work out of it. When I told her about my call to the lawyer, she didn't say anything. She stared out through the streaky windshield and picked at the plastic covering on the steering wheel. Over the years, she'd dug a small hole there, and the nail on her right index finger had a permanent black crown to show for it, a tiny marring of her natural beauty.

"Beach is undependable," she murmured after a while, as if it were just another unimportant fact about the lawyer, a detail that she'd known all along but hadn't bothered to mention.

I didn't tell her about my visit to Sergeant Tony.

Though the car was parked in the shade of an oak, and the windows were open, the front seat was suffocatingly hot. I slouched down, my knees pushing against the dashboard. Occasionally, someone walked along the sidewalk and looked down at us in mild curiosity.

Bunny rambled on about the country club, about the bickering between Beatrice and Millie, the other two waitresses, about how someone had stolen $42 from the pro shop, about Shorty's latest unhappiness. But it was imitation conversation. She was just following the routine, and there was no spirit in it for either of us.

Finally, I sat up and said, "Can we talk about Eddie for a minute?"

"Now?"

"Time's running out."

"I'm so tired," Bunny said. "I'm bone tired."

"I know."

"I can't sleep. I just can't fall asleep."

"Me, too."

"So tired."

"But Eddie—"

"I sleep when I'm with Eddie. I can fall asleep with him."

"He's the problem, Bunny. If you could get rid of him, I could get out of this."

Bunny rested her head on the steering wheel, facing away from me. "It's that simple?" she asked.

"Yes. At least, I think so from the way Mrs. O'Brien talks."

She waited. Seconds passed. Her head was turned away, but I could see how tired she was by the curve of her back and the slope of her shoulders. "But where'll I be?" she asked finally. "You'll go off, and then I'll be absolutely alone."

"Bunny, I'll never leave you," I said, though I knew I was lying. I told myself it didn't really matter. Things will change. I'll make it up to her. When she fell silent again, though, I grew frightened.

At last, Bunny straightened up. "Why's Dwayne always hanging around here?" she asked. He'd ridden past on his bike, and now, circling back, he was watching us as he passed on the other side of the street.

"I think he's looking out for me. Ever since that day on the square, he thinks he's been protecting me."

"I wish someone would protect me," Bunny said glumly.

Later that evening, I tried to call her. I didn't have anything particular to say, but I had the idea that the sound of her voice would still the jabberings that were filling my head. I tried all the numbers several times, but I couldn't find her. Finally, just to keep busy, I called Reverend Vaughn's number at the Congo. I knew it was hopeless, but I let the phone ring for five minutes, not giving up until the operator came on a second time to insist that no one was home.

The next morning, Mrs. Vernon was unusually perky. She'd been out to buy milk and had detoured past the fairgrounds. "People are already starting to go in," she said, as she set toast and tea in front of me at the kitchen table. "And the Ferris wheel was running. Can you imagine? Nine o'clock the first day. This is the biggest fair ever. They've got tents almost all the way out to Banyon's Woods, and lots more exhibits. Plus, the farm news is so good." She dropped a copy of the day's *Exponent* next to my plate. I glanced over the front page just long enough to notice an article about Percy Granville's former assistant. He'd been found in his home with a bullet in his head, a presumed suicide. I quickly turned the paper over and pushed it away.

"An article there says the corn grew eleven inches last week," Mrs. Vernon said. "That's almost fast enough to see!" She pinched out one of her dry, formless laughs. "It's the same in my garden. Plants are just charging out of the ground. Green things love that warm rain—the rain and then the hot, sunny days."

Mrs. Vernon puttered while she talked, consolidating two opened jars of peanut butter, rinsing off the cutting board, picking the bad strawberries out of a basket that had been sitting in the refrigerator for three days. From years of housework and neglect, the fingers on her hands were dried and cracked—gaunt, ruddy twigs of skin and bone. Yet her fingers and hands never rested, they darted around in movements unconnected to her conversation. Watching them, I couldn't help feeling that I was being reproached.

At about four that afternoon, Mrs. O'Brien showed up. I was in Sissy's room and didn't bother to come down. Mrs. Vernon let her in, and I heard their low, muffled talk in the hallway. Soon, the social worker climbed the stairs, and her footsteps thudded sadly toward Sissy's room. She knocked and entered before I could say anything. Her face was slightly flushed, and perspiration made dark stains under her arms. She came over and sat in Sissy's small, armless desk chair, sitting with her legs apart, in a faintly masculine way, and leaning forward, panting softly. I just lay there.

"Well, I think we've worked something out," she said. "I've been back and forth between your mother and Mr. Moon all day, and I think we've finally worked something out."

I rose on my elbows, like a patient in a hospital bed. Didn't she realize what she was saying?

"Judge Horner doesn't always follow my recommendations, but he usually does, and now we've got Mr. Moon along, too. The judge doesn't have to agree, though, so be prepared." She set one elbow on her thigh and rested the weight of her upper body against it. The desk chair looked like a milking stool beneath her. "In any case, I'm going to recommend that you go back to live with your mother, as long as the three of us—you, your mother, and me—keep up regular counseling sessions. We'll ask the judge to put an unlimited time frame on it, and just see how it goes. Is that agreeable to you?"

"Yes." I nodded frantically.

"Good. I must tell you, Martha, that your mother is a very stubborn woman. Very stubborn and, at times, disagreeable. She makes things hard for herself. I don't tell you this to make you feel bad, but to help you understand. She's agreed to change certain things in her life because she sees now that her family is at stake. But her agreement is a fragile thing, I can see that, and it's going to take work from all of us to keep her on track. To be frank, I've felt all along that the problem here was much more your mother than you. And I told your mother that. I told her that today in exactly those words."

She watched me for a reaction and I kept smiling. "We really haven't talked much about your problems, have we? About what got you into this," she said.

"No."

"It was a bad thing for a young girl like you. That little boy." Her eyes were dark and solemn. "You are ashamed, aren't you?"

I hesitated. I'd felt a lot of things since this all started. Confusion, fear, embarrassment, hope, fury, despair. But shame? There hadn't been time for it. I'd been too overwhelmed by emotions that were more real. No, I really hadn't felt any shame at all.

"Yes," I said.

Mrs. O'Brien sighed. "Well, that's a start, anyway." She stood slowly. Outside of the swimming pool, her body seemed only a burden to her. She pushed the chair back under the desk, and I walked her downstairs. "I've still got one client to see today," she said. "This case has thrown off my entire schedule. But don't worry, we've taken care of that now."

She stopped at the door. "Your mother will be around later. She's taken the night off so you two can be together. Relax a little for tomorrow." She put her hand on my arm and squeezed. Then she opened the door. "Goodbye, Mrs. Vernon," she called out as she left, though she knew Mrs. Vernon was out in the garden and couldn't possibly hear.

TWENTY-FOUR

After Mrs. O'Brien left, I went into the parlor. Copies of *Life*, *The Saturday Evening Post*, and *National Geographic* were stacked on the bottom bookshelves along the wall. Some of the magazines were very old, going back ten or fifteen years. I took a handful of *National Geographics* and sat in the middle of the sofa, looking at the pictures and reading the captions.

Leafing through the magazines, my movements were slow and limited to what was absolutely necessary. I was careful not to rustle pages. I hardly dared breathe deeply: I wasn't going to do anything to disturb the world. I felt as if the least commotion from me, a sneeze, a shout, an angry thought, could upset the arrangement that would let me go back to Bunny.

After about an hour, Mrs. Vernon walked in. "Oh, there you are," she said. "You startled me. Aren't you warm in here?"

"Not really."

She pushed the window up a few extra inches. "I thought I might try to get a little breeze flowing through the house. The air gets so stale in this heat." She stood above me, looking forlorn. "Some kind of blight has hit the garden," she blurted suddenly. "A whole batch of baby carrots is dead."

"Oh, no." I sat as still as I could.

"I hope it doesn't spread. Some of the tomatoes haven't come in yet."

"I'm sure it won't."

"You didn't notice anything yesterday when you were weeding, did you?"

"Not a thing."

"I'm quite worried. These blights are so mysterious, so hard to explain." She walked out, shaking her head.

By dinner, I hadn't heard from Bunny. Mrs. Vernon had a church meeting to attend, and Mr. Vernon was going to the VFW, so we ate in the kitchen: fish sticks, mashed potatoes, and peas from the garden. As soon as Mrs. Vernon set the plate in front of her husband, he got up and went to the refrigerator. He took out a jar of pickles and a jar of mayonnaise and chopped several pickles up in a bowl. Then he scooped two tablespoons of mayonnaise on top and mixed it all up. Mrs. Vernon watched him silently. When he sat down again, he arranged his fish sticks like logs on a bonfire and gobbed his pickle-and-mayonnaise mixture on top. He never looked up at his wife.

"I'm sorry, dear," said Mrs. Vernon. "I guess I was so upset about the garden that I forgot all about your relish."

He grunted.

"Walter loves fish sticks," Mrs. Vernon said to me. "They're practically his favorite meal."

"I like them, too," I said. "They're much crisper than real fish."

Mr. Vernon stopped eating for a moment and tilted his head to look at me. "They are real fish," he said.

Mrs. Vernon smiled and shifted in her chair. "What Martha means, dear, is that they're crisper than *fresh* fish."

"I heard what she said. She don't need you 'terpreting for her."

"I was only—"

Bam! He slammed his hand on the Formica table top. "You ain't no 'terpreter," he said harshly. "Let the girl speak for herself."

A smile flitted across Mrs. Vernon's lips, then disappeared. As she turned away, her eyes caught mine for just a second. "There!" they seemed to say. "See?"

The Vernons had both left by the time I heard Bunny's Pontiac rattle up outside. I ran down to the curb and hugged her and laughed, but her body felt weary.

"Isn't it wonderful?" I gasped.

"I knew it would work out," she said. She looked at me affectionately and stroked my hair. She was wearing a cotton housedress with a busy pink print, something she'd never normally wear out of the house.

"How did you do it?" I asked. "What did you have to promise Mrs. O'Brien?"

"Oh, she just wanted to hear me say some things. It's always the same." She dropped her hand.

"And Eddie?"

"Don't worry about Eddie. He'll be all right."

We were standing on the sidewalk. It was only about eight, but Oak Street was empty. A few of the houses had turned on their front lights. "It's creepy around here," said Bunny. "Why don't we go for a drive, or something. Let's get out of here."

"Do you think we should?"

"Why not? Mrs. Vernon told me we should relax tonight."

"But I'm not dressed to go out." I ran my hands down my sides. I was wearing a faded and formless old sundress, something I'd thrown in the suitcase without thinking the day I came to the Vernons'. This morning, when I'd spotted it in Sissy's closet, the dress's worn, familiar look had been comforting.

"You're fine," said Bunny. "You're dressed just like me."

I was uncertain about leaving, but Bunny was insistent and I didn't want to argue. Just in case, I scribbled Mrs. Vernon a note and left it on the table near the phone. Her church meetings sometimes dragged on until midnight, and I was sure I'd be back before then. But in an emergency I wanted her to know I was with Bunny.

We drove aimlessly for a while, down toward the center of town, past the News Depot, around the square, which was already shrouded in leafy darkness, up West Morgan, past the Congo. A light was on in the minister's study. Reverend Vaughn was back from his trip. I felt a quick pang that he hadn't called me.

"How's your boyfriend?" asked Bunny, when she saw me straining to catch a glimpse of him through the tiny window in the side of the church.

"Don't call him that."

"Why not? He's kinda cute, in a skinny way."

I folded my arms and didn't respond.

The lines at the Dairy Queen were surprisingly short. "I guess everyone's at the fair," said Bunny. "You want a chocolate dip?"

I shook my head, remembering what had happened the last time I stopped there. Bunny continued out Walker Street, past the farm equipment store, the Hide-Away Motel, the Dog 'n' Suds. After half a mile or so, the buildings stop abruptly and a field of corn spreads out, a cool green sea lapping up against the town. The sun was down now, and little islands of bright farmhouses or dark clumps of trees stood out above the flatness.

We followed Walker for a short ways, then turned off on a gravel road that slices between the fields. We were alone. Behind us, the taillights of Bunny's car made fiery clouds shining through the road dust. Bunny was quiet and seemed distracted. I guessed she was contemplating life without Eddie. She'd never understand, of course, that she'd be better off that way. I thought of all the nights that he'd yelled at her, or walked out, or just drunk too much and fallen asleep on the couch, a useless sack of a man. I'd wander into the living room Sunday morning, and he'd still be there, asleep and pathetic, curled up like a baby trying to keep himself warm. Now that he was gone, Bunny wouldn't remember any of that. Her capacity to forget unhappiness was incredible, maybe even a little crazy. As soon as the man was out of her life, the bad things had never happened.

Still, I knew, there was something different about Eddie. It wasn't exactly that he was sad—it was more that he was sort of separate, apart from the rest of us, as if there were a small space between him and everything around him. Reverend Vaughn was a little the same way. They both had that quality, and it was alluring, it gave you some place to crawl into.

Poor Bunny. I looked over at her without turning my head, so she wouldn't know I was staring. Lately, I'd been noticing that the lines at the corners of her eyes had deepened and spread. She'd smile or frown, and the wrinkles would suddenly appear, standing out like the angel's wings on Mercury's helmet. The skin over her cheeks was starting to get shadowy, too. You'd hardly notice, except in certain lights or at the times when she was feeling low.

I wondered—did she blame me? That wouldn't be like her, but maybe she really did believe that this was her last chance for a great love. Now, she has to give it up, because of me. Through all Tom's troubles and her problems with men, I'd always been there. She used

196

to call me her anchor, she'd say it all the time. I was the one she could rely on. I was always at her side. Once, when I was nine, I stayed home from school and cared for her for a week after Wayne Wadlinger betrayed her. She thought she was in love with Wayne, and he'd been making promises. Then he showed up at the Tennessee Lounge with a woman named Nora. Within ten minutes, three people called to tell Bunny, and the phone rang four more times that night after she'd stopped answering it. Bunny went to bed and didn't get up for a week. And the whole time, I was there—bringing meals in on a tray, fetching magazines from down at the News Depot. I even climbed in bed and slept with her, putting up with Bunny's constant thrashing. I'd wake up in the morning, and she'd be spooning me, her arms around my chest, her face in my neck, her heavy morning breath on my cheek. And then one morning, she got up and went back to work, as if a week had been set aside for mourning, and once that was over, life went on. But I'd been there. When she needed me, I'd been there.

Outside the car, the fields streaked by, smooth and regular. Mack Creek meanders around this part of the countryside, and Bunny slowed every now and then to cross one of the small stone bridges spanning the murky water. Frogs were croaking back and forth. The air was warm, but the young corn gave it a crisp, fresh smell.

Bunny came to a paved highway, took a right, continued for a few miles, and then took another right on another gravel road. She was making a big loop around one side of Katydid. Pretty soon, we were pointed back toward town and could see the dome of colored lights reflecting off the sky. Then we were just outside town, staring at the circle of colored bulbs on the Ferris wheel, spinning high above the fairgrounds.

"Why don't we park and go in for a few minutes?" said Bunny. It was the first thing she'd said in a quarter hour.

"I don't know," I said. But she'd already slowed down in front of the field they use for parking. A boy waving a red flashlight guided us down a bumpy lane, past a long line of cars. At the end, another red light swung back and forth, indicating our spot.

Bunny parked and started to get out. She could see I was reluctant. "We won't stay long," she said. "I just feel like getting cheered up a little. I could use a little cheering up."

Still, I sat there, staring at the dashboard.

"Jesus!" said Bunny, jumping out and slamming the car door.

"Sometimes you really depress me, you really do." She stomped around for a few seconds, then leaned back inside the window. "You really depress me," she repeated.

"Why can't I just wait here?"

"Jesus!" she muttered again, turning away. She started walking down the line of cars toward the entrance to the fair. She was taking short, jerky steps and swinging her arms rapidly. Her baggy dress rode up and down clumsily on her hips. From the back, I hardly would have recognized her.

She did blame me, I thought. She blamed me, and she's right, it's my fault. I'm all she's got and I depress her. I depress my own mother.

I hurried out of the car and ran after her. She heard me coming and slowed, taking my arm in hers when I caught up. "We'll only stay for a bit," she said. "Just enough for some cheering up."

The outside of the entrance gate was hectic and noisy. People milled around a cardtable covered with Eisenhower stickers and buttons. A balloon man stood in a colorful thicket of plastic. A man in a top hat offered little toy farm animals that dangled from key chains. People were laughing and calling out to each other, talking above the sounds of the fair.

"I hope I don't see anybody I know," I said, after Bunny had paid our way in.

"Why not? Hold your head high."

We wandered down the main path, getting used to the lights and commotion. Babies were crying, and dust covered everything. Each step on the hard, worn ground kicked up a little explosion of dry, yellowish clay. One year, I remembered, I wore sandals to the fair, and, when I got home and took them off, they were still on, in reverse—perfect white lines from the straps across the tops of my feet, and everything else dark yellow.

After a few minutes of wandering, Bunny bought some pink cotton candy and tried to nibble around the outside without getting her face all sticky. Soon she gave up and dumped it in a trash can. "I want to try a game," she said.

We came to a small, open tent, set in a clear space, so groups of people flowed around it. The tent covered a huge, pastel pyramid of little fish bowls, each filled with colored water—pink or yellow or blue. The pyramid was lighted from within and made a spectacular display, like some otherworldly rainbow hovering in the dust of the fairgrounds. To win at the game, you had to toss a Ping-Pong ball into a bowl. In the top few layers, each bowl contained a goldfish. If you landed in a bowl with a fish, you won the fish. Landing in a fishless bowl earned a water whistle, shaped like a chick, or a thick, hot dog-sized pencil with a hula skirt on it, or a hollow straw tube that locked your fingers if you stuck them in both ends and tried to pull out. The water whistles were something new and were proving quite popular. I'd already heard six or seven of them bleating around the fair.

"You want to try?" Bunny asked, after we'd admired the pyramid for a few seconds.

I shook my head. I've never been very good at games.

"Well, I'll try, then," she said.

A thin woman with dyed black hair was running the concession. She was wearing a money apron and standing inside a wood railing. "Try your luck," she kept calling out. "Three throws for a quarter. Try your luck."

"How can you miss?" whispered Bunny. The pyramid seemed to be nothing but yawning bowls.

The woman noticed us. "Come on, blondie, try your luck," she yelled. "Show these folks."

"All right," said Bunny. She gave the woman a quarter and got back three Ping-Pong balls.

"That's the spirit, blondie," said the woman. "Win a goldfish." A number of people who'd been listening to the lady's spiel now moved closer.

"Here we go, Martha," said Bunny. "This one's for you."

She leaned across the railing, lifting her left leg to help her keep balance. Her dress was pulled tight against her body. Her bottom stuck up in the air. The woman behind the railing frowned. Bunny brought her arm back behind her ear and let go with a hard, over-hand throw. The ball ricocheted off the side of a bowl and bounced way out to the side and onto the ground.

"Awww," said Bunny.

"Throw it underhand, honey," said a man standing behind her. "Nice and soft."

Bunny leaned forward again, stretching to get closer, wiggling her hips the way she does to get into her girdle. I would have been embarrassed, except that every eye was on her. No one even knew I was there. She held her arm out straight in front, gripping the ball with her fingertips. With a sudden, herky-jerky sweep, she tossed it underhand. The ball floated high above the pyramid, then looped down. It hit the lip of a top bowl, then bounced, plunk, plunk, plunk, off three lower bowls and onto the ground.

People groaned. "Hey," said Bunny, "this is hard."

"Come on, honey, nice and soft, you can do it," said the man who'd spoken up before. He was thin, with a wine-colored face and a blue shirt that buttoned up the front. The top few buttons were undone, exposing a perfect wine-colored "V" down his chest. The man was angling, trying to edge forward in the crowd. "Nice and soft, honey," he repeated.

Once again, Bunny leaned over the railing. Everyone was watching her and no one was buying a chance. Bunny held her last Ping-Pong ball in front of her eye, sighting the route she wanted it to travel. Then she stretched still further. With a quick thrust, she catapulted the ball toward the top of the pyramid. The little white sphere shot in a fast, straight line and plopped exactly into a bowl filled with pale blue water and one frantic orange goldfish.

"Hey!" said Bunny, sounding as if she expected the ball to pop out again.

People whooped and clapped. "Way to go, Bunny," yelled Mr. Fanzone, the man from the hardware store, who was standing in the back with his wife. I tried to slip behind a few of the people who'd pushed up front, but Bunny turned to find me. "Come on, we won a fish," she called.

The woman behind the counter hurried over to the pyramid and lifted out Bunny's bowl. The fish was swimming around in a tiny circle. Using two fingers, the woman scooped out the Ping-Pong ball and handed the bowl to Bunny. "Here you go, blondie," she said tightly. Then she shouted, "All right, who's next? Win a goldfish. If blondie can do it, so can you." Several people dug into their pockets and pulled out change. Suddenly, the woman was doing a brisk business. She didn't like Bunny, though. "Come on, blondie, move on," the woman said. "You got yours, now let some of these other folks have a chance." Bunny just stood there, holding the bowl up to her nose and trying to see eye-to-eye with the fish. Finally, she slid over to me.

"He's cute, isn't he?" she said. "He's got little tiny lips." She thrust the bowl toward me. "Here, you carry him."

"Oh, no. You won him. He's yours."

"Well, what am I going to do with it?"

Suddenly the man with the wine-colored farmer's tan appeared over Bunny's left shoulder. "Don't you girls want to take that good-lookin' fish home?" he asked. He had an angular face and a thin smile that moved diagonally from the right corner of his mouth to the left.

Bunny stared at him without saying anything.

He continued to smile. "Well, how about if I carry it, then?" he asked. "If you two don't want it, I'll take it home and give it to my little girl."

"You've got a little girl?" asked Bunny, screwing up her face in disbelief.

"What's the matter, don't I look like the kind of man who could have a little girl?"

Bunny shrugged and shoved the bowl into his hands. We walked away, but he followed right behind. "You got a name for this fish?" he asked after a few steps.

Bunny looked at me and rolled her eyes. "Moby Dick," she said. "I call him 'Moby' for short."

"Heh," said the man, catching up and walking alongside us. "You can't go treating a good-lookin' fish with that kind of disrespect. You got to treat him formal-like. I think I'll address him as 'Mr. Dick.' "

Bunny stopped and looked the man over. "Mr. Dick," she said. "Hah, hah, hah, hah." Her laugh came out in sharp, unnatural spurts.

"Let's go," I said softly.

Bunny stared at me blankly, as if she were confused, and then she turned back to him. He was smiling and nodding his head, letting his eyes drift down her body and then back to her face.

"Hah, hah," Bunny laughed again.

The man said his name was Frank. He tagged along as Bunny toured the 4-H tents—the sweet-smelling one where big-eyed calves stared out at us silently, the noisy one where pig families were crowded together in wooden enclosures like immigrants in the hold of a ship. In the food tent, the entries were lined up on shelves in glass-fronted wooden cabinets. Some of the food had already been judged, and the plates of pies, cakes, breads, and muffins dripped bright ribbons. The tent for the vegetable competition had an entire table of cherry tomatoes. Each entry of three tomatoes sat on a small, white paper plate, looking like an idiot's idea of a salad. Another table had the winner of the "Best Vegetable in Fair" ribbon, a pumpkin so big it was losing shape, melting under its own size.

Bunny moved quickly through the tents, and Frank hurried to keep up, all the time trying to make jokes and splashing water out of the goldfish bowl. I lingered behind, always keeping them in sight and hoping that Bunny would look back for me. She never did, and Frank eventually steered her away from the exhibits and into a beer tent. Three big, silver kegs were resting in troughs of crushed ice. A makeshift bar had been set up, and four men in Budweiser hats were serving beer in tall paper cups. I came up while Frank was saying that he worked on a farm over in Edenboro, and he was going to compete in the tractor pull tomorrow. Bunny barely seemed to be listening.

"Beer, miss?" one of the bartenders asked me.

"Oh, no," I said, hopping back. Did I really look that old? I stood near a tent pole, glaring at Bunny, though she didn't seem to notice.

"What's the matter with your daughter?" Frank asked after a while. "How come she's not out with her friends?"

"We're here together," said Bunny. She looked at me for the first time in minutes. Her face broke into a smile—the same proud, open smile that's hanging over my head like a moon, just out of reach, in my earliest memory.

"I don't think the girl likes me," said Frank.

"Of course she does. She's just a little shy."

"Let's go, Bunny," I said. I didn't care if Frank heard. "Let's get out of here."

"I just want to finish this beer," Bunny said, taking a small swallow.

"See," said Frank. "I told you she didn't like me."

"Oh, hush," said Bunny. "She likes you all right. Don't you, Martha? Tell Frank you like him."

I turned away and faced the tent pole.

"Martha," said Bunny, raising her voice. "Do what your mother says. Tell Frank you like him."

I crushed my eyes closed. Outside, you could hear the sharp clang of the strongman's bell and the tooty music of a merry-go-round.

After a few seconds, Frank said, "The hell with you two. You know what? The hell with you two." I opened my eyes just as he was stalking away. I noticed that he was wearing cowboy boots.

"Now look what you did," said Bunny. "You've offended him."

"Who cares. Let's get out of here."

"I told you, I want to finish my beer," she said flatly. She took another sip. "Oh, look, he left the goldfish. Think of his poor little girl." Bunny flicked her fingernail twice on the side of the bowl, and the terrorized fish began circling again.

"Well, I'm going," I said.

"So, go," said Bunny.

I turned and stomped away. I was angry, but frightened, too. I'd never seen her like this before. She was like another person—selfish, uncontrollable. Was this what it was going to be like from now on?

I decided to go back and wait in the car. Walking down a path, I passed a shooting gallery, another game where you tried to tip over three milk bottles with a baseball, another where the idea was to knock a furry doll off a shelf. People were standing around and playing in groups, I was the only person alone. The fair seemed dirtier than ever. Everything was cotton-candy sticky, and dust thickened the air.

The path ended suddenly at a tall, wire fence separating the fairgrounds from Banyon's Woods. I'd taken a wrong turn. Aiming for the entrance gate, I followed the fence for a while and came to a sausage-shaped silver trailer that was set apart from the other exhibits. A big-lettered sign on a sandwich board out front said, SEE THE TWO-HEADED BABY. Smaller printing added, A MARVEL OF NATURE! A SCIENTIFIC EXHIBITION! I stopped. A picture of the baby, done in bright, cracking paint, hung on a canvas sheet draped from the side of the trailer. The baby was a girl, and in the painting she looked out with two fresh faces, each surrounded by a halo of curly brown hair. The faces looked happy, the eyes firm and direct. The heads seemed almost eager to talk about their condition: Yes, it's complicated with two of us, I could imagine them saying, as they tripped over each other's words. But it's exciting, too, not at all what you one-headed people might expect. Think of the conversation, the companionship, everything shared.

Outside one end of the trailer, a woman sat in a ticket booth. She was reading a book and not paying attention to the people who stopped to stare. A bulb in a conical shade threw a spreading beam of light across the top of her head and over her book. The rest of the ticket booth was black. I dug into a pocket of my sundress and rolled around a few large coins.

I felt strangely excited, as if there were some useful secret, some kind of relief, inside the trailer. The two faces looked so open and willing. Elro had said the baby was kept in a jar, but, in the painting, she wore a pretty pink dress, with puffy sleeves and a flaring skirt. Two pink normal legs jutted out below.

I edged over toward the ticket booth. Nobody noticed me. People kept wandering by, shaking their heads at the trailer, uttering low words of disapproval, and then moving on. Walking sideways, I slipped up to the booth and placed a quarter in the cradle in front of the woman. She looked up only far enough to stare at the coin.

"It's fifty," she said in a scolding voice.

"Fifty?"

"Fifty cents." The light above her head made deep, skull-like shadows over her eyes.

I reached in my pocket and pulled out another quarter. Nothing else at the fair cost fifty c—— but I paid willingly; the expense seemed appropriate. I pushed the——quarters toward her. A hand darted out quickly and scooped them up. Another dropped a green ticket into the cradle. Her eyes never left the book. "The man inside," she said.

"What?"

"Give it to the man inside."

I backed away. The trailer had an open door at one end. A bluish light spilled out from the inside, but there was no sign of a man. I walked a few steps closer, and he came into view. He was sitting on a stool, spooning ice cream out of a quart container. He saw me watching him and stopped eating for a moment to stare back. Then he returned to his ice cream. How could these people be so relaxed? I felt feverish, knowing what was just a few feet away, behind those silver walls.

I stepped toward the doorway, but at that moment, a woman behind me spoke up in a loud voice. "The parents who did that ought to be shot," she said. I turned. She was about Bunny's age, with graying hair and wearing a checkered dress. She glanced around to see who'd heard her, and her gaze fell on me. "Don't you buy a ticket here," she said. "This place should be boycotted. Imagine, selling your baby like that. They should run it out of town."

I nodded hesitantly.

"They never used to allow things like that in the Katydid County Fair." She turned to the man standing beside her. "We should complain," she said. He stopped shaking his head and started nodding it. "*You* should complain," she said to me. "The more people who complain the better."

"Maybe I will," I mumbled, stealing a glance at the woman in the ticket booth. She was still reading, as if she hadn't heard a thing.

"Good," said the woman who'd been complaining. She stood there, planted, her hands on her hips, ready to take on anyone who made a move toward the ticket booth. I slunk away, all the time feeling she was watching me.

What had I been thinking of? This wasn't like me at all, I told myself. Being curious about the baby in a morbid kind of way was bad enough, but to give in to the feeling—that was unforgivable. Everything I knew, everything I believed in, had taught me to fight urges like that. Anger pounded at my stomach. Another mistake, another piece of bad judgment. What's happening to me? I wondered frantically. I can't trust myself anymore. Do I have to censor every mood and notion? How can you live like that?

I hurried past clumps of slow-footed people. I had to get Bunny, and we had to get out. It was ridiculous coming to the fair on the night before my trial. How do I let Bunny talk me into these things? I asked myself. She's as much to blame as I am. I'm so busy watching out for her that I don't have time to watch out for myself.

Almost at a trot, I passed the McCarthy family, strolling along with all six children. The four youngest were holding hands. "Hello, Martha!" yelled Jeannie, who's six and who was thrilled to see me.

"Hello," I said quickly, and hurried on, thinking of the look of disappointment on Jeannie's face.

Since I'd left, the beer tent had filled with a group of men, who all seemed to know each other. I pushed my way through to the counter. Bunny wasn't there. The men around me were talking loud and crowding me, holding their ground, as if they thought I wanted to butt in front.

"Mister, mister," I called out, trying to get the attention of the bartender who'd offered me a beer before.

The man to my right didn't like being jostled and frowned at me. "You're a little young to be that desperate for a beer, aren't you?" he said. He was wearing a shirt with parrots on it.

"I just want to talk to that bartender," I said, pointing. "I have to ask him something."

"Well, why didn't you say so?" He turned and yelled across the bar. "Hey! Jody!"

"Yeah?" said Jody, wiping his brow with his forearm. He was frantically filling cups with beer and handing them to other bartenders.

"Girl here wants to ask you something."

"What is it?" He didn't turn around.

I leaned across the bar and tried to talk clearly, without being loud. "Did you see where my mother went? She was here a little bit ago."

He stopped filling the cups for a moment and turned to see who was talking. Sweat was pouring down his face and under his collar. "Oh, hi. She went off with some guy, some skinny guy."

"The one who was here with her before?"

He stared at me and considered. One thing about Bunny, people always notice her. "No, a different one," he said finally.

"Hey, let's go," said another bartender. "I got people waiting."

The bartender named Jody turned back to the kegs.

"What did he look like?" I called out.

"Like I said, he was skinny," Jody yelled over his shoulder. He drew some more beer, then added, "He didn't have a shirt on."

"Thanks," I said softly, stepping back into the crowd of men. Eddie.

TWENTY-FIVE

An event in the arena let out, and a swarm of people, mostly farmers, came clamoring up a path between the tents. I slipped off down a smaller path to get away. On the side, a group of people was gathered, bending down. A woman was stretched out on the ground, her pocketbook for a pillow. Her eyes were open, but she was staring straight up. The people were trying to talk to her, but they seemed helpless. My heart raced, and I hurried on. Just get to the car, I thought. Bunny's got to come for it sometime.

Here, in the center of the fairgrounds, noise came from all around: shouting, clanging, crying, bleating. Strings of bulbs hanging between utility poles cast a brown light over everything. I paused to get my bearings, and a man bumped into me, then moved silently on.

"Martha!" a voice called out suddenly. I caught a flash of yellow, a shiny-white grin. "Martha! Hey, look, it's Martha Calhoun!"

Tammy Mirkov appeared in front of me. She seemed to step out of a brown fog.

"I haven't seen you since the pool," she said, smiling eagerly. "What are you doing *here*?"

"I came with Bunny," I mumbled.

"Look, it's Martha Calhoun," she repeated, turning to two boys lurking behind her. One was Art Harrington, her boyfriend. I didn't recognize the other. The boys nodded at her.

I started to walk away, but Tammy grabbed my arm. "No, wait," she said. "Did you meet Muscle? He's Art's cousin from Emerson. Muscle's not his real name, but that's what everyone calls him. He's on the wrestling team."

Muscle was a shorter, stockier version of Art, with a bristly brown crew cut. He smiled quickly at me.

"How's it going?" Tammy asked.

"Fine," I said.

She looked at the boys, and her eyes sparked. "You're kind of famous, in a way," she said, turning back to me.

"What?"

"You know, famous." She was smiling. I couldn't look at her directly. My gaze kept floating up to the top of her head, where her blond hair was pulled back tight and shiny and sleek. "Hey," she said, suddenly. "There's a party. A big party. Do you want to come?"

"I don't think so."

"Why not? It'll be fun. Right, guys?" She turned again to the two boys. Art seemed to be shaking his head, but she ignored him. "You can't pass up a party," she said. "Come on." She brushed past and gave my arm a tug, but let go when I resisted. She walked forward a few feet, then stopped and turned back. I pivoted to watch her. The boys were behind me now.

"Well, are you coming?" she demanded. She was talking to all three of us. I should have left, but her taunting manner held me there. She was being so open about it—she was testing me, and I suddenly felt that to walk away now would be to admit that everything they'd said about me, everything they'd imagined was true. I had to prove myself.

In the middle of the path, we engaged in a kind of tug-of-war, Tammy against me and the boys. I got the feeling that as soon as one side gave in by just a step, it would go sprawling toward the other. I stared at Tammy. She looked past me to the boys. For a few seconds the rope was absolutely taut, and I thought I saw her waver. But then, behind me, Muscle gave a little snort. "Well, okay," he said, and pushed past me. Art followed, shrugging his shoulders. With them in tow, Tammy turned and walked on, certain that I'd follow. And, of course, I did. I'd let myself get trapped, and now I had to see this through.

Tammy twisted and dodged through the crowds of people, leading us on a jagged course across the fairgrounds, without ever looking back. Where do you get that kind of confidence? Of course, she had it years ago, as a little girl with ironed dresses and flawless hair, the only child in the neighborhood who dared defy Tom. She once told him she "detested" him, using a word that none of us understood and that sounded adult and truly horrible. I expected Tom to slug her, but he just crept away. I think he secretly hoped she'd be his girl-friend.

After a while, we came to the animal tents and, beyond, to the fence that circles the fairgrounds. The lights in the tents were low, and the area was dark, but Tammy knew exactly where she was headed. She walked along the fence for a few yards and stopped. At a spot by her feet, the wire had been sliced and bent back, making a hole just big enough for one person to crawl through. On the other side, Banyon's Woods was black and cool. Tammy crouched and slid through the hole, moving on her hands and toes, like a small, four-legged animal, so she wouldn't dirty her white pants. Once through, she stood and brushed her hands against each other impatiently.

Art and Muscle and I looked from the hole to each other. Finally, Muscle scrambled through the opening. I didn't want to be last, so I stepped forward. The hole looked so small and so awkwardly placed, near the ground. I crouched, but I loomed hopelessly over the open-ing. I'm bigger than these people, I thought. I imagined I'd have to get down on my stomach and slither through, like a snake. "What are you waiting for?" said Tammy. I knelt and poked my head under the jagged wire. Then I pushed my shoulders through. I lowered my back and crawled. The dampness of the crushed grass pressed against my legs. I was ruining my dress. The wire scraped against my back. But in a second, I was through, standing on the other side, feeling as if I'd crossed some terrible distance and the fairgrounds was miles away.

"Aren't you coming, Arthur?" said Tammy.

"Take it easy," he groused. But he just stood there, eyeing the hole.

"We haven't got all night," she said. There was something familiar and resentful in the way they addressed each other. I remembered Mary Sue's story of what had happened in Art's car.

Art shook his head, but he dropped down and slipped effortlessly through the hole.

Before he was on his feet, Tammy had started into the woods, winding silently among the trees. Banyon's Woods, also known as Bang 'em Woods, rates with the Ledges as a make-out spot, and

Tammy knew her way. Muscle walked in front of me, holding branches back so they wouldn't snap in my face. Roots twisted across the trail and once I stumbled, falling into Muscle's back. "Oops, sorry," I whispered.

Behind us now, the fair gave off a cheerful, jumbled commotion, pierced every now and then by a single, powerful sound—the strong-man's bell, a rooster crowing, a particularly loud, high-pitched scream from someone on a ride.

Art reached out and poked my shoulder. "Don't pay any attention to this," he said quietly. "It's only some fun."

"What is it?"

"Only some fun."

Tammy heard us and looked back. "Don't spoil anything, Arthur," she said.

Ahead of us, the orange light of a fire flickered through the trees. Our procession moved silently forward, and I could see a bonfire with a group of dark figures huddled around it. Someone was talking in a slow, plodding voice. Tammy put up her hand, and we stopped in the trees, just beyond the circle of light. Art crowded up behind me, pressing against my shoulder.

In the fire's throbbing glow, a few of the faces were familiar—boys I knew from school. The boy talking was Gunnar Nygaard, and he was telling a joke involving three morons and a monkey. The three of us stood listening. The joke went on for several minutes, punctuated by an occasional hoot or shout or laugh from around the fire. Everyone was drinking beer. Someone threw a bottle into the flames, and an explosion of sparks billowed up and drifted off into the night.

Gunnar took great care with his story. He's a slope-shouldered, loopy boy, always slow on his feet. When we were young, people used to tease him and call him a moron; now, it seemed, he'd acquired a special attraction for the subject.

Finally, he came to the punchline. A great chorus of laughing and whooping erupted, and Gunnar stood awkwardly and took a bow. The celebration carried on for half a minute or so. Then a boy I didn't know jumped up, almost stepping into the fire. He pumped his fist into the air again and again. "Circle jerk!" he screamed. "Circle jerk!" The boys around the bonfire hooted and yelled.

At that moment, Tammy marched into the light. Art's hand tightened around my elbow, and I was guided out of the darkness.

Our entrance startled the group. In the sudden stillness, Tammy pranced up and back like a circus ringmaster. She swung her arm toward me in an extravagant arc. "Look who's here, folks!" she bellowed. "Look who I've brought! The girl you've all been talking about. The one, the only . . . Martha Calhoun!"

Art pushed me forward. I felt as if I'd stepped out of a doctor's office into a crowded waiting room: Every face turned to me, every patient was part startled, part pleased, part hoping to see evidence of some hideous disease. Then, quickly, around the fire, the yelling started again, a great thunderclap of noise that didn't abate. There was no place to go. I stood staring into the flames, letting the hypnotic flickerings close things out as much as possible. Beside me, Tammy was clapping and Muscle was waving his arms. Art had stepped away. The heat of the attention seemed to warm my skin and clothes. I wished it were possible to make myself die.

I don't know how long I stood there. The noise reached a peak and then screeched steadily, as if it came from a giant machine that would only quiet when it was turned off. People got up and moved around, anonymous dark forms hugging the shadows. From behind me, a hand appeared and perched on my shoulder. Neither friendly nor unfriendly, it sat there for a few seconds without moving, then went away. Close by, in the dark, a dog was barking.

Suddenly, the woods exploded in light. The shouting cut off instantly. Two huge spotlights, the size of full moons, bathed the bonfire in a fierce brightness. A man shouted: "Stay right where you are. This is the police. Don't move."

Of course, everyone did. The boys jumped up and scattered, screaming and laughing, dropping bottles of beer and tripping over roots and logs and each other. Three uniformed policemen appeared from the woods and started wading into the confusion, grabbing at arms and shoulders. Art snatched Tammy's hand, and the two of them tumbled off into the darkness. Muscle disappeared. A cop seized Gunnar by the neck and held him out stiff-armed, the way you'd hold a puppy that had got into mud. Another policeman, a big man, wrapped his arms around the necks of two boys, so they dangled from his chest like two enormous medals. I didn't move. People darted and dodged around me. Screams and hollers floated up from the woods. Finally, someone grabbed my arm, squeezing it with a grip that cut off circulation. I looked back and into a face I recognized: George, the cop who'd given me the Coke at the stationhouse the week before. He'd grabbed me with his right hand. With his left, he was trying to hold on to a boy who was wriggling like a monkey. George had the boy by the shoulder and, in frustration, he gave him two powerful shakes. The boy went limp and started whimpering. Then George looked at me. "You!" he said. In his surprise, he loosened his grip. The fingers that had been pressing into my arm went slack. His eyes, squinted tight against the spotlights, turned gentle. "You," he repeated, more softly this time.

I sensed my chance. Yanking my arm free, I jumped away, then turned and ran into the woods, beyond the beams of light.

"Hey!" he yelled.

After staring at the spotlights, I was blind in the woods. I ran as hard as I could for about twenty steps and ran right over a small tree. The thin trunk bent back under my weight, but didn't break, and I ended up straddling it, one leg on either side. The branches jabbed at me, poking all over and lifting my dress. My face was untouched, but burning scratches ran down my arms and legs. Worse, I wasn't sure how to get untangled. The tree and I were locked in a kind of clumsy embrace. At any moment, I thought, George's hand would clamp around my neck. I stood for a few minutes, breathing hard and feeling furious at the tree for being in the way. Finally, I backed up, slowly pulling my dress from the branches. By the time I got out, the thin trunk was bent lifelessly toward the ground.

I tried to pull myself together. My breath came in deep gasps, and my head felt light. I put my hand on my chest, hoping to slow my heart. The beams of the spotlights didn't reach this far, so I was safely in the dark, but I could see perfectly back to the fire. George hadn't bothered to chase me. He was still holding the whimpering boy, dragging the boy behind him as he stalked around the clearing. Another policeman had gathered Gunnar and some of the other boys and had made them sit by the fire with their backs against each other. After the chaos of the raid, the scene was strangely quiet. Behind me, the noises of the fair drifted up again.

I must be crazy, I told myself. Insane. I must have temporary insanity. I used to think that Bunny had a streak that made her do dumb things, but coming out to Banyon's Woods was beyond dumb, way beyond dumb. What's happened to me? I used to be so careful—I was about the most careful person I knew. And then Butcher and now this. Temporary insanity, that's got to be the explanation.

It occurred to me that I should go back to the bonfire and give myself up. It seemed so clear now, temporary insanity. I'd explain it all to George.

I took a step forward and tripped over a root, falling into a bush. I caught myself, grabbing a handful of leaves, but branches crackled under my weight.

"Listen!" hissed the other cop. "Someone's there." He stared out directly at me.

"Forget it," said George. "We got enough."

"Where's Mike?" asked the first cop.

"I guess he ran after them," said George. "He'll be back. We'll wait here."

The cops returned their attention to their captives, working silently, ordering people around by grunts and gestures. Watching from the darkness while the spotlights glared, I felt like a secret witness who was about to see some awful crime committed. I can't go back there, I realized. I can't go to the cops.

I waited a few minutes, until the silence of the woods settled around me. Then I began creeping back to the fair. I felt my way among the trees, not knowing where the path was. A bright moon sent some light through the leafy ceiling, and I followed the distant sounds. Going forward, my left hand was always in front of my face, open and palm out, to guard against branches, or worse, cobwebs. My right hand swung back and forth as added protection. With each step, my right foot edged out a few inches and planted itself on solid ground. With those inches safely established, my left foot caught up from behind, and the process was repeated. Moving like that, like a blind cripple, I maneuvered my way through the woods. Soon, the sounds of the fair grew louder, and the lighting began to show the way. After about fifteen minutes, I was again at the fence.

This area of the fairgrounds didn't look familiar, however. Several big, unlighted buildings stretched ahead in the darkness. No one was around. I found a faint path along the fence and followed that to the right, looking for something I recognized. After about a hundred feet I stopped. These buildings stored tractors and snowplows and other heavy equipment for the county. They were on the opposite side of the fairgrounds from the entrance, and, as far as I could recall, they weren't anywhere near the fence hole. So I turned and walked back the other way. After a while, the buildings ended and the animal tents appeared. The fence was in a deep shadow, and I walked close, my shoulder bumping against it, so I wouldn't miss the hole. I stayed hunched over, my eyes toward the bottom.

"Hey!" hissed someone close to my ear.

I jumped back, scraping my hand on the raw edge of the severed wire. There was the hole, anyway.

"Help," whispered the voice again. It was Muscle. He was visible only as a dark hulk, pressed against the fence. I couldn't even tell which side he was on.

"What are you doing?" I asked softly.

"Get me out of here," he begged. "The cop handcuffed me to the fence."

I couldn't tell if he recognized me, but I stepped closer. His left arm was attached to the fence at about the height of his head. He pulled on the handcuff and it rattled against the wire. "Do something," he said. He sounded as if he were about to cry.

"What?" I edged toward the hole.

"Get a saw, get a hammer. Get *something*."

"Hmmmm." I crouched down. I remembered how drowning people act, how dangerous they can be, grabbing at anything to save themselves. Muscle was just on the other side of the fence, just within reach of the hole if he stretched.

"Please," he moaned, shaking his tethered hand again.

"Sure," I whispered. I dropped to my knees and scrambled through the hole, then jumped to my feet on the other side. Muscle snatched out, and his fingers caught the left strap of my sundress. I pulled away and the strap ripped out.

"Wait!" he yelled. I ran off between the tents.

The loose strap flapped down, and my dress sagged, but I kept running, past darkened tents of calves and sheep, past a huge mountain of straw, past a long, fenced enclosure full of goats. Finally, I came to a main path and slowed to a walk. People were wandering by, chattering and laughing, acting as if nothing important had gone on in the world for hours, for days before. They seemed from another country, people I hadn't seen for years, or perhaps knew only from books. I was exhausted, my body ached all over. Just watching these people drained my last bits of stored energy. Without even talking to me, they seemed to be demanding so much.

A father walked by, holding his son by the hand. When the boy saw me, he stared, twisting his head back as the two went past. My dress was in ruins. Dampness and grass had stained the front, and the loose left strap drooped down over my stomach. I could have been wearing a toga. I felt in back and discovered that the button to hold the strap was gone. The only way to keep the front of the dress up was to pull the strap back over my shoulder and then tuck the loose end under my arm. That meant I had to keep my left arm tight against my side, as if I were wounded or suffering from some deep stomach pain.

I walked along looking for Bunny. I was certain she would be around; she wouldn't have left without me. I'd check the beer tent and the Ferris wheel, the only ride she'd ever go on. I had to find her. People swept past me, their faces blurs, their clothes just streaks of color. If I concentrated, I could focus my eyes, but I didn't have the strength. It was easier to move along in a fog. Don't think. Just find Bunny. Someone called my name—or was it just a memory, knocked loose behind the blur? It wasn't Bunny, so I kept walking.

The path swung around a big tent and then along a line of clattery game booths. Through the fog, my eyes caught a bare, sinewy arm: Eddie. I focused and found myself staring at the barker for a dart-throwing game. He was leaning over his counter, watching the people go by. He caught me staring. "Hey, honey bun, how about it?" He held up a fist with three dart points sticking out. "Three shots for a quarter. Win a bear." I looked away and walked past, back into the fog. "Come on, honey bun, where's your sense of adventure?" he called after me.

I angled left, hoping to get back to the beer tent. The path grew darker, and the crowd thinned. Another wrong turn, nothing but wrong turns. A bright, glittery object appeared in the path, an enormous precious stone blocking the way. I concentrated and saw that it was the silver trailer with the two-headed baby. The woman in the ticket booth was still bent over her book and the blue light still flowed over the man at the entrance. I put my hand in my pocket and felt the soft edges of the ticket I'd bought less than an hour before. Strange that it hadn't fallen out with all my crawling around. I shuffled a few steps closer, my eyes on the painting. The two beaming faces still seemed to promise something—some remarkable secret, a fantastic possibility just beyond my imagination. For a while, I stood there by the trailer, studying the painting. People came and went, stopping, staring, moving on. I could have been there ten seconds or ten minutes or an hour. Time had stopped.

Then a voice woke me up. "We weren't doing anything wrong, you know," it said insistently. "You can't arrest me." A cop was coming toward me down the path. Tammy was beside him, her back arched and her chin out. She was lecturing him, and he was sinking under the burden, bumping into her as he drifted from side to side. "My uncle won't like this at all," she said. "He's Ivan Mirkov, on the city council."

They hadn't seen me yet. There was still time to escape. I spun. Where to go? I couldn't let her see me—she'd betray me, maybe even offer me up as a kind of trade. I had to hide. Quickly, I slipped past the booth where the lady was reading. At the door to the trailer, the man had his chin on his chest as if he were sleeping. He heard me approach and slowly lifted his head, examining me with two tiny, round eyes. I thrust the worn, damp ticket at him. When he handed back the stub I walked up three thin, metal steps and went inside.

The trailer was bright with glaring light. On the left, someone had tacked a display entitled "The Story of Life." In faded color paintings, the kind you see in high-school science books, the sperm met the egg, and the fetus developed. I turned away. On the right, the wall was covered with magazine clippings about quintuplets and Siamese twins. I moved down the narrow walkway.

At the far end, a small metal table had been clamped to the floor. On it was a glass jar, about the size of a gallon pickle jar, fastened down by a metal garter. Three more steps and I was exactly in front.

The baby was floating in a yellow solution. Her skin was a dull red-orange, about the color of dried-up orange peels. Her hips were wide and hanging down between her legs was a third leg, slightly smaller than the other two and crooked. She had a wide chest, but her two arms were normal, and one tiny, flat palm pushed against the inside of the glass. The two little heads were on thick, short necks, side by side. The eyes on each face were squinted shut, the mouths barely open, showing perfect bow lips. The identical noses were perfect, delicate bumps. The baby was absolutely still in the jar, but the head on the right was tilted slightly, so its smooth forehead rested on the forehead of the other. In that pose, the heads could have belonged to two different babies, set down beside each other on a mother's bed, each lost in a wonderful child's sleep.

A note printed in careful black letters sat in a small picture frame beside the jar: "Ruth was born to a farm couple in Manfred, Idaho, on January 25, 1947. She lived for eleven minutes before her heart gave out. For that brief time, both heads were alert and crying. Doctors believe she has an extra lung, an enlarged stomach, and badly tangled intestines. Her middle leg is not attached to a hip. Had she survived, it would have dangled behind her like a tail." In larger letters below, someone had printed, "But for the grace of God, there go I."

I stood so still I hardly breathed. The long lights buzzed over my head. The inside of the trailer seemed crystalline, so fragile that the smallest shock, the least shudder would shatter the room and everything in it. After a minute or so, I heard voices at the door behind me. People were coming in. I moved around the table, past a tall, blue screen, and out the back door, which faced the fence and Banyon's Woods. After the glare of the trailer, the night was particularly dark, but I moved quickly and surely across the fairgrounds.

TWENTY-SIX

I hurried along the main path, still holding my dress strap under my arm and not bothering to look for Bunny. A man wearing a baseball cap was standing at the exit. "Do you want to get stamped?" he asked gruffly.

"Huh?"

He brandished a rubber stamp. "Are you going to come back?"

I shook my head and brushed past him. A steady line of cars was moving slowly toward Katydid, about half a mile away. I started walking along the side of the road, picking my way through the patches of gravel and tall grass. After a while, I came to a sidewalk, the farthest reach of town. I followed it along Altgeld Street, past several blocks of little houses put up for workers years ago by the KTD. I passed the Rock Creek Elementary School, Dixon's Corner Store, and Mayor Krullke's house, floodlit from the lawn, as always.

Eventually, I came to the square. The bandbox, the usual hangout, was deserted, and no one was around the drinking fountain. Along the paths, near some of the benches, the red tips of lit cigarettes brightened and faded like fireflies. The old people were out, people you'd hardly notice on busy days. I skirted the square to the north, avoiding the big, empty shell of the old Montgomery Ward building on the south side, and then turned up West Morgan Street, toward the Congregational Church. The streetlight at the corner was out and, in the darkness, the church building squatted on its small hill like a solid outcropping of red rock. I walked around the corner. A lamp was still burning in Reverend Vaughn's study. From the sidewalk, all you could see was a wall crammed with books.

My dress clung limply to my skin. In hurrying away from the fair, I'd started to perspire. Using the loose strap, I wiped off my forehead. I picked up the hem of the dress and flapped the air a few times. The breeze felt good curling up my legs and cooled some of the scratches. I knew I looked a fright, but there was something I had to tell Reverend Vaughn, something I'd held in for days now that had been released in the crystal light of Ruth's trailer.

"My God," the minister said, when he opened the door. "What happened to you?"

I glanced down at my dress. It was worse than I'd thought.

"Come in, come in," he added quickly.

"I'm kind of a mess," I said, stepping into the study. The room was lit by a single, bright ceiling light.

His eyes wandered from my head to my feet. "You look as if you fell off a hayrack."

"Actually, I was out in the woods. It's a long story."

"The woods?" He frowned. He was wearing a dress shirt and a dark, striped tie; instead of shoes, though, he had on sandals. Like his fingers, his toes were white and thin and very long. "Sit down and tell me about it." He gestured toward a couch. "Can I get you a glass of water?"

I shook my head and sat down. The study was comfortable, but spare. There were bookshelves on two sides, a compact wooden desk, several plain chairs. A nature calendar and a framed degree were hanging behind the desk, but otherwise there was nothing personal about the room—no pictures, no knick-knacks—except, of course, the books.

"How was your trip?" I asked. He was standing over me, still inspecting.

"Oh, fine, fine." Finally he sat in one of the chairs. "What happened in the woods?"

I didn't really want to explain. In a way, it didn't seem important now, or, at least, not important enough to waste time on. But I couldn't pretend it hadn't happened, so I told him about Tammy and the bonfire and the police raid. I told the story quickly and simply, leaving out details where I could. He asked many questions, fleshing out my account. In the end, he shook his head and combed his hair with his fingers.

"It's that factory," he said.

"The factory?"

"Don't you see? The whole town is panicked over the KTD closing, but instead of doing something useful, they take out their frustrations on you. It's not you personally—it's just that you're there, you're an easy target."

It bothered me for a second that he was always talking about the KTD. Even when he'd start talking about me, the factory always seemed to come up. "You really think so?" I asked.

"It's obvious." He paused and shook his head again. "Of course, no one in this town would understand the psychology of it, except you."

His eyes were deep blue—not pale, like Eddie's, but rich and unthreatening. He stood up and came over, sitting beside me on the couch. For a moment, I almost expected him to draw me close, even to kiss me. I felt pulled toward him, as if someone were lifting up my end of the couch, and I were falling inevitably into his arms. All he did, though, was take my hand—my left hand, which loosened the shoulder strap again. The dress sagged.

"Look," he said, ignoring the dress, "you're an obvious target. Someone like you is too full of life for a small town, too smart, too eager to learn. A town like Katydid can't hold you—you've got to experience the world, to taste things. You're not willing to settle for some mundane job and mindless life. The people here realize that. You're above them, and they resent you for it."

I nodded, staring into his eyes. Is this what love is like, I wondered. He was so wrong about me. I'm not like that at all. It was Bunny he was describing. She's the one who's full of life.

"You really think so?" I asked.

"Yes. You're special. You outgrew this place ages ago. What you're going through now is nothing. Nothing! In a couple of years, you'll move to Chicago or New York, some center like that, and you'll start a whole new life. Katydid will be behind you forever."

"Gee." It was wonderful hearing him talk like this. I could almost begin to believe him.

"Do you think you can hang on?" he asked. "It'll only be a couple of years."

I nodded. His hand on mine felt warm. I wanted to lift it to my cheek, to feel the softness of his skin, the bristle of his blond hair. He looked at me silently, and I thought about why I'd come here.

"There's something I want to tell you," I said.

"Something?"

"Yes, about you—"

"Me?"

"Well, me more, but—"

"You?"

"Sort of us, but—"

"Us?"

"Mmm-hmmm."

"Wait." He let go of my hand. We both seemed to be out of breath. He stared across the room toward his desk. On top, a book lay flat open, something he'd been reading when I knocked. The couch was unusually low, and his knees loomed craggily above it. Finally he said, "There's a story I never told you, something about me that might help you out. I had to go through something similar to you once—it was vastly different, of course, but similar in some ways. Do you want to hear?"

"Yes."

"When I was sixteen, back home, I had a very good friend, a boy. I'd known him all my life, but after we got in high school, we became very close. Too close, really, I suppose. And when my father realized how close we had become, he forbade us to have anything to do with each other. My father was a simple man but very forceful, and, of course, I had to do what he said. So even though my friend and I still saw each other in school, and we passed in the hall, we weren't allowed to have any contact with each other. For two years, we'd just see each other and never talk. Can you imagine? My best friend. Once, I remember, we were in the same gym class, and I came late. He was alone in the locker room. We had to get into our gym clothes standing ten feet apart, not daring to say a word to each other. I rushed to get ready and hurried out, but as I left I glanced at him for a second. He was watching me, and his eyes were brimming with tears, and all the time he was begging me, begging me with his eyes. But he never said anything."

"What happened?"

"The day after we graduated from high school, he joined the army, and I never heard of him again. He was gone like that." He snapped his fingers noiselessly. "The best friend I ever had, and he was gone."

"How did you do it?" I asked. "I mean, how could you see him and not talk?"

"I steeled myself. That's the point I wanted to make, since you can do it, too. I just steeled myself. It was as straightforward as that." As if to demonstrate, he looked into my eyes without blinking. I tried to stay with him, but I felt weak and quickly turned away.

He stood abruptly. "Well, that was just my experience. Maybe it will help." He walked over to his desk and sat against the front edge, crossing his legs.

"It will," I mumbled. But how? All I knew was that I'd been wrong again, another mistake. I can't seem to get anything right anymore. Was this what it was like for Bunny—always deluding herself, always misreading her men? Am I that much a part of her?

He rocked slowly up and back. "I might as well tell you something else, Martha, since you seem to be my only confidante. I haven't announced this yet, so you mustn't tell anyone, but I'm leaving Katydid."

The words hung in the air. I could have reached out and touched them. "Why?" I asked finally.

"The truth is, I've been asked to leave. That won't be part of the announcement, so that has to be a secret, too."

"But, who?"

"The church fathers decided they don't like my kind of ministry. They want more God-and-Bible stuff, more talk about right and wrong. The kind of sermons I give make them uncomfortable. Of course, they were very nice about it; they're good people. I just wasn't their type of minister." He shrugged.

"What'll you do?"

"Oh, I'll find another pulpit. The church organization will help me, and I'll find something, I'm sure. And if that doesn't work—well, maybe it'll turn out I'm not anybody's type of minister. But I'll give it at least one more try."

"Gee." I shook my head. "I'm sorry."

"Oh, don't be," he said cheerfully. "I'm not. I mean, I'm sorry I washed out here, but I'm not going to second-guess the way I worked.

That's the only way I could work. I'm not a God-and-Bible sort of person. I have to minister the way that's right for me. Besides, as I said, I've learned to steel myself."

He stood up again and drifted across the room, toward the window. I sensed he was making a signal, so I stood up and walked to the door.

"Are we still on for tomorrow?" he asked.

I looked at him blankly.

"For the hearing. Is your hearing still scheduled for tomorrow?"

I hadn't thought of that for hours. "Yes. At least, I think so." My mind tripped backward, trying to think what might have happened tonight to change the hearing.

"At eleven?" he asked.

"Yes."

He followed me to the door, his hands fluttering for places to rest. Finally, he grabbed the doorknob. "Are you all right?" he asked. "Do you feel better now?"

"Yes."

He opened the door, and I stepped onto the stoop. All around were shadows, and the lawn in front of the church fell down the hill into blackness.

"Wait," he said. "Let me drive you."

"No, no, I can walk. It'll be nice."

"It's so far."

"Not really." I ran down the steps. "Thanks," I said.

He hesitated. "Wait," he said again. He moved from behind the door and stepped onto the stoop. The light pouring from the study silhouetted his figure. His fine blond hair seemed afire. "I almost forgot," he called out. "Did you want to tell me something?"

"No," I said, turning away. I felt a sudden heaviness. Why did he have to ask me that? He'd known what I was going to say. Everything had been all right until then. Why'd we have to pretend now? "No, it was nothing," I called back.

TWENTY - SEVEN

The walk to the Vernons' took about half an hour. I avoided the square, to make sure I wouldn't run into anyone who'd wandered back from the fair. I went down Parker Street, behind the hotel, past the army recruiters' building, the bowling alley, the Sears catalogue store. Turning down Molly Street, I crossed to the other side to stay away from the bars—the Little Las Vegas, Tumble Inn, Murphy's, all lined up and spitting out bad smells and jukebox music. When I came to the tracks, I crouched and put my hand on a rail, feeling for a train. The metal was cool and still. Down Prosperity Street, I followed the hum of the KTD, letting my body absorb the vibrations from the air. Flashes of white welding light sparkled through the factory's squinty, stained windows. The midnight whistle was still about fifteen minutes away.

As I came down the Vernons' block, I saw someone on the curb under the streetlight, sitting slumped over, like a drunk. When I got closer, I realized it was Bunny. She heard my footsteps and stood, but waited for me to come to her.

"Are you all right?" I asked.

She put her arms around me and hung from my neck without saying anything.

"The man inside sent me away," she mumbled finally. "He growled. I heard him growl."

Bunny dangled from my neck for a few more seconds and then dropped down to the curb again. I sat beside her. Between her feet on the street was the goldfish bowl she'd won earlier in the evening. "He's still alive," she said, pointing to the fish.

"Lucky him."

Bunny rested her head on my shoulder. I braced my arms in back for support, letting my fingers slide through the cool grass. I told her all about Banyon's Woods, though she hardly seemed interested. I couldn't even tell if she was listening.

"I really am a good mother," Bunny said, when I'd finished. "Maybe Tom does have problems, but look at you—you're a perfect child, a perfect child."

"Stop it," I said gently.

"No, really. Every mother would love to have a daughter like you." With her head on my shoulder, she was talking across the street, and her voice had a distant quality. She was quiet for a minute or so and then said, "And, anyway, I love Tom, so I don't care."

"I know. I love him, too."

She was quiet again. The sharp squeak of a cricket persisted from the tree above us. A car nosed around the corner and down Oak. The driver, an old man, was gripping the steering wheel with both hands and straining to see in front. He went by without noticing us.

After a while, Bunny said, "You know, I've figured out what my problem is. It's really not so different from anyone else's. But when things go bad for other women, they drink or take pills. For me, when things go bad, I need to be loved. I can't help it. That's just the way I am."

"Maybe you should try to steel yourself," I said. "I mean, not everybody gets drunk or takes pills when things go wrong. Some people just learn to get by."

Bunny sat up. "You can't expect me to change," she said. "That's just the way I am. You can't expect me to be different than I am."

That wasn't really an answer, of course, since people are always being forced to be different than they are. But I didn't want to argue. I just looked away, and after a few seconds, Bunny put her head back down on my shoulder.

We stayed that way for about ten minutes, hardly talking. Finally, Bunny said she better get home and get some rest for the hearing tomorrow. She picked up the goldfish bowl and stood stiffly, like an

225

old person. I walked her to the Pontiac, parked up the block. She put the bowl on the front seat beside her.

"Won't it slosh?" I asked.

"He'll be more comfortable there," she said.

I closed the door behind her and watched as the car lurched away.

The Vernons' house was dark inside. A pale light from the street drifted through the front windows, making crisscross shadows on the wall. Without turning on a lamp, I could still make out my note, untouched on the table. I had to smile to myself. After everything that had happened tonight, I'd still got in before Mrs. Vernon's church let out. I tiptoed up the stairs and went softly to Sissy's room.

TWENTY-EIGHT

We made a strange, starchy party going to court the next morning.
Mrs. O'Brien, not taking any chances, had stopped to pick up Bunny
before coming by for me, and, for this hearing, Mrs. Vernon came
along, too. We were all dressed up, but no one had quite managed
to get it right—every outfit seemed half a season wrong, or half a size
off one way or the other. I'd put on my white blouse with the bow
in front and a navy skirt. The skirt was too heavy for the weather and
nagged against the scratches on my legs, but it looked very conserva-
tive and had seemed the right choice when I examined the closet early
in the morning. Mrs. Vernon was wearing a flowery violet dress, with
a white collar, something unexpectedly gay, and she'd pinned on a
white spring hat. Just after breakfast, she'd come down to Sissy's
room to primp and get my opinion.

"It's fine," I told her, though she was the picture of a woman going
to church on an April day.

"The last time I went to court, Josephine told me I looked too
dowdy," she said, frowning. "She told me Judge Horner doesn't like
dowdy women."

"I'm sure he'll like this," I said.

Mrs. O'Brien was wearing a huge, formless green shift that swept
around her legs when she walked and gave her the appearance of a

great broad tree with feet. But the most surprising outfit was on Bunny. She'd chosen to wear a dark blue linen dress—her good summer dress, as she used to call it, though the dress hadn't been out of her closet in years. Now, with its plain, boxy lines, the dress was sufficiently out of style to appear very proper. Bunny was sitting in the front seat of Mrs. O'Brien's station wagon when I came down the walk. Seeing her there I had to pause; the dress jogged loose a memory, something I couldn't quite grasp that saddened me nonetheless. I found myself fighting back tears, even before we'd got to court.

"That damn fish died last night," Bunny said, after Mrs. Vernon and I had settled into the back seat.

"A fish?" said Mrs. Vernon. "That's strange. A bunch of my carrots died yesterday for no reason. I hope there's not something going around."

"Probably is," said Bunny.

At the courthouse, we waited on the benches outside Judge Horner's courtroom. Unlike the last time, the corridors were almost empty. Shortly after we sat down, Reverend Vaughn appeared. I watched him coming down the long corridor. It cheered me to see him, but when he stood before us, tall and rickety, I found I could hardly speak. Bunny ignored him, and Mrs. O'Brien asked a few sullen questions about whether he'd seen Bishop Sheen on television lately. Finally he was reduced to listening to Mrs. Vernon jabber on about her church. After a few minutes, he managed to escape, and he sat down on a bench by himself, taking a paperback book out of his jacket pocket. Every now and then, I'd glance over at him. Engrossed in the book, he leaned forward, crossing his arms and legs, finally pretzeling himself into a loose, bony knot. "He's got too many joints," Bunny had said one time.

The start of my hearing was delayed. There was another group in the courtroom, and periodically an explosion of loud noises could be heard behind the thick wooden door. At one point, Josephine stepped out and came over to Mrs. O'Brien.

"These Mexicans," she said. "So emotional."

Bunny looked at her watch and shook her head.

"We've got all day," said Mrs. O'Brien.

At 11:30, Bunny said loudly, "I wonder where Simon Beach is?"

"I told you he's not coming," I said.

Bunny glared at me. "Of course he's coming. He's your lawyer."

I leaned toward her and lowered my voice, so Mrs. O'Brien wouldn't hear. "Don't mess things up," I said.

Bunny made a clucking noise with her tongue, then shook her head and looked away.

Shortly after noon, the courtroom door swung open to a procession of Mexicans. An older woman, probably somebody's mother, stumbled out first, sobbing into a handkerchief and talking in soggy bursts of Spanish. A man had her by the arm, trying to soothe her and hold her up at the same time. A dozen other people came out behind them. Most of the women were crying. Through the door, I could see Francis X. Moon and Sergeant Tony up at the front of the courtroom, huddled with Judge Horner.

My hearing was put off until after lunch, so Mrs. O'Brien, Mrs. Vernon, Reverend Vaughn, and Bunny and I made our own procession down the corridor and out to the square. Reverend Vaughn said he had some business to take care of and promised to return later. He hurried off toward the Congo, obviously relieved to be free. Bunny insisted she wanted to look for Simon Beach. I started to argue with her, then stopped. Maybe believing in him will ease things for her, I thought. So the four of us walked across the square and up the stairs of the hotel to his office. Bunny rattled the knob for a while, but the door was locked—even the secretary was out.

"Well, let's at least have lunch," said Mrs. O'Brien. She led us back out to the square and over to Paul's Front Porch. The restaurant was smoky and crowded. Everyone who works around the square lunches there, and, by the time we arrived, people were milling around the cash register, waiting to get seated. Bunny knows the head waitress, however, and we were quickly led to the first open table in back. Across the room, Judge Horner, Mr. Moon, and Sergeant Tony were together at a table. Judge Horner wasn't wearing a jacket, and he had on an unpleasant brown tie. In his rolled-up shirtsleeves, he looked rather slight. He nodded at Mrs. O'Brien, then went back to his conversation.

Bunny and I weren't hungry and only ordered tunafish sandwiches. Mrs. Vernon just wanted tea. But Mrs. O'Brien ordered a sliced turkey plate, which arrived with a huge mound of mashed potatoes, a dousing of yellow gravy, and a side dish of corn. The heat spell earlier in the week had passed, but outside it was still in the eighties, and it was particularly warm in the restaurant. The steam rose from

229

Mrs. O'Brien's plate and circled and hung over our table. My skirt itched and stuck to my legs. Little drops of perspiration appeared on Bunny's forehead.

"How can you eat all that hot food?" Bunny finally asked, drawing on her second cigarette of the lunch. She'd only nibbled at her sandwich.

"I believe in good breakfasts and good lunches," said Mrs. O'Brien. "Then a light dinner. That way, you get your full meals and a chance to digest them."

"Look at those potatoes," groaned Bunny.

"My conscience is clear," said the social worker.

At two, we gathered again in the courthouse corridor. This time, there was another group seated on a bench. I recognized Toby Warner, a boy my age who'd been caught breaking into Wally's Record Emporium last year. His mother sat beside him. From across the corridor, I stared at her feet. She appeared to be wearing a pair of beat-up old bedroom slippers. Even in first or second grade, I remembered, she'd always seemed overwhelmed.

Bunny and I walked down to the end of the corridor, near a window, to get as far away from Toby as we could. The window looked out on the parking lot, and below us I watched a boy, sitting by himself on the curb. He was playing jacks, a game you don't see much anymore.

Reverend Vaughn returned and came up to us. "Still hanging in there?" he asked me.

I nodded. Behind him, I saw Mr. Moon come out of the courtroom and gesture for Mrs. O'Brien to follow him. They walked a few steps down the corridor to be alone.

"Well, don't worry," said Reverend Vaughn. "I think it's going to work out." He was bouncing from foot to foot, trying to be cheerful. I smiled, but I kept glancing down the corridor, where Mr. Moon was talking intently to Mrs. O'Brien. The prosecutor's head shot up and back in short jabs as he made his points.

"And if it gets to that, I've got a secret weapon," the minister went on. He tapped his jacket, over the inside pocket. "I even wrote a little speech—a sermon—in your behalf. If we need to, I'll pull that out and give the judge some fire and brimstone."

"Did you pray?" asked Bunny dully.

"What?" said Reverend Vaughn.

Mrs. O'Brien, her head bowed to listen to the prosecutor, suddenly looked up at me. Her eyes were ice.

"You know—pray," Bunny said. She put her palms together and rolled her eyes up in her head. "That's what a minister's supposed to do, right?"

"Oh, pray. Yes, well, I've been doing that all along for Martha," Reverend Vaughn said.

Mr. Moon walked back into court, but Mrs. O'Brien just stood there, staring icily at me from down the corridor. I understood exactly: Everything was lost. It occurred to me suddenly that Reverend Vaughn had been all wrong in his sermon last Sunday. There is a giant wheel that just keeps rolling forward. Even if you don't see it, the wheel is always there, tracking you, bearing down. There's no escape, that seemed so clear to me now.

"I don't think prayers do any good," said Bunny.

TWENTY-NINE

Mrs. O'Brien returned to her seat on the bench without saying anything, and for the next hour she sat silently by herself, her shoulders pressed stiffly against the wall. At three, Josephine finally summoned us. Inside, the high, church-like space of the courtroom looked even more vast and unfriendly than before. Far down in front, Sergeant Tony and Mr. Moon turned to watch our entrance. Walking beside Bunny down the long center aisle, I had the feeling that I was participating in some momentous ceremony, like a wedding or graduation, and that I had to move with a slow, solemn step to keep the mood of it all.

Mrs. O'Brien followed us down to our table in front, just beyond the lip of the judge's bench. She took a chair to my left. Her anger billowed off her, and finally she said in a low, muttering voice, "You should have told me about last night." She couldn't look at me when she said it.

I started to say that I wasn't quite sure what to make of last night—that I'd had so much on my mind I hadn't really been able to digest everything. But I stopped myself. She'd just think I was making another excuse. "I'm sorry," I said.

"You Calhouns." She made a smacking noise with her lips. "I sometimes think you care more about embarrassing me than you do about solving your own problems."

Judge Horner came in reading from a handful of papers. In all the courtroom, for several minutes, there was only the sound of the papers he was rustling. I looked up and watched the overhead fans making their slow turns. It seemed they couldn't possibly do any good, couldn't possibly cool the air while moving at that lazy, silent pace, so far above.

At last, Judge Horner put the papers down. "This hasn't worked out, has it?" he said.

Mr. Moon and Mrs. O'Brien exchanged glances. After a moment, Mr. Moon stood. "I take it your honor is referring to the incident last night."

"Yes, last night. What was going on out there, anyway?"

"Drinking," said Mr. Moon. "All underage. Those parties out in Banyon's Woods are getting worse, and the police have decided to clean it up."

"Well, last night was one thing, and last week was another," the judge said. He picked a sheet of paper off his desk and waved it in the air. "This escapade with Boggs running around drunk and naked. I thought we were getting involved here to do some good?"

"They've made it worse," said Bunny loudly.

The judge glared at her. "I'm not going to have any outbursts today, Mrs. Calhoun. This isn't the country club, where you can just shout out when you want. Any outbursts like last time, and I'll throw you right out." He turned to the prosecutor. "The same goes for you, Mr. Moon. Today's going to be nice and calm and orderly."

"Yes, your honor," said Mr. Moon.

Bunny raised her hand. "Can I say something?" she asked.

The judge nodded.

"Why are we doing this without Martha's lawyer?"

"Her lawyer?"

"Yes."

"Where is he?"

"He couldn't make it."

"Well, who is he? Why didn't he contact the court?"

"Simon Beach."

Mr. Moon cleared his throat. "Your honor, if I may address that. Mr. Beach phoned me this morning from Carbondale, where he's been called on business. He warned me that Mrs. Calhoun may try to claim that she'd retained him in this matter. But he said he told her specifically that he doesn't handle juvenile matters and wouldn't take this one on. He's authorized me to make that representation to the court. He's not her lawyer, your honor. That's just a figment of her very active imagination."

Judge Horner turned to Bunny. "Well?" he said.

Bunny scowled and hunched down in her chair.

"The county is ready to proceed," said Mr. Moon.

Reverend Vaughn and Mrs. Vernon had sat down together in the first row of spectator seats, and Judge Horner now asked who they were. Mrs. O'Brien stood and made introductions.

"I didn't recognize you in that pretty dress, Mrs. Vernon," said the judge.

Mrs. Vernon blushed and fought with a handkerchief in her lap.

"I don't believe we've met," said Reverend Vaughn. "I hope I can be of some help here. I've spent a good deal of time with Martha lately."

"Yes, I know who you are," said the judge. "I hope you can help, too." He straightened the papers on his desk. "Well, let's get on with it and build the record. This is a fact-finding hearing to determine whether the circumstances justify the county getting involved on a long-term basis. If I so determine, we'll have a separate hearing on the girl's disposition. All right, Sergeant Tony, let's hear from you."

For twenty minutes, Sergeant Tony went over the police reports and read from his notes. He talked in a nasal, bored tone, one that I'd never heard from him before. His sentences were flat and run-on; there were no cracks to get in, no places to interrupt him. He was talking about me, though he had it all wrong. This Martha Calhoun was a stranger, a character out of a book or a movie. She had sex on her mind; she chased after little boys; she hung around with her mother's boyfriend; she stayed out at wild, teenage parties; she had no conscience. Sergeant Tony was like the last person telling a long story in a huge game of telephone—nothing but a few scattered facts were left of what had really happened. And yet, there was a kind of truth to what he said, or really, there were little pieces of truth all stitched together. It was as if he had taken a few twigs off a tree, woven them into a basket, and then held up the basket, saying, "This is a tree we're talking about." It would never have occurred to me to do that—it never occurred to me that you *could* do that. But when he was finished, nobody objected. Mrs. O'Brien sat with her chin on her chest. Bunny stared at the courtroom wall. Judge Horner thanked Sergeant Tony, and the officer sat down.

Francis X. Moon then stood up. He put on a pair of glasses with heavy black frames and proceeded to read from a long, yellow legal pad. He'd made a list, an accounting of every incident in the police files that involved our family, and the list went on for page after page. The incidents started before I was born, when neighbors called the police because of a loud argument between Bunny and my father. Later that same month, Bunny filed a robbery claim, saying Jeremiah P. Calhoun had run off with the car, the toaster, the silverware, and a bunch of other things. There was a gap of a few years and then a report about someone named Joe Burford driving a car over the sidewalk and onto Bunny's lawn and passing out on the horn. The next year, an unidentified man was seen yelling at the house in his underwear. The neighbors chased him away.

Soon Tom appeared, and his contacts with the police took up several pages: Tom painting names on a wall at the school; Tom caught breaking into the bowling alley; Tom throwing rocks at cars from the Hanson Street overpass; Tom digging holes in the Little League diamond; Tom over and over and over—more than I ever imagined. He'd been gone long enough now that I'd almost forgotten how bad it had been, how Bunny and I had driven down to the police station so regularly that it was almost like doing the laundry, a chore you expected every week.

Tom dominated Mr. Moon's list for those years, but Bunny was there, too. She bounced some checks; stores complained. And there was more boyfriend trouble. Once Wayne Wadlinger got mad about something and started throwing furniture and things out of the house onto the lawn. Half the living room was scattered over the front yard before the police arrived. Another time, Lester Vincent got drunk, climbed out a window on the second floor and stood on the edge of the roof, threatening to jump. He was only about ten feet off the ground and would have landed in nice, soft grass, but the police came that time, too.

Even I made Mr. Moon's list. Years ago, when I was about five, I was out at the country club with Bunny, and I noticed a small riding mower—one of the first I'd ever seen—sitting on a hill next to the clubhouse. Bunny was off somewhere and the mower looked enticing, so I climbed on and pretended to drive. I bounced on the seat and turned the steering bar. Of course, nothing happened. I reached down and pulled a lever. Suddenly, the mower started to roll downhill. I remember thinking for an instant, "Oh, boy!" and then smashing into the window of the basement pro shop. Glass rained down all around and people screamed. I wasn't hurt, but the pro shop was a mess. I've never forgotten that: "Oh, boy!" and then smash.

Beside me in court, Bunny managed to turn and smile when Mr. Moon got to the pro-shop incident.

When the lawyer reached the end of his list, he took off his glasses. He was a dark little man with shadowy olive skin. Even the top of his head had a dark, bruised look, where it wasn't covered by strands of black hair. "Those are just the *reported* incidents, your honor," Mr. Moon said. "There were others, too petty to make it into an official police report. And who knows what went on in that house that we never found out about. For five or six years there, we practically had to have an officer working full time on this family alone."

"Oh, come on," groaned Bunny.

I was afraid Judge Horner was going to throw her out, but he just asked if she wanted to comment.

"We weren't any worse than a lot of other families," Bunny said. "I know my son used to get in trouble, but so did a lot of other boys. The difference was that whenever anything went wrong in this town, the police would come knocking at our door, blaming Tom."

"Do you want to dispute any of these incidents?" the judge asked. "Mr. Moon is putting them in the record, and I'd be perfectly willing to listen to your challenges."

"Awww, what good would it do? You need a lawyer to dispute and mine isn't here."

"I've explained you don't need a lawyer in juvenile court."

"Well, he's got one." Bunny wagged her thumb at Sergeant Tony.

"Mrs. Calhoun," said the judge, raising his voice, "I'm not in the habit of arguing about something that's already been settled."

"Jeeezzz," hissed Bunny, looking away.

"Ah, perhaps we could go on," said Mr. Moon.

Judge Horner nodded.

"Your honor, I wasn't happy about the direction this case was taking even before the girl showed up last night in Banyon's Woods," the prosecutor said. "I know Mrs. O'Brien had some hope, but I frankly didn't see it. Look at the facts. We put her in a foster home and twice she goes off on a visit with her mother. Each time, they end up in a police report. What kind of a message is Mrs. Calhoun giving us?"

The lawyer paused to see if the judge would respond. When nothing happened, he went on. "The issue in this proceeding is whether the county is justified in intruding into the familial relationship. Obviously, we don't want to do that except in the most aggravated circumstances. But that's what we've got here. I look down the road and see nothing but trouble for this girl." He glanced quickly in my direction. "The question is, your honor, is the girl getting the kind of supervision and guidance at home that will ultimately be in her best interests? The answer is obviously no. Not only has Mrs. Calhoun raised one son who was a constant problem for the police and the people of this town, but when her other child gets in trouble, Mrs. Calhoun just acts more irresponsibly. She gets more reckless."

Bunny snorted and crossed her arms and legs. Her head sank into her shoulders.

The prosecutor looked down, rubbing the bridge between his eyes. When he looked up, he sighed. "Let me get it all out and on the record," he said. "I'm sorry to bring it up in front of the girl, but it's relevant to this matter. Two weeks ago, your honor, you yourself told Mrs. Calhoun to settle her affairs. Everyone in the courtroom knew exactly what you meant. Well, she hasn't settled her affairs, not by a long shot. Ever since her daughter moved out, Mrs. Calhoun has been maintaining an open and adulterous relationship with Edward Boggs. The neighbors know about it, the community knows about it, the police know about it. She stays overnight at his house, and sometimes he stays with her." The lawyer shook his head again. "It's, it's . . . it's enough to make you sick, your honor—and this, when her family is at stake."

Bunny thrashed in her chair, crossing and uncrossing her legs and shifting from one side to the other. Judge Horner asked if she wanted to say something.

"Yes, your honor. I want to say, 'So what?'" She sat up and pushed her head toward the judge. "So what? Lots of people who aren't married have friends, and what's wrong with that? I mean, we aren't in Russia here. These have been very hard times for me. First you send my son to jail. All right, so he had problems, but he was my son. And now you take away my daughter. What do you expect me to do? I felt empty, unhinged. I hated stepping into my house. Without my children, I didn't want to live there. I thought about burning it down, I really did. I needed someone to talk to, and Eddie was there. He was the only one. My mother's dead, you know." She paused. Her tongue darted out and moistened her lips. "Of course," she went on, "if my daughter comes back, I won't need Eddie anymore. I can live without him. Once Martha comes home, he's out of my life forever."

Judge Horner stared down evenly at Bunny. He had on the same checkered sports jacket that he'd worn at my first hearing. I remembered how innocent and unprotected he'd looked at the restaurant, in his white shirt and brown tie.

"Can I ask Mrs. Calhoun something?" said Mr. Moon. He was still standing.

"Certainly."

The lawyer turned to face Bunny. "Mrs. Calhoun, are you married?"

"Of course not. My husband left home years ago."

"Let me put it this way, Mrs. Calhoun. Are you divorced?"

"Well—"

The lawyer turned back to the judge. "That's adultery, your honor. What kind of example is that for a child?"

"I couldn't afford a divorce," shouted Bunny.

"All right, Mrs. Calhoun," said the judge, motioning for her to calm down. "Let's put that behind us for the time being. Let's hear from you, Mrs. O'Brien."

The social worker pushed herself up quickly from her chair. Her green shift rose and fell as her chest heaved. She looked at the judge and sighed, puffing her cheeks and blowing out air noisily. "I feel defeated, Judge Horner," she said. "There's no easy way to put it. I feel defeated."

"Go on," said the judge.

"I don't want to make excuses. The simple fact is that I haven't made any difference." She spoke in a calm, mournful voice. "Over the past two weeks, I think I've come to know these two well. Bunny Calhoun is willful and arrogant. She has little self-awareness, little understanding of the depths of her problems. But she does have a job, and she does run a household. She can function quite adequately if she puts her mind to it. Martha is basically a nice girl—a bit of a homebody, too lacking in confidence—but a good girl at heart. Her problem is that she's under her mother's sway—far, far too much under her mother's sway. She needs to become her own person, to develop her own values quite apart from her mother's. That's a serious problem, but something I felt I could deal with. Indeed, I spent hours working with both mother and daughter. We all worked hard. Bunny was difficult, but I thought progress was being made. Yesterday I even told Martha that I'd recommend that she go back with her mother." Mrs. O'Brien paused and looked fleetingly down at me. "And then I came to court today and heard about last night. I was shocked at what happened, shocked that Martha would get involved, shocked that she hadn't told me." Each time she repeated the word, the warm air in the courtroom took on an electric charge.

Mrs. O'Brien stopped to catch her breath. In talking, she'd unconsciously sidled over toward me, and now she was only inches away. With the exertion of the speech, her coldness had disappeared, and I detected a faint, warm fragrance coming off her, something not unpleasant, something close to the smell of a baby.

"What's discouraging, your honor," she went on, "is that I think I see a pattern in this family that's being repeated elsewhere. It's new and very worrisome. The Calhouns have problems, but they aren't like some families. They aren't like some families with a long history of crime and poverty and trouble. There are families I know—you do, too, Judge Horner—that you just look at and get discouraged. They simply don't have the ability to set themselves right, and you know there's nothing you can do to help. But the Calhouns are different. They're reasonably intelligent, they aren't poor. They have the ability to be an almost normal family. But they choose not to. I see this going around now, and I get very worried. It's something I never saw three or four years ago. People are choosing the wrong things. They've got the ability, they've got the opportunity, and they just choose bad over good."

Judge Horner nodded thoughtfully. "The whole country's getting that problem," he said.

"A social worker can only do so much," said Mrs. O'Brien. "You see where the trouble is, you diagnose it, you make suggestions, but you can't force people to make the right choices. In our system, people are basically on their own. And that's what we've got here, your honor. A mother who makes the wrong choices."

"So what do you recommend?" said the judge.

Mrs. O'Brien shrugged. "I think the county simply has to get more involved."

"All right," said the judge.

Reverend Vaughn suddenly stood up. "Can I say something," your honor," he asked.

"Of course."

I turned to look at the minister. Tall and assured, he seemed to provide a kind of balance to the judge. But behind him, the courtroom stretched back in row after empty row. He looked very alone.

"I must say, I'm a little bit mystified," Reverend Vaughn began. "I won't say there's been a misunderstanding, but there certainly seems to have been a . . . a loss of context here."

"Family matters *are* context," said Mr. Moon. "That's what it's all about." He looked around with bright eyes shining from his dark face.

"I realize that Martha's family has had some problems," the minister continued, "but she's smart and mature. From everything I hear, she's a fine student and, aside from this one incident, I don't think she's ever been in trouble before.

"Three incidents," said Mr. Moon.

"Three?"

"The boy and the two police reports."

"Well, I'm not sure how much credence to put—"

"Do you have any reason to doubt the accuracy of the police reports?"

"Only from what Martha has told me."

"So you're taking her word over an officer's, Father? Or, excuse me, Reverend. You'll have to excuse me, I'm a Catholic."

Reverend Vaughn turned to the judge. "Your honor, Mr. Moon keeps interrupting me. Couldn't I have a chance to say what I want without getting interrupted?"

"I'm sorry, your honor," said Mr. Moon. "I'll be quiet. It's just that I hear these things, and I feel compelled to speak up for our police department."

"Go on," said the judge.

"Well, I've never been involved in one of these proceedings before, so I'm not quite certain what standards you apply," Reverend Vaughn said. "But I listened to this long recitation of incidents involving Martha's brother and her mother's boyfriends, and I started to wonder whether Martha is being punished for problems that her family had, not for anything that she did herself."

"Oh, I can't stay quiet for that," said Mr. Moon.

"Your honor—"

"Officer Wesnofske spent twenty minutes detailing, *detailing*, what the girl had done," Mr. Moon said in a loud voice.

"Your honor." Reverend Vaughn was looking for help.

"The information about the family is relevant in these proceedings," Judge Horner said. "It helps me get the overall picture for my decision."

"Well, if you're looking for the overall picture, what about this town?" Reverend Vaughn said sharply. "The major employer is closing down. Hundreds of people are going to be out of work. And all anyone is worried about is this sixteen-year-old girl."

"What's he talking about?" said Mr. Moon.

"About opening your eyes," snapped the minister.

The prosecutor was on his feet. "Your honor, this is more of that stuff," he shouted.

"What stuff?" said the minister.

"Hold it," said the judge. "Hold it both of you." He cleared his throat. "Reverend Vaughn, the KTD isn't relevant in this proceeding. It's just not relevant. If you want to talk about it, you'll have to find another forum."

"Yes, your honor."

"Do you have anything else to say?"

The minister glared at the prosecutor. "I'd like to be able to say it without being interrupted." Mr. Moon smiled pleasantly and sat down.

"Go on," said the judge.

Reverend Vaughn reached inside his jacket and pulled out a folded piece of paper. He scanned it for a moment, then put it back. "Your honor," he said, "I'm sure that sitting in juvenile court day after day, you see some disturbing things. The relation of parent to child is not an easy one—I'd even venture to guess that the pathologies of that relationship account for almost all the cases that you get. But most of those pathologies, I'd bet, are rooted in some failure of love, some blockage in the pipeline of love between the parent and child."

Mr. Moon rolled his eyes and dropped his pencil on the table. It made a clattery noise that stopped Reverend Vaughn for a moment.

"When that love isn't flowing," the minister went on, "then it's your job—the county's job—to move in and repair the situation. That's when the authorities need to act. But what we've got here is a different situation entirely. There's love here between Martha and her mother such as I've hardly ever seen before. Martha is devoted to her mother. If anything, she's an idealization of what a loving child should be. Maybe that's too much. Maybe she should get out more, as Mrs. O'Brien says. I don't know. But to suggest that there's some failure on the part of Mrs. Calhoun, some unfitness that would justify taking Martha away—"

"He's getting into disposition, your honor," barked Mr. Moon.

"We're here for a fact-finding, Reverend," said the judge. "What you are saying may be more relevant to deciding what to do with the girl afterward."

"But the girl's relationship to her mother is relevant to the fact finding. We're talking about Mrs. Calhoun's fitness as a mother, and, by the measure of love, Mrs. Calhoun is very fit, wonderfully fit."

"What about seducing little boys?" snapped the lawyer. "Maybe she learned that from her mother, too."

"That's obscene!"

"You said it."

"All right, all right," said the judge. "Mr. Moon, I expect you to set a better example in here."

"I'm sorry, your honor, but I just don't like to let these things pass unnoted."

"Reverend, do you have anything else you'd like to say?"

Reverend Vaughn looked around the court. I remembered how flustered he'd become that time when Tom started speaking out during a sermon, how helpless he'd been when the polite world of the church was cracked in even that silly way. Now his eyes met mine, and for an instant we looked at each other like two burglars who'd been caught.

"Judge Horner, I think you'd be making a mistake if you took Martha away from her mother," he said simply.

"Thank you," said the judge.

Mr. Moon hopped to his feet. "Your honor, can I ask Reverend Vaughn a few questions?"

"Yes."

"Ah, Reverend," the lawyer said, stepping out between the tables to get a more direct line at the minister. "How long have you known Martha Calhoun?"

"Personally?"

"Yes, personally."

"Oh, I'd say I've known her personally—really well—about two weeks."

"In other words, since this incident with the Benedict boy occurred."

"Yes."

"And before this incident, did the Calhoun family ever come to your church?"

"Yes, they did. And the brother, too."

"They did. And tell me, was that more than one time, Reverend?"

Reverend Vaughn stared down at his hands folded in his lap. "At least once," he said finally, looking up at the lawyer.

"At least once, but would you say less than five times?"

Reverend Vaughn nodded. "Fewer than five times."

Mr. Moon turned back to the judge. He lifted his arm and for a moment it floated in the air, weightless, waving like a pennant in the direction of the minister. "This is the best the family can do," said Mr. Moon. His arm dropped suddenly. "That's my point."

Outside, a light rain had started to fall, and drops of water were streaking down the long, thin courthouse windows. Rainy summer afternoons have always seemed wasteful to me—a childish notion, I know, but something I've never outgrown. Now, my sense of loss expanded, opening a huge, hollow place exactly in my center. A car with speakers on top passed by the courthouse. The speakers blared a tinny message about a Republican rally on the square. A woman in the building across the street, alerted by the rain, pulled some potted plants off the window ledge, then slammed the window shut. Everything just kept on, as if nothing were happening.

At last it was Bunny's turn. She got to her feet, her hands working nervously to pull down the skirt of her dress. Her breath came in quick, hard gulps. She cleared her throat. Sergeant Tony took his chin out of his hand and swiveled to get a better look. Bunny cleared her throat again. Her eyes jitterbugged around the room. Still, she said nothing.

"Well, Mrs. Calhoun?" said Judge Horner.

Bunny shook her head. "I can't think what to say." Her voice came out so slight there seemed to be no breath behind it. In the half hour since she'd last spoken out, she'd been very still.

"Do you want to comment on this proceeding? This is your chance to talk."

Bunny stared back blankly at the judge. I realized suddenly why seeing her in that dress had made me sad. It was the dress she used to wear when she went out on dates on Sunday nights when the country club was closed. Tom and I would be in the living room, listening to the radio or playing with each other, and she'd appear in that dress. It meant she'd be leaving us, going off someplace with a boyfriend, and, for a night—a rare night when she wasn't working—other people would get to hear that voice, that laugh.

Judge Horner tried to be helpful. "There have been some serious accusations against you and the way you've raised your family," he said. "Try to respond to them, Mrs. Calhoun. Give us your side of the story."

"Everybody . . ." Bunny started and then stopped. She looked over at Sergeant Tony and Mr. Moon and then back at the judge.

"Say something," I whispered.

"I . . ." Again she stopped. She frightened me, she looked so frail. Her face was as pale as the blond hair she'd teased into lifeless waves around her head. She shrugged and slumped back down in her chair.

I reached for her hand. Her palm was covered with a cool film of moisture. I could have been squeezing an old, damp sponge.

Judge Horner waited a few seconds. "All right," he said, after a bit. "You don't have to speak." He turned to me. "How about you, Martha? Do you want to say anything?"

I shook my head. I was frightened and confused by Bunny's behavior. My mind was a jumble. I just wanted this to be over.

"Come, Martha," said Mrs. O'Brien loudly. "You must have something you want to say to Judge Horner. We've all been brought here for your benefit."

I stared down at the tabletop. To my left, Sergeant Tony whispered something to Mr. Moon. Then the lawyer spoke up. "Your honor, I think it's worth noting that Martha has never expressed the least bit of remorse about any of the events that have brought her here."

"Is that so?"

I glanced up and saw that the judge was staring at me, waiting for an answer. They were all staring. Even behind me, I felt Reverend Vaughn's eyes on my back. But I couldn't talk. It was one thing to sit there like a spectator, watching the hearing unfold as if it were happening to someone else—as it was, in a way, since it was unthinkable that I'd end up like this. But it was another thing to say something, to participate. That would put me in it, that was real.

Anyway, by then I'd caught the same muteness that Bunny had. There was nothing to say.

"You must have some explanations," said Judge Horner. "What were you doing with that little boy?" There was an edge to his tone. Dealing with these silent women was frustrating to him. It robbed the hearing of something, even I could feel that. He waited, staring. "Well, Martha?"

Bunny made a noise. She struggled to sit up straight, then made the noise again. "Judge," she was saying. "Judge."

"Yes, Mrs. Calhoun?"

"Can I have some water?" She aimed a limp finger at her mouth.

Josephine hurried out of the courtroom and returned a few seconds later with a tall glass. Bunny drank the water down without stopping, holding the glass in both hands like a baby. Handing it back, she smiled warmly at Josephine and blinked with heavy lids.

The water revived her. She sat up in her chair. A touch of pink returned to her cheeks.

"Feeling better?" asked the judge.

Bunny nodded. Suddenly, she started to talk—not the way people talk in court, but the way she does at home, when we're just sitting around, and the thoughts and sentences drift out almost unconnected. "She was a perfect child," Bunny said, "a perfect child from the moment she was born. Oh, it was a hard birth, much harder than her brother, which is strange, since the first is supposed to be the worst. I didn't even mind the pain, though. It was good in a way, you know what I mean? Good pain." She smiled at the judge. "And after she was here, she was perfect, a perfect child. She never once cried. Can you imagine?"

Josephine threw a nervous look at the judge. Mr. Moon cleared his throat. Mrs. O'Brien reached behind me and tapped Bunny on the shoulder. But Bunny kept talking. "I remember the day I brought her home from the hospital. I knew I was going to have a girl, I just *knew* it, so I'd fixed up the guest room next to mine, since I think a girl should have a room of her own, even if she's only a baby. I'd painted it pink and covered the walls with these decals of seahorses and fish and mermaids. It was sweet, an oceany kind of thing. So I brought her home and set her in the crib. It was a hot day, and all she had on were her diapers. She looked like a little roasting chicken, all naked and pink, with her arms and legs curled up. A little plucked chicken on her back there in the crib. But she was happy, so happy. All the neighbors came over to admire her, and she just looked up at everyone, looked right into their faces. You could just feel the joy she brought, you could feel it like it was something you could put your hands on. I don't think I was ever happier than that day." Bunny reached over and stroked my hair for a moment. "That's funny, isn't it? To be able to think back to your very happiest day."

Again, Mrs. O'Brien reached behind me to touch Bunny. Judge Horner waved her hand away. "There wasn't a woman who came that day who didn't tell me she was a perfect child," Bunny went on. "All of them said it, and some of them were no friends of mine, that's for sure. But they just couldn't help themselves, she was so wonderful. Of course, a mother can't take credit for her child—or at least not much. It's her flesh and blood, but a child's a gift, really, isn't it? You can't know what you're getting." She paused. "Still, I knew with Martha long before she was born that I was getting something special. Even before I was pregnant enough to show, when she was only that tiny hum deep inside, I knew."

Bunny's eyes had been wandering around the top of the courtroom, almost as if she had been reading from notes scribbled to herself on the ceiling. Now, she shifted and started speaking directly to the judge. "Afterward, your honor, you can't imagine the joy that child brought me. She was like a friend, a best friend, from the moment I brought her home. I had someone put rollers on her crib so I could wheel it around the house while I cleaned up or cooked. And then we just talked. Talked about everything. I'd be busy, but we'd just talk away for hours about any old thing that came into my head. Those were hard times for me, your honor, being a mother alone with two babies. But having her to talk to kept me in one piece, I really believe that's so. At night, I remember, her brother used to go right to sleep, but Martha would stay up with me, she just didn't want to leave me, even to go to sleep. I used to have this old radio. It had belonged to my mother, but she gave it to me for company after my husband left. Anyway, after Tom had gone to bed, Martha and I would sit up in the living room and listen to the radio. She was just a tiny little thing, but we'd sit there and listen to the news broadcasts to see how the war was going. The war was just starting then, and I knew a lot of boys who'd be fighting. Anyway, I'll always remember that. It was a bad radio, real crackly, but Martha and I would sit there together and listen every night, me on the sofa and her in the crib. Or sometimes I'd hold her in my lap. And she'd reassure me . . . I knew so many boys. . . ."

"Your honor." Mr. Moon pushed his chair back and stood up. "Your honor, I'd like to know what an old radio has to do with this proceeding."

"It's my turn to talk," said Bunny.

"You were wandering a bit, Mrs. Calhoun," said Judge Horner.

"Your honor, I think we ought to get back to the issue here," said Mr. Moon. Now that he was on his feet, he wasn't going to let Bunny run away again. "The issue is whether this young girl is in need of more supervision, and I submit the record is abundantly clear that she's not getting the type of supervision from her mother that a girl needs in these difficult times."

"What do you know?" said Bunny. "She's my daughter, and I love her more than anything."

The lawyer made a face like he'd bitten something sour. "That's not the issue, Mrs. Calhoun. The issue is whether she's getting adequate supervision."

"Love is supervision." Bunny's face was turning white again and her lower lip was starting to dance. "Love is all the supervision she needs."

"And what about last night?" said the lawyer. "Where was your love when she was off gallivanting around Banyon's Woods?"

"That was the others," said Bunny. Her voice sounded as if it were about to break. "The others did it, but she got blamed."

The lawyer took a step toward us and his arm shot out at me. "Your honor, that girl is driving this town crazy," he shouted. "She's driving the town crazy, and her mother's not doing a thing about it."

Bunny bounded up and shoved the table so hard it clattered across the floor and banged into the front of the judge's bench.

"Jesus!" said the judge.

"The hell with it," yelled Bunny. "The hell with it."

"She's nuts!" shouted Mr. Moon, jumping back.

"Please—"

"Hey!"

"Nuts!"

Sergeant Tony knocked over his chair getting to his feet. "Hey, lady!" he yelled.

Bunny stared wildly at the three men. She opened her mouth, and her lips moved silently. Finally, she made a noise. Maybe she'd wanted to say something, but it came out just a screech, a long, rasping sound that hurt just to listen to. It seemed to go on for at least a minute. Everyone waited. At last she snapped it off. She grabbed her pocketbook, whirled, and stomped down the aisle. She fumbled with the door, thinking it opened in and not out. Finally, she swung it open, stepped outside and slammed it shut. The crash echoed back through the huge, hushed courtroom.

THIRTY

"It's just craziness, that's what it is. Craziness." Mrs. O'Brien steered her station wagon along the rain-spattered streets and talked over her shoulder. "What did your mother mean—going on about having conversations with a baby? Didn't she know who she was talking to? Didn't she know where she was?"

"It's tragic," said Mrs. Vernon, from the passenger seat in front. "Simply tragic."

"And I think Judge Horner was sympathetic until the end," said Mrs. O'Brien. "He was listening, did you notice? Then all that craziness."

"Simply tragic."

The car bumped along Center Street. The windows, rolled up against the rain, started to steam over. From the back seat, I stared out through the blurry glass, half expecting to see an erect, elegant figure marching through puddles on the deserted sidewalk, her hair like a streak of sunlight breaking through the downpour.

After Bunny had banged out of the courtroom, Judge Horner sent Josephine into the corridor to find her. By the time Josephine returned empty-handed a few minutes later, the judge had prepared a small speech. "This is a sad case for me, but not a hard one," he said. "There's love here between Martha and her mother, but in six years on this bench and over three hundred cases, I've learned that love alone is not determinant, that sometimes you need more. Young people have to have guidance, discipline, examples. The world is moving too fast, with too many temptations, for us to sit by and ignore a worsening situation if we find a home that lacks those qualities."

As he talked, he looked only at Mrs. O'Brien, as if he were dealing with things so subtle and complex that only she could understand him. "The evidence I've heard," he continued, "clearly establishes that Mrs. Calhoun isn't providing adequate supervision for Martha. Despite her love for her daughter, Mrs. Calhoun refuses to make even the most basic sacrifices to straighten up her personal life. The girl is being exposed to things that are better left to adulthood. We're a small, country town here, and we don't like to push our children. But with the kind of home life Martha experienced, it's hardly any wonder that the incident with the Benedict boy happened."

Lowering his voice and speaking quickly, Judge Horner then said I was delinquent under the family law of Illinois. He told Mrs. O'Brien to prepare a report on possible dispositions, and he ordered another hearing in a week. In the meantime, I was to stay at the Vernons'. "All rise!" sang out Josephine, and we stood again. "Keep your chin up," Judge Horner said to me as he left the courtroom.

The rain drummed incessantly on the roof of the station wagon, and the women in front fell silent. Mrs. O'Brien sat forward and squinted through the windshield. I sensed she was exaggerating her concern over the condition of the road, overacting, trying to prove she really did care what happened to me. Finally, she steered the car to a stop along the curb in front of the Vernons' house and turned slowly to face me in back. "This has been the saddest day of my professional life," she said. "I feel I've failed." She paused, but the sound of the rain hurried her on. "I think you and I worked together fine, Martha, but I just couldn't reach your mother. Something about that woman was beyond me. I'm sure the failure was mostly mine." Another pause, while Mrs. Vernon shook her head. "Anyway, I'm thinking of recommending that your case be turned over to a colleague."

"If you do, we'll all miss you," offered Mrs. Vernon.

Mrs. O'Brien forced a smile. "I don't like to give up, but sometimes the fit on a case isn't right, and the best thing a social worker can do is let someone else try to help. Do you understand, Martha?"

She seemed to be speaking from miles and miles away, from a place so far away and unimportant that there was no need to respond. I jumped out of the car. The rain was surprisingly cold and beat down almost painfully, soaking my hair and blouse. Running up the walk to the house, I saw Dwayne just up the block—a wretched figure, dripping rain, standing with his bicycle under a tree.

By then, my plan was almost complete. It had probably been building in the back of my head for days, but I finally came to it as Bunny slammed shut the courtroom door. In the shock of that moment, I could feel, like a physical thing, the loss of everything I'd had. So that's the way it really is, I thought. Bunny had worried that the others were siding with me against her, but, in the end, it was Bunny who finally drew the line. She was the one who slammed the door, closing me in with them. She was the one who pulled away. After all this, that's what it had come to, I realized. Even Dwayne stood around in the rain, watching over me. Bunny just walked away. Well, if she can walk away, I thought, so can I.

In Sissy's room, I changed out of my wet things. Sitting down at the desk, I pulled some lined notebook paper out of a drawer and prepared to write Bunny a letter. The letter, too, had been building in my head, composed in bits of ideas and bunches of words even before Bunny had stomped out. Still, I had trouble getting started and sat for a long time with the blank paper spread on the desk top. I'd never written to Bunny before—maybe a note once or twice when I was playing, or a practice letter in school, but never something for real, something to keep. All that talking, all those words that had passed between us—gone, just sucked up in the air.

Finally, I wrote a sentence, then another. Looking them over, the words were clunky and wrong, nothing like what I'd say if I were just talking to her, even angry and frightened as I was. I crumpled the paper into a tight ball. I had to get this right. It would be so easy to misunderstand. Again, I wrote a few sentences on the lined sheet. They still weren't right. Words I could speak confidently, easily, knowing I could control them, seemed dangerous as shifty, black squiggles. What if she thought I didn't love her anymore? What if she thought I blamed her for all that had gone wrong? I might never see her again; this could be the last thing she knew me by. I balled up that sheet, too.

I'd been sitting there more than an hour by then. It was no use. On the next sheet of paper, I wrote: "Bunny, I'm running away. It's too hard to explain, but this is the only way. I still love you more than anything. Don't worry about me." Then I signed my name.

There wasn't an envelope anywhere in Sissy's desk, so I folded another piece of notebook paper into thirds and used Sissy's scotch tape to make an envelope of my own. I put the letter inside, sealed the envelope with more tape, and wrote Bunny's name on the front. Then I hid the paper packet in the pages of En Français.

By then, the rain had started to let up. I took out another sheet of paper and wrote out another message. This one was for Elro. I told him that if he still wanted to take me away, I'd go with him. All he had to do was come tonight to get me. I knew what I was doing, and I didn't doubt myself. Letting Butcher touch me was nothing compared to this—this was everything. There'd be no turning back. But all my life, I'd tried to be careful, tried to get along, and look what happened. I knew it was time to go the other way.

I folded the note and walked downstairs. I could hear Mrs. Vernon in the kitchen, chopping vegetables with that metronome beat. I slipped quietly out the front door and ran down the walk and up the block. A light, fine mist still hung in the air, and the leaves dripped rain. Dwayne wasn't anywhere around, but I stood under the tree where he'd been waiting. In a few minutes, he came down Oak on his bike. He stopped in front of me. His clothes were soaked, and his black hair had formed into the matted curls you see on pictures of Greek statues. He almost looked handsome. I pressed the note into his hand and told him to give it to Elro when he got a break from work at the KTD. Dwayne stared at the square of paper.

"C-c-c-can I read it?" he asked. His lips were turning blue from the chill of the rain.

"Yes."

While he held his bicycle between his legs, he carefully unfolded the lined paper and studied the side with writing on it. He moved his head back and forth, following each line of what, to him, were unknowable scratches. Finally, he smiled and folded the paper up again. "Okay!" he said.

"You won't forget? Elro Judy."

"N-n-nope." He climbed on the bicycle and pedaled furiously down Oak in the direction of the KTD.

Later, Mrs. Vernon knocked and brought a tray of food into Sissy's room. I told her I didn't want dinner, but she said she'd feel better knowing that food was there if I got hungry. She'd made a chicken salad and scooped it onto a bed of lettuce. Bright red tomato slices made a flower pattern around the plate. She put the tray down on the desk, then stood looking around nervously. It's possible she suspected something, because she didn't go through her usual ritual of straightening up.

"Do you want to pray with me?" she asked. "We can pray for your mother."

I shook my head and finally she left. Then I got into my pajamas and lay down for a few hours. At about ten, on her way to bed, Mrs. Vernon peeked in again. I told her I'd be fine. I waited another half hour and then got up and put on jeans and a blouse. I pulled the suitcase out from under the bed and packed a skirt and another blouse and some underwear. I wrapped a tissue around my toothbrush and packed that, too. The suitcase was barely a quarter filled, but I thought it was better to travel light. I'd brought a black leather purse along from home—an old purse that used to belong to Bunny and that I'd kept around for emergencies. I stuffed some tissues inside and all the money I had, around $15. Then I put the suitcase and the purse under the bed and lay down to wait.

At midnight, the whistle blew over at the KTD. Soon, a few vehicles puttered down Oak Street. I kept expecting to hear a tapping at the window, but there was nothing. An hour passed, then another. It was already after two. I couldn't bear lying down, so I got up and paced the room, walking back and forth from the door to the desk, until I realized that Mrs. Vernon might hear me. Then I flopped on the bed, lying crossways, and stared out the window. I just lay there and stared out for another hour. The night was remarkably still. The sky had cleared since the afternoon, and the rainstorm had polished the air. The stars came through sharp and bright. Across the dappled lawn, the Porters' house was sullenly blank, unbroken by any cracks of light. I hadn't seen Grandma Porter for a couple of days, I realized, but she must be all right. I would have heard if something had happened. After a while, the Porters' brown, furry cat slipped out of a shadow and padded halfway across the lawn. It stopped suddenly, sat down, and looked up at Sissy's window—spotting me, apparently, and curious to find someone awake. The cat watched me for a few minutes, but soon grew bored. It yawned and rolled its head, then slipped back into the shadows. Every now and then, a car would come down Oak Street, and my hopes would revive. But all the cars passed without stopping, and, eventually, none passed at all.

Elro wasn't coming, I decided. He might have had to go out to his father's house to pack up, but that would barely take half an hour—an hour at the most. He obviously wasn't coming. He'd obviously just been talking when he said he wanted to take me away. Now that I'd accepted the offer, now that I was really going to test his talk, he'd lost his nerve.

I squirmed and rolled on the bed. That's typical, I thought. Empty promises. I'd heard nothing but empty promises in the last two weeks. From Mrs. O'Brien, from Reverend Vaughn, even from Bunny. Promises that blew away and disappeared when the time came to live up to them. Now Elro. I should have known better. After all, he'd been drunk the times he said it. He probably didn't even remember. He'd probably looked at the note and wondered what in the world I was talking about. I pictured him there at the back gate of the KTD, standing against a post, trying to read what I'd written. Maybe he wasn't even able to read it. I saw the strain lines making circles around his eyes, his lips moving clumsily over each word. Why was that so familiar? Of course. In grade school, he'd been one of the worst readers in class, stumbling, struggling, fighting to make sense of even the simplest sentences. People would giggle—not so much because he was dumb, which he wasn't, really. They laughed because he tried so hard. An oversized, gawky, slow-talking boy, deadly serious about things the rest of us dismissed in a moment. A strange boy. He had a bullying older brother who was always pushing him, needling him, and still Elro followed the brother around, hoping for the least bit of attention. And the mother—thin and frail with the softest, gentlest voice I ever heard. I used to imagine that her words were a kind of cloth that I could reach out and run my fingers over. Mrs. Vernon said she died last year. What from? For some reason, I imagined breast cancer. Now Elro and his brother and father were alone. Alone at the Gardner place, in the tenant house, Mrs. Vernon had said. I thought of them sitting at a table, having dinner. Alone.

Like Bunny. She'd be alone, too, now that I was running away. Of course, she'd have Eddie, but that wouldn't last. Pretty soon, he'd be gone like all the others. Then the next man would come and the one after that and the one after that. But how long could it go on? She was getting older. The men wouldn't be chasing her forever. She used to joke that someday she and I would grow old together, just the two of us. She always said it with a laugh, but I could tell she was a little bit serious: Bunny and me keeping house, sharing secrets, always having each other. The idea comforted her. Of course, that's not something that I'd want. I always hoped I'd marry and have my own family. But I never stopped Bunny when she made remarks about the future that way. I guess somehow the idea comforted me, too. Now, that was all gone. I could get by. As long as I didn't get sent away, I could get by, I was sure of that. But what about Bunny? She was like a child, really. She needed someone to take care of her, to keep her out of trouble. I'd been doing that for years—almost since I could remember, I'd felt responsible for her. She was always on my mind: What was she doing? Was she okay? Did she need my help? Thinking back, I could see now that that responsibility could have been a burden, but I never resented it. I liked it, really. It made me feel important. Fussbudget. A fussbudget daughter. I was a fussbudget before my time. But who would look after Bunny once I was gone? Not Eddie, certainly. He was more of a child than she was. All her men had been children, none of them worth a thing when it came to responsibility. She'd be alone, truly alone. Like Edith, the old woman at the Buffalo Tavern. Alone and disgusting. How could I do that to Bunny? How could I leave her to that? Would her hair turn gray and frizzy, like Edith's? Would her clothes be rumpled and smelly? She'd already started to drink too much—would she turn into a solitary, slumped figure in the corner of a lonely bar? How could I abandon her to that?

My stomach was clenched up in knots, so I rolled over on my back and stretched on the bed, trying to relax myself. Elro wasn't coming, and it was just as well, I decided. This was a bad idea, one more mistake. More insanity. Worse, this was selfish. I'd be ruining Bunny, just to save myself. And what kind of life would be left for me, anyway? How far could I go with Elro? He was just a dupe, a way to get away. I'd be ruining his life, too. It was better he didn't come.

But was it really? I remembered how I'd felt in court today. I thought of Tom's letter. Running away had looked like the only solution an hour ago. I'd been so certain, I'd felt almost happy. At least I'd be *doing* something to help myself. I wouldn't just be taking it, letting them do things to me. There's something noble about taking control—even in my confusion I could sense that. Maybe suicide was the answer after all. That would be taking control. I hadn't thought of suicide since the night of the blackout, but now the idea started to seem reasonable again. I'd show Judge Horner. I'd show Mrs. O'Brien. I'd show the whole town of Katydid. I've got my pride, and I'm not going to take it.

I started making an inventory of things around the Vernons' house, trying to figure out the simplest, most painless way to do it. There weren't any pills, except for that one old vial in Mrs. Vernon's medicine cabinet—and who knew if they'd kill you. I couldn't take the chance. I'd never seen a gun in the house, and, anyway, guns scared me. I wouldn't want to end up feeling scared like that. A knife? Mrs. Vernon's knives were certainly sharp enough. Or a razor. I could even take the blade out of the razor I used to shave my legs. But think of the pain and the blood. Would I have the nerve to draw a blade deep across my wrists? There must be another way. Tom used to joke about licking the light socket. Would that really do it? I imagined myself on my knees, underneath Sissy's desk. What if it just burned my tongue? I've never heard of anyone committing suicide that way. How *did* people die? Old age, disease. Cars. That's it, I thought. A car crash. Kids are always dying in car crashes. I'll steal the Vernons' car, take it out in the country, get it going a hundred, and then aim for a tree. Just another teenage casualty. It would be so simple. Only I didn't know how to drive.

Something bumped the wall outside. I rolled over to look out the window, and Elro's face popped up. "My father wouldn't go to bed," he whispered. "He was up drinking coffee."

"That's okay." I was surprised at how glad I was to see him. I almost had an urge to throw my arms around his neck and kiss him.

"I got some money. Almost a hundred dollars."

"Great!" I scrambled off the bed and pulled out the suitcase and pushed it near the window.

"What's that?" he asked.

"My suitcase."

"That's too big. We can't get it down the ladder."

"But I've got to take some stuff."

"Find something smaller."

I looked around the room and remembered the brown Piggly-Wiggly bags that Mrs. Vernon used to line wastebaskets. Fortunately, she'd changed the one in Sissy's room just the day before. I fished out the crumpled letters to Bunny, the only things I'd thrown away. Then I took the clothes from the suitcase and stuffed them in the bag. Everything fit. I folded the top neatly.

"Hurry up," whispered Elro.

I put the money from the purse in one of my jeans' pockets, retrieved the letter to Bunny from the French book and shoved that into the other pocket. The letter would get crushed, but that was okay. I'd been barefoot all this time, and I started to put on my tennis shoes, but then I thought that my brown loafers would go with either the jeans or the skirt I was taking. So I dug the loafers out of the closet and slipped them on. For a moment, I stood by the bed and let my gaze circle the room. I'd been there two weeks—two weeks of staring at Jesus statues, at the world's ugliest wallpaper, at things that a dead girl had touched, slept on, lived in. Two weeks, and already the place seemed almost normal and safe.

"Come on," hissed Elro.

I climbed onto the bed and handed him the bag. He backed partway down the ladder. I leaned out. This wasn't going to be easy. The ladder stopped two feet below the window ledge, and somehow I had to get to the top rung. I pushed the window open as far as it would go and sat on the sill, so I could dangle my legs along the wall. Scrunching down to get into the space of the window, though, I couldn't get my legs outside.

"I'm too big," I whispered.

Elro came back up the ladder. "Maybe you should just sneak out the front," he said.

"Mrs. Vernon would hear me."

"Then you're gonna have to back down."

I turned around, lying face down on the bed. Luckily, the bottom of the window was just a few inches higher than the mattress. Wiggling back slowly, I pushed my legs out the window, scraping my shins on the metal ribbing. I couldn't see, but I knew my legs were sticking straight out into the air, fifteen feet above the ground. It was frightening, but not entirely unpleasant. Moving backward like this, pushing painfully against the windowsill, I had a strange sensation of something difficult and uncertain and yet somehow exhilarating. Was this what having a baby was like, shoving off blindly into the unknown?

Moving slowly, I maneuvered my waist over the sill; my legs finally bent down toward the ladder. Elro reached up and grabbed my ankle, guiding me. I still clung to the sill, but soon I was balanced with both feet on a top rung. This was going to be all right. Elro let me catch my breath, and then, still holding my ankle, he guided my right leg down an additional rung. I let go of the sill and let my hands slide down the scratchy shingles on the side of the house until I could grab the top of the ladder. I took another breather and stepped down again.

"Stop!" hissed Elro. Behind us, a light had flicked on suddenly, throwing our shadows against the side of the house. "Someone's up," he whispered.

We stood on the ladder without moving. The light had come from the Porters' house across the lawn. I waited a minute—waited for a voice to shout, a door to slam, a phone to ring. Nothing. Finally, I turned and crouched, peering under a low, heavy branch of the oak. I found myself looking into the eyes of Grandma Porter. She was pressing her face up against the window, the way a child does on the morning of the year's first snowfall. Her jaw moved slowly, worrying, but otherwise she just stared.

"It's okay," I whispered to Elro.

"But she's watching us."

"Just keep going."

"What's she want?"

"Just go."

I started backing down toward him and Elro again moved down the ladder. At the bottom, he let his hand slide up my back as I stepped off onto the lawn. The ground was soft from the rain, and the grass felt cool and damp. He handed me my bag and picked up the ladder. Side by side, we moved silently around the house, all the time under Grandma Porter's silent gaze.

Elro had parked his pickup a block up the street. I threw my bag on the seat and climbed in. The truck wasn't new, but Elro and his brother had kept the cab neat. The seat was patched in spots with pieces of green canvas. A clean rubber mat covered the floor. Someone had attached a little plastic cow to the dashboard in the place where people put statues of Jesus.

"Where's your luggage?" I asked, after Elro had climbed in.

"In back."

I looked through the rear window. Besides the ladder, the only thing in the truck was a small, battered suitcase—actually, it wasn't any bigger than a briefcase. The handle had been replaced by a few strands of rope. Even compared to my Piggly Wiggly bag, it seemed a thin, pathetic way to start an adventure.

Elro was still feeling spooked by Grandma Porter. "Do you think she'll tell anyone?" he asked.

"No. Now drive me to Bunny's."

"There? Why there?"

"I have something to drop off."

He glided the truck down Oak, then left on Charles, and back up Sycamore. No one else was around. The streets, with their ceilings of leaves and lamplight, were deep, quiet tunnels. Elro stopped about fifty feet from Bunny's driveway and I got out and walked in the grass so as not to make any scuffing noises. The house was dark. It's the smallest house on the block, just a box really, plopped in the middle of an unruly yard. Tiptoeing over the lawn, I thought of the summer days I'd spent playing on this patch of ground. Tom and I would be let out like ponies, and we'd only come in for lunch and dinner. There was the glittery, gray rock—bottomless, since we'd never been able to dig it up—on which Tom had cracked his head open; the spot near the stoop where we'd held a burial service for a mouse Bunny had caught; the circle worn permanently bare from being home base. Now, even the grass over home was luxuriant, almost to my ankles. I'd mowed the lawn the day before I went to the Benedicts', and Bunny probably hadn't thought of it since.

At the front door, beside the three concrete steps, I paused for a moment to listen, not really sure what I'd hear—the familiar creaks and groans of the walls, perhaps, or the clunk of the refrigerator revving up to cool itself off. Voices, maybe—some assurance. But the house was dead quiet. I lifted up the mail slot in the bottom of the door and silently dropped in my letter.

THIRTY - ONE

When I got back to the pickup, Elro was drinking out of a bottle, and the medicine smell of whiskey filled the cab.

"I swiped this from my old man," he said. He thrust the bottle toward me. The whiskey inside looked black. "You want a drink?"

I shoved it away. "You shouldn't drink if you're going to drive."

"I'm used to it." He started the truck and let it roll quietly past Bunny's house. "Where should we go?" he said.

"I thought you had a place."

"No place special." He took another gulp from the bottle. He was holding it with one finger crooked around the neck, and he tilted his head back when he drank, as if swigging from a jug. "What about Chicago?" he said.

I remembered Mrs. O'Brien's story about the girl who'd run away to Chicago with her boyfriend. Chicago sounded remote and dangerous. "How about Wisconsin?" I suggested. "You mentioned Wisconsin once."

"Yeah! Wisconsin. I been fishin' there." He guided the truck down East Morgan and turned onto the deserted square. A few spots of all-night neon enlivened the storefronts but only made the place look emptier. The tall concrete Civil War monument, a lone soldier with a rifle, stood out in the center of the park like a black, hulking scarecrow.

"Why'd you come to the square?" I asked.

"Don't know. Just habit, I guess."

"Well, let's get going. I want to get out of here."

"Yeah, yeah, take it easy." Gulping another drink of whiskey, he misjudged a corner, and the truck's tires screeched over the concrete.

"Elro!"

"Shit." The beams of a car's headlights suddenly swept onto the square. The car hurried and came right up behind the pickup. "Cops," whispered Elro.

Looking back, I could see the bubble on top. "Go slow," I said. Then, remembering the trouble Bunny had had on Sunday, I added, "But not too slow."

"Shit," said Elro again. He was rattled and kept looking back over his shoulder at the police car.

"Don't turn around," I said. "They'll suspect something."

"Shit."

As we looped around the square, the police car stayed behind us, its headlights bathing the cab of the truck in brightness. "That old lady must have called them," said Elro. "I knew she was trouble."

"Calm down. Just turn off."

"Where?"

"Anywhere."

We passed the old, boarded-up Ward's building, a somber black wall, and Elro turned right on South Harrington. Suddenly, the cab was dark again. The police car continued on around the square.

"Now we're going the wrong way." I said.

"Huh?"

"We're headed south. Wisconsin is north."

"Just shut up for a minute," Elro said. "Just shut up and let me think."

"Okay."

"Shut up." He drank some more whiskey and wiped his mouth with the back of his hand.

The excitement of escaping had given me a temporary lift, but now the dread came back, a deep familiar ache. For a moment, I imagined that I was trapped in this pickup with Elro, that I was condemned forever to glide the streets of Katydid, pursued by the police.

"The Dells," said Elro. He sounded calmer.

"The Dells?"

"The Wisconsin Dells. I've always wanted to go there."

261

"Okay." Better humor him, I thought. Keep him calm.

"Ride the ducks."

"What?"

"Ducks. They've got these amphibious vehicles called ducks. They go anyplace—on land or water. They're left over from World War Two. You see billboards for them all over Wisconsin. I always wanted to ride one."

"Sure." Was he drunk already?

"Anyway," he added, "there's lots of people there. No one'll ever notice us."

Suddenly, I realized Elro was right. The Dells was the perfect place for us—a big tourist attraction, with people coming and going all the time, lots of kids around, a favorite date spot. We'd blend right in. Why, we could probably even get work. Me as a waitress, and Elro— well, maybe in a gas station or something. The Dells was perfect.

"Great," I said. "That's a great idea."

He looked at me and smiled. "We'll get a motel room."

"Okay," I said, and I turned to stare out the window as the houses of Katydid passed in the darkness.

We drove for an hour. Elro said he was afraid the police might come after us, so he took an out-of-the-way route, zigzagging north on gravel roads and dodging even the smallest towns. We hardly saw another car. As the miles ground on, I started to think how easy it had been—escape had been little more than a matter of deciding to do it. Aside from the soul-searching, there was no trauma, not even much tension. Now here I was on the other side, and I didn't feel different. It was a bit of a letdown. I guess I'd been expecting a burst of courage, or an outflowing of passion, or a new, frightening guilt— something to confirm that I'd taken a momentous step. Instead, there was nothing. If anything, I was a little bored by the trip so far.

A pale film of purple appeared along the horizon. "Sun," grunted Elro, as if he'd just learned the word. He'd finished almost half the bottle, and, though his driving still seemed steady, the liquor had made him talkative. On and on he went, mostly about cars and trucks, about cams, piston rods, bearings, fuel pumps. And ducks. He kept returning to the ducks. Once he told me that the ducks had won the war for America, that they'd been the critical factor in a crucial battle. The Germans had retreated to a river somewhere. They'd crossed over on a bridge and then blown the bridge up, thinking they'd ensured their escape. But then an army of ducks came scudding up to the riverbank and swam right across to the other side. The Germans were surprised and defeated.

"You sure about that?" I asked.

"Of course I'm sure." He frowned, unhappy that I'd doubted him.

After a few seconds, his face brightened again. "You know, this thing will do ninety, ninety-five when I really goose her up," he said, patting the dashboard of the pickup. "My brother and me bored out the engine so the thing's faster 'n most cars."

"Yeah?"

"Yeah. You want to see?"

"Not really."

"Watch." He stomped on the gas pedal. The pickup paused for a second and reared back, as if taking a breath, then shot forward with an animal roar. "Whoooo-eee!" yelled Elro. The back end skidded sideways on the gravelly road.

"Don't!"

"See?" His face was flushed. "See what I mean?" He let up on the gas, and the truck straightened out. "If some cop wanted to chase us, I'd give him a hell of a ride."

When we were back to normal speed again, I said, "What do you think they'd do if they caught us?"

"I tell ya, they wouldn't catch us in this thing." Again, he touched the dashboard, this time stroking it gently. His hand was broad and thick, with stubby, coarse fingers. I found myself staring at it. I couldn't imagine being touched, or, worse, held by that hand. It was like something not designed to come into regular contact with other people, like a boot, a heavy leather boot. I thought of Reverend Vaughn's slender, delicate hand, and my stomach burned. Running away wasn't that easy after all.

"They'll have to shoot us," said Elro.

"Shoot us?" The smooth, dark fields were coming clear in the sunrise. The horizon was now splashed with orange.

"Yeah. The law says you can shoot fleeing felons. We're fleeing felons."

"Fleeing felons?"

"Yeah."

"We're just kids."

"Don't make no difference. They shoot fleeing felons all the time."

263

"Where'd you hear that?"

"I heard it."

I turned to him, but avoided looking at his hands. "You've got a lot of stupid stories in your head, you know that? You're like an old man who believes in superstitions and ghosts."

"I just remember things." He picked up the bottle and thrust it toward me. The whiskey sloshed inside. "Sure you don't want some?"

I shook my head. "Let's talk about something else, something besides cars," I said.

He swigged from the bottle. "Like what?"

"Oh, I don't know." I thought for a moment. "Remember how in fourth grade, Mrs. Kirkpatrick used to talk about her pets all the time, how she'd spend half the morning telling what her cat did the night before? We were supposed to start the day with current events, but she just talked about her cat or her dog. And she had a parakeet, right? She brought it to school once. I used to time her. Once she talked all the way up to the first recess. Remember?"

"Nah, not really." Elro's face had sunk into a pout. "I didn't like her much."

"Really?"

"Nah."

"Why?"

"I just didn't."

We fell into silence. "Oh, I know what I wanted to ask you," I said after a while. "Did you really go out with Sissy? That seems kind of strange to me."

"What a bitch." He made a noise, half laugh, half grunt.

"I thought you liked her."

"She liked me, you mean. She wanted it."

"Don't be crude. Anyway, she was a religious fanatic."

"That don't mean she don't get urges. Everybody does. My brother used to mow the lawn out at the convent, and he says they won't even let the nuns order bananas there."

"Ugh! Shut up."

"It's true."

This was hopeless. Elro started humming to himself and drumming with his fingers on the whiskey bottle.

"But still," I said, more to get him to stop humming than to keep up the conversation, "her mind was so full of Jesus that she wouldn't have had time to think about things like that."

"A lot you know."

For some reason, hearing him talk that way, I felt offended for Sissy. "You really ought to be more considerate, Elro," I said. "After all she went through—dying and everything."

"Hah!" he took another drink.

"Why'd you laugh?"

"I didn't laugh. I said, 'Hah!' "

"Why'd you do that? That's cruel."

"She didn't die. She drowned."

"I know that. I was there. It was awful."

"I was there, too. I drowned her."

I waited a few seconds. "What are you saying?" I asked. "That's crazy."

"I drowned her. She was botherin' me, so I drowned her. Tough." He drank again from the bottle. "Tough, tough, tough."

"How can you say that? How can you even think to say it? That's the ugliest thing I've ever heard."

"It's true."

I turned to get a better look at him, shifting until the door handle pressed into my back. He kept his eyes straight ahead, locked on the path of the pickup's headlights. For a second, I imagined his eyes *were* the headlights.

"You're just drunk," I said, though he seemed more sober than he'd been for miles.

He shrugged. I watched his face for a while. The whiskey had covered his lips with a moist film that gave off a glinty shine in the darkened truck. "You know what a cock-tease is?" he asked.

"Of course."

"Well, she was a cock-tease."

"She was not. Anyway, a lot of girls do that."

"I didn't like it. She kept leadin' me on and then stoppin', over and over, the same thing. She didn't know what she wanted."

I thought of her in her silly bangs and ankle-length dresses, always carrying her books in front like a shield. What she wanted had always seemed so simple and pathetic.

"Elro, you're upsetting me."

"Can't help it. You asked, and I told you."

"But wait a minute. We were all at the pond the day she died. Someone would have heard her scream."

"Nobody did." He was like Eddie in his pleasure in direct, plain answers that told you nothing.

I thought for a second. "How'd you do it, then? I want to know."

"Simple. I took her out beyond the float when no one was around, and I told her I was tired of waitin'. Then I put my hand down her suit and told her if she screamed, I'd hold her under. When she started to scream, I held her under, just like I said. I figured she'd let up and go along with me, but she just kept fightin' until . . ." Elro looked at me and the corners of his mouth twitched up in a smile.

I didn't say anything for a long time. My chest was starting to heave, so I pulled my arms tight around myself. "I don't believe it. You're drunk," I said finally.

"Am not." He swigged again. "She was cock-teasin' me. A man's got certain needs, and you mess with those needs, and who knows what can happen."

"You're lying."

"You don't have to believe me."

"Elro, you tell me you're lying or I'm gonna jump out of this truck."

He braked sharply, slamming me against the dashboard. My left wrist hurt from bracing my impact.

"So get out," he said. "But I ain't lyin'."

The truck had stopped along the side of the road. In the half light, I could see a ditch and, beyond that, a field of low-growing plants. Elro wagged his head at me. Now I could see the effects of the whiskey. His mouth was hanging open, and his eyes were wild. He reached over and poked me in the shoulder with his finger.

"Ouch."

"So you still think I'm lyin'?" He poked me hard again.

"Cut it out."

"What's the matter?"

"I'm getting out."

"Go ahead," he said. But I didn't trust him. He was too twitchy and excited, too dangerous.

"Go ahead," he taunted. "What are you waitin' for?" His lips were wet, his eyes were BBs, rolling around in his head, but always settling back on me.

I worked my right hand slowly to the door handle and sneaked my left hand under my bag of clothes. Suddenly, I gaped out the window. "Look! A cop!" I yelled, and in that instant, I was out the door, pulling away from his clawing fingers. I ran down the side of the ditch and took a leap across the bottom, hoping to make it in one bound. My foot sank in mud up to the ankle. I pitched forward, keeping my balance by splashing down with the other foot into a worn-out stream that was trickling through the weeds. The truck door slammed. Elro was coming. Leaning forward, I hauled my left foot out and planted it, dripping muck, on drier ground in front. Still, my right foot was sinking. With a heave, I pulled forward and shot free, stumbling onto the bank on the other side. But something was wrong. I'd lost my shoe. My right foot had slipped out, and now the loafer was buried under six inches of mud.

There wasn't time to fish for it. Elro had walked around in front of the truck and was standing in the beams of the headlights, squinting in my direction. "Wait up!" he yelled thickly. Seeing me pause, he scrambled down the ditch after me.

With the weeds stabbing into my bare foot, I ran up the other side and slipped through the loose strands of barbed wire on the fence at the top. Before me was a pink-purple sea, a field planted in clover. The soft moist leaves felt soothing on the bottom of my scraped-up foot. I ran a few steps into the field and stopped to take off my other shoe. Elro had given up and was slowly climbing back to the pickup. I started running again. The clover was cool and downy and the stems slid in between my toes, tickling up a wave of excitement, as if I were doing something terribly fun but wrong. I ran for fifty yards, a hundred yards, until my chest was pounding, and my Piggly Wiggly bag seemed weighted with cans. Finally, I stopped and drew deep gulps of air. The opposite edge of the field was still far off, marked by a long ridge of trees that turned the sun's rays into orange spikes. Close by, a handful of small, graceful birds darted over the clover, their morning songs rippling the air.

Back at the pickup, Elro was framed by the headlights. Bending down, one arm braced against the hood, he was retching in agony. Every few seconds, the deep, rasping sound rolled across the field, answering the clear lilt of the birds. His body shook. It was painful to watch him. By now, he'd emptied everything and was just having spasms. After a while, I sat down in the clover. He went on for about ten minutes, passing through periods of calm before the agony hit

267

him again. At last, he was quiet for a long time. He slumped against the fender of the truck, and his head drooped down over his chest, as if his neck were a long, loose rope. Eventually, he straightened up, got something out of the cab and walked around to the back of the truck, away from where he'd been sick. He stood on the edge of the ditch, looking out over the field. He couldn't see me, and after a few seconds he called out my name. His voice was high and weak from all the wretching. I just sat and waited and listened. He called again and again. Shading his eyes from the early sun, he searched methodically from one side of the vast field to the other. It must have been terrible for him, like looking out at a sea into which someone had disappeared.

"Martha!" he yelled.

I waited.

"Martha, come back!" He sounded like a little boy. "Martha!"

What was I to do? I had hardly any money, no place to go, no way to get anywhere, and only one shoe. Even the short run had exhausted my panic, and now there was something touching in hearing my name called like that. I took a deep breath and stood up. He saw me across the clover and waved. Now we were really in this together, I thought. Once you cross the line, the biggest misfit, the worst outlaw is your ally. Who else do you have? Walking back, I paused to snap off a clover stem and chew on the sweet flower. Already, the sun slanting over the horizon felt hot on my neck. Anyway, I thought, I'm not scared of Elro. I knew I could cope, even if Sissy couldn't. Poor Sissy—maybe she really was a cock-tease, though I'm sure she didn't even know what the word means. She probably just got hit with some strong feelings. Even out there in Jesus-land, you can't escape the feelings. Elro may have been right—she wanted it, but she didn't, she was pulled both ways. Well, that wasn't my problem. Getting frightened and running had cleared my mind. I owed Elro one. He'd helped me escape, and now he had a right to collect. I'd pay off, at least once. Sorry, Sissy, I thought, but nothing I can do will bring you back.

"That was stupid," said Elro, as I clambered up the bank to the pickup. His hair was damp from sweat, and he was chewing a giant wad of gum.

"I lost my shoe."

He turned his back and walked around to the cab. "Serves you right."

I had to step over the vomit to get in the truck. "It wasn't as stupid as drinking half a bottle of whiskey," I said.

He started the pickup off hard, kicking up dust and gravel. "It only happened 'cause I had to run. If you hadn't got crazy, I'd've been fine."

A few miles down the road, he picked up the bottle with what was left of the whiskey in it and flung it sidearm out the window. "There," he said.

THIRTY-TWO

We bumped along for the next hour or so, and Elro didn't say much. There were fields all around and occasionally a farmhouse, but the country was wilder than around Katydid, or if not wilder, at least less fussed over. The fields were bigger, and they were separated by tangled patches of woods so dense you couldn't see more than a few feet into them. In the distance, tree-covered hills poked out of the flatness like mountains. Crossing streams, we'd drive over rickety bridges made of lumber that buckled and clattered under the weight of the truck. Once, near a barn, we had to stop while a boy steered a herd of brown cows across the road to a pasture. The boy was about twelve, and he was wearing overalls and carrying a broom handle that he rapped on the ground to keep the cows in line.

"Mornin'," he said to Elro after the last lumbering cow had crossed in front of us.

"Mornin'."

"You goin' to town today?" The boy stood beside Elro's window. His hair was the color of straw and stuck up in tufts on his head.

"You better watch your cow there," Elro said. The last heifer had missed the gate and was following the grass down the side of the road. The farm boy took off after the animal.

"Hee-awww!" he yelled, waving his stick and circling around to head the cow off. "Hee-awww, baby!"

Elro waited for the straggler to be walked into the pasture and then started out slowly, so as not to spook the herd.

"Thanks," called the boy, saluting with his stick. "Maybe I'll see you in town."

By now, the sun was above the trees. We started passing men on tractors, and we passed one man riding a wagon pulled by a horse.

"Are we in Wisconsin?" I asked.

"Guess so."

"Do you know where we are?"

"Maybe."

"It's so rural."

"So."

As we drove along a cornfield, my eyes ticked off each perfect row, stretching into a green infinity. It was hypnotizing, and I had to pull myself away.

"Elro, I'm sorry that I ran away back there," I said.

He grunted, not looking at me.

"I'm sorry about that, but there's still something I have to ask you, okay?"

He said nothing. His face was gray and droopy, as if the skin were sliding off.

"Okay?"

"What's that?" he muttered.

I took a breath. "When Sissy drowned—afterward—didn't you feel bad? I mean, even I felt guilty. Didn't you feel—when you thought about it—didn't you feel a little bit bad?"

A fine yellow dust had settled on the windshield, and Elro started the wipers to clear the glass. He watched as the worn rubber blades left streaks of dust that stayed there, defying the wipers as they swept again and again over the same course. Finally, he shut the wipers off. "No," he said.

We came to the outskirts of a town, probably the one the farmboy had talked about. We passed a square brick high school sitting surrounded by a lawn of unshaded brown grass. At a feed store, a line of wagons and trucks was already backed up against a loading dock. A sign said MINNIEFIELD POP. 707.

"Let's get some food," said Elro.

"I need a pair of shoes."

"First food."

The town was just a treeless strip of road, with a few buildings on

271

either side and a railroad crossing at the far end. Everything was painted white and, under the bright sun, the buildings gave off a hard shine, like bleached bones.

Elro parked along the sidewalk beside several other pickups and just down the street from an untended horse and wagon. The straps from the horse's harness were tied around the parking meter. The horse's head was down and he was snorting around in the dust in the gutter. Elro went on ahead, but I stopped in front of the horse. I'd taken off my remaining shoe and was standing in my bare feet on the hot concrete sidewalk. The horse's nose looked cool and velvety and, without thinking, I stuck my foot out and ran my big toe down it. The horse shook his head quickly, and his long tongue lolled out and licked the bottom of my foot. I looked up and down the street. Aside from some children playing on the sidewalk on the other side, the street was empty. So I offered up my other foot. The horse obliged again, sending shivers down my back.

Minniefield had one restaurant, Coogan's Dinette, which faced the street with two dark windows made of small panes of glass. A bell connected to the screen door tinkled when I went in, and a half dozen customers—all men—looked up from their coffee and eggs. A counter with stools ran along one side, and fifteen or so small tables were scattered across a dark wood floor. Elro was sitting at a table in the corner, studying a cardboard menu.

"I hope no one notices my bare feet," I said softly when I sat down.

"Keep 'em under the table."

"Do you suppose the police have put out a bulletin about us yet?"

"Shut up."

A waitress in a white smock came out of the back and sauntered over. "So this is your friend," she said to Elro. She held her head back and laughed with an overloud, wet sound. "It's a little early in the day for a date, isn't it?" She was about Bunny's age, but way too made up, with her hair twisted into a loose knob and flaky powder covering old acne scars on her cheeks.

Elro mumbled something and stared harder at the menu. The waitress bent down between us and spoke in a whisper. "Well, if you kids are elopin', don't worry, 'cause your secret is safe with me." She nodded at each of us in turn. "I had an offer to elope when I was sixteen, and I turned it down, and I've been stuck here ever since. Been stuck in a town that don't know nothin'." She pointed to her ring finger, which was bare. "Of course, I've had other offers," she said to me, "but nothin' to take me away from here."

"I'll have fried eggs and pancakes," said Elro.

The waitress straightened up. "And milk, lots of milk," she said, winking at me.

"We ain't elopin'," Elro said.

"Listen to him." The waitress cocked her knob of hair at Elro. "You stay out all night, and you're elopin', that's for sure. You may not know it yet, but you're elopin'. Wait 'till you try to take that pretty girl back to her daddy. Then you'll see what I mean." She shook her head and leaned over me. "Ain't I right, honey?"

Her dress fell away in front, and I could see a small ball of cotton stuffed between her breasts. The cotton had been soaked in perfume, and the sweet, heavy fragrance curled up around my head, tugging at me like a rope. I sat back. "Tea and toast," I sputtered.

She laughed again. "Don't worry, I told you your secret is safe with me." Still laughing, she turned and walked away, shaking her head.

"What was that all about?" I whispered to Elro.

He shook his head.

"Are we that obvious?"

"Shut up."

The food perked him up. He ate a big plate of eggs and pancakes and drank lots of milk, since the waitress kept coming back to refill his glass. His color returned, and his eyes came alive. Eventually, he started talking again.

"Can't wait to get to the Dells," he said. "They got great stuff there, caves and things."

"Great." It cheered me to see him brightening.

"And, first thing, we'll take a tour on a duck."

"Great."

"I'm not really tired, you know. Been up all night but I'm not really tired."

"Me neither."

"We'll stay there tonight."

"Great." Tonight. It seemed so far way it might never come. I wouldn't think about it.

"Ride the ducks," said Elro, mopping a spot of egg yoke with a last piece of pancake.

The doorbell tinkled, and everyone looked up. A fat policeman in a broad-brimmed hat and blue uniform stood in the entrance. He nodded a few greetings, then walked over and sat at the table next to ours, setting his hat on the extra chair. His stomach pushed out against his shirt, exposing a small, hairy triangle of skin just above the belt buckle.

Elro stiffened and searched the room for the waitress. "Let's pay," he said. He took a worn leather wallet from his back pocket and set it on the table. From the corner of my eye, I could see that the cop was studying us. Elro squirmed and shoved his wallet around the table. The waitress had disappeared somewhere in back.

"It looks like it's going to be hot again today," I said, trying to make conversation to calm Elro.

"Yeah." Elro ran his hands down the sides of his jeans and rocked up and back.

"Good for the corn." The cop was still staring, so I turned to him and smiled. He had a wide, soft face, plain and unemotional. He nodded.

Finally, the waitress banged out of a door in back carrying a tray of plates. She distributed the food at a table on the other side of the room and then bustled over with coffee for the cop.

"Want something this morning, Stan?" she asked.

"Just coffee."

"Yell if you change your mind." She started to walk away.

"Hey!" said Elro, grabbing the hem of her smock. "We wanna pay."

"All right, all right, but what's your hurry? You got the whole day ahead of you."

The bill came to sixty-five cents. Elro counted the coins out of a pocket in his wallet.

"Don't forget the tip," I whispered.

He frowned and took out another nickel. We both stood up to leave.

"Say, buster, come here," the cop said.

Elro froze. His back formed a taut arc, and his arms were locked in strange angles at his sides. The cop was between him and the door, but I could sense that Elro was figuring the odds, betting he could sprint around the table and be out the door before the cop was out of his seat. What about me, though? I was already close enough to be within grabbing distance. If Elro bolted, I'd be trapped. Reaching out,

I snatched Elro's hand. "Come on, dear," I said, trying to sound peppy. "It's only a policeman."

Elro lifted his arm hopelessly, as if discovering that the fingers twisting through his were an iron chain. Then we shuffled the few feet over to the cop's table.

"There somethin' wrong, buster?" the cop demanded. He talked by jiggling his cheeks. His lips hardly moved.

"No."

" 'Cause if there's somethin' wrong, we want to know about it."

"No, sir, nothin' wrong."

"Well, you come here then." The cop crooked his finger to draw Elro closer. "That's right, let go your girlfriend there for a second."

Elro looked at me and dropped my hand, then took a halting step toward the table. The cop hoisted himself up a few inches. He spoke under his voice. "You tell your girlfriend that we've got an ord-nance in this town that says people gotta wear shoes in public extablish-ments. Tell her that if she comes in here again, she better cover up her pretty toes."

"Yes, sir," said Elro.

"Got that?"

"Yes, sir."

The waitress came up again with a fresh pot of coffee. "Are you botherin' these nice kids, Stan?" she asked. "Now, you just let them be."

"I was just tellin' the girl here that she better learn to wear shoes in a extablishment like this."

The waitress stared at my feet. They looked huge and shamefully pink against the scuffed wood of the restaurant's floor. I felt as if I were in one of those dreams where you suddenly realize you've arrived at school wearing your pajamas. "Why, you're a regular poet," the waitress said.

"Whaddaya mean?" demanded the cop.

"See?" she said to me. "I told you this town don't know nothin'." She shooed us away. "You kids run along. Leave us old folks to argue."

"Why a poet?" huffed the cop, his cheeks jiggling.

Outside, Elro grabbed me by the elbow and pulled me toward the truck.

"Wait," I said. "I've got to get shoes." My embarrassment in the restaurant had punctured my confidence. I could have cut off my feet at the ankles.

"Not now, we gotta get out of here." He continued to pull me along the sidewalk.

I shook my arm free. "I'm not leaving without shoes. It's your fault I lost my others, and I'm not going barefoot anymore."

"Jesus!" Elro stomped over to the truck and jumped into the cab, slamming his palm down on the steering wheel. Behind me, the waitress rapped on the restaurant window. She'd apparently witnessed our scene, and now she shook her head knowingly. The knob of hair flopped back and forth above her.

I turned and scurried down the sidewalk in search of a place to buy shoes. In a two-minute walk, I passed a grocery, a tavern, a hardware store, another tavern, and a tiny post office whose front was almost covered by two gigantic white columns. Beyond the post office came several boarded-up buildings, a vacant lot, and, at the end of town, a wood building whose whitewashed walls had weathered into the dirty, smudged color of old snow. Stenciling on the window said DEMARZO'S DEPARTMENT STORE. Kitty-corner across the street, a sign on a brighter, newer building said FINNEGAN'S FIVE AND DIME. But the children I'd noticed before were playing in front, and I didn't want to walk past them in my humiliating bare feet. So DeMarzo's was it.

Inside, the lighting was dim. I didn't see anyone around and wandered down one aisle. Away from the front, the air was stale. Dry goods were stacked on the shelves in neat piles that looked as if they hadn't been disturbed in years. I picked up a man's white dress shirt packed in a clear plastic envelope. The envelope had gathered a coating of dust, and the shirt inside was turning faintly yellow, like an old photograph.

At the far end of the aisle, a door opened into a small room with a rumpled sofa pushed against the wall. "Anybody here?" I called out, and to my left a voice suddenly crackled. Tucked in a corner of the store, an old woman was sitting in a ladder-back chair. Her dress was a shapeless mass of black, and she was sitting with her thighs apart, resting one hand on a cane.

"Hello," I said. "I'm looking for shoes."

"Got shoes," she said, speaking with a strong accent. "Lotta shoes." She pointed with her cane to the wall nearby, where one whole section was taken up with shoeboxes. I went over to have a look. The boxes, too, had yellowed with age. I started flipping through them, looking for shoes that might fit, but all I could find were men's shoes, black and brown and all very plain.

"No, no," said the woman. Pushing herself up with her cane, she rose to her feet. I saw that she was extraordinarily short, the top of her head barely came to my chest. She shambled over and again using her cane, she poked at my feet, taking the measure of them. Then she bent slowly at the waist and pulled a box from the bottom shelf. "Here," she said. Cradling the box on her hip, she took off the top. Inside, unprotected by any tissue paper, two ankle-high black shoes nestled against each other like napping puppies. The shoes appeared to be made of some thin, shiny material, and black, wiry laces ran up and down the fronts.

"Try, try," she said.

I lifted one out. Though it must have been sitting there for decades, the shoe was in perfect shape. The leather sole was stiff, but flexible. There was a short, thick heel. The woman didn't seem concerned that I was barefoot, so I sat in a nearby chair and slipped the shoe on. It was narrow, but the right length. I laced it up over my ankle.

"Fit good," the woman said.

"Yes."

"Very fine shoes, very beautiful. The beautiful women, they wear this shoe."

"I can imagine." I turned my ankle round and back, studying the effect. In fact, the shoe was ugly, I thought. It was grim and indelicate, and it looked preposterous on me. The high, blunt top came to the cuffs of my jeans. Still I liked having the shoe on. I felt sort of honored, as if I'd been entrusted with something treasured and pure.

"It's ancient!" I said.

"Made good," said the woman. "These new, they break." She swung her cane to indicate the rest of the contents of the store.

I ran my fingers up and down the shoe's silky sides. "How much."

She considered for a moment. "Five dollar."

Five dollars. I only had fifteen. This was ridiculous. I couldn't walk around the Dells in a pair of shoes like that. I couldn't walk anywhere without everyone noticing.

"Made good," she said again.

"I'm sorry, I need something newer. And cheaper." I quickly took off the shoe and handed it back.

"Okay." She stared at the wall of boxes and reached up with her cane to tap one above her head. "You get," she said.

The box contained a pair of orange canvas espadrilles with rubber bottoms. The shoes looked a little unstylish, but they weren't antiques. I put on one, then the other, and took a few steps. They fit fine.

"How much?"

"Three dollar."

"Okay."

Wearing my purchase, I followed her to a counter along the wall and took three dollar bills out of my pocket. She rang them up in a mountainous cash register.

"Summer shoes," she said, smiling and indicating the espadrilles. "Summer and fun."

"I know," I said. I thanked her and walked outside. The new rubber soles squeaked with every step. Part way down the sidewalk, I stopped. I could see Elro up ahead, sitting in the cab of the truck, staring blankly down the street. I watched him for a moment, then I went back into DeMarzo's Department Store and bought the old shoes, too, carrying them away in their box, under my arm.

THIRTY-THREE

Outside of Minniefield, Elro took the first main road that headed north, and we drove for several hours. The sun pounded down on the pickup, and the inside of the cab grew hot. I started getting drowsy. I lay my head back on the seat, but I was caught in that never-never land, just short of dozing off, where real thoughts and dreams fade in and out of each other. I was thinking about Bunny: She'd be up by now, probably at the kitchen table drinking coffee, having gone around the house first thing, checking all the doors and windows. Her "tour of the property," she used to say—who knows what she expected to find. Nothing, I suppose. She just needed to make sure that everything was exactly as she'd left it the night before. Anyway, there she'd be, sipping coffee at the kitchen table, maybe reading my note—she'd find it on the tour—but probably just sitting and staring into space, wrapped in her green terrycloth bathrobe. No, she hasn't had that in years. The robe she wears now is beige. How could I forget? She'd be in her beige robe, and someone would call. Mrs. Vernon? No, Mrs. O'Brien. Mrs. O'Brien on the phone. Mrs. Calhoun, your daughter has run away. With a boy! A dumb, danger-ous boy. We told you she was bad. You didn't believe us, but we told you. Now, you've raised two bad ones, a son and a daughter. What do you say to that, Mrs. Calhoun? Where's your talk about a child being a gift now? And you said this one was special. Specially bad, maybe. Specially like her brother. You can't keep the badness out, can you, Mrs. Calhoun? You try to hide it, you try to dress it up, you try to talk around it, but, in the end, the badness comes through, doesn't it, Mrs. Calhoun? Mrs. Calhoun? Mrs. Calhoun?

"Ride the ducks!"

"Huh?" I blinked my eyes open. The sun through the windshield weighed a ton on my chest.

Elro pointed to a billboard that showed what looked like a barge with wheels crawling into the water, carrying a load of joyous passengers. The passengers were waving ecstatically, with their hands above their heads, as if they were doing some kind of African dance. The sign said we were twenty miles from the Dells, "nature's wonderland." "Ride the ducks!" the sign commanded.

"The only thing they can't do is fly," said Elro.

Soon the roadside was littered with billboards—signs advertising a water show, a frontier village, motels, miniature golf, restaurants, a river tour. But nothing was advertised as much as the ducks. Duck billboards were everywhere, and soon I started seeing bumper stickers on cars. The message was always the same. "Ride the ducks!"

"Those words," I said. "Maybe I'm just getting giddy, but they're starting to sound really crazy."

"Yeah?" said Elro.

"Yeah. It's like they're telling us to do something wild and amazing. They make my heart speed up."

"Yeah?"

"Like a war whoop, except not for war."

"A nut whoop," said Elro.

"What?"

"A nut whoop. You know, you yell it before going nuts." He paused. "Ride the ducks!" he yelled suddenly, and he bugged his eyes and started shaking like an idiot.

"Don't." I grabbed his arm. "We'll crash." He settled down, and I let go. "Where'd you hear that?" I asked.

"What?"

"Nut whoop."

"I made it up. Just now."

"Really?"

"Yeah, really. Why not?"

280

I turned to stare out the window, smiling to myself. I *must* be getting giddy, I thought.

From the outskirts, the town of Wisconsin Dells doesn't look much like nature's wonderland. The road we were on was banked by restaurants, stores, gas stations, and motels. Cars were backed up at the first big intersection, and we had to snake in a long line past a traffic cop who kept blowing his whistle, as if someone could do something about the whole mess. It was probably one of the busiest weekends of the year. "They'll never find us here with all these people," said Elro.

"I don't know. We look like the only ones without kids."

"Don't worry."

Elro followed the signs for the ducks, and eventually we came to a parking lot filled with cars. A man in a brown uniform told us a duck had just left—the next one would go in half an hour. Elro bought two tickets, at two dollars apiece, and parked the truck. With time to kill, we wandered over to a hot dog stand and sat at a table outside under a parasol. Elro bought two hot dogs, some fries, and a Coke for himself, and fries and a Coke for me. Before starting to eat, he tucked a paper napkin in the neck of his shirt to catch any drops of mustard. Again, I smiled to myself and turned away, sipping my Coke through a straw and looking out over the parking lot.

The sun burning down on the roofs of the cars created a shimmery glare, a glittery silver lake. Here and there, a human boat cut through the dancing water. A man wearing a baseball cap and trailing a wife and three kids tacked back and forth, apparently in search of the family car. I couldn't hear what was being said, but I could see. The father was getting frustrated and blaming the mother, whose job it probably was to mark down the location whenever the car was left in a lot. The mother was squawking at the kids, who risked getting lost as the father hurried in his search. The smallest child, a girl, was crying. At one point, she stopped in a clear area, put her hands together, threw her head back, and let out what must have been a frightening wail. By the time it rolled over the cars and wound through the shimmering, rising heat, however, it came to me as a sweet, short gust of soprano. It could have been a glorious snatch of opera, heard from afar. While she was still crying, they found the car. The mother fanned the doors to cool the inside, and the father came back for the little girl. He lifted her high off the ground, and she put her arms around his neck, holding her little head close to his. Watching them, I remembered a moment from when I was very young. I was in a huge, noisy building, perhaps a bus station, and like the little girl, I was crying uncontrollably. Suddenly, a strange man, a friend of Bunny's, lifted me above his head and put me on his shoulders. In the terror and the strangeness of it, I stopped crying. I gripped the man's head, my nose in his rough hair. There was a musty, leathery smell to his hair, so strong that I thought it must be a bad smell, though I rather liked it. Bunny smiled up at me. "See? That's better," she said. "Now you're happy." It occurred to me there at the hot dog stand that all I ever knew was Bunny, then and now.

Beside me, Elro had dozed off. His legs were stretched out in front, and his chin had dropped to his chest. After a while, the duck drove up, moving clumsily along on black tires that poked out of the hull. A bright garden of tourists sprouted from under a canopy on top. After parking, the duck unloaded several dozen passengers, who fanned out slowly through the cars in the lot. To the side, a line of riders for our trip was forming.

I shook Elro's shoulder. He dragged his eyes open painfully.

"The duck," I said.

He sat up abruptly and fumbled in his shirt pocket for the tickets. "Let's go," he said.

We filed past the ticket-taker, walked up a ramp and took two seats on the side. Families milled around, scrambling to find places together. A young man and woman fussed over various seats, testing the views, before sitting down in front of us. Finally, we were ready to go. The driver, a broad-backed man in a red shirt, spoke to us through a microphone. "Welcome to the Wisconsin Dells and to a ride on a duck—an *original* Wisconsin duck." The motor started up, and the vehicle rumbled forward. "The Dells is a scenic treasure created by Mother Nature, the greatest architect of them all," the driver went on. "It's a wonderland of cliffs and caves and sculpted rocks, carved over centuries by glacial waters eating through the area's soft sandstone. Using these unique Wisconsin ducks, we're able to show you the most magnificent sights on both land and water."

We turned past a sign marked "Duck Trail" and headed off through a pine woods. The driver put down the microphone and stepped on the gas. The duck bolted forward, and everyone gasped. Our seats were only ten feet or so off the ground, but speeding along in the open made them seem much higher.

"This thing really moves," said Elro.

The young man sitting in front of us suddenly turned. "Some ride, huh?" he said.

"Yeah," said Elro.

We drove on through the woods. The pine trees were tall and full and densely packed, and they streaked by in a long, even curtain of green. The trail was bumpy, but the duck was heavy and moved in looping bounces that sometimes left your stomach up around your chest. I held my head out to the side, letting the wind with its clean pine fragrance billow through my hair. There *was* something wild and amazing about the ride after all, and I was glad we'd come on it.

After a few minutes, the man in front again turned to Elro. "You ever do this before?" he asked.

"No, first time."

"Some fun, huh?"

"Yeah."

The man was perhaps in his early twenties, with frizzy brown hair and beaverish teeth. He shifted in his seat to get a better look at Elro, virtually turning his back on the woods. "You two just up for the day?" he asked.

Elro wiped his palms on his jeans and stared into the pines.

I nodded.

The man persisted. "Where ya from?"

I thought for a moment. "Illinois."

"Hey! Me, too. Where in Illinois?"

I glanced at Elro, but he was off in the trees, his face twisted as far away from me and the man as it could get. "Emerson," I said. It's a town not far from Katydid.

"Oh, I know Emerson. A pretty town. We ate at a restaurant there once. What was the name of that place, honey?" He tapped the shoulder of the woman with him. She gave him a bored smile that told him to go away. "Oh, you know," he said to me. "The famous place. Everybody knows it."

I hadn't been in Emerson in three years, and I'd never eaten there.

"You know, the big one, with the porch. It's got a little statue of a nigger jockey out front." He was getting excited. "You know."

"Ahhh." Nothing came. I was too tired to lie. I glanced again at Elro, looking for help, and the man saw something in my face. His eyes tightened with suspicion.

"The Rose Bush," said the woman. She had delicate, pointy features.

"Yeah, the Rose Bush," he said, relaxing again.

"Oh, of course, the Rose Bush," I said.

The driver flicked on his microphone. "Hold onto your hats," he announced. "Here's Suicide Hill." At the top of a small bluff, the duck wavered for a second, and then dipped and streaked downhill. Children screamed. The duck plunged jarringly along the steep trail. We were all pushed against the backs of our seats.

"Jesus!" said the man in front, grabbing the woman. He spun back around, and I hoped that would be the end of it.

On level ground, we passed some rock formations—cliffs that jutted out to form craggy profiles. "Some people see Abe Lincoln over there," said the driver.

"I see him, I see him," squealed a little girl behind me.

The man in front turned to us again. His beaver teeth gnawed at the air. "You two married?" he asked.

I glanced down at my ringless left hand, in full view on my knee. "No."

"Oh, just up for the day? The Dells is a pretty long way to come on a date, isn't it?"

Was this the way it was going to be? Endless questions that produced endless lies that curved and twisted and cut back, forming a maze as jumbled as the piles of rocks all around? It seemed so hopeless. Everyone knew—they just looked at us and knew. And Elro wasn't any help. He was still thrashing his thighs, refusing to talk. Why was it up to me?

"We're part of a church group that left early this morning and came on a bus," I said. "We sang hymns all the way up."

"Oh." He was quiet for a second. I was exhausted. The lie had taken all my strength.

"What church?" he asked.

"Methodist."

"Really? That's our church. Hear that, honey?" The woman nodded her head slowly. Her tiny lips were locked in a perfect straight line. "Who's the minister there?" the man asked. "Maybe we know him."

"Jeremiah P. Calhoun."

"Calhoun, Calhoun." He scrunched his face to show he was thinking hard. "Don't really know him, I guess. Calhoun. That's funny. It sounds like a Catholic name."

"Oh, he's completely Methodist."

"Well, I guess he has to be."

"Yes." How could I stop him? What did he want? I felt too tired for this. I couldn't go on. Better to confess it up, tell him everything. Maybe behind those shiny front teeth there'd be some compassion. Suddenly, from deep inside my weariness, a thought popped up. "Are you two here on a honeymoon?" I asked, smiling.

He tipped his head and pretended to blush. "Hear that?" he said to the woman. "She thinks we're on our honeymoon." Again he shifted in his seat, turning around so he almost faced me. "We've been married for four years," he said. "Actually, we're here as a kind of reward—one I'm giving myself for some work I did in Chicago a few weeks ago. I spent four days there. Can you guess what I was doing?"

"No."

"Come on, guess. Think of the newspapers. Chicago." He jiggled in his seat. It had worked; he only wanted to talk about himself.

"Something with money?"

"No, no," he said irritably. "The convention. The Democratic Convention. I was a delegate."

"Great."

He rocked back. "A delegate! Me! A baker! A delegate to the Democratic National Convention. I actually ate breakfast with Adlai Stevenson."

"Wow."

For ten minutes, while the duck bobbed along the trail, the man described how a friend had talked him into going down to his local Democratic club, how he'd run errands, walked the streets, handed out leaflets—done all the low-level jobs a beginner has to do. And then, last spring, when the president of the club died suddenly, and the vice-president went bankrupt, they'd put him on the ballot as a delegate. And he'd won!

The man was completely turned around, kneeling on his seat. I felt safe, since he'd clearly lost interest in quizzing us, but Elro didn't understand that. He'd slowly gone rigid as a firecracker. Only his hands and arms moved, rubbing methodically up and down his thighs.

"Now they want me to give a speech at the high school on opening day," the delegate said. He gripped the metal bar between us. "And you know what I'm gonna tell those kids?"

"No."

"Guess."

"I can't."

"What's holdin' ya back? You know?" His eyes were burning. "That's what I'll tell 'em: What's holdin' ya back?"

With that, Elro blew. "Shut up!" he screamed, his face brilliant red. "Shut up. Just turn around and shut up!" His hands were clenched in tight fists.

Everyone stared. A little dark-faced boy, across the aisle on his mother's lap, put his face next to hers and clung nervously to her sleeve.

The delegate flinched and leaned back, holding onto the bar. "You don't need to be so touchy about it," he said. He looked Elro over, then looked around, apparently assessing what stake he had in facing up to the challenge. When his wife pulled on his arm, he turned and settled back into his seat.

Elro was panting, so I put my hand on his leg to calm him. His jeans were still hot where he'd been rubbing.

We rode on quietly for another mile or so. Elro's outburst had silenced the other tourists. Where before there'd been noisy chatter, now there were only soft murmurs and occasional glances to see how Elro was bearing up. Once again, in our eagerness for anonymity, we'd managed to draw the attention of everyone.

Soon the woods opened up and the duck slowed to approach the edge of a large lake. We crawled down a concrete ramp that disappeared under the blue-green water. Hitting the surface of the lake, the duck was lifted gently, and we seemed to be floating in air. Then the propeller started up with a muffled roar, and we pushed on.

Here was the real Dells—the high, red cliffs lining the lake, the rocks balanced impossibly at crazy angles, always on the verge, it seemed, of breaking loose and clattering murderously into the water far below. After the flatness around Katydid, the wide, tended stretches of green, the cliffs looked incredibly harsh and unfriendly. They were spectacular, but almost too much so, as if they were man-made or inauthentic, nature's equivalent of a platinum dye job.

Sitting there beside Elro, I gradually came to realize how ridiculous this was. I'd just changed my life forever, abandoned my mother, run away with a boy I didn't even like, and now I was sailing around in a weird boat in the middle of a resort. Nothing ever turns out the way you expect. No matter how hard you think, no matter how carefully you plan, things always end up differently. There's no imagining that works. I mean, riding a duck! That's what it always seems to come down to.

The boat puttered along the shore, here and there nosing into a small cove, while the driver crackled away about the sights. Compared to the constant bumping on the Duck Trail, the ride on water was pillowy. The duck moved slowly and the waves drummed rhythmically along the sides. The delegate ignored us. He said a few quiet words to his wife, but mostly he stared coldly off at the cliffs. Elro didn't talk, but I sensed him starting to relax. His body slackened, then rocked with the regular motion of the boat. Eventually, he slumped down, put his head on my shoulder, and went to sleep.

He woke again as we pulled into the parking lot. To avoid any confrontations, we waited to get off until everyone else had left. People filing out inspected us carefully. The delegate permitted himself one quick peek our way. The corners of his mouth were stapled tight, and he shook his head for our benefit.

"What a bunghole," muttered Elro.

"Shhh," I said, patting him on the arm.

When we got to the pickup, the cab was filled with superheated air, and the seat was too hot to touch. I fanned the doors for a few minutes, the way I'd seen the mother do earlier, and Elro took a towel out of his suitcase for me to sit on. Finally we started off and pulled into a line of cars easing onto the road. After a few minutes of starting and stopping, a loud, insistent honking erupted behind us. I looked back. A blue convertible was trying to butt into the line of cars just in back of us. The driver hollered and honked again. It was the delegate. He'd spotted us and was trying to catch up, though parked cars were blocking his way in front, and the cars in line weren't letting him in.

"Hey! You!" he yelled, waving at me. "Hey! I thought you said you came on a bus?"

He inched the convertible forward, but the car behind us held its ground. The delegate stood, pulling himself up by the steering wheel. He pointed toward me. "She said she came on a bus," he yelled to the other drivers, as if that alone were reason to let him in line. Still, no one made room. So again the delegate honked, and this time he held it, sending out a long, mean howl that hung in the air.

Again, Elro blew. He looked back wildly, his face clamped in a fierce mask. Then he rammed the gearshift into low. The pickup roared and shot out of line. It jumped a curb onto a grassy median, churned over the ground, and hopped the median at the far end. Turning and digging into the main road, the truck spit pebbles at the parking attendant, who had jumped behind a signpost. Both lanes of the road were packed with cars, but Elro headed down a shoulder, zooming past cars stuffed with faces set in wonder. After about fifty yards, he cut behind a street sign, ran over a sidewalk, and bounced onto a side street. It, too, was busy, but he stayed on the pavement, swinging into the oncoming lane to pass several cars. He went a few blocks, then cut left across traffic onto another side street and soon turned and turned again. We were in a subdivision. Small, frail summer houses were crammed side-by-side. Here and there, a thin pine jutted out of a lawn. The street was quiet, and Elro finally slowed down.

"Fuck the duck," he said.

THIRTY-FOUR

"What are we going to do now?"

"Get a motel room."

"But, I mean, beyond that."

"What beyond that?"

"You know, we can't stay anywhere near the Dells now, and I was going to get a job as a waitress."

"Don't talk about it." Elro's hands clutched the steering wheel. His eyes were outlined in red, as if someone had taken a crayon and run it around the edges of his lids. Another narrow country road stretched out before us, disappearing ahead into the darkness of jaggedy pine shadows. We'd arrived at this route, heading north, after winding tediously through back alleys and side streets. Now we weren't just fugitives from Katydid, but also from the Dells, whose police were undoubtedly eager to find the hotrodder responsible for disrupting their busiest Saturday. Elro had slipped into one of his silences again; in fact, he'd already passed a few motels without even seeming to notice.

"It's getting late," I said.

A slight shrug of his heavy shoulders.

"I'm tired," I added.

A grunt, perhaps an approximation of "Me, too."

"We're never going to find a motel on this road." Aside from a tractor pulling a hay wagon, we hadn't seen a vehicle in ten minutes. Even the farms seemed forsaken. Coming over one hill, we'd driven past the crumbling remains of an enormous barn, whose rotting, caved-in sides looked skeletal, like the ribs on a huge, fallen beast.

"We're really in trouble," said Elro.

"Well, if you hadn't panicked back there."

"Me? If you hadn't lied, we'd have been all right. Why'd you have to lie to him?"

"What was I supposed to tell him?"

"Nuthin'."

"Well, you weren't any help. You just sat there rubbing your pants."

"That's better than blabbing. You're as bad as your mother."

"What's she got to do with this?"

"She's got a big mouth."

"She does not."

"Does too. Every time she came to school, she acted as if she owned the place."

"Did not."

"Did too."

"Shut up, Elro."

"You shut up."

We swung around a sharp curve cut into the side of a hill. The pebbly, rust-colored soil had bled onto the road, leaving thin, red fingers on the concrete.

"You know something?" I said. "I don't really understand why you did this—why you ran away with me. I mean, I think I know why, but that doesn't seem like enough."

"Huh?"

"I mean, really, Elro. What were you thinking?"

He shrugged. "Nuthin'."

"Do you know Eddie Boggs?" I asked.

"Know who he is."

"Well, last week, we were out at a picnic on the Little Carp, Eddie and Bunny and I, and he tried to explain to me how he felt, and it just didn't make any sense at all. I couldn't understand. He ended up getting mad at me."

"So?"

"Now you. I can't figure out what you're thinking. I mean, I'm grateful and all, but I wonder." I started talking fast and using my hands. I was tired and suddenly I was getting too many ideas. "Are you just thinking about tonight, about doing it? But what about tomorrow or the day after that or the day after that or ten years from now? I mean, I can hardly make a move anymore without my head filling with these questions about what the move will mean for tomorrow and the future. It's as if for every move I see these dominoes falling, and I try to follow where the last domino will drop. I don't like it necessarily, but that's the way I think. And the few times, the few, tiny moments, when I don't think like that, I end up in Butcher Benedict's bedroom. But I wonder—in those moments, am I like Eddie and you are all the time?" I paused. No response from Elro. I was talking to an ear, a big, meaty catcher's mitt of an ear.

"It's so hard to figure out," I went on, a bit more slowly. "Sometimes I think it's as if there's some code out there that men are following, something invisible, you know? And I can learn the rules, like football, I can learn how the game is played, but, still, overall, it doesn't make any sense. I can't see the purpose. You know what I mean?"

"Nope," said Elro, shaking his head. But he was softening. I could see the corners of his mouth slackening and his grip easing up on the steering wheel. Slowly the tension was seeping out of him. After another mile or so, he said, "I always wanted to get away from that town. I never liked that town."

"How come?"

"I don't know. The people, I guess. And the way it looked. It always looked wrong to me. It's like everything was there, but in the wrong place. The square, the park, the Ward's building, the library—they were all in the wrong place. It hurt my eyes to look around. It gave me a headache."

"That sounds awful."

"Ever since I can remember," he said, "I wished I was someplace else."

We drove a few more miles and came to a larger road. Elro hesitated, then turned down it, following signs for a town called Fullerton. After a while, the farms along the road gave way to a nursery, an equipment store, a Ford dealership. On the left, we spotted a sign, JIM'S FLORIDA MOTEL AND MINIATURE GOLF. Elro turned into the driveway. The motel was a single, long, low building that stretched away from the road. The building was painted pink, and the front edge of the roof was decorated with blue trim cut to resemble waves. In a couple of places, the trim had broken loose, and the waves dangled down like stray curls on a girl's forehead. The golf course curved around in back of the motel. In front was a small, battered lawn where a couple of children were playing with trucks, and a man and a woman in bathing suits were sitting out on beach chairs, taking in the sun. Elro parked down the line from the office and looked around.

"What do you think?" I asked.

He considered for a moment. "You wait here," he said. He climbed out of the truck and walked slowly to the front of the building, disappearing into the office through a flapping screen door. A few minutes later, he came out. He was walking fast, and when he caught my eyes, he couldn't restrain a smile.

"Got it," he said at the truck window. "Get your stuff and let's go." He reached in back and pulled out his suitcase. Beyond him, in the window of the motel office, a face appeared. An elderly bald man was watching us closely.

I followed Elro down the walk past each pink motel door, every one marked with a blue number: six, seven, eight, nine, ten, eleven. At twelve, on the far end, he stopped and opened the door with a key. The shades were drawn, and the room was dark. A damp, moldy smell hovered over the thin rug and the few pieces of dark, low furniture—two padded chairs, a bureau, a broad, undulating bed.

"Wow!" said Elro. He put his suitcase down and walked over to the side of the bed. "Look at the size of this thing."

"We need some air in here and some light." I went to the back wall and pulled aside the heavy, green curtain. Sunlight bounded around the room. The walls were actually aqua; we could have been standing in a swimming pool. I opened the window a crack, and in seconds the air and light had burned off the moldy odor and even brightened the ominous barge of a bed. But there was a problem. The miniature golf course came right up to the back of the motel. Not ten feet away sat a huge, spotted frog, each eye a red blinking light bulb. The frog's pink tongue stretched down its front and onto the green carpet of the putting surface. While I lingered at the window, a boy about Elro's age stood hunched over a ball. His girlfriend leaned on a putter and watched. With a quick, hard stroke, the boy sent his ball rolling up the tongue and into the hole of the frog's mouth. Moments later, the ball popped out a small opening in back, rolled over the flat, green carpet, and plunked into the cup. The boy looked up to celebrate his hole-in-one and looked right at me. He had a crewcut and a bright, clear face, and, in a moment, he'd taken in me and all of room twelve, including Elro, now stretched out on the bed. The boy's smile quickly twisted, as if he couldn't quite control the muscles in his face. I pulled the curtains closed again, plunging the room back into semidarkness.

"That's better," said Elro. "I like it better this way." He had his hands behind his head, and he was staring at the ceiling. "My brother and his girl did it fourteen times the first night," he said.

"Who was she?" I started unbuttoning my blouse.

"You don't know her. She goes to the Catholic school."

I took off my blouse and slipped out of my shoes. "Do they still go out?" I asked.

"Nah. They hardly went out after that. She was kinda fat."

I stepped out of my jeans. I was standing in the middle of the room in my bra and panties. Elro hadn't noticed. He had closed his eyes, and he was humming a song, "Tutti-Frutti," to himself.

I wasn't scared, and I didn't have second thoughts. Other girls had talked about saving their virginity as a "gift" for their husbands, but that had never made sense to me. Women get divorced all the time or become widows and then marry again without any "gift" for the second man. It couldn't be that important. Besides, Bunny never talked about it. Everything I'd ever heard about the sacredness of virginity had come from other girls.

Still, standing in the center of room twelve, I hesitated for a moment. I guess I was concerned with history in a way—my first time—and I wanted to make sure I had taken in the setting: the pale walls; the white bowl of a ceiling light, with its crown of dust; the painting of a palmy beach hanging above the bed; the small pile of clothes left at my feet; the laughter of the boy and girl, still putting around the golf course.

Elro opened his eyes and stopped singing. "Jesus!" he said. "Come here."

I stepped toward the bed, still hesitating, hoping to save a moment or two. "Elro," I said, "what do you know about Little Richard?"

"Huh?"

"You know, the singer. You were just humming his song. Who is he?"

"I don't know. Who cares. Some nigger probably. Who cares?"

293

I climbed onto the bed. My knees sank into the soft mattress. "I was just wondering."

He grabbed my arm and pulled me toward him. I was on top of him, and his arms were around me. He kissed me with his mouth open, and I could taste the mustard from his hot dogs. He rolled over on me and put his mouth near my ear. "I love you, I love you," he whispered. He thrust his left leg between my thighs. He pressed himself against me. It was hard to breathe. He rubbed against me, his hips moving up and down.

"Oh, Elro," I said, though I didn't feel anything. I just wanted to be part of it.

"Ohhhh," he moaned. His pumping became furious. His leg was wrapped tight around mine. He paused for a moment and reached down to unbutton his pants, but he couldn't wait. He gave up and went back to pumping, harder and harder, so hard the side of my leg got raw from rubbing against his jeans.

Finally, he stopped. His whole body went limp and sprawled over mine. He was incredibly heavy. His face was turned away, and I couldn't feel his breathing. I wondered if he were dead. We lay that way for what seemed like an hour. I stared up at the ceiling. It was white and cracked, and huge flakes of paint were curling down. A water spot made rust-colored circles just over the bed. Outside, in back, an occasional group passed through the frog hole, always laughing as the ball ran up the tongue, always waiting in silent excitement as it clunked down through the huge frog body. Elro started to snore softly. I fell asleep.

I woke when he rolled off me. He swung his feet over the side of the bed and put his head in his arms, rubbing his eyes.

"I gotta go," he said.

"Go?"

"My father's gonna kill me for takin' his truck."

"Oh."

"Here." He reached in his pocket and took out his wallet, then he counted out eight ten-dollar bills, dropping them on the bedspread. "You can have the money." He thought for a moment and took one of the bills back. "Well, let me have this to get home."

He stood up and tucked in his shirt. "You ought to go home, too. They're just gonna catch you. This whole idea was crazy to begin with. They just would've found us and taken us back."

"I can't go back."

"What are you gonna do?"

"I don't know. I'll figure it out."

He stomped around the room, as if looking for something. Finally, he picked up his suitcase, which was right beside the door, exactly where he'd left it when he came in. "My father's gonna kill me," he said again.

I suddenly felt a chill, so I slid between the sheets. They were starched and clean. I thought of a hospital, though I'm not sure why—I've never spent a night in a hospital. Elro walked over to the bed.

"Another thing," he said slowly. "That stuff with Sissy that I told you about—it didn't happen quite like that."

"I didn't think so."

"It was sorta like that, but I really didn't drown her. She drowned herself, really." He stared at me. "You believe me, don't you?"

"Yes."

He put his suitcase down. "It was mostly like I said. She really did want it. She was watchin' me all the time. It was obvious. The guys were teasing me about it, even my brother. The day of the picnic, she and I were out behind the float, and no one was there. I kissed her, and she got scared or something and started pullin' away. She panicked. It was like she thought I was gonna rape her or something. She swam away and then she started wavin' her arms and splashin' up the water. And she splashed up a wave that just swept into her mouth. Her mouth was open for a scream, and the wave went right in. Then she started chokin', and she sank. I knew she was dead because she sank like a rock. It was real scary. We were together, and then, all of a sudden, I was all alone. There was nothin' else on the water, and it was real quiet."

"What did you do?"

"I swam around tryin' to find her, but I couldn't remember where she'd been. The top of the water all looked the same. I dove down a couple of times, but it was no use. Finally, I just swam under the float and sort of sneaked back to the beach. No one noticed. And then, a while later, someone spotted her." Elro rubbed his forehead with his hand, an old man's gesture. "You won't tell anyone, will you?"

"I'm never going back to Katydid."

"But even so, you won't tell, will you?"

"Maybe. I don't know. But I don't blame you."

He managed a smile. "Good." He picked up his suitcase again. "And you can see why I didn't feel that bad, can't you? It was the scream that killed her. She opened her mouth, and she drowned. If she'd been quiet, she would have lived." He searched my face. "I mean, I felt bad, but not as bad as if I'd done it myself."

"I understand."

"Do you believe me?"

"Yes."

Elro walked toward the door. I realized that I wasn't surprised to see him go. It was as if I'd had a very clear picture of it, as if I'd seen it happen once before. I wondered if I'd been dreaming when he was lying on top of me on the bed. Maybe I'd already dreamed his departure.

"Well, I gotta go," he said. He put his hand on the doorknob. "The room's paid for, you know." He saw me staring at the wide, damp stain on the front of his jeans. "It's a good thing . . ." he started to say, and then he stopped himself. He held the suitcase up in front of the stain. "This whole thing was pretty stupid," he said.

I didn't respond, and he opened the door. The low, late-afternoon sun pushed past him and made the room too bright. I covered my eyes, and in that moment, he was gone. A few seconds later, I heard the truck start up and drive away. Soon, I fell back asleep.

Much later, the sound of laughter on the frog hole woke me up. The room was dark, except for a slat of yellow light streaking past the curtain. Lying under the covers, I'd grown too warm, and now I was soaked by perspiration. My mouth was dry, and my eyes were scratchy. Again people laughed, this time right outside the window. I got up and peeked out through the curtain. Two couples were there, kids about my age. One girl putted the ball up the frog's tongue, but didn't do it hard enough. The ball rolled back down, setting off more peals of laughter.

I left the window and turned on the ceiling lamp. The bulb was dim, and the room too vast to be lit adequately. A low, gray illumination, almost too weak to make shadows, covered everything. Except for a slight mussiness on the bedspread and my few things—the pile of clothes, the Piggly Wiggly bag, the box of shoes—the place looked unused.

I went into the bathroom and splashed cold water on my face, studying myself in the mirror above the sink. The mirror was broken in one corner and had a ragged, glassy edge that made me uncomfortable. I needed a shower, but that could wait until I decided on my next move. But what would that be? I was alone, abandoned with nothing in the world but $70, maybe $80 if you counted what was left of the money I'd brought. I suddenly realized how much my idea of running away had depended on Elro. Together, it was almost an adventure. Alone, it was—what? More craziness?

I went back into the room. It was important to stay orderly— orderly and reasonable. Maintain patterns, as Mrs. O'Brien would say. Something would come to me. I'll unpack my bag, I thought. No, that's stupid, not enough clothes in it to bother unpacking. I'll sit on the bed and write a letter. No, that's stupid, too. Who can I write to? What can I say? I started spinning slowly, inspecting the room as if expecting, with each half turn, to find some doorway or sign that would lead me to my next move. Bureau, bed, window, door. Bureau again, bed—suddenly I had an idea: I'll get some cigarettes. I'd never smoked before, but this was an occasion. Things had changed, and I might as well have a new habit to go with my new situation. Besides, Bunny used to say that smoking helped her focus.

I got dressed quickly and fished in my pocket to make sure I had a few coins. Then I took the key from where Elro had left it on the bureau and went outside. It was a nice night, moonless and starry and noisy with bugs. Five or six cars were parked along the walk, pointing at their owners' rooms.

I walked down to the motel office. It doubled as the office for miniature golf, and one side was cluttered with putters and boxes of colored golf balls. The bald man who'd watched us before stood behind a counter, reading a newspaper. To his left, on a table at about the level of his knees, a television threw off a flickering light. *Gunsmoke* was playing to itself. I walked over to the man, and he looked up from his paper. He had a wide, flat face to go with his bald top. His eyes were so far apart they seemed to come at you from two different directions.

"I want to buy some cigarettes," I said.

"What kind?" he asked dully.

"Luckies." Bunny smokes Luckies when she smokes.

He searched under the glass counter. He had rows and rows of cigarettes and candy lined up, cigarettes on the top shelf, candy on the bottom. He picked out a pack of Luckies and set it on the counter.

"And a Turkish Taffy," I said.

"What kind?"

I studied the display. The tall, thin Turkish Taffy packages, each flavor with its own color, were fanned out like a hand of cards. The man must have a wife, I thought. "Strawberry."

He took out a red package and put it next to the Luckies. I handed him a quarter and and a nickel, and he dropped them in the cash register. On *Gunsmoke*, Kitty was telling Matt that a young man, a stranger, had been in the saloon that afternoon, asking about him. She talked in that throaty way she has, with her head thrown back, so you can't quite tell if she's flirting or teasing or just acting normal.

I scooped up the candy and the cigarettes and started to leave.

"Where's your husband?" the bald man asked.

"Pardon me?"

"Your husband."

"Oh. He had to go. He'll be back."

"We don't want any trouble," the man said.

"Oh, no. No trouble at all." I jammed my left hand into my pocket and backed toward the door.

"See to it you're gone in the morning."

"Yes, we will be. I promise."

"We don't want any trouble."

I started out the door and then stopped. "Say, can you tell me, does a bus come through here?"

His eyes bore in on me from both sides. A stupid question. Why didn't I think? "I thought you said your husband was coming back," he said.

"Oh, he is, but he's got to get his truck fixed, and I'm supposed to be in Chicago tomorrow for my mother's birthday. She's turning sixty, and all her kids are coming from all over the Midwest. I can't miss it, and I thought, just in case . . . ." So simple. He didn't believe a word of it, but even before I'd finished, his eyes were drifting back to the paper.

"Down the road half a mile. In Fullerton. A bus depot."

Back in room twelve, I sat on the bed, propped up against the headboard, and smoked a Lucky. I sucked the smoke in and swirled it around my mouth. It was hot and sharp and tasted bad, but I liked the look of the cigarette between my fingers. With my wrist bent and my fingers straight, I practiced sweeping my hand through the air, leaving a thin trail of smoke. I'd never been pleased with my hands, but, holding a cigarette, they looked almost pretty, I thought.

After a while, the smoke made me dizzy, so I put out the cigarette and chewed off a piece of the Turkish Taffy. Then I took the old, ankle-high shoes out of their box. I ran my fingers along the shiny sides and over the smooth, leather soles. Finally, I slipped the shoes on. All the lacing took several minutes. When I'd finished, I stretched my legs out on the bed to admire the results. I hadn't really noticed before, but the shoes didn't quite fit. They were long enough, but very narrow—left over, I guess, from a time when feet, like people, were more delicate. I took the shoes off and set them beside me on the bed. They were best for just looking at.

Then I sat back and puffed on another cigarette. I'd go to Milwaukee, I decided. I'd take the bus in Fullerton, and when I got to Milwaukee, I'd find find a room at a cheap hotel, and I'd get a job as a waitress. I'd live alone, and they'd never find me. I'd be too quiet. They've probably stopped looking for me anyway, I told myself. I was gone now, and that was what mattered. Bunny would care, of course, but she'd bury herself in Eddie or some other man, and I'd become a distant memory, a light bill she forgot to pay, an old book she'd read once. She was right—she was like a drinker that way, a love-aholic, loving away her memories. Tom might care, maybe Tom. Maybe I'd see him again sometime. But as for the others—it was funny, really. *In re M.C.* was supposed to be about me, and yet, in the end what happened was that I got to know them: Mrs. O'Brien, the Vernons, Sergeant Tony, Reverend Vaughn, Sissy, Elro, even Ruth, poor Ruth, with her two heads touching—it seemed I saw them all so clearly now.

I stubbed out my Lucky. I'll go to Milwaukee, become a waitress like Bunny. Live alone. I'll always be alone. That's the way, the only way.

THIRTY-FIVE

It didn't happen that way, of course. Nothing turned out as I'd expected, though, for a time, for a couple of weeks, I thought I'd managed to work it out. Everything went by so quickly, however, that now it hardly seems worth mentioning.

Early the next morning, I slipped out of the motel and walked the half mile into Fullerton. I found the bus depot in the center of town and caught a nine o'clock bus heading east. Shortly after noon, I stepped onto the streets of Milwaukee. I remembered Reverend Vaughn's talk about his first moments in Chicago—about his feeling that a whole new world had opened up. Nothing like that happened to me. For one thing, Milwaukee didn't look like Chicago; it didn't even look that different from Katydid. The buildings were small and the streets quiet. There was none of the honking and pushing and yelling I think of when I think of the Loop. Mostly, Milwaukee just looked neat and empty.

I wandered for a while and passed a hotel. I paused, but some men were standing around the doorway, and one man was sitting in a chair on the sidewalk. I decided to walk on. Later, I came to the Viking Hotel. A sign said "$6 A NITE—WEEKLY RATE $35. The lobby was barren, but clean, so I went in. A boy not much older than I stood behind the front desk. His face was scarred with terrible acne, and as he talked to me, he looked down at the counter with his chin tucked into his right shoulder. I gave him $35, almost half of what I had left, and signed the register "Lily Richards," a name I'd thought of on the bus. The boy gave me the key to room 43, on the fourth floor. The elevator was run by a very old Mexican named Will who had snow-white hair and dirty white stubble on his chin. He rode up and down on a little round seat that folded out of the elevator's wall. At each stop, he hopped up and opened the elevator's grate door, which moved with an incredible clatter.

Room 43 was toward the end of the hall. A single bed with a prominent valley in the middle took up most of the space. There was a bureau, a chair, and a wash basin to go with the toilet and shower in the tiny adjoining bathroom. A window looked out on the tops and backs of several plain, brick buildings. I could lie in bed and watch pigeons dive and swoop from one rooftop ledge to another.

The second day I was there, Will saw me carrying a newspaper folded open to the want ads. There were only a few ads for waitresses, and the places I'd called were looking for people with lots of experience.

"Yob?" asked Will. "You wanna yob?" He pointed at the paper and I nodded. "My son restaurant, very beeg." He shrugged. "Maybee wash deeshes, maybe wash floor." With his arms held out, he bounced from foot to foot, doing an imaginary dance with a mop.

"Okay," I said.

He stopped the elevator between floors and taking the ballpoint pen and the newspaper out of my hands, he scrawled an address over the newsprint. "Numero seex booss," he said.

I thanked him, and after going back to the bus station to find the address on a map I took the number six bus to Will's son's restaurant. The ride took almost an hour and led, finally, to an industrial area of big, windowless buildings and smokestacks puffing out grayish fumes. The restaurant turned out to be the American Diner, one of a couple of diners on the block. It had a long counter and booths along the windows.

I got there in the middle of the afternoon, when the only customers were a couple of men, sitting far down the counter, whispering together and sipping coffee. Will's son, Lou, was behind the counter, going over figures in a book. He was dark and compact and wore a white counterman's shirt. I told him that I was looking for a job and that Will had sent me.

"Will? How the hell do you know that old man?" he asked in perfect English.

When I explained, his eyes narrowed. "Do you have a Social Security card?" he asked.

"No."

"Ever waited tables before?"

"Yes, at a country club."

"Summer job?"

I nodded.

He leaned over the counter and looked me up and down. "Well, you sound smart," he said finally, "and I can always use smart people. You get yourself a Social Security card, and I'll put you to work. Seven in the morning until three in the afternoon. Be here ten minutes early. I got a uniform you can wear until you can afford to buy your own. Okay?"

"Yes."

I left, not knowing what to do. How could I get a Social Security card when I was using a fake name? But at 6:50 the next morning, I showed up for work, and Lou never said another word about a Social Security card.

Lou's wife, Angela, got me started. She gave me a clean white uniform—too short, but she later let out the hem—and taught me Lou's system. I worked eight booths along the wall. Actually, they had been Angela's booths, but my arrival meant she could move back behind the counter with Lou; that way there'd be two people on the cash register. Two middle-aged women, Judy and Maria, handled the other booths.

The work was easy. The food was much simpler than the country club's, and the customers were less demanding. There were three fast times during the day: breakfast, from seven to nine; midmorning, when men would come in with boxes to take coffee and pastries back to their co-workers, and we all had to help behind the counter; and lunch. In between, we straightened up, filled salt shakers and napkin dispensers, or else we just sat around. Nobody talked much. In fact, Angela told me that Judy and Maria hadn't been speaking to each other for three years. Angela couldn't remember why.

Every day at 3:15, I'd catch the number six bus back to the Viking.

Will was very pleased that he'd found me the job, and one day, to thank him, I bought him a tie. It was blue with red stripes, and I thought he could wear it to church, but he put it on right there in the elevator and wore it every day from then on. For meals, I'd eat breakfast and lunch at Lou's, and in the evening, around six, I'd go out to another diner, down the street from the Viking. Always the same dinner: a tuna salad plate and a Coke. After the first three days, the waitress didn't even have to ask me. Sometimes, after dinner, I'd walk over to the bus station. There was a newsstand there, and I'd browse through the magazines. Occasionally, I'd buy one and bring it back to my room. Except for Will and the customers at Lou's diner, I hardly talked to anyone, and no one seemed to notice me.

On Friday afternoon, Lou gave me an envelope with $60 in it. With tips, that meant I'd earned about $90 in the week. That was more than enough, I figured, to keep me going at the Viking. Feeling rather encouraged, I tried twice that weekend to call Bunny. I went into the phone booth in the hotel lobby, closing the accordion door behind me. Each time, I let the phone ring for ten, maybe twenty times, without getting an answer. She must be at Eddie's, I decided, and I wasn't about to call her there. After the second attempt, I concluded it was better not to try to reach her at all, and I never called again.

The second week went even more smoothly than the first. By then, I was used to being on my feet all day, and my legs didn't ache. I was starting to recognize most of the regular customers, and they were starting to call me by my name—that is, by my new name. It was Lily this and Lily that. How you this morning, Lily? Lily pond; Lily pad; Lily-of-the-valley; silly Lily; chilly, Lily (referring to a plate of eggs I'd just served—the comment broke up the entire booth). Martha had been so simple.

Still, I was getting used to it. Going home, my pocket would be bulging with a heavy load of nickels, dimes, and quarters. The number six bus started near the restaurant, so I was usually one of the first passengers on. The driver asked my name the second day and ever after greeted me as Miss Lily. I'd always take the same seat, third from the end on the right, and stare out the window as we passed from neighborhood to neighborhood. In the middle of the run, the bus would be crowded, but by the time we arrived in front of the Viking, most of the seats were empty again.

On Friday of the second week, the only other passenger left on the bus as it rumbled through traffic for the last few blocks was a heavy-set woman with straggly, graying hair. I'd noticed her before. She always got on the bus toward the end of the run, usually carrying a shopping bag. Because she was overweight, she always paused to catch her breath after climbing the steps of the bus. Once she'd sat down, she stared out the window with a particularly blank, unthinking look on her face. I never heard her say a word to anyone, and I came to think of her as a kind of grown-up orphan, someone who moved through life without any connections to the world around her. Like me. I imagined that she, too, had once come alone to the city and was now using up her days in safe isolation. Watching her day after day, I always felt a slight wave of contentment pass over me.

On this particular Friday, she took the seat directly in front of me. Her stringy hair looked uncombed, and she was wearing a faded print housecoat. For several blocks, she stared out the window as usual. Then she bent down and rummaged through her shopping bag. When she straightened up, she was holding an envelope with an address written on it in a goofy, childish scrawl. The envelope had already been opened, and she pulled out several sheets of note paper, all covered with that same embarrassing handwriting. As she read, I leaned forward, trying to catch a glimpse of the message. I only saw one sentence, and it was enough to make my head snap back: "So what do you think, Mom, should I buy the blue Chevy?" By the time I got off in front of the Viking, tears were streaming down my face.

I walked around the block once to pull myself together. Then, hurrying past the Viking's front desk, I was stopped by the boy with acne. "There's someone here to see you," he said. The boy nodded toward the wall behind me. Crooked old Chief Springer was struggling to get up out of a frayed, sunken sofa, the only piece of furniture in the lobby.

"Let's get your things and be going," he said.

On the way up in the elevator, Will avoided my eyes, as if he was afraid to let on that he knew me. But on the way down, when he saw I'd packed to go, he came to my defense. "She a good girl," he said to Chief Springer. "No breeng boys eento room." Chief Springer smiled without saying anything.

"Goodbye, Will," I said. "Thank Lou for me."

Will followed us into the lobby, the first time I'd ever seen him out of the elevator. "A good girl," he called after us.

The ride back to Katydid took about three hours. The inside of the police car was cluttered with sections of crumpled and torn newspapers. Every so often, the police radio would break into a loud, terrible cackle—a noise that had started out somewhere far away as somebody's voice. Chief Springer just ignored it. After a while, I asked him how he'd found me. "When a sixteen-year-old girl runs away, it's just a matter of time before we catch up," he said. "The world's not a very big place when you're a sixteen-year-old girl off by yourself."

Halfway home, we stopped for coffee. The arthritis in Chief Springer's back is so bad that he has trouble getting in and out of cars. He asked me to lend him a hand. I hurried around the police car and held his arm as he pulled himself out from behind the steering wheel. It seemed like a lot of trouble for a cup of coffee, but perhaps he had something else in mind. At the table in the restaurant, he asked me how things had come to this—how a nice girl like me had got into so much trouble. His face was puddled and spotted in red, and I felt relieved to be with him. So I explained what had happened that day with Butcher, and I told him about the harassment I'd received and about the bonfire out at Banyon's Woods. I also explained about running away with Elro. When I told him that nothing had finally happened, Chief Springer didn't seem surprised—maybe he'd already heard the story from Elro. "It's not fair," I said at the end. "Once I'd made one mistake, things just seemed to multiply, and then I got blamed for everything."

As I talked, the chief chewed on the frame of his glasses, sometimes letting the glasses dangle down from his mouth. Over time, he'd eaten away most of the plastic at one tip, exposing the frame's wire skeleton. "I'll tell you something," he said. "That town's only got six thousand people in it, but it lost eight boys in World War Two and three more in Korea. At this point, it gets kinda confused about its children and doesn't always know what it's up to. You can't really fault the town for that."

"But what's going to happen to me?"

"You're just a child," he said. "You'll grow up and move away. Nothing bad can happen to you. Think about me. I'm an old man. I can't even stand up straight."

They put me in the Children's Home, as I'd expected they would, but it hasn't turned out to be so bad. I'd forgotten that my great fear of the Home came from when I was six or seven, when the possibility of being an orphan was terrifyingly real to someone with only one parent. Over the years since, I'd kept the fear without realizing that it's really just a child's notion. Living here isn't the worst thing that could happen.

A man named Mr. Noren runs the place. He's a frantic sort of person, always late, always hurrying down the hall with his shirttail flapping out the back of his pants. He apparently sees me as someone he can confide in. He tells me how tired he is and complains about the orphans he gets these days: all without manners, all badly educated. Once, we were walking down a hall, and he stopped and put his hand on my shoulder. We were alone and I was frightened, but all he did was lift up his foot and show me the ribbed rubber sole on his shoe. "I have to go all the way into Chicago for these," he said. "They're the only things that keep me from sliding all over the floor."

Most of the children are far younger than I. Mr. Noren put me in a tiny room with one of the few girls my age, Mary Lewis—Crazy Mary, as she's known. She's actually two years older, and she's lived in the Home nearly all her life. Her parents were killed in a car crash. She has straight black hair and black eyes, and she likes to wear black clothes—black stockings, black sweaters, black skirts. She explained to me once that black soaks up the light. She almost never talks, though. Days go by, and she never says a word.

The room itself is very plain, with pale green walls, two single beds with terrible, itchy, gray-wool blankets, and two small wood desks. The desks are old, and their tops are so marked up and nicked that you have to put a piece of cardboard under the paper if you want to write something. Over the years, instead of being sanded down, the desk tops have simply been recoated with varnish, which has sealed in the scratches and made them seem almost historical—the archives of countless orphans from the past.

The day after I was brought back to Katydid, another hearing was held down at the courthouse. Chief Springer was there this time instead of Sergeant Tony, and my new social worker, Mr. Lowry, came up and introduced himself. He is young, with unruly brown hair and horn-rimmed glasses, and he looks out of place, somehow, as if he should be playing the smart kid in a very old movie. "Mrs. O'Brien sends her best," he said. "She'd be here but she has a conference to attend in Fogarty." He frowned, and I gathered he expected me to be unhappy at this piece of news. Then his face lit up. "I'm in such a good mood," he said. "I got married this summer, and my wife is wonderful!"

Judge Horner scowled when he came into the courtroom, and he told me I was a fool for thinking I could run away from my problems. But his scolding could have been worse. In the end, he said he wanted to "take another look at this thing," and he told Mr. Lowry to prepare a new report "in light of how circumstances have changed."

Judge Horner didn't say it outright, but he was referring to the fact that Bunny is in a hospital in Rockford, recovering from exhaustion. She was checked in two days after I ran away. I haven't seen her, but I've talked to her twice, using the phone in Mr. Noren's secretary's office. The first time, Bunny sounded dreamy, her words were loose and she had trouble following the conversation. The second time, a few days later, she sounded much better.

"Why *him?*" she asked. "I can't imagine what you saw in *him.*"

I explained that it didn't have anything to do with Elro personally, that he was just the only one who would take me away.

"I should have taken you away," Bunny said. "We should have left when we had the chance."

"How's Eddie?" I asked, to change the subject.

"Oh, he's all right, I guess. He's been over to visit a few times. The doctors don't like him, though. They say he stirs me up, and I'm supposed to have complete peace and quiet." Her voice cracked. She started to cry. "It's true, he does stir me up."

"Bunny—"

"No, it's true."

"Don't think about it. You're supposed to relax."

"I've grown old. I look at myself in the mirror here—they took away my compact, but there's a mirror in the bathroom. I look at myself, and it's an old woman's face looking back. I could be fifty, sixty, seventy years old. It's all the same. I'm an old woman."

"Bunny—"

She snorted, a laugh bubbling through the tears. "And you know what else? My bottom's got fat. I sit down now, and it spreads out like a bag of sand. I'm an old fat bottom."

"Bunny, you're beautiful, you're the most beautiful woman in Katydid."

"I was, my darling, I was. But that's all gone now, that's the past."

Not long afterward, Mr. Lowry arranged for Bunny's doctor, Dr.

Wheeler, to talk to me. Sitting at Mr. Noren's secretary's desk, I made the call at the appointed time, eleven in the morning. The doctor wasn't in his office, and in the background, I could hear the paging system calling his name. After several minutes, he picked up, but he sounded rushed and irritated. "I recommend that you write your mother from now on and not call," he said. "Her condition is still very delicate, and conversations tend to upset her. Keep your letters to unimportant subjects—the weather, school, that sort of thing. Don't mention anything that might make her worry."

"When is she going to be able to come home?"

"We can't know that, but she won't be home soon. She's been living on borrowed emotional energy for years, and now she's paying the price. I suggest you just go about your life in your own regular way and hope that some day she'll be ready to catch up with you. Now, I've got to go. I've got lots of patients to see in addition to your mother."

"Wait!" I yelled. I was holding the receiver in both hands, dreading the click on the other end. If he hung up now, the silence would be unbearable. "Dr. Wheeler?"

After a long pause—perhaps he had heard me but was considering hanging up anyway—his voice came slowly. "Yes, I'm still here."

"Dr. Wheeler, I was wondering. You know, I got in trouble here this summer and then ran away, and now I'm worried that maybe I caused this to happen to Bunny, that I made her sick."

"You know perfectly well it's been a traumatic summer for her."

"Yes."

"And your brother—"

"Yes." Please help me, I begged silently.

"But illness like this isn't set off by one thing or even two. It's an accumulation of things over time. Some of them are obvious, and some aren't. It doesn't do any good to backtrack. The best thing is to accept this and go on with your own life. You aren't to blame." He sounded efficient, clipped, even bored. How many sons and daughters had heard this speech before? "Now, I really must go."

"Thank you, Dr. Wheeler."

"Goodbye."

I hung up and sat at the desk without moving. I tried not to think. Mr. Noren's secretary believes in neatness, and everything has a container with its own place—pencils, pens, stamps, paper clips, coins, thumbtacks, tea bags, sugar packets, throat lozenges, hard candies. I scanned the candies in their small, round tin. Cherry, strawberry, lemon. Ahhh—I took a lemon, unwrapped it, and threw it in my mouth. Suddenly, Mr. Lowry burst into the room, his face crimson, his arms flapping. "Guess what? The tests are positive! My wife's pregnant!"

On the same day that the *Exponent* carried an article saying that the owners of the KTD had decided to keep the factory open for at least another year, Reverend Vaughn called me up. The phone connection was distant and crackly, and he sounded a bit uneasy, talking too fast and asking too many quick questions. I got the idea that he thought I'd run away because of him, because of the story he'd told me that night in his study. Explaining would have been too hard and too tiring over that scratchy phone line, so I just tried to steer the conversation to other things. He told me he was in Chicago, staying with a friend until he found another church.

"Are you worried?" I asked.

"Actually, it's rather nice," he said. "I hang out at the Art Institute, read a lot—I really sort of wish I never had to work again."

"Did you hear about the KTD? It's going to stay open."

"For now," he said. "It got a reprieve, not a pardon."

"But you helped. That ought to make you feel good. You did something, and it helped."

His familiar light laugh trickled over the wire from Chicago. "You're sweet, Martha, but no. What I did didn't help a goddamn bit."

School has started, but they won't let me go back yet; they're waiting to see how Judge Horner resolves my case. That's fine with me, because it means I have the dormitory room to myself during the day. Mr. Lowry brought me some textbooks, and every now and then I look through them. But mostly I've used the time to write—that's where all this comes from. In the late afternoon, after school has let out and the kids are coming back, I hide the pages under the mattress. We eat at six, spend an hour and a half at study time and have to be in bed, with the lights out, by nine. Someone always comes around to check. Then I lie on my back, staring at the ceiling. Usually it takes hours to fall asleep.

On nights like that, I can't help thinking about the past, wondering about it all. I remember something Bunny said last winter, after she'd bounced a check and they'd shut off our electricity. We came home to a dark and icy house, and I was furious. "How can you be so careless?" I demanded. "How can you live like this?" Bunny just smiled. "Because of you," she said. "Everything's possible because of you." At the time, I didn't really understand. She'd just started going out with Eddie, and I thought her new love was making her larky. But lately, thinking about it, I've begun to see what she meant. As long as we had each other, nothing else really mattered. The checks could bounce, the boyfriends could disappear, Tom could even go to jail— in the end, we always had each other.

Lying here in the darkened room, listening to the slow, snorting breaths of Crazy Mary on the bed a few feet away, I try to bring back that old feeling, to make things the way they were just a month ago. But it doesn't work. I still love Bunny with all my heart, but I know now that love like hers is dangerous. It makes you a little crazy.

Sometimes, though, if I'm still awake when the midnight whistle blows over at the KTD, I play a little game with myself. I imagine that I'm free from here, and I've gone to pick up Bunny. As a present, I bring her the old shoes that I bought in Minniefield. They're just right for her—as special and romantic as she is. She loves the shoes and tries them on right there in the hospital, parading around the ward, showing them off to the bewildered patients, coming back again and again to hold me in her arms. "A perfect child," she tells everyone. "A perfect child." And then I pick up the battered old suitcase in which she's packed her things, and we walk down the marble stairs and out the heavy front door. The day is cloudless, and the air smells of mowed grass. Outside the hospital, across the street, a huge meadow spreads out, with low hills in the distance. Bunny and I walk toward them, talking the way we've always talked, touching occasionally, lost in each other, until, in my imagination, we're two tiny dots disappearing into the perfect green horizon, and I drift off into a sweet sleep.

FOR THE BEST IN PAPERBACKS, LOOK FOR THE

In every corner of the world, on every subject under the sun, Penguin represents quality and variety—the very best in publishing today.

For complete information about books available from Penguin—including Pelicans, Puffins, Peregrines, and Penguin Classics—and how to order them, write to us at the appropriate address below. Please note that for copyright reasons the selection of books varies from country to country.

In the United Kingdom: For a complete list of books available from Penguin in the U.K., please write to *Dept E.P., Penguin Books Ltd, Harmondsworth, Middlesex, UB7 0DA.*

In the United States: For a complete list of books available from Penguin in the U.S., please write to *Dept BA, Penguin*, Box 120, Bergenfield, New Jersey 07621-0120.

In Canada: For a complete list of books available from Penguin in Canada, please write to *Penguin Books Ltd, 2801 John Street, Markham, Ontario L3R 1B4.*

In Australia: For a complete list of books available from Penguin in Australia, please write to the *Marketing Department, Penguin Books Ltd, P.O. Box 257, Ringwood, Victoria 3134.*

In New Zealand: For a complete list of books available from Penguin in New Zealand, please write to the *Marketing Department, Penguin Books (NZ) Ltd, Private Bag, Takapuna, Auckland 9.*

In India: For a complete list of books available from Penguin, please write to *Penguin Overseas Ltd, 706 Eros Apartments, 56 Nehru Place, New Delhi, 110019.*

In Holland: For a complete list of books available from Penguin in Holland, please write to *Penguin Books Nederland B.V., Postbus 195, NL-1380AD Weesp, Netherlands.*

In Germany: For a complete list of books available from Penguin, please write to *Penguin Books Ltd, Friedrichstrasse 10-12, D-6000 Frankfurt Main I, Federal Republic of Germany.*

In Spain: For a complete list of books available from Penguin in Spain, please write to *Longman, Penguin España, Calle San Nicolas 15, E-28013 Madrid, Spain.*

In Japan: For a complete list of books available from Penguin in Japan, please write to *Longman Penguin Japan Co Ltd, Yamaguchi Building, 2-12-9 Kanda Jimbocho, Chiyoda-Ku, Tokyo 101, Japan.*